ELODIA'S KNIFE

Elodia's Knife

Copyright © 2023 by Robert S. Phillips

Cover Art by Bob Paltrow Design

Author Photo by Audra Lee Photography

Contact Information: RobertSPhillipsAuthor.com

ISBN: 979-8-9884074-0-9 (paperback)
ISBN: 979-8-9884074-1-6 (e-book)
ISBN: 979-8-9884074-2-3 (audio book)

Historical Fiction/Antiquity

ELODIA'S KNIFE

Book One of the Visigoth Saga

By Robert S. Phillips

Dedication

To my Melissa, late, beloved and sorely missed, who always supported my scribbling.

Contents

Maps

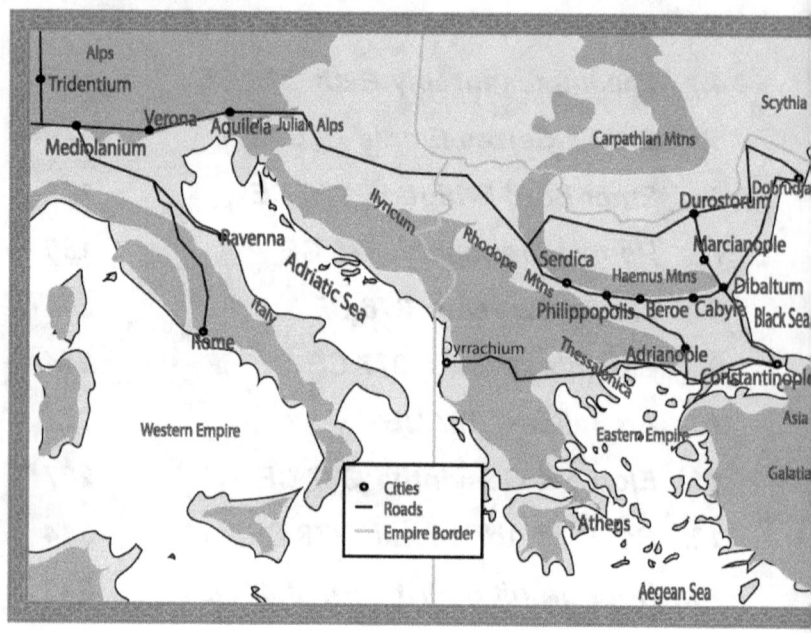

Roman Empire 376 CE

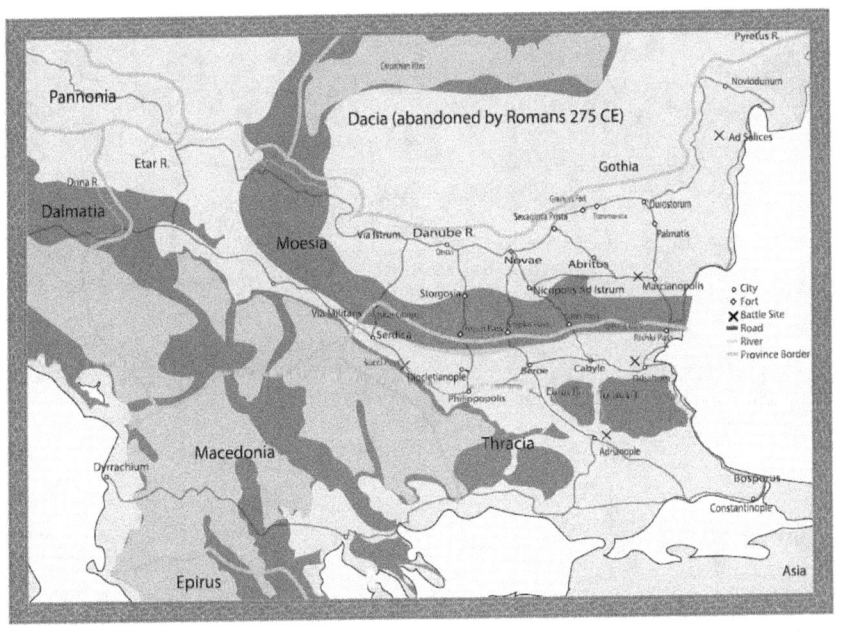

The Balkan Peninsula 375 CE

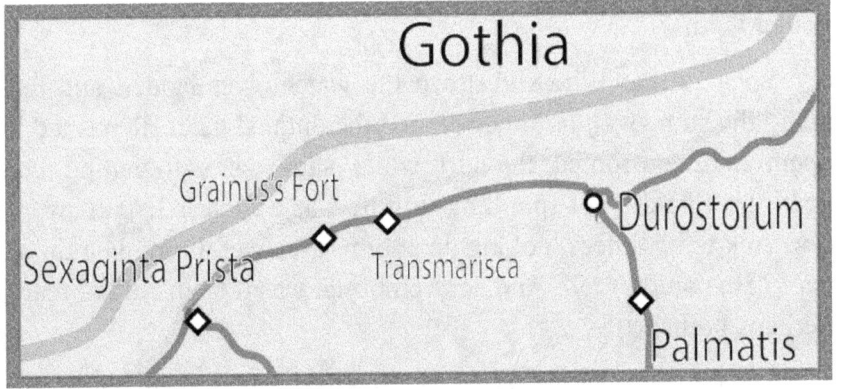

1. Elodia Seeks Refuge
375 CE

The raft materialized like a ghost from a grave and grated ashore at the foot of Grainus's watchtower. He would have missed it if he had been asleep, but he never slept on his watch. He had learned better. Anyway, the six-foot square platform he stood on, atop the fort's thirty-foot watchtower, was too small for napping. Instead, he stomped his feet, chafed his hands, and sang; anything to ward off boredom and the bitter cold.

A single passenger, a cloaked girl, stepped off the raft and disappeared behind the riverbank. Moments later, she emerged onto the outpost's frontage road. A gust of wind flipped back her hood, revealing her long black hair, but the mirky darkness concealed her face. She peered through the gloom, looking this way and that.

He would not sound the alarm. Not for just a single woman. He could manage alone. Would someone chide him for it? Breaking his own rules? Perhaps, but he was the squad leader, the *decanus*, and he could do what he liked. It was a kindness, really. His men were asleep in the barracks, a dozen yards away. He saw no reason to bother them.

Spear in hand, he slid down the watchtower ladder, and ran along the stone wall until he reached the outpost gate. He pushed it open, and confronted the girl while she was still getting her bearings. She did not spot him until he was a spear's length away. She sank to her knees looking up at him, eyes wet. From the rain or tears? He couldn't tell. And her trembling, was it from cold or fear? Perhaps both.

She struggled to her feet, revealing the garb of a wealthy Goth. The dawn's sharp light flashed on the gold thread that edged her black cloak and revealed stripes of yellow, green, and red. Rain streamed off her leather trousers and dripped onto her bare feet. She had a narrow face, a strong nose, and a high forehead. Thick eyebrows shielded her wide black eyes. Her tears, running freely down her cheeks, did not mar her beauty.

She tried to move past him toward the outpost wall, where he'd left the gate open.

"Stop. Go back. You cannot come here," he said in Greek.

He blocked her way with the shaft of his spear. So, she doesn't speak Greek. He wasn't surprised. It was the common trade language and most local folk spoke it, but she wasn't from here. He repeated his command in Latin, which he spoke very poorly. He knew all the military commands and not much more.

Still, she showed no sign of comprehension. She grabbed his spear shaft and pushed it back against his chest with surprising force. She raised one shaking hand, pointed to the gate, and uttered a pleading cry. Gothic, of course. That was a tongue he recognized but didn't speak.

She was a Goth. Now that was a problem. It would be better if this young woman just turned around, got back on her little raft, and pushed north for her Gothic home.

For ten years, the Roman frontier troops had striven to maintain Emperor Valens's prohibition. It banned all interaction between Roman subjects south of the Danube River and the Gothic barbarians to the north. Young barbarian raiders, trying to prove their manhood by crossing in search of adventure and plunder, instead encountered the frontier troops and death by sword and spear. Smugglers met the same end. Refugees who encountered the Romans met a grisly fate, being sold to a slave trader.

She must know those are her only two options. Death or slavery. He would hate to kill her, but that might be kinder than selling her to the slave traders. Those insidious scum had a sixth sense for misery.

Their tug-of-war continued, much to Grainus's surprise. She was short, robust, and about the same size as him, but she could not outmatch a strong legionary. She argued with increasing volume and panic, though he understood none of it.

He looked over her shoulder in time to witness a tall man emerge from the riverside shrubs. Seeing Grainus's distracted look, she followed his gaze, released the spear, and shrieked. Then the man was upon them.

The warrior was a head taller than him and fifty pounds heavier. Grainus feared he'd met his match. The warrior reached for the woman, but she ducked behind Grainus, keeping him between them. The bear-sized brute moved around him with surprising speed, but Grainus turned, holding his spear at the ready, and the woman shifted to stay behind him. She shouted to the warrior in her language, babbling the same thing over and over.

Whatever she said, he ignored it. He paused and looked down at Grainus's spear. Its point grazed his chest. He looked up, caught Grainus's eye, and looked sharply left. Grainus followed his glance, distracted, and realizing too late he'd been tricked, allowing the warrior to brush the spear aside with one hand and snatch it with the other.

Rather than immediately impaling Grainus, the warrior came nose to nose with him and shouted—a warning or a threat?—in his face. Then he howled and stepped back and clutched his shoulder.

The woman, taking refuge behind Grainus, was jumping up repeatedly to reach over his shoulder and jab the brute with a knife. He paused momentarily, only long enough to see the wound was only a scratch, then charged her. Grainus stood in the man's path, but that did not matter. The warrior simply bowled him over.

The legionary fell, cracked his head on the cobblestones, and blacked out.

Caius lay in his bunk bed, looking up at the rocking shape of Polybius, asleep in the bed above. Why was he stuck with the bunkmate who snored the loudest? There were eight men in the squad, and he was given the noisiest. Jesus! He shakes the bedframe!

Well, they all snored. All except Evander, sleeping like a baby over there in the corner, far from the drafty door. But he was young. Give him a few more years of frontier service, and he might out-sing them all.

The bitter night air journeyed down Caius's neck, traveling beneath his two blankets and finding an arctic home on his stomach.

He pulled the blankets close and tight. Warmer. Better. Oh, let the cold travel down Polybius's neck, wake that bugger, and give him a chance to sleep again.

The storm moved off to the north. Rain no longer rapped on the barrack's door. The wind finally stopped whistling through chinks in the walls.

There. Yes, he could faintly hear Grainus singing off in the distance. He did that when he was on watch and bored. He sang so very badly. Evander once joked Grainus's voice helped defend the frontier, disarming would-be attackers. No one, he said, could attack with their fingers in their ears.

Grainus enjoyed a ribbing, which endeared him to the squad. He could laugh at himself. A fine fellow. He was even taking the watch duty of the two men who were on leave in Transmarisca. He could have assigned it to other men, but, no, he took it himself. Even knowing that tonight would be nasty and freezing. That's the kind of man the decanus was. If their roles were reversed, would *he* take the extra watches? Not likely.

Caius snuggled a little deeper under his blankets and listened to Grainus's razor voice shred innocent songs.

But his voice changed! He was no longer singing, but talking. To who?

Caius sat up in bed, careful to avoid banging his head on Polybius's low-hanging butt.

No, there was another voice. Fainter, higher. Shrill. A woman. Speaking in… Gothic?

It was too distant for Caius to make out the words. But he heard her shriek.

"Awake!" he called. "Something's happening." He swung off his bed, slipped into his hobnail sandals, and darted for the door. He donned a stout leather vest—should he put on armor? No time for that—seized a spear off the rack and bolted into the outpost's courtyard. He ran across the yard to the wall, trying not to slip in the thick mud, passed through the open gate, and stepped onto the road. There were three people tussling, Grainus sandwiched between a girl and a barbarian warrior, a massive man. Caius gripped his spear and watched.

The melee ended when the warrior knocked Grainus down. The girl cowered behind his prone body, though it provided no protection from the huge warrior advancing, spear in hand, preparing to run her through.

His unprotected back was to Caius, a back that inexplicably sprouted a spear. He turned to face Caius, revealing the spear's point protruding from his chest. Then he collapsed as blood seeped from his tunic.

Where was *his* spear? Then he recognized it, saw it jutting from the warrior's body. Hurling it had been a reflex.

The tension drained from him when he realized Grainus, his friend, his decanus, was safe. And the girl too. Though she looked at him with wonder, as if he were the legendary Ajax come back to life.

She watched as the big man who killed Hathus took her by the arm, helped her to her feet, and led her through the outpost gate. The sun had risen, so she could see all there was to see, which wasn't much. A square compound, fifty feet on a side, surrounded by an eight-foot-high stone wall. Inside the compound was a barracks building where the soldiers dwelled, a latrine, a well, pens for livestock, and a stable.

She stumbled as she walked, feeling tired. The big man kept her from falling. Sharp gravel jabbed her bare feet.

Looking back at the other legionaries, she saw several assisting the injured man. Others dragged Hathus's body to the river's edge, and without ceremony dumped him in. *He was not an evil man. He deserved better.*

She silently prayed to Odin, asking him to admit Hathus to the hall of heroes.

The man holding her threw open the barracks door and guided her to a seat by the fire. *Warm.* She closed her eyes, only to open them when he pushed a bowl of soup into her hands. She lifted the bowl and gulped a long draft. Salty. Too salty but also delicious, such a vile concoction, but she could not consume it fast enough.

"My name is Caius," he said. He spoke Gothic with what she later recognized as a Latin accent.

"Elodia," she said. When she emptied the bowl, Caius replaced it with a large mug of warm ale. Other squad members were making their way into the building, sitting on stools, the edge of the bunk beds, or anywhere heat from the fire might reach.

Caius sat down and said brusquely, "Why are you here? Who are your people? Who was that warrior?"

She paused her drinking to answer. "That was Hathus, a brother of my dead husband. He found my husband's body this morning. He thought I killed his brother. He followed me across the river to kill me."

"Did you kill your husband?"

Should she lie? There seemed no point. "Yes. He hurt me. He beat me." She took a long draft of ale. "This time, I waited until he got drunk and fell asleep. Then I put my knife in his throat."

"Couldn't your family protect you?"

"I have no family, not nearby. I cannot go back. Anyone in my husband's family would kill me. Torture me and then kill me. I cannot go back."

Did the other men understand her? It didn't seem so. Just this *Caius* spoke her language.

"Wait," he said, "while I explain this to Grainus."

Caius spoke to the man who'd been knocked down, the man called Grainus. She could tell they were talking in Greek, which she didn't understand.

They talked on and on, but she was tired, so very tired. She listened as they spoke, grasping none of it until she could not keep her eyes open. They were still talking when she fell into an exhausted slumber.

Caius had just finished recounting Elodia's story when she slumped over in her seat and began to softly snore. "Grainus, what do we do with her?"

Grainus said, "First, you'd better find a place for her to sleep."

Caius grubbed around in the back of the barracks, choosing some old but serviceable garments from a bin. Tucking them under his arm and grabbing one of his blankets, he picked up the young woman with no more effort than he'd spend lifting a cat. He slung her over his shoulder and disappeared out the barracks door, returning ten minutes later holding Elodia's still-damp clothes.

"In the stable?" Grainus asked.

"Yes. I made her a bed of straw in the loft. She never woke up."

"Not even when you stripped her?"

Caius kept a straight face. "Her clothes were still wet." He proceeded to hang them on a line near the fire.

Grainus said, "Of course. And ... how does she look?"

"Quite common, quite unkempt. Rather beat up."

Marius said, "What Grainus wants to know..."

Caius said, "I *understand* what Grainus wants to know."

The other members of the squad snickered.

"What about tomorrow? What should we do with her then?" asked Grainus.

Although Grainus led the squad, he leaned heavily on Caius for ideas and advice.

"First, we inform Bitorix." Military Tribune Bitorix commanded all the frontier outposts along this stretch of the Danube.

"Of course. He gets nasty if he's kept in the dark. Then what?"

"We wait for his orders. He'll probably want her sold. She's young, and when she's clean, she might look pretty. Any slaver should offer a good price for her. And Bitorix will want his cut."

He could see the look of distaste on Grainus's face. The man hated slavers. Two years earlier, when a slaver passed through the local village and kidnapped a little girl, Grainus pursued him relentlessly. The decanus caught up with them under the walls of Durostorum. Without uttering a word, he slew the slaver and returned the girl to her parents. Not all the empire's enemies came from across the Danube.

Grainus said, "Polybius, run to Transmarisca and talk to that shit Bitorix. Tell him about the girl and get his instructions. And while you're there, tell him we've waited a month for a replacement for Eutaius. Say that we're entitled to a replacement soldier, and we want one. Now!"

Polybius feigned shock. He said, "Surely you mean 'make a polite request' of our esteemed Military Tribune Bitorix."

"Yes, that's what I said. And don't let the shit give you 'no' for an answer."

Eutaius was the squad's cook and provisioner. He was in the legion's hospital in Transmarisca, sick with the lung disease. The latest report said he was hacking up white chunks. Grainus had no hope that he would recover.

"Decanus, sir, I am next on the leave rota," Polybius said. "May I take my leave while I'm in the city?"

"You know the rules. You don't get your leave until the Pannonian brothers return from theirs." Minicius and Arruntius, born and raised in the province of Pannonia, were due back the next day.

Caius, speaking softly, said, "What's the harm? We're in no rush. I can put the girl to work cooking and so on."

Grainus laughed. "Now that you've had a good look at the girl, a really good look, you're not keen to be rid of her?"

Caius stiffened. "No such thing."

10

"Fine. We'll put her to work around here until Polybius returns with orders."

Clodia awoke at dusk. She had straw in her hair, in her mouth, creeping up under her tunic and poking her legs. Her tunic? She had never seen this garment before! It was big enough for two of her and had been stained black by the gods know what. But she was dry and warm. Much better than this morning.

She remembered the frightening river crossing and the fight with Hathus, the salty soup, and ... the big soldier ... Caius. Who had saved her.

Caius must have brought her here. Put her here, up in this loft. The Romans had not killed her, as the people back in her village predicted. They had not bound her hands and feet and locked her up as they would if they were planning to sell her. What was their plan?

She struggled out of the loft and climbed down to the stable floor. She felt dirty and ugly. She picked the straw off her garment and out of her hair, ran her fingers through it, teasing out the tangles. She found a comb meant for currying the stable's mule, but it wouldn't mind if she used it. She stepped out of the stable into the yard. It was late in the day. The morning's drizzle was gone, but it was overcast and cold.

She found a bucket filled with fresh rainwater. She scooped out handfuls, scrubbing at her face. Would the Romans let her bathe? Give her back her clothes? The oversize peasant tunic looked ugly but there was nothing she could do about that. There, finished. This was as presentable as she could make herself.

"Good, you're awake." Caius approached carrying a pair of worn sandals. "Put these on. I have work for you to do." They were too large, a man's sandals, but any sandals were better than walking through the mud and shit in bare feet. She slipped them on and stooped to tie the straps. When she stood, she saw him studying her. How dreadful did she look?

"You look better. A day's sleep has helped. Yes, you'll do."

"Do?" she asked, "Do for what?" They must mean to sell her.

Caius ignored her question. "Here are your duties. First, muck out this stable. It hasn't been done in days, and it stinks. Next, the barracks…"

"Please, sir. Caius. Please tell me what will happen."

He stopped talking and looked down. A foot taller than her, he opened his mouth to speak. He had good teeth. And a sweet breath. He kept his black hair short and his beard trimmed, unlike the other outpost soldiers. They had looked more like barbarians than her own menfolk.

"Your condition is your own fault. Grainus gave you the choice of going back. You refused."

Because I would be dead now.

"If you were a man, or if Grainus were not Grainus, we would have killed you. That is what we do. Goths who cross the river are killed." He spoke without emotion, with the flat tone of a litany one utters every morning of one's life. "That is the emperor's law and has been for decades. You should know it. We kill raiders, smugglers, and intruders. Occasionally, we capture and sell them."

Unable to meet his gaze, she studied the stable floor. "And me?"

"I don't know," he said. "Grainus has sent a man to Transmarisca, where Bitorix, our military tribune, resides. We await his orders. In the meanwhile, Grainus has charged me with making you useful."

"I'm to be killed or sold?" He did not reply. "Could you not just hold me hostage? I am Elodia, daughter of Gordric, chieftain of the Fontal clan," she boasted, proudly raising her chin.

"My father will pay a large ransom for me. He has talents of gold." A lie. Gordric had little gold and none to spare for a daughter who had just murdered her lawful husband. She ventured to look up at him.

Raising an eyebrow, Caius uttered a skeptical "Umph."

He talked on. "You will care for this mule and all the other livestock."

Easy work. "Growing up, I owned a horse and cared for it myself. Mules and chickens? I would be happy to care for them." She smiled.

"You *will* care for them."

Her smile dissolved. Why was he so harsh and disrespectful? She was not some sloven peasant girl.

"In addition, you will keep the barracks clean and tidy and wash the squad's clothes. Also, you will purchase any supplies we need from the nearby farmers and villagers. It is your responsibility to cook the squad's meals, two meals daily. In addition, perform any other tasks ordered by Grainus or me."

Trying to keep her breathing slow and steady, she clenched her teeth. These tasks were not appropriate for someone of her class.

"You will keep our armor in good shape, free from rust. You will not touch any legionary's weapons without his permission. You will not stray from the outpost without permission."

It was too much. "Fryken!" she spat on the ground. "I do not cook, clean, buy things, or the rest of it. The animals are one thing, but the rest? I am no slave. You forget who my father is."

"You are *nothing*. Obey Grainus and me. If you vex us, we will sell you now without waiting for Bitorix. There are always slavers nearby, looking for merchandise."

How could she argue? The giant soldier had a sword. She had only a little knife. Yes, for now, she would do as he demanded, but once she knew this area and the nearby farms and villages, she would run. This Caius giant would never see her again.

"And don't even think about running. Yes, I see the idea written on your face. A little Gothic girl with no Greek and no money? The locals would catch you in a day, and Grainus would sell you to the slavers on the next.

"Start with cleaning these stalls. When it's too dark to see, come into the barracks. Tonight, we will cook for you. Tomorrow you will start cooking for us."

He watched until she began to work, standing in a mule stall, pitching out its filth.

She looked up and saw him staring at her. With a smile. A small smile, but still. Why was he smiling? It was not a cruel smile. He was not gloating. Did he take pleasure watching her shovel shit? Perhaps he was too long away from a woman. She was pleased she'd combed her hair.

14

"You're late! Again!" Caius interrupted his climb up the watchtower when Minicius and Arruntius, returning from Transmarisca, staggered through the outpost gate. Arruntius leaned on his brother, who, none too steady himself, jerked him upright. It aggravated Caius that they habitually overstayed their leave. The two brothers, the most useless members of the squad, in his opinion, were required to be back by midnight from leave or a mission. Instead, they would wander into the outpost at dawn, often half drunk, incapable of doing anything worthwhile. Grainus would punish them, but it made no difference. Even lashing had no effect. It just left them disabled for several days. They valued the extra time off more than the skin on their backs.

"But Caius, we're late for a good reason," Minicius said. He was the more articulate of the two. "There is a new barmaid at the Tortured Tortoise, and she is black! Taller even than you and black as Hades. Not dark like an Arab but midnight black. From Aethiopia, she claims. And thin. Not a trace of fat anywhere except where a girl should be fat. The delicious tricks she learned in Aethiopia are well worth the extra sesterce she charges…"

"Enough," Caius said. "You have just missed the squad. The semaphore spoke of a boat crossing." The frontier outposts along the Danube were carefully spaced. This allowed signals from any watchtower to be visible to its neighbors, relaying a message over hundreds of miles in a few hours. "Grainus has gone to intercept them. You may escape another lashing if you can catch up before the action starts."

Minicius said, "Aye," and saluted. Arruntius said, "I feel sick," and vomited on his sandals. They drifted toward the barracks to collect their armor and arms.

15

"One other thing you should know," Caius called. "There's a girl, a prisoner, working in the stable. She showed up yesterday."

Minicius said, "A prisoner?"

"Yes. We captured her after her raft landed on our doorstep."

"She's a Goth?" asked Arruntius.

"Yes."

"Tervingi Goths?"

"Of course." The frontier troops only encountered members of the Tervingi tribe of Goths. The other major tribe was the Greutungi Goths, who rarely came this far west. Whereas the Tervingi were farmers who fought on foot, the Greutungi were herdsmen who lived on the open plains north of the Black Sea and fought from horseback.

"Grainus should have killed her." The brothers blamed the Goths for destroying their village in Pannonia and leaving them orphans. "Why didn't he kill her? Doesn't he always kill them?"

When Caius didn't answer, Minicius said, "You saved her, didn't you? She must be pretty. Did she remind you of your girl back in Aquileia?"

They were correct on all counts. Yes, he'd saved her. Yes, she was pretty. Very pretty. But how did they know about the girl in Aquileia?

Caius didn't respond to their jibes except to say, "If you hurry, Grainus might not punish you. Next time, get back on time."

Elodia was busy using the curry comb to brush the mule. The animal quietly whimpered with pleasure.

"You like that, Bridie, don't you!" While growing up, Elodia had had a favorite cat by that name, long since gone to bite the heads off heavenly mice in cat paradise. "But you don't bite, do you, Bridie?" It was a good name, suitable for reuse on this young mule.

The animal's coat had revealed its long neglect. Elodia slowly removed the knots and thorns from its pine-yellow hair until the animal gleamed in the morning light. After brushing, she turned her attention to its hooves. She lifted each leg in turn and, using her knife, no longer stained with Hathus's blood, cleaned the debris and stones lodged in the hoof's groove. The horseshoes looked good, but the hoof walls would soon need trimming.

Last night she'd started to clean the stable stalls until it grew too dark to work. Now, she picked up a shovel to continue the job. One shovelful of mixed straw and shit flew out the stable door, followed by another.

"Whoa, girl, watch where you toss that crap," came a voice from outside. A thin scruffy man followed the voice into the stable. After him came a stout, equally scruffy man who stood silently on the threshold, leaning on the door frame. Similarly featured, both had blond hair, its length roughly bundled at their napes. Blue tattoos covered their faces and arms. Brothers.

She had no idea what he'd said. She stopped just before pitching a shovelful of steaming shit in their direction. The thin man said something more in Greek. "Who are you?" she asked in Gothic. They did not understand.

The stout one laughed and replied, "Blacka bortle snork." The thin one giggled as if his brother's mock-Gothic was the height of hilarity. Stout One stepped into the stable. Thin One walked right up to Elodia. He blew in her face, his breath foul, reeking of old ale. As she moved to step back, he seized her breasts, pinched them, and smushed his mouth into hers.

She staggered back. With a leer, Stout One babbled a few words at her. She didn't need an interpreter to understand his intentions.

While Thin One gabbled, she pulled away, still holding the shovel handle. A quick flip threw its contents into his face. He recoiled as shit went into his gaping mouth, and mule piss stung his eyes. He tried to curse her, but his mouth was busy spitting. He hacked and puked.

When Stout One came forward to aid his sibling, Elodia flicked open her knife and jabbed Bridie's thigh. The mule's kick caught Stout One in the chest. His body arced out the stable door onto the courtyard's muddy ground. Thin One, still spitting shit and scarlet with fury, moved to attack Elodia again. She waved her knife in his face, but when he didn't back off, she darted forward and sliced his cheek. She stepped away again. From outside, Stout One moaned and called for help. His brother, blood dripping from his wound, turned away from Elodia toward his sibling and left.

She stood panting, feeling sick. She had attacked a Roman, a legionary, and drawn blood. What would Grainus do? Could there be any doubt? She would be killed. *O, Ithunn, save me.* But she doubted if the goddess of youth could save her.

Caius responded to Arruntius's call for help. Together with Minicius, they carried the moaning man to his bunk. "A broken rib or two," Caius said. "He'll probably live." *Too bad.*

He jabbed a finger into Minicius's chest. "Leave the girl alone. She's not your plaything. A mule kick could be the least of your punishments." He stared angrily at Minicius, who, rather than looking back, studied a tattoo on his arm.

Returning to the watchtower, Caius chuckled. Not only was she pretty, very pretty, but she had spirit. And he would never forget the image of Arruntius trying to spit out flecks of mule crap. It was all too funny. Life at the outpost promised to be more interesting with Elodia here. If he could keep her.

"I see you've started assaulting Emperor Valens's limitanei," Caius said, as Elodia sat on a stool in the stable, head between her knees, crying softly.

She looked up. "What is a limitanei?" she asked.

"That's us. The limitanei are the legions of us second-rate soldiers destined to spend our lives guarding the empire's frontier," he said.

He was talking about those two men. They were certainly second-rate. Wait, was he not angry? Was he just here to talk and not punish her? Or kill her? Perhaps if she could keep him talking…

"Are you second-rate?" Elodia sat up and started to dry her eyes.

"We don't think so. We train hard. We always beat your lot when they venture across the river. But, in truth, we are not a match for the Roman field armies. Those troops are better armed, better led, and better paid. They are not stuck in a fixed place. They see action wherever the empire needs them."

"If you are limitanei, what are they?"

"In Latin, we call them comitatenses," he said. "But let's talk instead about your knife. You keep jabbing it into people."

Elodia sighed. She knew the talk would have to return to stabbing. "Only people who need it," she said.

"This must stop. You must never again attack a legionary, not even scum like Minicius and Arruntius. Regardless of provocation. If it happens again, I will take your knife."

"But I need it, if you want me to look after the mule." She gestured toward Bridie, "Or to strangle chickens and clean your dirty clothes and wash your butt. I will need my knife."

He laughed. Looking down at her, he saw a slight smile cross Elodia's face. And then she laughed.

"What will those men do to me? What will Grainus do?" she asked.

"I've ordered Minicius and Arruntius to leave you alone. The other men will too. As for Grainus, he'll likely overlook it this once, given the circumstances. I think he will also be amused. He might seem as rough as bark, but he admires spirit."

It was dusk when Polybius entered the barracks and sat at the table. Caius ordered Elodia, "Serve Polybius." Though he'd spoken in Greek, she appeared to understand because she filled a wooden platter with roasted pork and set it before him. Everyone else had already eaten, but there were plenty of leftovers. No one wanted seconds of Elodia's cuisine.

Polybius grimaced as he bit through the charred skin and into the raw flesh by the bone. The others watched with grins, waiting for his reaction.

"It's not bad if you smother it with salt and wash it down with strong wine," he said. They all laughed, but Caius could see her cringe. Polybius pretended to take another great bite.

Fidgeting impatiently, Caius waited to hear Bitorix's order. Grainus's fingers beat an equally eager cadence on the tabletop.

Grainus said, "Never mind the food. What happened in Transmarisca?"

Polybius said, "Oh, about the same as here, I suspect. We got a spot of rain which, by the mud on the road, I see you got too. But it's clear now, and the sun is warm. I felt it in my bones on my walk back."

Grainus's fingers kept tapping.

"When I reached Transmarisca, I felt frozen through and through. Mind you, I quickly made my way to our favorite tavern—the Ruptured Duck, do you remember?—where a lovely young barmaid served me mulled ale. That melted the ice in my guts."

Caius saw that Grainus was turning red.

Polybius went on. "When I call her a 'maid,' that's just me being polite. For a little extra coin, she took me upstairs and warmed me from head to toe, if you catch my meaning."

Grainus finally lost patience. "And the news? What did Bitorix say?"

"Bitorix? I didn't see him until the next day after my money was gone. You see, when the maid and I were done, she introduced me to some gentlemen downstairs who were playing dice. At first, I won. Quite a lot. Enough to buy a round for the house and another bout of upstairs warming from the barmaid. But then Felix," the Roman god of luck, "turned against me. I returned to the dicing table and lost every sesterce! Which was fine with me. I have no regrets. A little drinking, dicing, and whoring, what else is money for?"

Grainus took a deep breath and exhaled slowly, the air hissing between his pursed lips. "Enough! Did you *finally* see Bitorix?"

Polybius nodded. "Yes."

"And…?"

Polybius said, "The military tribune directs you to sell the girl and send him half the money."

A verbal order. Caius was not surprised. Bitorix would not want it in writing that he skimmed fifty percent of slave sales.

Caius watched as Elodia, hearing the name "Bitorix," bit her lip and turned to listen to the conversation. She couldn't understand it, but she knew it concerned her. Oh, how she must wish she knew Greek. He would talk to her later.

When Polybius finished, she looked around the table for the men's reactions. Minicius and Arruntius looked pleased. The other men seemed indifferent.

Grainus said, "What of Eutaius?"

Elodia reacted to another name she recognized. Caius had explained Eutaius was the squad's provisioner, responsible for all the chores she'd been given. The provisioner was dying in the legion's hospital. She felt no sympathy for him. He'd neglected Bridie.

Polybius said, "No change. Still taking his sweet time to die."

Caius, deferring to Grainus, said, "May I ask a question?"

Grainus nodded, "Yes."

"Did Bitorix order Grainus to sell Elodia *immediately*?"

Polybius scratched his head. "I don't believe so. No, he never mentioned *immediately*."

"Then," Caius said, directing his remarks to Grainus, "I suggest we keep Elodia until Eutaius returns. Then you can sell her. She has started to perform his duties and does them better than he did. Without her, we'll have to spread the work among us again. Do we want that?"

All the men shook their heads except Arruntius.

He said, "If we sell the girl and divide the money eight ways, what would be my share? Or would it be nine ways? I suppose Grainus, as decanus, should get a double share."

Grainus said, "Arruntius, what the fryken hell are you talking about? You are *such* a fool. Answer the question, 'yes' or 'no.'"

The fool looked around the table. Everyone was shaking their heads, so he said, "No."

Elodia showed no sign of understanding the discussion. She turned to Caius. "What is happening?"

"You are to be a slave." He watched as her face crumpled. What news had she expected? The only alternative was death. Still, watching tears stream down her face made him wince.

23

"But," he went on, "we will not sell you immediately. You will continue to do Eutaius's jobs until he gets better and returns."

"And then?"

"Then Grainus will sell you."

He watched as her face began to crumble again. "But, Elodia, don't cry. Eutaius is dying. No one recovers from the lung disease. You will probably stay until Bitorix sends us a replacement for Eutaius."

"And when will Bitorix do that?"

"Maybe never. He just refused Grainus's request for a replacement."

Elodia was confused. They would keep her until something that won't happen happens? In the meantime, she was warm and fed. And Caius made her feel safe.

Nothing more could be decided that night. Caius sent her back to her straw bed in the stable's loft. Before she left the barracks, he gave her another blanket. "Be careful on the porch," he said. "The decking is slick with frost."

She smiled in appreciation. His lips curved up just a little in response.

Over the next four months, Elodia's life fell into a routine. She got up before dawn, stoked the barracks fireplace, and prepared gruel for the squad's breakfast. After they'd eaten, she would clean the barracks and chop wood. In the afternoon, she always faced a mountain of soiled, bloody, or torn clothing, which she washed at the riverside and mended. There were provisions to buy from the local village, a mile away, and dinners to prepare. Dinner remained a problem. She hated cooking because the men hated her cooking.

But at noon, she had time for her mule. She liked the mule, and the mule liked her. She talked to the mule, sang to the mule, and hand-fed oats to the mule with extra oats if the mule responded to her name, "Bridie."

Elodia made a point of taking Bridie out for exercise every day. They rode along the Via Istrum, the imperial road that ran along the Danube shore. Vast marshlands separated it from the river. The rushes and sedges quickly grew tall in the spring, recovering from the harsh winter's punishment. The grasses came alive with birds, either making nests for their young or just stopping briefly on their way back north, filling the air with their calls. Soon, the towering bullrushes made it difficult to view the river from the road, but from the back of her mule, Elodia could see the Danube flowing fast and deep. The far bank, a half-mile distant, flat and featureless, showed few signs of life except some wisps of rising smoke. From this distance, she could not make out any huts or see any indication of her late husband's clan.

Caius showed up one day with another mule, a young filly. Elodia helped him brand her, as required to mark her as legion property. The mule did not take kindly to having her butt burned. She squealed and complained for so long that Caius named her "Fortis," Latin for *brave*. To settle her, Elodia hand-fed her sweet white beets.

Elodia would whistle and sing whether she was feeding, grooming, or exercising her charges. She even sang while mucking out their stable, a small stone structure with two stalls, a thatched roof, and the loft where she slept.

Evander came to listen when he heard her sing. She sang the songs of her people. The lyrics were Gothic, which he didn't speak, but when the melodies were familiar, he would hum along. They shared many tunes, which bards and traders carried across the river and wherever they went. He, in turn, sang to her.

When she believed Evander's lyrics might be interesting, she asked Caius to translate them from Greek. Over time she learned more Greek, and Evander learned more Gothic. During the short days of early spring, when the nights were still bitterly cold, singing became an evening entertainment. Most of the squad could sing passably well except Grainus. He had no ear for a tune. Folk said he had a voice like scraping gravel.

One day as she was saddling Fortis for the mule's daily exercise, Caius asked if he might ride along too. "Yes," she said in broken Greek, adding wryly, "Who is slave telling master not to ride? Other thing, won't other mens joke you?"

"They might tease me," he said with a grin, "but only once."

Riding became a daily event. She taught him the Gothic names of all the plants and animals they spotted. He would speak Greek, telling stories of growing up in Aquileia, and she, in halting Greek, told of her childhood north of the Carpathian Mountains.

"Where Akeela? What you did there?" she asked.

"Oh, I could talk for an hour about Aquileia," he said and began. "It is situated at the head of the Mare Adriaticum, the Adriatic Sea in Greek. It is one of the world's great cities, with a hundred thousand people or more. It has vast walls with tall towers and has never been conquered. The people are the most industrious in the world. We have a settlement of Jews who produce exquisite glassware. We produce armor and weapons. Wine, olive oil. Even amber. Its port can harbor the whole Roman fleet, and traders sail there from all over the world. The roads… "

He looked at her and saw she was laughing at him. With a grin, she said in her stumbling Greek, "Yes, yes! You love Akeela! Someday you take me there."

That gave them both pause. She was a slave, and his contract with the legion ran for another eighteen years.

They would never go to Aquileia together.

"Talk," she said. "What you do there?"

He laughed at her. In Gothic, he said, "I have trained many recruits who knew no Greek. Your Greek is worse than any of theirs. You sound like you're gargling and coughing at the same time."

Elodia laughed too. She did not take it personally. It was probably true. Replying in her pidgin Greek, she said, "I learn fast. You never learn Goth better. You not talking better than a baby. Little baby speaking little baby Goth."

They laughed together. She repeated her question. "What, lovely master, you doing in best Roman town Akeela?"

"I trained under my father as a blacksmith and armorer."

"Why you get here?"

Over the next few weeks, Caius, speaking Greek, spun out the story of his youth, bit by bit, as they rode the mules along the roads and paths around the outpost. In short order, she became fluent in that tongue. She noticed when his story approached his adulthood or touched on the events leading to his joining the legion, he became reticent. He veered his tale to some subject he found less sensitive.

Elodia realized the men in the squad were lonely. When they watched Caius and her riding near the outpost, talking, laughing, and singing, many asked if they might ride too. She always agreed. They were eager to know more about her life north of the river and the customs of the Goths.

Glabius feigned surprise to hear they cooked their meat. "So, Goths *do* know how to cook! All of them but you."

"My cook slave doing it," she said humorlessly in her weak Greek.

The legionaries had their own stories, often sad stories, and she listened. No one in the squad had ever listened before.

Marius had no interest in riding, but he and she enjoyed bow hunting, a skill she'd practiced since childhood.

Polybius wanted nothing more than to fish. She joined him one day and learned that he demanded complete silence once his hook was in the water. She'd wrongly assumed he would carry on his usual rambling, one-sided conversation. After a single afternoon of silent dullness, she was done with fishing.

With each legionary, she made a point of speaking Gothic, hoping that in time they would learn her language. She wanted them to treat her as a friend, perhaps a younger sister, but not as a slave. Growing up, she'd had slaves. She did not want anyone treating her cruelly as she'd treated her own.

Sometimes, Caius would ask her about her life in the outpost. By then, Elodia felt at home living among and taking care of eight strong hairy men dressed uniformly in gray woolen tunics who banged around in hobnail sandals. All of them (except for two) were growing accustomed to and even friendly toward her.

Caius asked, "You like living with us?"

"The work isn't hard. I am safe and fed. I feel valued. The men leave me alone. And you are my friend. It is good for now." She gave him a warm smile and added, "Life for many slaves is much worse."

After years of tension and trauma, her tranquil life on the edge of the great river soothed her spirit. She attributed this blessing to her favored goddess, Ithunn. Every night up in the stable loft, she prayed as she burrowed into her bed of straw and pulled her blankets up to her chin.

Please let me remain here. And teach me how to cook.

Caius could see that dinner remained the bane of Elodia's existence. She simply had no clue. Between a lifetime of being waited on and having no great interest in food, she was perhaps the worst cook he'd ever met.

Eutaius, the late provisioner, had taken indifferent care of the animals, but his cooking verged on competency. Though he set a very low bar for acceptable, it was higher than Elodia could jump.

Breakfasts were easy. Every morning she would serve the same warm, nutritious slop, a large bowlful of oat porridge, which they wolfed down before being fully awake.

But they expected her to provide variety, flavor, and quantity for dinner. She didn't know how. It aggravated the squad every day, day after day, like a pebble caught between foot and sandal.

Caius would laugh if it weren't so sad. She struggled trying to help the squad, being friendly and entertaining, and accumulating the squad's goodwill. Then every evening, she would squander it by serving something revolting. She understood her failing, but she was too proud to ask for help. Until after she ruined Polybius's catch.

Polybius entered the barracks one afternoon with five salmon on a line, the most beautiful pink salmon, each one enough to feed two legionaries. He told Elodia she should grill them. She did not know what a grill was. It had something to do with cooking on or in an open fire.

The two salmon she carefully placed in the flames were incinerated before she could rescue them. She was more careful with the other three fish, placing their fileted halves on hot rocks near the flames. They were hot but raw when it came time to eat. Polybius was furious.

Among the others, there was no yelling, no open revolt but, one by one, the men stood and emptied their largely untouched meals into the fire. Minicius said to Grainus, "You should trade her for one who can cook."

After dinner, Caius found her moping in the stable. She looked so miserable. To his surprise, he was miserable too. "Why don't you ask for help?" he said.

"Ask who? I am the slave. Soldiers do not help slaves. Especially soldiers do not help slaves cook."

"I would help you."

"You? Why would you help me?"

He couldn't possibly tell her why, so he said, "Because you taught me the Gothic word for 'frog.'" It was an absurd reason, but when she looked at his face, she understood.

"Thank you."

30

With Grainus's permission, Caius was relieved of other duties in the late afternoon, freeing him to help Elodia with cooking. "I'm not doing it," Grainus said, "because I think you want to spend more time with her, which, by the way, I do believe, but because if we don't start seeing some edible meals, I'll have a mutiny on my hands."

After that, Caius and Elodia spent hours together every day cooking. But also planning meals, visiting the nearby village to buy supplies, and exercising the mules. They talked and teased and joked with each other. Minicius said, "They're like an old married couple." Arruntius said he didn't care so long as the meals tasted good.

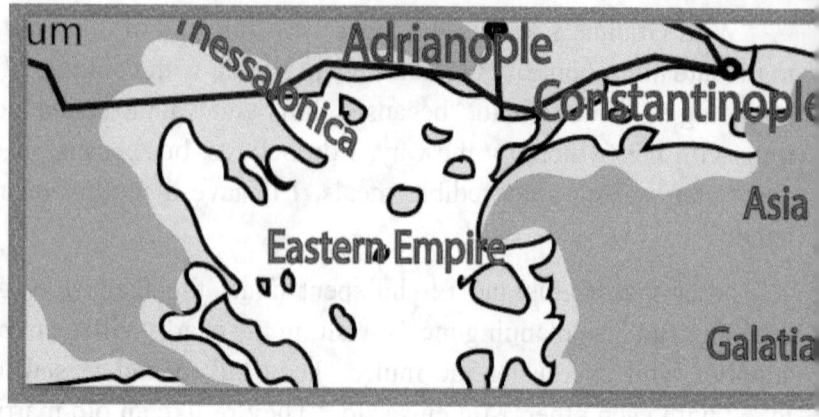

2. Bitorix Notices Elodia
375 CE

Military Tribune Bitorix was negligent of many things, but forgetting unpaid debts was not one. Yet, he'd overlooked a payment for half a year. He had ordered Decanus Grainus to sell a slave—a young girl, was it?—and send him half the proceeds. He had not.

All this came to mind during the military tribune's inspection tour. With almost seventy-five frontier outposts along the Danube from Durostorum to Oescus, stopping at each took him the better part of a long rainy month. Soaking wet and cold, he reached Grainus's outpost at dusk on an endless day, having just reviewed three others. All he wanted was shelter from the blowing rain, not a tent but something more solid, a fire, and a good hot meal. The outpost's squad stood at attention in the rain outside the small fort's wall. Its decanus saluted and welcomed him. The fellow's name was… Well, did it matter? These scum were all the same.

"Decurion Grainus, sir," the man prompted him. "Welcome to Outpost Quadraginta Quinque," forty-five, this being the forty-fifth outpost west of Durostorum, "and our barracks hall is yours." After tossing the squad's personal possessions out onto the porch, Bitorix's lead men had moved in the military tribune's gear. Polybius carried their things to the stable for safekeeping. Marius and Glabius were busy setting up tents for the squad's use that night.

Elodia was occupied roasting her second deer of the day, having accidentally reduced the first to a mound of venison jerky.

Is this one adequately cooked? No time left to check, here comes the big man himself, ready to eat.

Grainus's squad ate in their tents while Elodia served the military tribune and his men at the long barracks table. She caught Bitorix's eye. He studied her. Young. Long jet-black hair, braided and pinned under a net cap. A long tunic embroidered in silver thread. It hid her figure poorly. He could see she had no breasts to speak of, an insignificant flaw in his opinion, and an aspect balanced by her chubby round rear. Yet it was her face that captivated him. Angelic. From her exquisite mouth came a clear voice, resonant. Just listening to her speak, and she did not say more than a word or two to any of his men, made him shiver. She approached him, refilled his wine cup, and asked if he needed anything else.

Yes, I need you to live with me. From tomorrow until the day I die.

"No, thank you, dear. But, if I may ask, do I detect a slight Gothic accent?"

"Yes, my lord. My late mother came here from Gothia," the lands north of the Danube, "as a young woman. That was before she married the man who is now our village duumvir," the local mayor. This was the cover story she had concocted with Caius that

33

afternoon, one that hid her actual status while presenting her as a respectable young woman of good family.

"Do you sing?"

"Aye. I know a song or two. Shall I sing after dinner?"

"No, sing now. Sing to me while I eat."

Elodia sang for an hour. After each song, Bitorix, leading his men, applauded, and demanded another. He would never tire of her singing. When her voice finally grew hoarse, she begged Bitorix to be excused and asked Caius, "Please walk me back to the village." The pair's exit was the final act in a play of deception that neither Caius nor Grainus imagined would go so smoothly.

Bitorix felt stunned.

I should not have let her go. She should be with me tonight. And every night.

When the rest of his men retired to the barracks bunks, he remained at the table, wondering, thinking, and drinking.

It is no coincidence that God has brought me here to the very place where she dwells. Where she lives, breathes, and sings. God help me.

Only when he could no longer keep his eyes open did he stagger to the nearest bunk, evict the man sleeping there, and collapse.

In the morning, Bitorix and his entourage meant to continue the inspection tour. But they first detoured to the local village. Bitorix, stopping the first person he encountered, an old woman, asked, "Where might I find a young woman named Elodia, the duumvir's daughter."

"My lord," she said, "the duumvir has no daughter. You must be referring to Elodia, the slave girl who services the local limitanei squad. Their outpost is but a mile upstream on the river road. The decanus is a good man, Grainus by name."

Grainus. A slave girl. An unpaid debt. It all clicked into place. A ruse, a clever ruse. Bitorix snarled like a bear worried by hounds. Did they think to keep her? No. She was meant for him, and he would have her.

The rain began again.

"He didn't suspect a thing, did he!" Elodia said to Caius. They were in the stable; she collecting eggs from the chickens, and he brushing Fortis. Her face beamed as she recalled the previous night's deception.

"Why are you so surprised? You looked nothing like a slave. Salonia fixed you up very well. That thing she did with your hair! And the clothes she put you in. Very nice." Salonia was the village baker's wife, an ethnic Goth with a young daughter, who Elodia had befriended during her many provisioning trips.

She understood Caius had no words for describing a woman's appearance, but he was right. She had looked appealing, much more like a wealthy merchant's daughter than a slave girl. Elodia appreciated his clumsy compliments, his fumbling words. Putting the last egg in her basket, she looked at him and found him watching her. A warm look. Caught staring, he colored and returned to currying Fortis, just missing her smile.

"Perhaps," Caius said, "Bitorix has truly forgotten you."

Bitorix had not forgotten Elodia. A few days later, when a warm wind brought more rain north from the Mediterranean Sea, a soldier arrived at the outpost bearing a message for Grainus. He rode a mule and led another. But Grainus was not immediately available. He had taken a few days' leave to spend time with his mistress in the village. Caius felt at liberty to open and read Bitorix's order.

"Decanus Grainus, You are to immediately return these two mules carrying, respectively, the messenger and the slave named Elodia. *ℬ*."

The final stylized letter was Bitorix's mark. For once, there seemed no way to ignore this order.

Caius and Elodia went to the stable, where he helped pack her few possessions into a leather satchel.

It is a wonder she does not weep. If she does, I will too.

"I know you promised to protect me," she started, and when Caius tried to interject, she hushed him. "I know you've done your best, but we both know in this case you are—we are—powerless. Urth," the Gothic goddess of fate, "has acted against us."

"Elodia… It will be all right, I'm sure." His shaky tone belied his words.

"You do not know that!" Her bitterness was not directed at him. "I prayed and asked for so little, just to be allowed to live peacefully here with my squad. And with you." Now he could see her eyes turn red and wet. "I have prayed every night to Ithunn. She has failed me."

He took her limp hands in his. Her gaze seemed to be focused on some spot on his chest. He said, "You must go. The messenger is waiting." He kissed her forehead. She squeezed his hands and shook hers free.

The distance from the stable to where the messenger waited in front of the barracks was short. It was long enough for Elodia to arrange her expression. To the other members of the squad standing on the porch, she gave an impression of calmness, a face blank and wooden. She mounted her mule and, with the messenger, departed the gate, not looking back.

The messenger and Elodia hurried their mules along the river road. He whipped her mule when she fell behind. They entered the fortress at Transmarisca and dismounted. Using the butt end of his whip to steer her, he pushed her through the passages and courtyards until they entered a small room, featureless except for a window overlooking the Danube River. Dull white foam dotted the black water, where the icy wind whipped it up. The messenger announced her, turned, and left. A man stood behind a plain wooden desk. Bitorix.

Tall and blond, muscular, well-built, a man of great beauty, spoiled only by his eyes. Blue, cold, and dead, like fish eyes. They frightened her.

He asked a few questions—name, family, how she came to live with Grainus's squad—but he only half-listened to her answers.

While she spoke, his eyes wandered over her body from head to foot. He got up and came around the desk. He stepped closer. His breath smelled sweet with mint. His breathing grew shallow and fast, almost panting. He took her chin between his thumb and forefinger. Tilting her head back, he studied her, working his way up from her neck to her mouth to her nose. When his gaze reached her eyes, she shut them. "Open them," he said. She obeyed but looked beyond his face to the ceiling.

He released her and stepped back. He seemed winded as though he had run a mile. Puffing with passion? "Would you like some wine?" Without waiting for an answer, he took her arm and hurried her up a flight of stairs into a room. His bedroom. A large, well-lit room with a west-facing window admitting the dim afternoon light. Colorful rugs covered the flagstone floor. A large bed occupied the room's center. A small couch stood off to the side.

"Sit," he ordered, pointing to the couch, "while I pour the wine. Make yourself comfortable."

She was anything but. This was not the treatment meted out to a slave meant for sale. His intention was clear. She froze. He attempted casual conversation. She could not speak but just nodded and shook her head. He gave a long and rambling speech with many forgettable details, but its general thrust was clear. He wanted to impress her. More than that, he *hungered* to impress her.

"I am a Gaul from Galatia province," he said in Greek, "descended from a long line of Galatian royalty. My people fled Gaul rather than submit to Roman rule and moved across the Bosporus centuries ago. I have the blood of kings in my veins." Did he glance at her to judge his speech's effect? She would not know. She was eyeing the wine in her cup, swirling it round and round.

When she failed to show any interest in his pedigree, he tried a different approach. "Our military count is a man named Lupicinus. He controls Thracia, Lower Moesia, and Macedonia. He has only six military tribunes, and *I* am one!" She finally raised her eyes and studied his face. He stood waiting for some response. Having nothing to say, she just nodded.

38

"You are so quiet. Have my lineage and position left you in awe? Would you be more at ease if we spoke another language?"

She shrugged.

"I am fluent in many tongues," he added.

Switching from Greek, he tried his native tongue, Gallic, the language of Gaul and Galatia, which she didn't understand. He tried his minimal Gothic, pronouncing so poorly she could comprehend nothing. He tried Latin. She pretended not to know it. Was he testing her? In this half of the empire, few people used Latin except the Roman military. They used it as a secret language, thinking the locals would not understand. Elodia spoke it fluently but kept that a secret, fearing someone might consider her a spy.

When she did not respond, he grew quiet. He finished his wine and poured himself more. Finally, reverting to Greek, he told her that she was beautiful. He told her he loved her. Ever since the banquet in the barracks when she served him dinner, he'd thought of her constantly. He could not sleep. He had no appetite.

She did not believe a word of it.

He said he would free her and wed her. He was rich, he said. He had a small chest, which he claimed was full of gold Roman aurei. To impress her, he opened it and allowed her a glance. She saw that he had placed a few gold aurei on top to conceal a chest full of brass sesterces. Everything about him was a lie. She'd met men like him before. He just wanted to bump her. He hoped to charm her, so she would desire him.

Lies, all lies. Except for his looks. "My ancestors were all tall and blond, like me, not dark and short like Romans from Italia," he claimed. To her, his looks meant nothing. He was a snake.

She could see his frustration mount when nothing he said drew a response.

She tried to scrub what followed from her memory. She fought. She tore her fingernails into his back; she bit his arms and shoulders. She reached for her knife, but he had taken it. When he finally overpowered her, she tightened every muscle in her body, lying as rigid as timber.

When he finished, he wept. Yes, to her astonishment, he cried.

Those were real tears that flooded his face! Was she indeed that important to him? Was he speaking honestly? He must be sincere, saying he would free her and wed her. Why else would he weep?

Perhaps he honestly thought he loved her. It didn't matter. She hated him now, and she would hate him forever.

She could see his disappointment turning to anger. Denial stung.

A man of his self-importance could not tolerate rejection, not from anyone, especially from a slave girl like her.

When he brought his crying under control, he called an aide.

"She does not please me," he said. "Lash her and send her home."

Agonizing lashing. She could tolerate that because he would then send her home. Home? Imagine thinking of her little stable as home. Yet it was.

day later, early in the morning, the same pair of mules carrying the same riders returned to the outpost. They entered its small gate before anyone noticed them. In a loud voice, Elodia's escort ordered her to dismount. His voice brought Caius to her side, where he helped her down. Her face was every bit as blank and wooden as when she left. When he questioned her, she said only, "I am back." As short as this conversation was, it was long enough for the escort to lean over to her mule, untie her bundle of possessions from the saddle and push it off into the muddy courtyard. He grabbed her mule's reins and rode back out the gate.

Caius led her into the squad's barracks. It was empty except for Grainus and Marius, who sat talking at the long table. She moved to the fire and squatted to warm her hands.

Grainus, startled by her unexpected appearance, asked, "You are back! Why?"

"He didn't want me."

"Because?"

"I did not please him."

Before Grainus could ask more, Elodia said, "May I go to my stable?"

He could see the girl looked exhausted. And crushed. There would be time later for more questions. "Yes."

She rose to go, and Caius, unbidden, rose too. He picked up her muddy bundle. Once outside, he brushed off the mud as best he could.

"What happened?" he asked.

"He took my knife."

Caius was puzzled. He reached to put his arm around her. She pulled away. They made their way to the mule stable, Caius waiting for Elodia to speak, but she said nothing.

"Elodia, tell me what happened to you."

41

"I just want to lie in my bed, Caius. We will talk later."

"Can I get you food and drink?"

"No, just let me sleep."

Elodia slept the whole day through. When she awoke, Caius was waiting, squatting on his heels in the loft. "You need to drink."

She took a long draft from his flask. He offered her stew he'd made himself, chicken and fried onions, liberally spiced. She waved it away, whispering, "Thank you, Caius." She went back to sleep.

That evening he helped her down from the loft and walked her to the latrine. She moaned in pain. Though she protested, he insisted she lift her tunic. "Jesus!" he exclaimed, seeing the slash wounds crisscrossing her back. He helped her back up the ladder to her loft bed, then went to the barracks to fetch bandages and salve.

"How is she?" asked Grainus.

"That fryker had her lashed. She can scarcely move."

Back in the stable, Elodia did not protest as he cleaned and smeared oil on her wounds before bandaging them. For the next few nights, while her wounds seeped, Caius slept by her. He wanted to be there with food and wine whenever she woke. When she wept in the night, he held her hand.

Elodia, you need to eat," Caius insisted. But she was too tired, and the food he brought was tasteless. It had been many days, but when he looked at her wounds, he claimed they were healed. He was wrong. She still felt great pain. She told him she could not move, but he compelled her to get up. He forced her into resuming her routine. "Bridie needs you," he said.

Elodia said she'd care for her in the morning. "It *is* morning," he said. *Then why is it black? It is always black. Even at noon, it seems black.*

She buckled under his pressure. Every day she did as he told her. Life became an endless cycle of Caius shaking her awake, her stoking the barracks fireplace, and preparing gruel for the squad's breakfast. Caius was always there encouraging her to eat; please eat.

After breakfast, she would sweep the barracks and care for the animals. *How can I clean Bridie's hooves? I have no knife.*

Caius helped her make the men's dinner and—if you would please eat just a few bites—let her retire after to her loft.

It took a week before she could perform even the lightest work. The other squad members covered for her. When Minicius grumbled once too often, citing the advantage of selling her, his brother, Arruntius, knocked him to the ground. Arruntius's new independence astonished everyone.

Three weeks on, her back had healed, though it would be scarred forever. Caius no longer had to coax her into performing her duties.

"Every day, she mentions her knife," Caius said to Grainus. "She finds some task or other she claims she can't do without her knife."

"Give her a knife," Grainus said.

"I fear she will use it on herself."

"If she means to die, she will do it, knife or no knife," Grainus said pragmatically.

Caius agreed. Within a few days, Grainus brought her a knife to replace the one seized by Bitorix. It was fine steel with a narrow double-edged blade about ten inches long. She accepted it graciously, saying, "Thank you. Bitorix shall receive this one when I get my own knife back."

Caius shuddered to imagine precisely how Bitorix might *receive* the new knife.

That marked a turning point. Elodia's outlook improved once she had a knife.

Just as Elodia thought her life had returned to normal, she found making the squad's breakfast an impossible challenge. Even the smell of oatmeal porridge made her vomit. She immediately recognized the cause. This was not the first time she had a baby growing in her belly. Gods, how she hated that shitty snake Bitorix.

Grainus understood her condition. His mistress had suffered similarly with their first child.

Elodia considered telling Caius. She no longer had any doubts about his feeling for her. Those ended when Salonia chided her. "Are you stupid, girl? The big man goes all a-quiver when he looks at you!" Yet he might feel jealous. Would Caius wish the child were his? She did not want to hurt him.

On the other hand, she knew the months ahead would be difficult. She would be dependent on Caius even more. As hard as telling him might be, it was necessary, and the sooner, the better.

They were together again in the stable, she mucking out the stalls, and he just watching. She didn't mind the task but she knew he really disliked it, so she didn't ask him for help.

I might as well be blunt.

"Caius, I'm pregnant. It's Bitorix's fault."

"I know," he said. "Grainus told me. I've been waiting for you to tell me."

She dropped her shovel and her eyes flooded with tears. She walked to him and rested her head on his chest. She squeezed her eyes tightly, leaving damp spots on his tunic.

In a quiet voice, she said, "I would want it if it were yours."

"You should want it regardless. The child does not choose the father."

"It will be hard, so hard, in the months to come. I am fine right now, but I know this will change and be more difficult. It will be worse, knowing it is his." She reached up, clutched Caius's shoulders, pushed herself back to arm's length, and looked him in the face. "You have always helped me. But this time is different. How can you help when it's another man's child?"

"That makes no difference," Caius said. "I will stand by you."

She wrapped her arms around him and raised her mouth to kiss his chin. To her surprise, he lowered his head and kissed her on the mouth. A first for the two of them.

The issue became moot when, a week later, she miscarried. The unformed baby leaked out as clotty blood, leaving her confused and miserable. In truth, it was something she'd wished for. She had feared the specter of raising Bitorix's child and seeing the father every time she glanced at it. Now, having that vision gone was a great relief. But how could she find comfort in an innocent child's death?

Caius did his best to calm her. He claimed she had no reason to feel guilty, but what did he know? Nothing. His opinion was slanted...colored...to be honest, by his love for her. Ithunn bless the man.

By the time of the solstice, Elodia appeared fully healed in both body and spirit. With her energy and enthusiasm returned, she made the solstice celebration a grand affair. She purchased good-quality ale and the best cakes from the village baker. Grainus invited his mistress and other village notables. Caius visited the adjacent frontier outposts, told their respective decani of the event, and promised them a warm welcome while adding, "Please bring your own beer."

All drank a libation for the new year, the 1229th year since the founding of Rome. They drank another to honor Emperors Valens and Gratian. The village's Christian priest led the crowd by proposing a third libation. This one was to celebrate the birth of Jesus, which the priest claimed happened three hundred seventy-six years ago. As his source, he cited "the famous astronomer Victorius of Aquitaine," whom no one else had ever heard of.

Elodia led the throng in poetry, song, and dance. She demonstrated a surprising tolerance for ale, drinking many legionaries under the table. Yet, come dawn, she drove a mule cart filled with those too drunk to walk back to their respective homes and outposts.

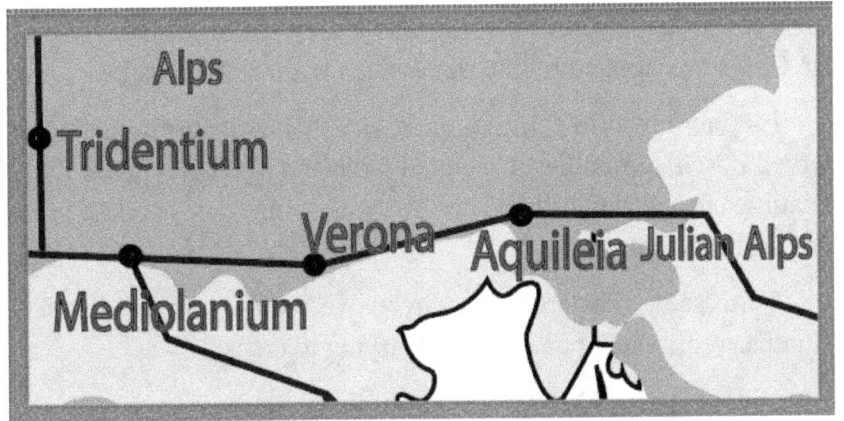

3. Refugees on the Far Shore 376 CE

On the order of Military Tribune Bitorix, Grainus traveled to Transmarisca, leaving Caius in charge of the outpost. The military tribune had brought in all his officers for a two-day meeting, which he claimed was for planning and preparation. The first morning, Bitorix passed essential information to his men. This was news he'd received a few weeks earlier from his commanding officer, Military Count Lupicinus, in Durostorum.

That afternoon and into the evening, Bitorix led his men through the seamy quarter of Transmarisca and treated them to drinks and whores. He got so drunk that the second day's agenda was canceled, and Grainus went home.

Once there, he convened a meeting of his squad. "First," he said as men gathered around the barracks table, "the Huns continue to massacre Goths north of the river. Men, women, and children. The Goths are fleeing south, but the Huns are coming this way. This has been confirmed by our spies. Reliable men, Bitorix claims. Once the Goths are stopped by the river, some will try to cross it."

Elodia moved to refill the men's cups. It was morning, so she served posca, a mixture of watered wine and vinegar. It was a vile mixture, in her opinion. She was reserving the good ale for that night's meal.

Caius said, "That explains why we've been so busy the last few months. With many boats and rafts trying to cross."

Glabius said, "All we've caught and killed are men. Are the Goths abandoning their families, leaving them behind?"

"Not likely," Grainus said. "They know our law. Crossing the Danube means death. They might risk their own lives but not their wives and children."

"I expect they are testing our defenses before they dare to bring their families," Caius said.

"Probably true. Or they have heard their king has petitioned Emperor Valens for permission to cross. Perhaps they hope he's granted it. Which, according to Bitorix, he has not."

Minicius, in his low authoritative voice, said, "Well, *I* heard the emperor tore up the Goths' petition and threw it in their envoy's face!"

Glabius looked across the table at his comrade-in-arms. "Where did you hear that? You just make up crap. You're an idiot."

Caius intervened before the insults spread. "Quite likely, the emperor is not in Constantinople. If he plans to battle the Sassanids this season, he will be in Syria. Then it might take months or even years for him to receive and respond to the Goths' petition."

The others understood. Constantinople was only a ten-day ride away, whereas a trip to Syria could take months.

"Why are we waging war on the Sassanids? Their country is just worthless desert land, full of snakes and scorpions," Glabius asked.

Not even Caius knew the answer to that.

"The Goths must be cowardly warriors if they won't stand and fight the Huns. Instead, they flee like women!" Minicius said.

Elodia could not stand by and let her tribe be maligned. "You know nothing about Huns! I do! My father had a Hun slave. I learned a lot from him."

"Such as?" Grainus asked.

"To start with, many things people say are simply not true. Half the stories are false. It is true they ride well and are excellent archers, but it is not true they drink only raw horse blood. I saw my father's Hun drink raw blood, but he also drank water and ale."

From Arruntius came, "Eww!"

"It is not true their height is half that of a real man. Father's Hun was small, like all Huns, but not *that* small. But *he* said they breed their children small because their horses are small. Most newborns are as small as a dog pup, and a Hun woman can bear two litters of four pups each year. Each Hun child grows to full size in two years."

Evander whistled in wonder.

"They are born knowing how to ride. Riding is so important that, on its second birthday, a Hun child is put on the back of a pony. If it falls off, it is left to die. As for archery, Hun children, both boys and girls, can draw a bow and shoot from their ponies by age three."

Grainus nodded. "I've heard of stranger things. Still, with so many Huns breeding so fast, it is no wonder their hordes are beyond number."

But Caius raised an eyebrow. "Are you sure this is true?"

"These things my father's slave told me, so I know they are correct," Elodia said.

"Thankfully, we will never face the Huns. They are so terrified of water they will never cross the river," Minicius said.

The other legionaries looked at him and shook their heads in disbelief. Minicius was always saying crazy things.

The shrill note of the alarm pierced the morning quiet. Elodia left behind her cleaning chores in the barracks and ran outside. "What is it?" she called up to Marius, who was standing high in the watchtower.

Grainus and the others sprinted from the courtyard where they'd been training and gathered beside her. They all watched Marius, waiting for an answer. He pointed out to the river where a confrontation was quickly developing. "Two patrol galleys are chasing a Gothic boat. No, I see *two* Gothic boats."

The frontier troops, like Grainus's squad, did not form the empire's first line of river defense. That honor belonged to the dozens of sleek, fast galleys that patrolled from the Iron Gates, far upstream, to the downstream delta where the Danube drained into the Black Sea. Many of these guard ships were berthed at the town of Sexaginta Prista, Latin for "the city of sixty ships," twenty-five miles upstream from Grainus's outpost.

The action quickly moved allowing those on the shore could see it. One of the barbarian boats turned back, heading toward the north bank as fast as its oarsmen could row. The other rapidly approached the shore just west of where Elodia and the others stood. The Roman ships also separated, each chasing one of the Gothic boats.

Grainus called his men to arms. They darted into the barracks, donned their armor, seized their weapons, and emerged a minute later, ready for combat. The decanus quickly inspected them—even Arruntius was correctly turned out, having remembered his helmet for a change—and marched them double time up the river road.

From across the water, Elodia could hear the Gothic rowers shouting and cursing as they pulled hard, trying to outpace the galleys. Gothic rowboats were no match for the Roman ships, designed and manned for just this kind of interdiction.

Strain as the Goths might, the Roman ships quickly closed the gaps and moved at ramming speed. The crack of splintering timbers reached Elodia's ears. The massive bronze ram mounted on the bow of the more distant galley smashed into the retreating Gothic boat. She watched as the broken boat heeled onto its side, turned turtle, and sank. A few warriors escaped the doomed vessel, jumping into the water and clinging to chunks of shattered timber. At an order from the Roman captain, his oarsmen shipped their oars, and the galley stopped. The archers on board quickly picked off the floating survivors.

Elodia watched as the last arrow-festooned body sank beneath the waves.

A second crash caught her attention. The galley closer to her finally caught its prey and rammed it. That boat, having reached shallow water, did not flip. Instead, it rocked gently back and forth

51

as it settled to the river bottom. The galley, also in danger of going aground, slowly backed off.

The Goths jumped off their foundering craft and waded ashore while dodging arrows fired by the galley's archers. Despite the distance to the receding galley, many shafts hit their targets, though two dozen Goths managed to reach the shore. The steep riverbank funneled those survivors to a spot where a path led upward, but Grainus and his men were waiting with sword and spear at the top to welcome the barbarians ashore.

Realizing they were scrambling up into a trap, they backed down to the riverbank. The galley carefully moved closer to the shore. One by one, the galley archers picked off the men. Marius stood above and shot point-blank into the cluster of warriors, killing more than seven. By noon, the barbarians were all dead, their bodies floating downstream.

High on the riverbank, Grainus studied the bodies his squad had killed. "Look," he said. "They are all emaciated."

Caius agreed. "They came to the Danube expecting to find food," he said. "In most years, the winter crops would be ready to harvest, but this year there were none. Our high spring flood destroyed them. No wonder they did not wait for permission to cross. They were starving."

Grainus shook his head. "It is a pity. Look, you can see some of the dead were once strong warriors before hunger sapped their flesh. In earlier times, we would have welcomed them and drafted them into the legion. Now they are just invaders, hungry invaders. Hunger certainly made them easier to kill."

One fine afternoon, with Grainus's leave, Caius and Elodia went to the local village to purchase provisions. To their surprise, the usual marketplace was empty, but they could hear cheering and singing a short distance away.

They made their way down the street toward the noise. It looked as though the whole village was there. When they reached the crowd's edge, Elodia's view was blocked, even when standing on tiptoe.

"I can't see," she said. "I'm too short." One advantage of being accompanied by a giant legionary, even when he was out of uniform and unarmed, was the throng parted to let them through. They moved forward to see a circle of dancers.

There they saw everyone chanting and beating in tempo as the dancers twirled and the circle revolved, turning this way and that, accompanied by drums and flute. At the center of the ring were four people. Elodia identified one as a Jesus God priest, judging by the silver cross hanging from his neck. He was dressed in cheerful bright red robes, which contrasted with his grim and severe face. Another person in the ring who did not look joyful or happy was a young man whose hands hung limply by his sides except when he wiped the sweat from his brow. The groom, she guessed. A pretty girl, a few years younger than Elodia, stood by his side, wearing a plain tunic and a big grin. She was unadorned except for flowers pinned in her hair. Finally, there was a straight-backed gray beard, who had to be the girl's father.

Elodia watched as the dancers sang, clapped, and circled to the rhythm of the music. The sound swelled each time the chorus came around, which everyone (except Elodia) knew and joined in. There were many words she didn't fully understand, but finally, catching the rude bits, she sang and joined the rest performing lewd gestures: clap, jump spreading feet, jump bringing feet together, thrust hips, clap again, and so on. Caius didn't sing, but he did laugh during the vulgar chorus when the bride blushed and covered her eyes.

When the song finally ended, the priest summoned the bridal party. He had to shout twice before the crowd quieted down.

The priest's rich voice carried to the far edge of the crowd. "Who speaks for the bride, Portela, daughter of Portel?"

The gray beard responded in an equally forceful voice, "I, Portel, her father, do." Elodia considered this silly since the older man was right there, standing in front of the priest. Who else could possibly be speaking for her?

The priest turned to the groom and asked, "How will you care for this woman, Portela, daughter of Portel?"

The groom addressed the bride's father in a high, quavering voice. "I, Bengham, son of Bengher, in the face of God, do vow to faithfully protect and provide for Portela, daughter of Portel, and our children until the end of my days."

Then the bride's father, upon a signal from the priest, spoke directly to the groom. "I, Portel, in the face of God, do vow that I have taught my daughter, Portela, obedience and fidelity. She will be faithful to you, love you, and bear your children and raise them in the Christian faith until the end of her days."

Elodia suppressed a snicker. She'd seen similar vows made and broken innumerable times among her people. What was the point of making such vows when everyone knew they would not be kept? Especially since the bride was not vowing to do anything. Her father may have taught her to keep her knees together, but she wasn't promising!

But a moment later, Elodia was proved wrong.

The priest took her hands, placed them in the groom's hands, stepped back, and nodded at her. The bride, Portela, said in a quiet voice, almost too low to be heard, that she vowed to do as her father and husband commanded. *Damn, now she really is committed.*

The priest waved at a pretty little girl standing just inside the circle of dancers. She came forward and presented the priest with two floral crowns. He solemnly placed the crowns on the couple's heads and intoned a prayer. "These crowns signify the oaths you are making to each other, oaths you are making in Jesus's name, and which you must keep from this day forward until you die or until you join Jesus when he returns again." The groom then took the bride's face in his hands, pulled her to him, and kissed her firmly on the lips. When they broke, she smiled and blushed. The crowd cheered, and as the singing and dancing resumed, she pulled his face to hers and returned his kiss. *Even with all the Jesus God nonsense, aren't they a beautiful couple?*

After the ceremony, the crowd dispersed. Barrels had been set up, and there was ale. Caius and Elodia made their way to where they'd spotted Salonia. As if reading Elodia's mind, Salonia said, "Yes, they certainly are a beautiful couple. I've known them all their lives. What about you two? Will you stay and dance?"

Caius said, "No," just as Elodia said, "Yes," so they danced and drank, not the usual watery brew made by the local innkeeper but a fine batch from kegs purchased a few miles east. That brewer's customary consumers, the officers of Caius's legion, were more discerning.

Elodia and Caius danced for hours until even she admitted her feet were sore. It was dusk before they got back to the outpost.

Grainus was irritated. Though he'd given them leave, he had still expected Elodia to return and prepare the squad's dinner. In her absence, the men ate cold mutton. But she presented them with a large loaf of Salonia's sweet bread, which dispelled their annoyance. Caius brought out a sizable barrel of the fine beer. When she poured each soldier a large mugful, they cheered her. Then she led Caius back to the stable for their dinner.

Caius lit the campfire outside the stable. Elodia heated cold mutton with salted gravy, which she served with a thick slab of wheat bread. He ate it with relish, smacking his lips and washing it down with a mug of the good beer. She followed up with a bowl of honey-sweetened rice. He moaned when the food was all gone. "I am so full! If I move, I'll vomit!"

By now, it was dark. She said, "I'm getting cold, and there are mosquitos. Let's go inside and huddle under my blanket. We can share more of this fine beer."

Elodia had never extended Caius such an invitation before. A quizzical look crossed his face. She kept her face blank.

He lit a torch from the fire and led the way inside. He walked across the dirt floor and waited by the ladder. She pointed up to her straw mattress in the loft. He started to climb when she grabbed his tunic. "Take off your boots! No dirty boots in my bed, you meatball!" While he bent to untie them, she kicked off her sandals, clambered up onto the bed, sat sideways across the mattress, feet dangling, and wrapped a blanket around herself.

When he got up, she was sitting comfortably on the mattress, leaning back against the back wall. By the flickering torchlight, he could see she was smiling at him. He sat beside her, his bare feet over the edge, and pulled some of the blanket onto himself.

He shuffled sideways so their legs and bare feet rubbed against each other. She leaned against him and kissed him on the cheek. He leaned into her, sighed, belched, relaxed, and exhaled a deep moan of contentment, having finally reached a place where he'd long dreamed of being. He put an arm around her neck, pulled her head to him, and was preparing to kiss her when she stopped him with her hand on his chest. "Where's the beer?"

"I thought you had it!" he said.

"I left it down below on the shelf."

"Do you really want it?"

"Yes."

Caius moaned softly but then dug himself out from under the blanket and slithered down to the floor. In the dark, he couldn't see her looking down from above, grinning.

"There's only one mug here," he called up.

"That's right."

By the time he climbed up, she'd repositioned herself at the end of the bed. She sat cross-legged with her back against the wall, and the blanket wrapped around her shoulders like a cloak. He handed her the mug. She drank while he sat facing her, cross-legged with their knees almost touching.

"May I have a sip?" he asked.

"Of course." She handed him the mug. He no sooner put it to his lips when she said, "My turn."

He handed it back. "It's cold up here. Do you have another blanket?"

"No." She handed him the mug and tucked the blanket more tightly around herself, but she wiggled a little closer to him so their knees rubbed. They continued passing the mug back and forth keeping his turns short, so he only got sips. On her turns, she drank heartily. With each hand-off, she moved closer to him until she could wrap her legs around his waist. Finally, she emptied it. "All gone!"

"I'm cold, and I'm still thirsty," he complained.

"I'll share the blanket," she said magnanimously, "and I shall let you taste my beery lips." With that, she lunged forward, pushing Caius onto his back. She straddled him and pulled the blanket over them both. After licking her lips, he said, "No beer flavor there. Perhaps somewhere else?" He proceeded to lick her elsewhere, everywhere, removing her garments when they impeded his search.

Later, as they were falling asleep, he said he'd tasted other flavors but not beer. But he claimed he was not disappointed. Neither was she.

Initially, the rest of the squad, apart from Grainus, teased the two relentlessly. Their new relationship was greeted with crude jokes, puns, and even riddles. Caius ignored the jibes. Elodia blushed but did nothing more. Grainus was the only one who took their affair seriously.

He took Caius aside after he started sleeping in the stable loft. "Caius, I need to talk with you," he said, an opening that did not augur well. "You can't marry her, you know."

Caius shrugged. He'd expected this conversation and had already recited it in his head. "Who said anything about marriage?"

Elodia and he *had* talked about marriage. "Up here on this frontier, who would care?"

Grainus ignored his question. "It is the law. It is illegal for a Roman citizen to marry a slave, also for a Roman to marry a Goth."

"The baker is married to Salonia. Isn't she a Goth?"

"Yes," Grainus said, "but she was born here long before the emperor's decree. Anyway, we're only talking about you and Elodia."

"Suppose we did want to marry. Not saying we do. We could marry secretly using the Gothic ritual."

"Yes," Grainus said. "That would work until someone betrayed you." Caius flinched. "I'm not saying anyone in the squad would reveal your secret," by which Grainus meant Minicius who would do so intentionally, or Arruntius who might do it accidentally. "But sooner or later, Bitorix would find out. I shudder to think what he would do. He still lusts for her, you know."

Caius did know. During Bitorix's recent staff meeting, when Bitorix was blind drunk, he'd wept on Grainus's shoulder. He declared, "I will love Elodia until I die," and "Why, oh why did you sell her?" thinking her sold and forever beyond his reach. An amusing misunderstanding.

Neither Grainus nor Caius mentioned this conversation to Elodia or anyone else.

Caius and Elodia were busy day and night. By day, it seemed, the squad was forced to intercept raiders trying to cross the river. Not that the fighting affected her directly. There was blood to be cleaned off swords and shields, not usually the blood of her men, and the occasional slash wound, which her stitching skills could manage. Every day she prayed to Ithunn and the Jesus God for her men's safe return.

By night, they were busy doing what new lovers do. After several months, it occurred to Caius that Elodia had failed to conceive. One morning, after they'd finished bumping, Elodia noticed Caius looking preoccupied. He opened his mouth to say something, then closed it.

"What is it? What's bothering you?"

"You're not with child, are you?"

"No. Is that a problem?"

"We have been lovers for months, and yet no child."

"Do you question whether you're a *real man*," she joked. "I can assure you, you are." But her jest had affected him.

"Yes. I do wonder whether I can father children."

Caius lay there for a while. He became lost in thought. "There was another woman. Back in Aquileia."

Elodia stiffened and nodded. She stopped grinning. "Who was she?"

"She was the daughter of my father's assistant. A pretty girl. A good Christian. I liked her a lot. She supposed I would make a fine husband. Her father and mine agreed. By the time we all agreed, she and I had been lovers for months. No baby."

Elodia was afraid to ask but needed an answer. "What happened to her?"

"My father made enemies among our competitors. They hired thugs who murdered him and destroyed our shop. I was left penniless. When she found out, she dropped me like a stone in a pond. She wouldn't have done that if she'd been with child."

Elodia had only known hints of this story. Caius always avoided discussing that period of his life.

"You were left wondering if you could father a baby."

"Yes and she may have wondered too. Perhaps it was another reason for breaking up with me. Anyway, we both knew my father's creditors would soon be coming after me. She and her father wanted no part in that mess. Rather than being arrested as a debtor and condemned to the life of a galley slave, I fled far away to Thracia and joined the legion."

Elodia lay back in bed and put her head on Caius's chest. Relieved. *One more mystery about this man is put to rest.* Perhaps their next bump might yield the results he wished for.

Grainus's squad could not ignore what their eyes could see. What appeared to be the whole tribe of Tervingi Goths was now camped across the river from their outpost. Elodia looked upstream and down, and the sight of their tents and wagons extended until they were hidden by the river's mist.

Some were brave or desperate enough to try crossing. The river took many. Of those Goths who survived, the frontier troops killed the men and sold the others. All were famished.

Elodia managed to speak with two women before the slavers took them away. Caius stood by her side, ensuring no slavers arrested her "by accident."

"You were fleeing the Huns?" she asked.

"Aye, they are devils on horseback. There is not one family in our village who has not lost kin to them," one woman said.

"And now there is no village," the other mourned.

"Did your men not stand and fight?"

"Oh yes, they fought. When King Athanaric called the clans to resist, our clan answered," the first said.

"And died," her friend said.

"I am sorry. What do you know of my clan, clan Fontal?" Elodia asked.

"I've heard of them. Yes, I believe they joined the king's guard and helped him survive when the Huns trapped the others in the fort."

This was all news to Elodia. The two captives explained how their men went east to join the fight. Athanaric led his army to the frontier at the Pyretus River and put them to work building a fort to stop the Huns. However, the Huns crossed the river upstream and attacked Athanaric's army from the rear. They trapped most of the men inside the fort and killed them all. Those not killed, including the people of Elodia's clan, fled with Athanaric up into the Carpathian Mountains. The remaining survivors turned to Fritigern, chieftain of the Balti clan, who now claimed he was the leader of all the Tervingi Goths.

Besides killing many people, the Huns destroyed towns and farms and burned the year's harvest. Fritigern's hungry people gathered on the riverbank and looked south. "We imagined a rich land that would provide us with food and protection," the first captive said.

"What about the crossing ban? Didn't you see the Roman forts and legionaries?" Elodia asked.

"Yes, but Lord Fritigern went to the emperor in person and begged for permission to cross. We believed the emperor had granted it."

The other captive said, "Well, we *hoped* so. We have waited for so long."

Grainus received a new report from Transmarisca that confirmed what Elodia had heard. "The legion reports this Fritigern fellow carried a petition to Emperor Valens himself, requesting permission for his people to cross the river. When he found the emperor was not in Constantinople, he traveled all the way to Syria, hoping to catch him there."

"What are Fritigern's terms?" Caius asked.

"I bet he's desperate. I'd wager if Valens demanded the Goth lick his toes, he'd do it," Minicius said.

Grainus ignored him. "Fritigern said if his Goths are permitted to cross the river, then all his people will become Christians. They will disarm and return to farming. Soon, he promised they would grow wealthy and provide the emperor with silver in taxes. And because Goths make good soldiers, they will provide many men for the legions."

Caius asked, "What are Fritigern's demands? I mean, besides being allowed to cross?"

"My report doesn't say, but the Goths will want land and, more immediately, food. They are already starving to death."

"And what should we do? Anything different?"

"No new orders came with the report. Until then, we stay here and enforce the law."

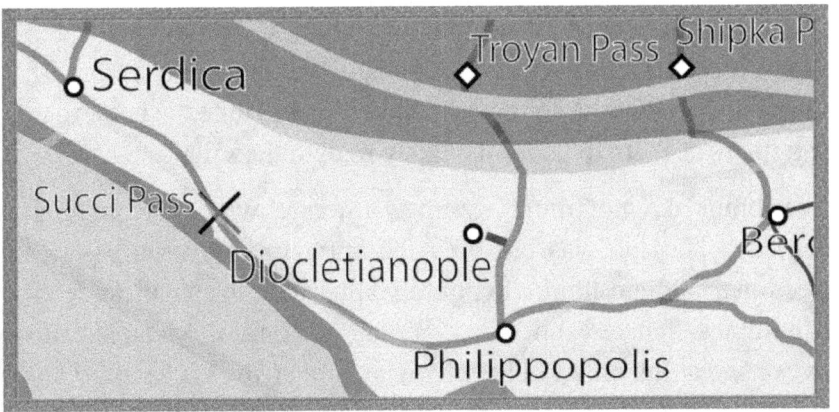

4. The Immeasurably Rich
376 CE

When measured in miles, the distance from a frontier outpost on the Danube to a wealthy plantation in western Thracia was not far. Perhaps a hundred thirty miles, about a week's march for a barbarian army. Yet the distance between Grainus's view of the world and that of an aristocrat like Licinius Sabinus could not be more pronounced.

Licinius Sabinus was rich, fabulously, extraordinarily, ultra-rich. His vast estates—fifty thousand acres—made him one of the largest landowners in Thracia, if not all the Balkans. He owned upwards of a thousand slaves. He was not some nouveau riche senator from Constantinople.

Land and slaves, Licinius ruminated on these as he settled himself onto a couch on his villa's portico.

These are the proper measures of wealth for a man like me. A patrician. Not trade and assuredly not manufacturing. And breeding. I have breeding. No amount of gold can buy that.

He relaxed while he waited for his guest to arrive. Senator Tosca Volesus. He had spotted the senator's entourage from far off, coming up the drive. A long way away. It would take the better part of an hour for them to cover the dusty road to the villa.

Sabinus did not mind waiting. It was a warm late autumn afternoon. The sun was brushing the horizon, so everything was bathed in a singular light, the light that picks out the smallest detail of buildings, fences, and crops. Biding his time, he watched his slaves harvest his broad fields of wheat. *The yield will be good this year if we can gather them before the snows come.*

He looked off to the north. There, he fancied he could distinguish individual trees on the foothills and, beyond the foothills, the Haemus range, the rugged mountain chain that separated Moesia to the north from Thracia to the south. No sign of new snow yet. The final remnants of last year's snow reflected the day's late light. When it was gone, the coming winter would refresh it.

Now the senator's train was close enough for Sabinus to distinguish individuals. Volesus. Now there was a man of no family. Rich, to be sure, wealthy enough to buy the title he flaunted so proudly. But where were his people when Gothic King Cniva ravaged Thracia? Sabinus's grandsire, six generations ago, another Licinius Sabinus, had fought Cniva and died at the side of Emperor Decius. Since then, we have stood by every emperor as we confronted the Goths, racking up victory after victory.

Licinius was filled with pride for his father, who had accompanied the current emperor, Valens, ten years ago in a campaign across the Danube River. His father said Valens gave the Goths a good thrashing and sent them fleeing back into the Carpathian Mountains.

"*Salve Pater.*" Licinius's son, Julius, climbed the marble steps from the gravel drive to the portico. A young man of seventeen, Julius showed the vigor of one already grown to full strength. He wore a simple coarse tunic that showed off his strong arms and thick thighs. The garment was black from perspiration. When he flung himself into a couch near his father, a spray of sweat flew wide. A few drops landed on his father.

Irritated, he said, "You spray like a dog shaking itself."

Julius ignored the comment. He signaled for a drink.

"For Jesus's sake, boy, go bathe yourself. See there?" Licinius pointed down the drive. "My guests will be here shortly."

"They won't be here for a quarter-hour. I have time." A slave, knowing the young master's preference, was prepared and stepped forward with an iced mug of ale. "Or perhaps I'll greet Volesus just as I am."

"You wouldn't!"

"I certainly would if I worried he might try to foist his ugly daughter on me."

Licinius laughed. "And suffer a rebuff like last time? Not likely." The father watched as his son drank deeply and belched. "What has made you all wet and stinky? Sword training?"

"No, I have been helping build the wall. Plying my hand at the mason's trade."

"Not fit work for a son of mine!"

"Perhaps not, but I am eager to complete the project. Time is short."

"Humph!" Licinius was not interested in reopening this debate. His son enjoyed this game, playing the soldier, reenacting the glory

67

of their forefathers. In Licinius's mind, the boy exaggerated the appearance of a few starving Goths into another invasion, like the one that Emperor Decius faced.

Licinius admitted the Goths were a threat, a minor one. They always had been and always would be. But in this day? Under Valens? Who had already bested them once? The Goths would not affect him, his family, or his property. Not in his lifetime.

But if it made the boy happy, where was the harm? Well, there was the wall, to be sure. Julius had engaged a builder from the small city of Diocletianople to build a wall around the villa. The builder came with a dozen skilled masons and a small army of slaves. His team had already completed most of the project.

All that remains, grumbled Licinius, is to raise the wall so it completely spoils my view.

Julius interrupted his reverie. "I'm off tomorrow to Diocletianople for a week. More militia training." Licinius's son, convinced that the Gothic threat was real and imminent, spent days recruiting and drilling a local militia to guard that city and nearby estates.

His father said, "What about Philippopolis?" Diocletianople was a smaller city just to the north of Licinius's estate. In contrast, Philippopolis, a day's journey south of the estate, was a major stopover on the Via Militaris. That Roman military road spanned the Balkans, running from Pannonia to Constantinople.

Julius shook his head. "The duumviri of Philippopolis have no interest in local self-defense. They said, 'We trust our safety to the army, as we've always done.'"

Licinius nodded as if to say, *as one should.*

Julius said, "Volesus is almost here. I'm off to bathe, so I'll be clean for his ugly daughter."

This was not the first time Senator Tosca Volesus had exploited Licinius Sabinus's hospitality. The senator made regular trips to his own properties in Moesia each summer. He traveled east to west, following the river road upstream until he reached the fortress at Oescus. Then he went south across the Haemus mountains to Thracia, stopping at Licinius's estate, a convenient break in his trip, before following the Via Militaris south to his home in Constantinople. It allowed his host to boast of his estate and demonstrate his hospitality.

On this trip, Volesus bypassed the lure of Diocletianople, famous for its hot springs and quality brothels. He felt an urgency to get home. He would only stay one night with Licinius. Well, a week at most.

In time, the procession of a carriage and ox carts drew up in front of the villa. Licinius descended the marble stairs and walked to the carriage just as a slave opened the door and assisted Volesus out. After a warm embrace, the two men entered the great house and proceeded into the atrium, the central open-air courtyard around which the villa was built. Volesus paused to admire the impluvium, a large rectangular pool in the center of the atrium.

His guest said, "You've redone the pool!"

"Yes," Licinius said. "I became bored with the old mosaic."

Volesus peered down through the clear water at the artwork below. "The Rape of Leda?" The bottom of the pool was paved with hundreds of tiny colored tiles. They depicted the image of Zeus, king of the gods, who had taken the form of a swan, having sex with a naked distraught Leda, Queen of Sparta. Masterful workmanship! And glaringly vulgar.

"Indeed," Licinius said. "I had the artist include the image of King Tyndareus looking on, even though that's not part of the original story. I like my addition." In one corner of the pool, the mosaic depicted Leda's equally naked husband, obviously aroused by watching the rape of his wife.

"Very tasteful," lied Volesus. He settled himself into a comfortable chair beside the impluvium.

Warm air descended from the open roof and picked up a fine spray from the pool, keeping the men refreshed on this warm day. A lissome slave girl supplied them with cups of iced wine. Volesus quaffed his drink and announced, "We have much to discuss! Things in Moesia have changed greatly since I visited you in the spring."

Licinius said, "No doubt. But surely that can wait until you're settled. Your usual room is prepared, and a bath drawn."

Volesus allowed that a bath and a change of clothes would be most welcome. "I must stink. I am covered with dirt and dung," he joked. His carriage kept him clean, but it couldn't keep him cool. A bath, that's what he needed, and that slave girl. He licked his lips.

As the slave girl led Volesus to his room, Licinius added, "Your favorite masseur, Marcus, is standing by if you'd like."

It was an hour before Volesus returned wearing a smile, looking much cleaner and very relaxed. "Between the services of Marcus and that girl," he said, "I'm surprised I can walk!"

The two men retired to the triclinium, where they met Licinius's wife, Cornelia, and son, Julius, who were already there.

The dining room had three couches configured in a *U* shape. The three men each found a couch. Volesus took the couch of honor at the bottom of the *U*. While the men lay comfortably, Cornelia sat upright on a chair facing her husband's couch.

Once settled, Licinius gave a signal that initiated a parade of slaves entering with food. Most of the food was raised on the estate: pork, lamb, root vegetables, and bread made from Licinius's wheat fields. For dessert, Cornelia had arranged for a sweet frozen fruit concoction using local apples and blackberries blended with ice from the estate's cold house.

Volesus appreciated the cold dessert. He knew having ice still available this late in the year was a treat.

He would wager Licinius saved it for his visit. Were it any other host, he would say the host was generous. But Licinius always tried to impress him with his opulence.

As if to echo his thoughts, Licinius said, "That's the last of the ice. No matter. Within a month or so, when streams high in the mountains begin to freeze, I will send my slaves out to cut and refill the cold house."

Cornelia asked after Volesus's wife and daughter.

"I have sent them back to Constantinople to prepare for my daughter's marriage." The girl's husband had died of a fever two years ago, leaving her a childless widow.

"I grew tired of having her around the house, but I wasn't going to marry her to just anyone. I rejected several suitors but finally found a young man of good family and secure fortune."

Volesus remained a little bitter that Licinius would not consider a match between their families.

Just because he could not trace his antecedents back one thousand generations? Yes, ancestry is significant, but he had something better; he had connections in the palace. If the emperor admits the Goths, let us see whose land he settles them on. Not those with friends in high places. Of that, he was sure.

Then the conversation turned to the situation in Moesia. Cornelia excused herself, claiming domestic arrangements required her attention, and left the three men to discuss topics "of moment," matters of no concern to a Roman matron.

"Now," Licinius began, "tell me of these momentous events in Moesia."

Volesus watched him yawn. He was not going to listen to him. He would be asleep in two minutes.

"You will not credit the sights I've witnessed. My wife and I parted company at my estate west of Marcianople. She went south to Constantinople, and I headed north to Sexaginta Prista, where, as you know, I own property. After spending a week there, I rode west along the Danube to Oescus city, to my glass and ceramics factory. For that entire week, the scene on the north side of the Danube was remarkable. A year ago, the riverbank was just forests and swamps. Mile after mile of nothing except the occasional village or isolated hut. But this year, that bank appears to be one continuous settlement. When our road rose to provide a view, I could see masses of hovels and tents stretching well back from the river."

He took a drink of wine before continuing. "Our military river outposts were busy indeed. I spoke with several of the limitanei officers. They all told the same story. The far bank is now infested by Goths in their tens of thousands. The Goths claim to be fleeing their homes in Scythia, far to the northeast. It is either run, the barbarians claim, or be butchered by the Huns. They say the Huns kill women and children as eagerly as they kill men."

He could see Licinius's head nodding. The man was asleep. But perhaps Julius would learn something.

"The Goths simply fled, carrying nothing but their weapons. They had hoped to forage for food along the river, but there was none. The floods this year wiped out the crops. Even the birds and fish have fled. The limitanei face a starving mob of barbarians with only the river separating them. Fortunately, it still flows high and fast."

Julius said, "So they can't boat or raft across?"

"Well, they can try. The limitanei officers say they intercept a few rafts each week."

"And what happens to those people?"

"They don't release them, to be sure. Emperor Valens's prohibition against immigration still stands, though the Goths have petitioned for admittance. As for the invaders, what happens to them depends on each limitanei officer. Usually, they are sold if there is a slave trader who will buy them; otherwise, they are killed and thrown in the river. I saw many bodies along the shore."

"Do you think Valens will let them in?"

"Holy Jesus, I hope not!" said Volesus energetically. His loud voice startled Licinius awake.

"Can you imagine," he continued, "Moesia with a hundred thousand of those pigs flooding in? They don't know Greek, let alone Latin. They are heretic Arians, not real Christians. They have no law. They wear skins instead of proper clothes. They have no culture. Their idea of culture is to get drunk and fight. The emperor might as well surrender Moesia to them just as Emperor Aurelian surrendered Dacia!"

Licinius shrugged as if he'd heard it all before. "I don't think it would be so bad. The empire needs warriors. We wouldn't settle them all in Moesia. We would put some in Gaul to protect the Rhine frontier, others in Syria to face the Sassanids, and so on. In a generation, they'd become productive citizens. That's how we've handled refugees in the past."

"Perhaps," Volesus said, "though I suspect the question is moot. The emperor is in Antioch. By the time he receives the Goth's petition, and they receive his answer, most of them will have died of starvation. And good riddance."

"You don't think, in their desperation, they'll surge across the river?" Julius asked.

"It's possible. Some of the limitanei commanders think so. They have always complained of being undermanned, but the ones I just spoke with seem particularly concerned. They send out press gangs to recruit any fit men they can find, be they farmers, tradesmen, or whatever. Anybody except slaves. They would have stripped my entourage of all the young men had I not been a senator," Volesus said. "I truly believe this."

He shook his head. "What worries the commanders more is the opposite: that the emperor *might* grant them refuge. How would we control such an influx of barbarians? We would have to strip all the river forts of their garrisons. And even if all those limitanei are gathered at the crossing site, which would likely be at Durostorum, the commanders say we would be hopelessly outnumbered if fighting broke out."

Julius nodded. "If, as you say, they are starving, then fighting is sure to break out. They will resist our usual practice of disarming them. They will fight when we try to disperse them to various towns where they can be supported. We must be prepared."

His father shook his head. "All this is known in Constantinople. The bureaucracy can deal with this kind of thing. I'm sure food will be stockpiled and accommodations made before any Goths cross the river." With a slight grin, he added, "After all, this is why we pay such high taxes."

His final comment produced a smile from Volesus. Paying taxes—or, more accurately, not paying taxes—was a shared joke. They bribed provincial bureaucrats so they could postpone paying their taxes. Year after year, their tax obligation would grow. But the aristocrats knew that a tax holiday would wipe out their debt in time. Typically, each new emperor tried to gain favor by declaring such a holiday. One of the privileges of great wealth was to avoid taxes. Taxes were for the little people.

Similarly, military service was for the little people. The great landowners had ploys to avoid conscription for themselves and the people on their estates. When the press gangs appeared, they could be countered using lies, bribes, and intimidation.

Good farm workers were the favorite candidates for military service. A landowner would hide them when necessary. If the recruiting officer demanded a quota be met, the landowner would dump his weak or sickly farm workers. He might even manumit unneeded or problematic slaves. Freeing them would make them candidates for conscription.

Julius asked Volesus, "What are you doing for security?"

"That's a thorny question. I have a dozen bodyguards accompanying me. In addition, I keep another twenty or so men to guard my properties. Some are ex-gladiators, while some barely know how to hold a spear. But they all train hard. I expect them to be ready if some emergency arises."

He continued, "But really, why should I have to maintain a private army? Isn't that why we have the legions?"

The young man said, "Yes, ideally so. But recent history shows it hasn't worked. The army can thrash any invaders but not fast enough to save our estates. If the Goths come across the river at Oescus, they would be here before the emperor is aware of the incursion. And by the time the generals have brought forces to bear, our estates would be smoldering ruins."

His father looked bored as if none of this could possibly happen.

Their guest contemplated his wine goblet. It was gold, which was good, but it was empty, which was bad. Gazing into his cup was sufficient to have a slave notice and quickly refill it.

Though the older men were not paying much attention, Julius spoke with animation. "I have been talking with other young men in this area. We have formed a local militia centered in Diocletianople. We have asked the town and all the estates hereabouts to support us with men and money. And weapons."

Julius finally caught Volesus's attention. An amateur militia of bored young men. How charming. How naïve.

He asked, "How many men have joined so far? And how many are trained fighters?"

Julius proudly said, "Over three hundred men have promised to come within one day when summoned. Of those, almost twenty are retired legionaries. We have two captains, both with experience fighting barbarians."

76

Volesus nodded, which Julius took as a sign of approval though the senator felt the whole endeavor foolish. He had been a legate a decade earlier when the Romans defeated the Goths under their king Athanaric. He had seen first-hand how fierce and brave the Goths could be. Could an untrained army of a few hundred stand against the vast numbers of Goths he saw camped along the Danube? It was ludicrous.

"Let me caution you," Volesus said, "if you stand against the Goths in open battle, you will lose. Your only hope is to fortify any town or villa you hope to save."

Julius replied, "Many agree with you. That is why the people of Diocletianople are working feverishly to repair and raise their wall. Even my father agrees. He has a work party here building a wall around our compound."

Licinius laughed. "*Julius* has a work party building a wall. I think it is pointless. However, with the last of the crops coming in, we need something to keep the slaves busy. Anyway, we've only just started. The builder assures me that within a month, all our major buildings will be protected by an impregnable wall, four feet thick and ten feet high."

"And you think that will keep out the barbarians?" Volesus sounded dubious.

"Not forever, but it should be effective until the legions can relieve us. Also, when the Goths face a stoutly defended wall, they will simply bypass us and seek some more accessible target."

The discussion carried on for another hour until long after sunset. The three men talked about weapons and armor, mercenaries and wages, and legionaries and emperors. It only ended when Licinius started snoring while Julius was talking. Licinius then woke up and called his slaves to help them all to bed.

In the morning, after a late breakfast, Volesus started for home after thanking his hosts. Just before his final farewell, they agreed to meet at the same time the following year.

That never happened. By then, two were dead, and one had fled.

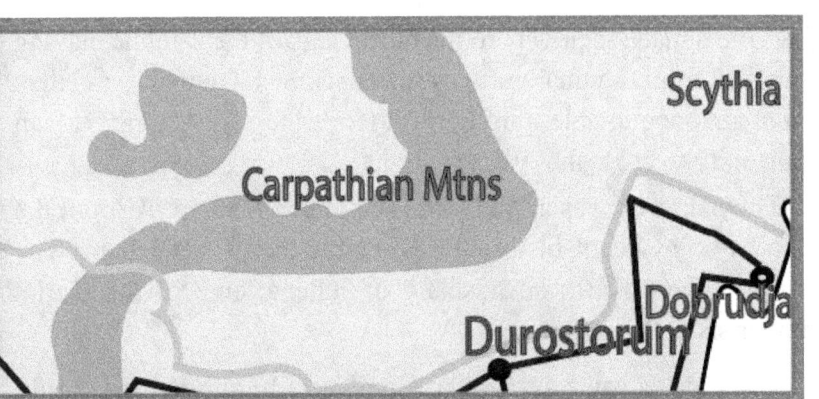

5. Bitorix Seizes Elodia 376 CE

*A*ccordingly, having by the emperor's permission obtained the privilege of crossing the Danube and settling in parts of Thracia, they were ferried over for some nights and days embarked by companies in boats, on rafts, and in hollowed tree-trunks and because the river is by far the most dangerous of all and was then swollen by frequent rains, some who, because of the great crowd, struggled against the force of the waves and tried to swim were drowned; and they were a good many.

From Res Gestae, Volume XXXI, 4-5, by Ammianus Marcellinus, Roman soldier, and historian (lived 330 CE to circa 391 CE)

Six Goths made their way to the north bank of the Danube, having walked from Scythia, north of the Black Sea. On their way, they joined an uncountable throng of their tribe, all hoping for an opportunity to cross the river.

The patriarch was an old man, the father of three: Arbrun, the oldest by a few years, his brother Bort, and their sister Jellena. The other two were Karl, the husband of Jellena, and Silvan, Karl's younger sister.

When news came saying the Huns were burning villages only a few days away from the family's farm, Arbrun took control and ordered the family to flee. His father had protested. The old man had never traveled more than a day's distance from their village. As far as he was concerned, if the eastern barbarians were still a few days away, what cause was there for panic?

But Arbrun had been anticipating this news. They had been preparing to flee for many days, knowing the trek to the river would be arduous. Arbrun had heard that once there, the Romans would boat them across, feed them, and give them new land near their capital city, Constantinople, the most magnificent city in the world.

Every day's walk took a toll on the old man, who kept trying to go back. "We forgot to bring my ard!" he would say, turning about, ready to make the journey back home. His iron-tipped plow had been his prized possession.

"No, Father," Arbrun would say, taking him by the elbow and steering him southward again. "The Romans will give us a plow," he assured him, knowing it was unlikely the Romans would be so generous.

It made no difference. By now, the Huns would have reduced their hut and everything in it to ash and cinders. And what would they do with an ox plow?

80

In their days of preparation, they had butchered the family ox. Its meat would sustain them in the days to come.

It had irritated Arbrun when Jellena and Karl laughed and joked as they helped prepare for the family's flight. Take, for example, butchering the ox. It was a job he'd assigned to Karl. The man had no idea how to start. "Brain it with the axe," Arbrun shouted. His friend approached the beast as if he were going to chop wood. "No, on the head! With the butt end!"

He loved his friend but could not understand what Jellena found attractive in him. She had adored Karl for as long as anyone could remember. Once, when they were little, Jellena pushed Karl into a dirty pool and began slathering him with muck. He reciprocated until both, exhausted from laughing, lay down in the mud. The two approached butchering the ox the same way.

Karl tried twice to stun the ox with the blunt end of an axe, missing once and irritating the animal on the retry. Jellena laughed, seized the axe, and brought the beast to its knees with one well-placed blow to its skull. The bloody task of dismembering the carcass resulted in a—Arbrun didn't even have a word for it—a *gore fight?* which left the couple, now newlyweds, bathed in red and howling with laughter. He had turned away, disgusted.

Arbrun had seen Karl's sister, Silvan, as she watched and laughed. That bothered him. He expected to marry her soon, further cementing his ties to Karl and Jellena, but what kind of a woman would be amused by a *gore fight?* Silvan was no beauty, but she had broad hips, suitable for bearing him sons. He had hinted at his interest, but she had not responded. He was not a subtle man. Did she expect a formal proposal? An order? She had complied with his demands to pack provisions for the journey, but ordering her to marry him was different. That order would have to come from her brother.

As soon as Jellena was old enough to marry, she pressured—demanded!—that her father allow her to marry Karl. He had resisted. Karl and Silvan were orphans with no money. Karl would bring nothing to the marriage, Father said. Ultimately, when the family's flight was imminent, Arbrun overrode his father. "Let them marry," he said, and it was done the day before they departed.

Usually, it would be a celebration enjoyed by the whole village, but many in the village had already left. Most of those who remained were either too old or infirm to travel. Others stayed, scoffing at the danger posed by the Huns. *All are dead now.*

Silvan waited in the family's little tent, not far from the river. There were no ferries, no boats to carry them across. There weren't any Romans. Everywhere within her view, there were Goths, upstream and down. Her family was lucky. They had a tent and the food they'd brought from their village far to the north. Or what remained of the food. Arbrun's father lay in the tent, sheltered from the incessant rain. Rain mixed with sleet whenever the gods chose to increase their misery.

Arbrun had ordered his father to get up, get out, and move around, "or you will die here in this tent." Silvan knelt by the old man, holding his hand, talking to him. He looked at her but said nothing.

Arbrun was probably right. Dying. She expected that was what the old man wanted. But did Arbrun need to treat his father so harshly? The son had no gentleness about him. If she married him, she should not expect any.

82

When they reached the river, Arbrun began actively wooing her. Silvan did not encourage him despite pressure from the others.

It was not that she disliked Arbrun. Much. But he was a bully. He always dominated her brother, Karl. If she married Arbrun, would she face a lifetime of being ordered about like a slave? On the other hand, could she avoid this marriage with the others pushing her?

She was not strong like Jellena, who'd demanded her father allow her to marry the man she loved. Her? She would be forced to marry Arbrun, whom she could barely tolerate. She just knew it.

Silvan did not understand what Arbrun found attractive in her. She was every bit as tall as her sister-in-law Jellena; both were tall for women, but they carried their height differently. Whereas Jellena and Arbrun were tall, strong, and graceful, no one could fail to see they were siblings, Silvan was plump and awkward. At the very suggestion that she and her brother resembled each other, Karl denied it, saying his sister looked like a cow made for breeding. Indeed, Silvan had large breasts and wide thighs. She was shorter than Karl by a head. Her face was plain, with a nose too long. Her teeth were crooked, so she avoided smiling. Her hair was a mousy brown, whereas her brother's beard and hair were a vivid red, so very different from hers.

Jellena loved everything that made Karl different. She called him "my ginger dwarf." She would wrap her long pigtails behind his head and, pulling on them as if tying a knot, draw his face to hers for a kiss. Silvan could not imagine doing that with any man. Certainly not with Arbrun.

A cavalry troop galloped up the river road in the middle of the night and stopped at Grainus's outpost. Marius was on duty up in the watchtower while the rest of the squad slept in the barracks below. As the troop watered their horses, Marius climbed down to talk to the legionary in charge. Even in the dark, he recognized Bitorix. He listened as Bitorix barked orders at him. Within minutes the troop was on its way, riding off into the dark.

Marius went into the barracks and, whistling sharply between his fingers, woke the rest of the squad. Caius and Elodia came in, sleepy-eyed, from the stable just as Marius told Grainus the squad's new orders.

"Bitorix said we're being redeployed to Durostorum. Not just us. All the frontier outposts west of Durostorum, all the way to Novae. Bitorix didn't say whether any frontier forts east of Durostorum are included, but what he did say was he would be back soon after dawn, and we'd, in his words, 'fryking-well better be ready to march' and to 'not take any fryking thing that might slow our march' and to 'destroy any fryking materials left behind that the enemy might find useful.'"

Grainus asked, "Is this a temporary move? Did he say when we'd be returning?"

"No, he didn't say. But since he said to strip the outpost bare, I'd guess we'll be away for weeks. Maybe months."

It did not take long for the squad to get ready. Each soldier packed three days of food, water, mess kit, blanket, and extra clothes.

When they were done, the men sat by the outpost gate, waiting for Bitorix's return. After an hour, just as the sun was rising,

Arruntius stood up and said, "I just realized. This means this whole stretch of the frontier will be left undefended!" No one responded.

While they waited, Elodia took all the surplus goods, packing what she could onto Fortis, the squad's second mule, and hauled it into the village. The villagers had caught wind of what was happening. They recognized she was in a hurry to sell, so they could buy the goods for trifling prices. Only when selling the mule itself did Elodia insist on receiving a fair price. She was sorry to see Fortis go. She'd grown fond of both mules, but Grainus said they could only keep one. She kept Bridie.

Elodia took a few minutes to drop by the bakery, bid Salonia farewell, and kiss her little girl. Salonia wept and said surely, they would return, wouldn't they? Elodia agreed, though privately, she wasn't confident. When she returned to the outpost, she turned the sales proceeds over to Grainus. Except for the tenth she kept as a "commission."

Grainus instructed Elodia to pack all the squad's remaining food into the mule cart. He'd had enough experience with the legion's commissariat to avoid relying on it for victuals. In addition, she helped load the cart with the squad's tent, cooking pots, and extra weapons.

The men waited all day in vain for Bitorix to return. "A typical Bitorix cockup," Grainus commented. At dusk, a messenger rode in, saying Bitorix would arrive late the following morning. Elodia dreaded that she might see him again.

That evening Grainus gathered the squad "for one last drunken evening at our riverside villa," as he sardonically called their spartan outpost. "That messenger says we won't be returning any time soon." He announced that the emperor had finally responded to Fritigern's petition. He would be allowed to lead his Tervingi Goths across the Danube at Durostorum, but only there. The imperial permission lay down harsh conditions for the Goths, tempered by the promise of immediate relief. First, the Goths had to allow the Romans to disarm them. Second, they could only settle in Thracia. But to alleviate their starvation, the empire would provide them with food, enough to meet their current needs. The food aid was temporary; the Goths were expected to quickly grow their own.

Elodia asked, "What about the eastern Goths, the Greutungi, under Lords Alatheus and Farnobius? Will they cross too?" Fritigern's (and Elodia's) tribe of Goths, the Tervingi, had close ties to the other important tribe of Goths, who were herders and horsemen.

"No. Only Fritigern petitioned the emperor, not Alatheus, so only Fritigern's tribe may cross. Military Count Lupicinus has said if the eastern Goths try to cross, they will be sent back or killed."

The emperor's decision had come only two days earlier. Immediately, the Goths started braving the Danube River in their hundreds and thousands, despite the river's swift current and choppy water. They crossed by Roman naval craft, by small boat, and even by makeshift raft. They came in such large numbers that dozens of lives were lost. A brief snowstorm showed that Skadi, the goddess of winter, was on her way south. Thousands arrived in Moesia, cold and starving. It was chaos.

Grainus went on, "To control the Tervingi, we limitanei are needed at Durostorum. This should be a job for the comitatenses, but those bastards must be botching it. The Goths who manage to cross are getting unruly."

Elodia almost laughed. Hers was a tribe of barbarians. What did they expect?

She asked, "Has there been fighting?" She pictured her boys, as she now considered them, marching into a horde of Goths, becoming surrounded and overwhelmed.

"No, no," he answered. "Not really. I heard a few Goths have been killed, but not many, considering how many thousands there are."

"What happened?"

"It started over food, of course. Lupicinus ordered the locals to provide bread for the Goths. They set up tables to sell bread, with the comitatenses providing security. Things were going well; it was a profitable business. The Goths had lots of gold and silver torcs, rings, and bracelets, but they were hungry. And you can't eat silver—ha, ha. Then the merchants ran out of food. It turned out some of the comitatenses were hoarding it, waiting for the price to go up."

Elodia ground her teeth. This was so typical of the comitatenses. Unlike her boys, the field army soldiers got the best wages, best weapons, best food, and best of everything and could enrich themselves with loot. Now the greedy frykers were impoverishing her people.

Grainus said, "When the food ran out, some Goths tried to leave the area to find food for themselves. Well, we couldn't allow that. Those barbarians would pillage the local farms. The comitatenses already had manned a perimeter to keep the Goths near the landing site at Durostorum. When their warriors began pushing against our men, we had to kill a few."

Elodia was outraged. She would have pushed too. What of the Roman promise? Lupicinus had promised them food!

Grainus said, "Some of the Goths drew weapons, which, of course, they shouldn't have had. They'd promised to disarm. The comitatenses should have taken their weapons before allowing them ashore. But they did have weapons, so our men drew theirs and killed some. That calmed them down."

Minicius said, "So we're on our way to rescue the useless comitatenses." He sounded smug.

Grainus said, "Just so. Lupicinus is pulling in all the limitanei. He thinks that should be enough to control the barbarians. The plan is to move them south into Thracia, where the emperor has promised them land. They will make good farmers and good soldiers. In a generation or two, they'll make good Roman citizens."

After the squad had finished drinking all the remaining beer, Caius and Elodia retired to her stable. She explained how this news excited but also terrified her.

"Perhaps I might see my family again. Sample my mother's cooking. Even arm wrestle with my brothers. We could have a family feast, and you could come too. You, my brother Boltus, and I could try to drink each other senseless." Then Elodia grew quiet.

Caius asked, "Something is troubling you?"

"What if I encounter my dead husband's family? If they see me, they will kill me."

"I won't let that happen," Caius promised.

"They will kill you, too," she said. "I will pray every day, and when an opportunity arises, I will sacrifice a young goat to Ithunn."

She paused and then asked, "And what about Bitorix? What will he do when he sees me?"

"Who can say? Just try to stay out of his way and hope he doesn't notice you. Mention that when you sacrifice to Ithunn."

She reviewed in her mind the exact words to recite when making such a sacrifice, words and promises that would go a long way to ensure her safety.

Then, being a practical young woman, she dismissed the matter. The gods being all-powerful, if it was Ithunn's will that Elodia be spared, then the goddess would ensure it. Otherwise, she was meant to die. There was no point in worrying.

Elodia turned her mind to other religious mysteries. "Why," she asked Caius, "would Lord Fritigern neglect all the gods except the Jesus God? Why depend on a single god's protection when so many might provide aid?"

Caius explained, "First, Fritigern is a soldier, and soldiers understand the gods. The gods do not give a damn about mortals. Christians, Jews, pagans, it doesn't matter. The gods just do what they please. You can pray, you can butcher a baby goat to Ithunn," here he looked at Elodia pointedly, "it makes no difference. Ithunn doesn't care. Fritigern knows this. If to get permission from the emperor, the Goths must worship Jesus, then Fritigern says the Goths will worship Jesus."

Elodia didn't interrupt him, but she knew he was wrong. She and Ithunn had talked more than once in the quiet hours of the night. The goddess said she would protect her, and so far, she had. If only she had saved her unborn babies too. Their deaths still grieved her.

"Second, Fritigern knows the emperor wants to absorb the Gothic people. In a generation or two, the emperor expects the Goths to speak like Romans, act like Romans, and, most importantly, worship like Romans. Fritigern understands this, so he claims, 'Fine, my Goths are all Christians now.'"

Elodia said, "What about King Athanaric? He hates Christians. He has killed many Goths who dared to worship the Jesus God."

"Athanaric is not with Fritigern. If your late husband's people followed Athanaric, they are not camped across the Danube. They are now up in the Carpathian Mountains, hiding from the Huns."

Elodia gasped in relief, knowing her dead husband's family was far away... thank Ithunn!

Elodia didn't get much sleep that night. By mid-morning, villagers began to arrive. Rumors were rampant. Some just came out of curiosity. Where were they going? Durostorum. When would they return? They didn't know. The villagers eyed the mass of barbarians across the river and realized those Goths would raft across once the outposts were unoccupied and the limitanei were gone. The villagers saw the soldiers, their security and protection, leaving. Who would defend them? They had all witnessed barbarian raids in the past, raids the local forces quickly suppressed and could only imagine how badly events would have turned out but for the limitanei.

Salonia, her baker husband, and child arrived driving a cart loaded with bread, grain, and a small stone mill. She told Elodia they would also head to Durostorum, where it was safe. The Christian priest showed up leading a pony, which carried his pregnant wife. In one hand, he held the pony's reins; in the other, his little boy's hand. They, too, planned to flee to the city. But most were staying. Bakers and priests could move, but farmers could not. Still, by noon there were dozens of villagers swarming about, one with a horse-drawn wagon, some with hand carts, and even more with bags and backpacks.

It was afternoon before the horse troop returned, leading many other squads from the west. Its arrival was announced from afar by the legionaries' hobnailed boots tramping on the cobblestone road and the squeal of ungreased cart axles.

The crowd scattered when the military tribune finally appeared on horseback, leading what seemed like an endless column of legionaries. Each had his sword, javelin, pack, and shield. Grainus's squad, similarly equipped, stood at parade rest with him at its head. The military tribune brought the column to a halt when he reached Grainus. Grainus hailed the tribune who returned the salute.

It was Bitorix. Elodia studied his face. Even at this distance, he was just as she remembered; beautiful and proud, though flawed by a recent scar and stitch marks along the further cheek. She remembered other scars along his sword arm. This was a man who had seen much action.

Elodia stood behind her mule, her hood hiding her face. Thankfully, Bitorix didn't notice her. He ordered Grainus's squad to fall in immediately behind him.

"Follow at the rear if you must," he ordered in a loud voice for all the civilians to hear. Grainus, Caius, and the rest of their squad arrayed themselves into two ranks of four abreast at the head of the column, and Elodia followed, leading the mule cart. The column set off again with Bitorix at its head, marching along the river road.

She heard Arruntius say, "Goodbye, cesspit outpost. I spent seven years there, and every day was a misery. Jesus willing, I will never set eyes on it again."

"Now perhaps we'll get a chance to kill more barbarians," said his brother, Minicius.

Elodia suspected it was likely the last time they would lay eyes on the little outpost. But her perspective was different from the Pannonian brothers. She avoided dwelling on the bad times and the sad times. Instead, she was thankful for this period of security. She had never gone hungry and never suffered during the bitterly cold winters. She had been able to buy small things for herself, soaps, combs, and nice clothes, from the bits of money she filched while serving as the squad's provisioner. She also won a small but constant flow of coins from the nightly dice games, taken from all the squad members except Caius and Marius, the only two men who understood numbers. She would miss her friendship with Salonia and her baby. Perhaps they would see each other in Durostorum.

She prized her friendship with the squad members. She liked them, and they all liked her, more or less. *Less* for the Pannonian brothers. *More* for the rest of the squad. And there was Caius, who was in a class of his own. Her fondness for him… was beyond words. If leaving the little outpost behind meant they would be separated…well, that was unthinkable. But as they marched along, she could see him ahead.

Several miles down the road, the column stopped at another river outpost where its garrison joined the column. This happened every few miles. All the Danube outposts were being abandoned. Most of the garrisons had a single mule cart. Some had two. All the drivers were uniformed legionaries. None were civilians, and certainly none were women.

The civilians who tried to join the column were brutally pushed back. Bitorix ordered Grainus to send his men down the column, flanking it to prevent civilians from sneaking in. After one such encounter, two legionaries who Elodia didn't know spotted her in the column leading her mule. Thinking she was a civilian, they blocked her.

"Civilians at the rear, girly," said an ugly one, his nose was scarred where some weapon had nipped off the tip.

He held his javelin like a staff, blocking her way. She tried to push past him while explaining she was part of Decanus Grainus's squad and this was the squad's mule. She looked around for Grainus or Caius. They had moved down the column, out of sight. She turned Bridie to point out the legion's brand on its hip, hoping that would prove her point. The second soldier whacked her mule's nose with his javelin. The poor animal bucked and cried a plaintive hee-haw, which made the soldier jump back. She jerked the weapon from his grip, made easier since he had only a thumb and finger on his right hand, and used it to whack at his nose. She missed his nose but gave his helmet a ringing blow.

"You've done it now, girly!" shouted Nipped Nose. "First, you steal the emperor's mule; now you strike his soldiers."

A slight exaggeration, since she'd only struck one soldier, just Finger Free. As Nipped Nose swung weapon toward her, she stepped back and held Finger Free's javelin in guard position. Snot bubbled out the top of Nipped Nose's nipped nose. She fully expected he would try to gut her. Even if she gutted him first, she still had a thousand other legionaries to defeat. The troop column in front of them stopped so soldiers and wagon-masters could watch the show. Everyone enjoyed a good gutting.

Before Finger Free could thrust, someone shouted, "Stop!"

Nipped Nose, Finger Free, and everyone else looked up and jumped to attention. She did, too, after first ensuring Nipped Nose had lowered his weapon. She worried he might sneak in a last-second poke; she did not want her insides leaking out.

Military Tribune Bitorix appeared. Elodia gasped and hoped beyond hope that he hadn't recognized her. Calling down from his horse, he said, "Let the mule pass. As the slave says, it belongs to the squad of Decanus Grainus."

Nipped Nose and Finger Free strode off, she assumed, to harass someone else. Elodia supposed they felt humiliated, called out by a military tribune, and put in their place by a "girly."

Bitorix used his riding crop to slash at the man in front of her. "What are you staring at? Get moving! Keep moving!" The rest of the column got the message, and they all resumed marching. Bitorix rode back toward the head of the column. Had he recognized her? If so, he gave no sign.

The column trudged on for several more hours, stopping again and again as it passed more riverside forts to collect additional limitanei squads. It was getting colder, and the wind was picking up, but the steady pace kept her comfortably warm. The river was wide here, perhaps a half mile, and running high. The road skirted ponds that were normally swamps. Entire trees quickly floating by showed the speed of the current. She looked for Goths on the far bank, but it was too far away.

At first, no one spoke to her, but over time, the men relaxed. When someone started singing, she joined in. She knew the songs. They were ones the squad had sung while standing around the cookfire and when sheltering in the barracks from rain or cold. Her boys said she had a good voice. Apparently, the men in the column agreed.

She found herself singing the verses by herself, with the others joining in only on the chorus. When the first song ended, they gave her a round of applause. An awkward silence followed as though the men expected her to start the next song. One muleteer made the point explicitly, saying, "Come on, *girly*, sing us another." The other men laughed at "girly." Apparently, Nipped Nose's slur had not gone unnoticed.

She began a song, an old one Polybius taught her, of the boy who tripped and spilled a jar of plum jam down a girl's tunic. The first verse described how the sticky stuff spread from her neck down her chest to her groin, and the other verses described how she insisted he clean it up with his tongue, working from top down, with a verse for each portion of her anatomy. Again, she sang the verses, and the men around her joined in the chorus, showing much enthusiasm.

She'd just finished the fourth verse, where the boy had lifted her tunic and was licking her stomach, and she sang the chorus, "Lickety-lick, lickety-lick, the jam in my navel was inflating his dick," when she found she was singing alone. Everyone else was looking up the road at something she couldn't see; her view blocked by a wagon in front.

A moment later, she stopped singing too. Emerging from around the wagon came Bitorix, followed by three of his bodyguards, all mounted.

"Don't stop singing on my account," he said. "Please, carry on." When she hesitated, he ordered, "Carry on!"

She sang the following verse all by herself. "No," he said, "Sing that verse again, and this time *everyone* sing." He indicated all the men marching beside her.

They sang, but reluctantly. Only Bitorix did not sing, but he nodded in time as she led the group through the last two verses, where the boy and girl moved beyond jam and licking. Finally, the singing stopped. All one could hear was the tramping of hobnailed boots.

Bitorix maneuvered his mount up next to her. "Your singing is excellent."

She turned her head and looked up at him. Ignoring his compliment, she answered, "You do not sing at all."

"It is a matter of dignity." He was silent for a period. Then, in a stern but quiet voice, he said, "Why are you here? I told that mentula Grainus to sell you!"

Submissively, she cast her gaze to the ground. "I cannot say, my lord."

"But you still live with his squad and work for them?"

"Yes, my lord." She did not explain that, in fact, she slept separately.

"And do you service them?"

"Yes, my lord, I do whatever task Decanus Grainus orders." She knew what he was driving at but played dumb.

"I mean, you stupid Gothic slut, do all the men in the squad bump you?"

"No, my lord." Well, not *all* of them, but one certainly did.

"Did Grainus keep you for himself? He's the only one who bumps you?"

"No, my lord, he does not." She still hoped they could leave Caius out of the conversation.

They walked on for a few minutes. She could feel Bitorix staring down at her. Finally, he said, "I am sorry for how you were treated."

She ground her teeth. *How you were treated?* As though some other person was responsible? She did not react but kept her eyes downcast. What did he want? Forgiveness? He had not asked for it, and she was no Christian to simply grant it for the asking. No, she had vowed to kill him. She kept her silence.

"Well, have you nothing to say?"

"No, my lord."

He rode alongside her. She could feel his gaze drilling into her head. At last, with a tone of frustration, he said, "You shall be sold when we get to Durostorum. Grainus and his squad will see none of the proceeds. They had their chance. Now I claim you."

Another minute of silence elapsed. "Continue leading this cart. When we reach Durostorum, I will send a man to come and collect you. Do not try to flee unless you want more scars on your back."

Caius could tell they were approaching Durostorum when the command came, "Ready arms!" The legionaries operated in unison, like a single massive machine, donning their helmets and loosening their swords in their scabbards. The pounding of kettledrums stepped up the pace of the march and set the beating of his heart. The column was now ready to confront any threat.

Before seeing them, he could smell the Goths, a sullen mass of people camped in filth on either side of the road. Their tents and fires stretched far off into the dusky distance. They said nothing, but those near the road stepped back out of sword range. The limitanei, too, were silent. The time for singing had passed.

The city of Durostorum was surrounded by a moat, fed by the Danube, and a thick high wall of stone. It was a small city by Roman standards but one of the larger cities in Moesia. The column broke step crossing the moat bridge and entered by the river gate. The interior, laid out as a square, was a quarter mile on a side and divided into fourths. The soldiers' quarter was surrounded by its own shorter wall, about ten feet high.

Grainus's squad, marching in formation again just ahead of Elodia and her mule cart, only began to relax when the city wall separated them from the festering slum of barbarians. They halted in the soldiers' quarter. Up against the walls were wooden barracks and stables on each side. An ordinary legionary of the comitatenses stepped in front of Grainus and ordered him to follow. Grainus led his squad after the man, though it was grating for the decanus to receive orders from a subordinate.

Walking ahead of them, the guide pointed out the central fountain and the latrines. He said, "You limitanei frykers have probably never seen a latrine before. That's where you crap. If you crap in your barracks, I'll force you to lick it up." It was typical of field army soldiers to mock those in the frontier army.

"Military Count Lupicinus requires you be ready for action tomorrow at first light," he said, when he finally dropped them off. Their squad was given two rooms, one for storage and the other for sleeping. The sleeping room had three triple-high bunk beds; the storage room was empty. The legion quartermaster had carefully arranged a barracks for each squad but made no arrangements for food. Thankfully, Grainus's men had prepared for that possibility.

They were just settling in when a centurion accompanied by four comitatenses entered their room. "Decanus Grainus?" asked the centurion. Grainus saluted in acknowledgment. "Come with me."

They escorted Grainus to a stone building just off the parade ground and into a room, which turned out to be the office of Bitorix. Bitorix, sitting behind a desk, looked up when Grainus saluted.

"Decanus Grainus reporting."

Those were the only words he uttered during the interview. Bitorix said since Grainus had failed to sell the Gothic slave girl as ordered, he was seizing her as he'd threatened, and she would be sold at auction. As punishment for disobeying orders, Grainus would be fined. The amount would be equal to whatever price she fetched. *Dismissed*! With those words, the centurion's men hustled Grainus out of the room and the building. He had no chance to react or protest.

He found his squad in an uproar when he returned to the barracks. While away, another field army officer with a half-dozen comitatenses had entered and seized Elodia. She was gone.

Several comitatenses were still there, blocking the door to prevent Grainus's men, especially Caius, from going after Elodia and her captors. It took time and a lot of yelling for Grainus to restore order. Once his men were settled, he could dismiss the remaining comitatenses, leaving the squad alone.

"She fought like hell," Minicius said with pride. He might not have been partial to the Gothic girl, but he loved watching her pound the legionaries.

Caius looked distraught. "She fought until one of them pulled out a lash. She recognized the man holding it as the one who flogged her before. Then the fight went out of her. I should have saved her."

"Then you would have received a hundred lashes," said Grainus.

With a heavy heart, he explained Elodia's fate and his own punishment. Glabius and Marius volunteered to pay a share of his fine.

Caius nodded, but he couldn't talk. He sat with his head hung down, desolate. Grainus tossed Elodia's effects into his pack. Her knife landed on top of her other possessions. He took that as an omen that there would come a day when she could reclaim it.

The officer in charge of Elodia's arrest had been warned by Bitorix that she would resist. Several of the comitatenses held her immobile, or tried to, while the officer gagged her. Tightly. He was angry. She had taken a good bite out of his arm. She landed one last punch before they pinned her arms behind her back. The officer succeeded in tying her feet together, but not before she'd kicked him in the groin.

Her struggling ceased when he pulled out a lash. She collapsed when the terrifying memory of their previous encounter filled her mind.

The largest of the comitatenses, one of the few she hadn't injured in her fury, took her knife from its sheath, dropped it and her pack on the floor, then picked her up and flung her over his shoulder. He took her out of the barracks accompanied by the officer and one other soldier. The remaining soldiers stayed behind to keep the members of her squad, all enraged and shouting, from following. She saw Minicius and Glabius trying their best to restrain Caius. He fought them until she told him to stand down, which, muffled by her gag, sounded like, "And dowwn." He was a brave and kind man who often acted without thinking. She was more than fond of him.

The officer and his men carried her to a block of buildings set back from the wall. They entered a two-story timber-framed building. The lower story was brick, and the upper level was wattle and daub. A soldier on guard stood aside to let them pass. The large soldier put her down, untied her feet, and the officer herded her upstairs by poking her with the handle end of his lash. She went down a long dark hall lit only by sputtering rushlight. At the far end, he opened a door and waved her in.

The last of the setting sun, entering through a small window, lit the room a faint pink.

The officer said as he left, "Someone will be along shortly. Stay here."

She tried the door. He'd bolted it from the outside. She opened the window shutters. The opening was wide enough for her to lean out and see the cobblestone yard far below, far enough that any jump would break her legs. The room was cold, the outside colder, so she closed the shutters.

"Someone will be along," he'd said. To do what?

The room was sparsely furnished. It held a bed, an empty tub, a large wooden table, and a fireplace already set with kindling and wood. There was a trunk, which she peeked into. It contained clothes neatly folded. Above the trunk, a crimson cape hung from a hook on the wall.

Within minutes the sunlight faded. She kicked off her sandals and lay on the bed. She sank into the mattress, a down-filled mattress such as she hadn't enjoyed since leaving her father's house. She pulled a blanket over herself and relaxed.

She didn't remember falling asleep. She woke when someone flung the door open with a bang. A troop of slaves came in carrying buckets of steaming water, which they emptied into the tub and a slave who applied a torch to the fireplace. They were followed by a fat old woman who turned to her saying, "His lordship says you're to bathe and put this on," and flung a tunic on the bed, "and give your tunic to me."

It was a long plain tunic of good-quality cotton, dyed olive green, far better than her old gray one. And much cleaner. A fair trade. Elodia got off the bed, stripped, and handed hers to Fat Old Woman.

"You'll get it back once it's cleaned."

I hope they'll let me keep the new tunic.

"And your smallclothes, too," Fat Old Woman added. She did not offer a clean loincloth. Elodia untied her loincloth and handed it to her. *Perhaps they'll wash and return it too.*

The slaves left as quickly as they'd come except for a tall, slim young woman who stayed behind to help her bathe. She steadied Elodia as she stepped over the tub's high side. Once seated, the young woman applied a small amount of perfumed soap imported from Arelate in Gaul and washed and rinsed her hair. Using more soap and a rough sponge, she scrubbed her body. Elodia purred like a cat. When the water was cold and dirty, the young woman helped her out.

The woman put her fingers between her lips and whistled a soft signal. A pair of strong young men came in—apparently, they'd been waiting in the hall—carried the tub to the window and dumped out the water. The young woman rubbed her down with a towel, then laid it on the tabletop. "Massage, Domina." At her signal, Elodia climbed onto the table and lay facedown on the moist towel. The massage began.

After hours of walking, her legs and feet were sore. The young woman massaged them in an excruciatingly pleasurable way. Elodia moaned as the woman worked the stiffness out of her feet. She finally began to relax as the woman moved her way up her back, shoulders, and neck. To avoid falling asleep, she asked, "What is your name?"

"You may call me 'slave,' Domina."

"Fine. What is your name, slave?"

"The master calls me 'Albia,' Domina."

"Tell me, Albia, whose room is this? And why was I brought here?" Based on the cape and trunk of clothes, she could guess the answer to the first question. Based on the bath, massage, and new tunic, she could also guess the answer to the second.

"This is the room of my master, Military Tribune Bitorix, Domina. He ordered you be bathed. He likes his women to be clean."

Yes, and yes. Two correct guesses. "And why am I *his* woman?"

It took time for Albia to answer this question, and her answer showed she didn't understand it. "Oh, you would not want to be owned by someone else, Domina," she finally said. "The master is good to his women and boys. To all his slaves, really. We are rarely beaten and never without cause."

That was false, as she knew firsthand. Her back provided the evidence. "He is gentle in bed and never bestial," Albia added. "He protects us from the men slaves and only shares us with his special friends."

It was as she suspected and feared. Albia was here to clean, dress, and primp her so her master would find her pleasing. Elodia began to prepare herself to be raped that night. She considered fleeing, but there was no escape, either out the window or past the guards in the hall. Rescue? There was no prospect of Caius rescuing her. Even if he could locate her—an unlikely event—there was the matter of the guards.

"And if I reject him?"

"By the gods, you cannot! You must not! He will beat you and then take you anyway. If you anger him, he may sell you. I've seen him do it. Even slaves almost as beautiful as you!"

Nice compliment.

Albia went on, "You seem concerned, Domina. Really, you should not. I am sure you will look back and think of this as the day your life got better.

"He is kind," Albia repeated. "He is a gentle lover. Please don't anger him!"

She continued babbling, which Elodia ignored while considering how she should respond to the impending assault. She would have to struggle; otherwise, Bitorix would believe he'd seduced her. He needed to know the truth: she was not his slave and did not want him.

Her struggle would not prevent the rape. As Albia said, he would have her with or without a fight. How hard to resist? Not so hard that he would beat her again. Just a symbolic struggle. Justice would come later. That idea provided a scrap of comfort.

Albia was still talking. "When Concordia had his child, he gave her new clothes and a silver necklace. He told her he wouldn't sell her child. And he didn't until the boy was seven. To one of his special friends."

To interrupt Albia's never-ending talk, she asked, "Albia, are you a Goth?"

"No," she said, "My mother was an Alan. I don't know about my father. A noble Roman, my mother said."

A very unimportant Roman, more likely. "Have you met any of these Goths, the ones coming across the river?"

"Just the three Gothic children my master has purchased. Two boys and a little girl. They will all be beautiful once they are fattened up. Now they are just skin and bones."

"What? You say the Goths are selling their children?"

"No, only the Goths who have no silver. Or who *say* they have none. Everyone knows the Goths are rich. They all wear gold and silver necklaces. Gold rings with jewels. But most have no food. The Romans can sell it for a good price. A loaf of bread will fetch a gold necklace. Or a virgin boy or girl. Some Goths hide their silver and then beg for free food. It is typical of Goths; they would rather trade a child than give up their silver. That's how my master bought his three new slaves."

Rubbish. There are rich Goths and poor Goths, just as in any nation. Goths love their children, like everyone else. Clearly, Albia doesn't know I am a Goth.

"Why," Elodia asked, "don't the Goths buy their food from someone else?"

"The soldiers are forcing them to stay near the city so they can be controlled. To prevent pillaging. Goths always pillage. But leaving wouldn't help. The Romans bought up all the food near here. My master, our master now, says if the Goths want to eat, they must give up their wealth or starve. He has many soldiers guarding his food sellers. Otherwise, the Goths would steal it all."

Albia indicated it was time for Elodia to sit up so she could brush and fix her hair. She braided it into a long black ponytail, which came down to the middle of her back. Albia went on, "Do you see how clever my master is? If he does really well, he may give each of us a denarius to spend as we want!"

I will spend my denarius on a knife.

But even with a knife, this rape would happen. She needed a miracle. She prayed to Ithunn, then to each of her other gods individually and to the lot collectively. She prayed for a miracle without much hope. Would the gods listen, knowing she had nothing to sacrifice? Even with a sacrifice, her prayers were rarely answered. Yet she prayed.

Albia interrupted her prayers. "We leave soon for Marcianople," she said brightly. "It is a much nicer city than this. Master has a bigger house. The rooms for us women are larger and have finer windows. Even the food is better."

"What about all the Goths?"

"Oh, they will be coming too. Marcianople is on the way to their new farms in Thracia. It makes me wonder if anyone will be left here in Durostorum in a day or two."

Now Elodia understood why the Romans brought all their forces here. They needed many men to herd the Goths south. Thousands of people walking for days on empty stomachs and angry, having just been robbed of their wealth and their children. Unless the Romans were strong, there would be pillaging, starving people searching for food. If the Romans appeared weak, any spark would set off a conflagration. Given half a chance, the Goths would massacre every Roman. She imagined her Caius lying dead or dying. She shuddered.

Just then, the door opened again with a bang, and as before, the small army of slaves came in carrying buckets of steaming water. The tub was refilled, the slaves departed, and a tall man stepped into the room.

Bitorix.

The torchlight emphasized his short, blond hair and neatly trimmed beard. In this light, his face was beautiful, though he did not smile. She could easily spend time studying his face, but she cast her eyes down once she recognized him. Bitorix was followed by a slave who carried a platter of meat and fruit and another who brought in a pitcher of wine and two cups. The slave poured the wine and placed the cups and platter at the end of the massage table.

Elodia, still naked, perched on the edge of the massage table with her legs dangling. She felt uncomfortable though none of the slaves looked at her. The Romans viewed nudity differently than her people. Often their slave women wore just a loincloth or nothing at all. That might be understandable in the lands around the Roman Sea and hot desert places like Egypt. But in Gothia, the land of the Goths, it was cold. Goths stayed properly clothed.

She considered covering herself with the towel even though it was now damp and cold. But since men found a concealed body more alluring than a naked one, and alluring was the last thing she wanted to seem, she just sat there with a straight back, not covering herself, not saying anything, but clutching the edge of the table.

Bitorix stared her up and down as if seeing her for the first time. When his study was finished, he said, "You look nothing like the smelly, dirty barbarian girl I bumped two years ago. You are magnificent." After further reflection, he said, "I shall call you Helen." She knew he was comparing her with Helen of Troy, who, as Caius told the story, lived a thousand years ago. Helen, considered the most beautiful woman in the world, had the misfortune of falling in love with Paris of Troy, a prince doomed for angering the goddess, Athena.

"Greetings, Helen." Bitorix said nothing to Albia, who left Elodia to minister to his needs. She helped him strip off his armor and clothes and knelt beside him when he was seated in the tub to soap and scrub his body.

He, too, was silent. Albia washed his hair and beard, sluiced him down with a pitcher of water, and used a clean towel to gently pat and press the water off his face and out of his eyes. Blinking, he turned to Elodia. "You got your new garment?" She nodded silently. "Put it on."

She hopped off the table, plucked the tunic off the bed, and pulled it on. It was cut low around the neck, revealing a small amount of cleavage, which, with her small breasts, was all it could possibly show. The sleeves were short and airy. "Do you like it?"

She nodded.

"Answer me," he commanded.

"I like it," she said in Greek.

"You may keep it after tonight. Now, come drink and enjoy this fine food."

Elodia wanted to refuse on principle. But her stomach had no principles. She helped herself to a slab of delicious pork, a good portion of hot fresh bread, and enough wine—unwatered, she could tell—to make her head swim. She hoped tonight's rape might be less intolerable if she were thoroughly drunk. Or at least less memorable.

"Albia, wine." She brought him a full cup and a meaty leg of pork. He sat in the tub, eating and drinking. He waved the cup, and she refilled it. He dribbled pork juice and wine down his chest. Albia knelt and washed him clean. He drained the wine cup again, then stepped out of the tub.

Albia whistled. The same two slaves entered and emptied the tub out the window. Bitorix stood with arms raised while she toweled him down.

"Are you enjoying this meal?" he asked Elodia.

"Yes."

"Our previous encounter ended badly. That was unfortunate."

She assumed this was as close to an apology as she would get for being raped and having her back lashed open.

He said nothing more for a long time. She sat still, feeling awkward, while he resumed studying her. When she could no longer stand the silence, she asked, "When may I return to my squad?"

"Oh, that's not going to happen," Bitorix said. "You were an enemy alien who entered my frontier section. You should have been captured, enslaved, and sold. I ordered Decanus Grainus to sell you. He disobeyed my order. I purchased you. You are mine. You cost me one denarius, which I may pay Grainus in time."

She knew this day wasn't going to end well. Owned by Bitorix? The idea made her sick. If she were the type of person who could tolerate vomiting, she would vomit her meat, bread, and wine all over Bitorix. Unfortunately, her stomach refused to release her meal.

"Albia, tell Helen what kind of master I am."

Looking at the floor, Albia spoke softly. "I have told her already you treat your servants kindly and gently. That we are beaten rarely and never without cause. That your men servants are not allowed to molest your women."

Bitorix nodded and said, "Go." Albia left the room.

Elodia could hear the bolt being thrown. He turned to her. "Disrobe and lie on the bed."

Her heart sank. This was it. She looked him square in the face and paused. He arched an eyebrow and nodded toward the bed.

"No," she said. "I do not agree to this. I reject you. I reject being bumped by you. Will you rape me again?"

Bitorix laughed. "It won't be rape, not under Roman law. Legally, a slave cannot be raped." She knew this. It was indeed the common law. A slave was property like a cow; you can damage someone's property, but you cannot rape it.

"I will bump you now whether you like it or not. It will be more pleasant if you do not resist. Please be an obedient slave," he said in a soft consoling way. "Otherwise... well, you already know the consequences."

She had witnessed this scenario in her father's household. Slaves did as ordered. But she would not sink to pretending enjoyment.

She didn't suppose Caius would break through the door and rescue her. If the gods were planning to intervene, they'd better hurry. There was little time left for a miracle.

She disrobed and lay on the bed, facedown. If she was to be treated like an animal, let him take her like one.

"I bought you for your beauty. Turn over so I can enjoy your face, Helen," Bitorix commanded.

She muttered, "It is Elodia," into the mattress as she rolled over. Where were the gods tonight? Maybe the Jesus God had vanquished the old gods from the empire. Perhaps he was the only god listening tonight. She did not know how to address the Jesus God nor what kind of sacrifices he liked. But maybe, if she requested just a small favor tonight, he might accept her degradation, her humiliation as a sufficient sacrifice. And so, she silently prayed, "Jesus God, if I must endure this Roman bastard's bumping, please spare me having his child."

And her ordeal began.

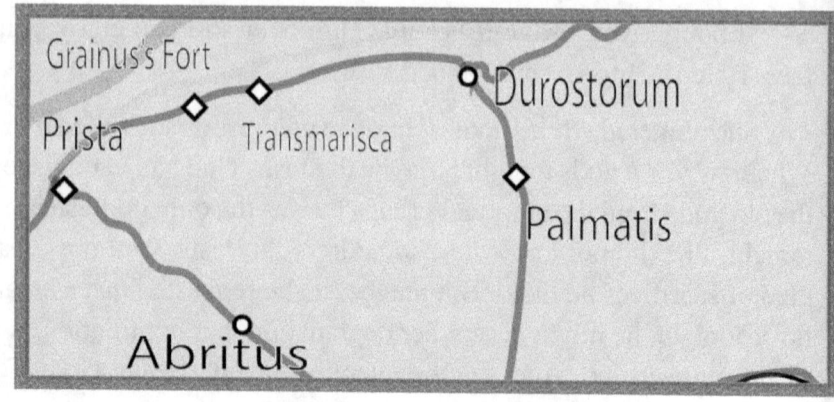

6. Enter Lord Fritigern 376 CE

When the barbarians after their crossing were harassed by lack of food, those most hateful generals [Lupicinus and Maximus] devised a disgraceful traffic; they exchanged every dog that their insatiability could gather from far and wide for one slave each, and among these were carried off also sons of the chieftains.

From Res Gestae, Volume XXXI 4.11, by Ammianus Marcellinus

The next day, Grainus's squad stepped out of the city's river gate into a scene from Tartarus, the deepest region of hell. The stench of the Goths, unwashed bodies and rotting corpses, was enough to make Grainus gag. The noise was deafening: a thousand people shouting, screaming, and crying, all pushing toward the wooden booths near the gate where food was sold.

Their initial assignment took them away from the gate and down to the riverbank to control the crowd. Getting there was an ordeal. The squad members lifted their shields, formed a *V*, and bulled their way through the mass of humanity, knocking down more than a few people and trampling on several.

When they reached the riverbank, they joined with other soldiers already attempting to perform an impossible task. The Goths were still crossing the river in great numbers using every imaginable means, anything that could float. The squad's job was to intercept the barbarians as they stepped ashore, disarm them, and direct them to the land booths where Gothic families were allocated a village—their new home—in Thracia.

The job was ludicrous. The number of people stepping ashore every hour outnumbered the soldiers many times over. Attempting to disarm a starving and angry Gothic warrior was so dangerous they didn't even try. Perhaps the soldiers on the guard galleys could disarm their passengers, but even that seemed doubtful.

Trying to direct them to the land booths was equally fruitless. Many of the Romans spoke only rudimentary Gothic or none. They could not convey the purpose of the booths, especially to people whose immediate need was food, not land. A few who understood walked to the land booths only to return, complaining the booths were in shambles and unmanned.

The Goths did learn, by word of mouth, the location of the food booths. They surged in that direction. An officer, recognizing the shoreside effort as useless, reassigned Grainus's squad to guard those booths. They pushed their way back toward the city's river gate, back to where they'd seen a dozen booths, side by side. A dozen booths weren't enough. The press of the shouting crowd would have overrun those stalls but for the legionaries who stood shoulder to shoulder using shields to keep back the unruly mob.

Caius saw horrendous things that day, which troubled him for the rest of his life. He saw the continuous train of food from the city to the booths, the food the emperor had promised the Goths. A corridor of soldiers lined the route from the city gate to the booths. Each food-laden cart was guarded as it was pulled by slaves down the corridor. Caius saw one man try to vault over Grainus onto a cart. Just as one spears a fish jumping a waterfall, Arruntius impaled him in the air. Legionaries along the corridor laughed and applauded Arruntius's skill. A legionary finished off the flopping Goth.

Within the food train, Caius witnessed shameful deeds. He saw a Roman merchant carting a cage of dogs to the booths. Shortly after, he saw him heading back to the city with his cage emptied of dogs but containing six little Gothic children. It was hard to miss them since they were all screaming for their mothers. Caius never believed he'd see people so hungry that they would trade their children for dogs. He hadn't known Goths would even eat dog meat.

He made his way down the corridor to the back of the booths. It would seem like a typical market if it weren't so chaotic. The Goths with something to trade—a gold or silver coin or some valuable artifact—waved it above their heads and shouted for attention and, after some noisy haggling, received a loaf of bread or a small packet of flour or lard. He spotted the same merchant returning with another cage of dogs and watched in horror as he traded a plump dog for a cute little Gothic girl.

Caius could identify the girl's mother; she was the one screaming at the girl's father, now holding the plump dog. As Caius watched, she punched the father in the face, causing him to drop the dog. A melee ensued as all the nearby folk scrambled for the dog. A slave trader who had witnessed the exchange must have felt the girl was worth more than a dog. He quickly bought her from the merchant for a handful of coins. The slave trader had cages where he could safely store such human purchases. He also had a contingent of thugs to protect his property.

By the end of the day, only a trickle of food was coming from the city. The crowd of hungry Goths had not diminished. The deluge of barbarians had happened so quickly that the quartermasters could not bring enough food to meet the demand. They said the nearest large stockpile was in Marcianople, two days' walk to the south. That, they said, was where this horde had to go next.

*B*ut he [Fritigern], with his natural cleverness in foresight protecting himself against anything that might happen, in order to obey the emperor's commands and at the same time join with the powerful Gothic kings, advanced slowly and in leisurely marches arrived late at Marcianople.

From Res Gestae, Volume XXXI 5.4, by Ammianus Marcellinus

A rap at the door awoke Elodia just before dawn. The Fat Old Woman barged in, pointed at her, and said, "We march in an hour." Albia entered, followed by a slave bearing a bowl of steaming water, which he placed on the table. Bitorix and she both arose to piss, her in a chamber pot, him out the window. Then he stood in front of the table while Albia wiped him down with a hot, damp cloth. When done, she handed the cloth to Elodia and helped him dress. Elodia stood, rinsed the cloth, washed her face, and wiped off the mess of the previous night's ordeal.

Fat Old Woman stood impatiently waiting, then handed her a bundle and a small loaf of bread. Elodia sat at the end of the bed and, while eating the loaf, opened the bundle. It contained her old tunic, newly washed, and a new loincloth.

She studied the loincloth. It was a long flap of material hanging from a simple belt, but unlike her old one, the cloth was dyed cotton, and the belt was leather. The bundle also contained a wool overshirt, a cape, woolen trousers, socks, and boots. The day was going to be cold.

She stood to put on the loincloth and donned last night's tunic and the other clothes from the bundle before pulling on her new boots. She was dressed and ready to go in less time than it had taken Albia to dress Bitorix. Albia was fastening his chest plate behind his back when she caught Elodia's eye. She nodded toward the bed and raised an eyebrow as if to ask Elodia, "How was the bumping?"

It was an event Elodia wanted to forget, not describe in detail. She raised her shoulders and gave an exaggerated shrug which Bitorix, unfortunately, noticed out the corner of his eye. "She was less than satisfactory, Albia," he said, "Now attend to *me*."

Seeing Elodia ready to go, Fat Old Woman gestured for her to follow. They descended to the city square, joined a half-dozen other slaves, and waited. She stamped her feet to keep them warm. It was an intense cold, one that froze the sun and kept it from rising and warming the world.

Already a column of soldiers was marching out the city's south gate. She craned her neck, hoping in vain to catch a glimpse of her squad. When the supply train left, she looked but didn't see her mule, Bridie.

Bitorix left the building along with Albia, who joined the slave group. An aide had been standing by with Bitorix's horse. He mounted and rode toward some officers who had gathered by the gate. He never looked at his slaves or at her. He was done with her for now. *Hopefully forever.*

Among the officers was a massive man on an equally massive horse. Both he and his mount were festooned with gold. Bitorix hailed him deferentially, a salute the large man mechanically returned. This was her first glimpse of Military Count Lupicinus, master of Moesia, Thracia, and Macedonia. There was no person of greater rank except the masters of foot and horse, and the emperor himself. She later came to know there was no greater ass or, as Caius would say, *podex.*

After an hour—Fat Old Woman's estimate was accurate—a marshal waved the slaves into the column. The supply train was in front, the rear guard behind, and a double column of legionaries on each side. They were there for her protection but had the additional effect of quashing any idea she had of escaping.

The march from Durostorum to Marcianople would take two long days. There were about fifty slaves, the property of the various Roman officers. All were household slaves except a dozen children. These were the new slaves acquired at bargain prices from the families of starving Goths.

The slaves walked along in groups, with each officer's slaves staying together. By then, she had met most of Bitorix's slaves: Albia, the bath attendants, the cook/waiter, and the Fat Old Woman, who had a forgettable name. They walked behind Lupicinus's slaves. There was a definite pecking order based on each owner's seniority. The slaves of Lupicinus assumed an air of superiority and led the way.

Her single attempt to socialize was quickly thwarted. She started talking to one of Lupicinus's new child slaves, a pretty little girl. The girl spoke only Gothic, which no one in her group could or would speak. Elodia learned her name was Gelvira. She did her best to avoid weeping, but when Elodia asked about her mother, the little girl's eyes filled with tears. They spoke for only a few minutes before Lupicinus's Fat Old Woman—it looked like every group of slaves was bossed by a Fat Old Woman—told her to "Get the fryke back to your group." Elodia rejoined Albia and the bath attendants.

The ground south of Durostorum rose steeply toward a ridge of low hills. From the top, she paused to look ahead and back the way they'd come. The land nearby was blanketed by a thin cover of bright white snow. The only green was provided by occasional pines and spruce trees. Looking ahead, she could see the evergreens growing thickly, forming woods on either side of the road. Looking back, she saw the end of the column, a full mile away. There the rear guard's polished armor glittered in the sun. Beyond them, in the distance, the mist rose from the Danube. On this side of the river were green hillsides where the sun had melted the nightly frost and brilliant white slopes that still lay in shadow.

Beyond the rear guard was a mass of people. It followed closely on the heels of the rear guard, and it stretched back to the horizon, filling the road and fields on either side. In the distance, she could just make out the city through the morning mist. The mob packed all the distance back to the city walls and beyond, even to the river. This was the Gothic nation on the move, or at least the portion that called itself the Tervingi, her tribe. Smoke rose some distance from the road, both to the east and west.

Seeing her gaze, one of the older bath slaves said, "It has begun. The pillaging and looting. Angry, hungry people looking for food. And revenge."

"And killing?" she said.

"Probably. Many locals have taken refuge in the city since the barbarians started to cross. A few Romans living in walled compounds may have stayed to defend their homes, if they have henchmen they can trust. Enough henchmen and those who know their business. Like veterans."

Elodia considered the people who lived near Grainus's outpost: the villagers and farmers. None of them lived in a walled compound. Did they need to flee? Did they know to run? That village was a long day's walk from Durostorum. Perhaps they would escape or hide until the army could return and reassert control.

"When will the army restore order?"

He laughed. "The army? You're looking the wrong way, girl. There's no army back there anymore. Oh, there are a few hundred men in Durostorum, enough to defend the city, but the army? You're marching with it to Marcianople. It will be weeks or months before the army comes back."

Are we safe? The mob is right on our tail. Will they attack us?

She took some comfort in looking at the legionaries. They were marching in the ready position—helmeted, shields in front, swords not drawn but loose in scabbards—and flanked by cavalry. No, the Goths would not attack the column when there were easier targets. In fact, she wondered whether Military Count Lupicinus intentionally left the nearby homes and farms undefended, a strategy

119

meant to provide the Goths with easy targets while allowing the army to move unmolested.

The column moved at a good pace. It was a pace a legionary could easily maintain all day, but it was too fast for the fat, old, or very young slaves. After a few hours of walking, the children were flagging. Perhaps because the senior officers were concerned the long walk might damage their new assets, they provided an ox cart for the purchased children. Later, Bitorix and Lupicinus, with their guards, rode by to check on their young investments. Bitorix owned three, Lupicinus owned six, and Elodia didn't know who owned the other three.

When the senior officers appeared, Elodia had been walking beside Albia, putting up with her incessant babble. Since Albia was taller than her, she tried to avoid being seen by putting Albia between the officers and herself. Her attempt failed. Bitorix pointed out his new "bump slave," his words. Lupicinus did a quick double-take and stared at her. Here again, her physical beauty was more of a curse than a blessing.

The officers rode into the column just ahead of her, forcing slaves to scurry out of their way. Now that she could get a closer look at Lupicinus, she saw he was not just enormous but also obese. His chest armor was split along the sides, allowing fat to bulge out. His sword belt was hidden by a fat roll as though he had a giant sausage wrapped around his waist.

Lupicinus and Bitorix approached each other to talk privately, their heads almost touching. As if one gawp wasn't enough, Lupicinus turned his head toward her from time to time for additional inspections. Each started at her feet and slowly made its way up to her face. *How humiliating.* As Bitorix and Lupicinus finished talking, she could almost make out Bitorix guffawing, "An (unintelligible) pity though. She *is* such a beauty. But boring in bed," to which Lupicinus scoffed, "Perhaps she'd do better with a better lover." Bitorix scowled but remained quiet. He knew better than to contest the military count's wittiness.

The officers' party blocked the column, forcing it to a stop and allowing a gap to open in the ranks. The pause was short. Bitorix reached down to her and said, "Take my arm." When she did, he swung her up behind him onto his saddle. They left the column, which resumed walking quickly to close the gap. Lupicinus and his bodyguards trotted up to the column's head.

While she and Bitorix rode to the front, she studied the supply train as they passed it, looking for her squad's mule. She recognized one she was sure was Bridie, but she didn't recognize the man leading it. After passing the supply train, they rode up by the ranks of legionaries. Again, she scanned them as she passed but did not recognize her boys. If she could spot even one of them, the others would be nearby, and, with luck, she'd get a glimpse of Caius.

Last night she'd fantasized it was Caius pressing down on her, not Bitorix. Regardless, she did not see any of them. Not surprising. There were thousands of legionaries dressed uniformly in steel helmets, all of whom looked the same when approached from behind.

Lupicinus rode close alongside Bitorix and Elodia, and began asking her the same questions she'd previously answered for Bitorix: who was her father, who were her people? Lupicinus did not ask for her name. He simply called her Helen. She didn't know what story Bitorix had told him, but based on his questions, he knew Grainus had rescued and enslaved her, and she'd worked as a provisioner for the intervening years. He also wondered aloud whether the squad had used her as a bump slave.

She didn't answer directly, which probably left him thinking it was true. After all, why wouldn't she provide that service? In fact, since most squads would have used her that way, she marveled at her good luck in crossing the river into Grainus's sector even as she cursed her bad luck in coming to this man's attention.

As bad as being bumped by Bitorix was, the idea of bumping this gross pig nauseated her. But if he wanted her, there was nothing to stop him. He outranked Bitorix as much as Bitorix outranked her. Lupicinus's word was law. She answered him as politely and deferentially as she could.

Soon his questions moved away from topics of lust. Instead, they centered on who she knew, what she knew, and what she'd done.

"What is your birth name? Who are your people?" he asked.

She looked back up at him. He was still staring into her eyes. "My name is Elodia. I serve as the provisioner for the limitanei squad of Decanus Grainus. I am the daughter…"

Bitorix interrupted, "She no longer serves Grainus. I own her now."

Lupicinus looked at Bitorix with irritation. "I am speaking with her, not you."

"Please excuse me, my lord."

"Helen, can you stay on a horse all by yourself?"

She said, "Yes, my lord."

"Military Tribune Bitorix, dismount and give Helen your horse. If you need a mount, go and take one from your own staff."

Bitorix reddened in humiliation. "Yes, my lord," and slid off the mount, handing her the reins. She effortlessly took control of the horse.

Once he was gone, Lupicinus turned to her. "You served my limitanei, but your accent says you are a Goth," he said.

She resented this man. He asked gently, kindly, but still, he asked and asked. Would she be forced to talk with him for the whole day? Perhaps if she answered sweetly, he would just move on. "I am the daughter of Gordric, chieftain of the Fontal clan of the Tervingi."

"Are your people among those who have just crossed the river?" he asked.

"No, I am told my clan has followed Athanaric into the Carpathian Mountains."

"Those are the pagan Tervingi?"

"Pagan?" Christians spat the word like an insult. "It is true we do not worship the Jesus God. We remain faithful to Odin and the other gods of our fathers."

He snorted. "Yes, that's what I mean by 'pagan.'"

After an awkward pause, he continued, "How did you come to Grainus's squad?"

"Several years ago, nothing was left for me on the other side of the river after my husband died. I rafted across. Decanus Grainus rescued me, gave me shelter, and hired me." She was not going to tell him the whole story. He did not need to know she was a murderer and an outlaw. Yet he continued to stare at her. Could he see the holes in her story?

"No children?"

"None. I have had two, but Freya took them from me before they were born." She expected him to offer sympathy or consolation, but he did not.

"I can see you were brought up to ride," he said. "Do you prefer a proper horse or a stupid mule?"

She was startled. Where had this question come from? Rather than debate the relative intelligence of her quite clever mules and his large stupid horses, she said, "Yes. My father, Gordric, had many horses. I grew up riding them." Doing it now felt good. Getting off her feet was a relief.

"Shall I call you Helen or Elodia?" he unexpectedly asked. *Why must he call me anything? Why couldn't he go away and leave me in peace?*

"My name is Elodia."

"Why 'Elodia'? It doesn't mean anything."

"Yes, it does. It is Gothic for 'lilac.' My mother felt the lilac has the most fragrant blossom of spring. Elodia is a good name."

"Helen is better for someone with your beauty. After Helen of Troy. She was the most beautiful woman in the world."

"I have heard of this woman. She married a king but caused a war by bumping another man. That is not me. I am not such a beauty."

"Yes, Helen, you are." He proceeded to tell her the whole story from the Greek poet Homer, though she'd already told him she knew the story. He said Troy was a city in Egypt, and Helen was the queen of Athens whose magical wooden horse was stolen by a Trojan prince. She did not correct him. *This is a man who likes to talk and never listen.*

He talked and talked. She held onto the saddle and tried to avoid falling asleep. She shivered in the cold. At least walking would have kept her warm. And she could have reached into her pack for an additional garment. Instead, she was bored and cold.

When he tired of hearing himself speak, he turned his attention back to her.

"Do you know the Gothic Chieftain Fritigern?"

"No, I only know him by name as the leader of a clan of my tribe. Or perhaps he is now king of the Tervingi?"

"Not yet. The tribe's king is a doddering old man named King Alavivus, but, in practice, Fritigern is the leader. Now let us talk about him. Do you speak the same dialect as Fritigern?"

"Yes. I mean, he probably speaks with an eastern accent, but we could easily converse."

"Have you any allegiance to him?"

"Good gods, no. I've never met the man."

Lupicinus went on to ask what work she had done for Grainus and his squad since her capture. She didn't explain that she was rescued, not captured. She mentioned her loyal work as a provisioner. She emphasized her dedication. Lupicinus nodded as she spoke, so her answers seemed to please him. His questions were leading somewhere, but she had no idea where.

"Bitorix says he bought you. For how much?"

"He boasted it was only one denarius."

Lupicinus raised an eyebrow. "So little?" She explained the auction was held yesterday, and Bitorix was the only bidder. Lupicinus laughed out loud. "That mentula!" Her opinion exactly.

Would she be willing to swear an oath of loyalty to the emperor? "Of course," which was only a partial lie. She would promise anything he asked, willing or not.

Had she ever killed a man? She shuddered, recalling the dreadful night when she helped her squad defend the outpost from an attack by Gothic raiders. She saw no reason to lie, so she answered honestly. "Yes, several."

Romans or Goths? "Just Goths."

Would she be willing to kill again? "Yes." She considered giving a more detailed answer, but her brief answers seemed to satisfy him.

He asked what would she do to get her freedom? She pondered this. What should she say? That she would bump whoever they wanted her to? No, she was already forced to do that, and it had yet to buy her freedom. But she suddenly saw the drift of his questions. "I would kill a Goth."

He nodded. Then he spoke to one of his bodyguards, "Escort her back to wherever Bitorix is."

Rather than acknowledging her, Bitorix ignored her for the rest of the day, which was fine. She had a lot to think about. Was Lupicinus expecting her to become an assassin? Who was his target? Lord Fritigern? She had killed before and had no qualms about doing it again, but only in her own interest. She would kill if it helped Caius or her squad. She would not kill some random person at the bidding of this Roman. Not that she would say so to him. She might live longer if she played along. If he offered her freedom, she would act suitably surprised and agreeable. But she was no assassin.

Growing up, Elodia never expected to end up a slave, let alone have three owners in one day.

In the late afternoon, they traveled through a high, bleak, uninhabited area to the fortress of Palmatis. It was cold. There were no trees, only the occasional shrub. The last leaves had been knocked down by rainstorms, so there was no shelter from the bitter wind. The damp air suggested the next storm would bring more snow and the onset of deep winter. The long column followed a dry riverbed, and looking up, they could see the fortress wall peering down from a plateau far above. The road wound up out of the river valley onto a rocky plain and around the low hills leading to the plateau's foot. Now Elodia realized the fortress, high on its plateau, was surrounded by the river on three sides. The fourth side, directly ahead, was a ninety-foot cliff into which the road had been cut. It rose, zigzagging up until it emerged at the top. After the last switchback, she could see the fortress was protected by a tall stone wall sitting on an embankment. A deep ditch in front provided additional protection.

They entered the fortress through a stout wooden gate set back a hundred feet from the precipice. Gate guards closed the gates after the last Romans entered. The long procession of Goths would have to camp on the rocky plains below in whatever shelter they could find.

With some squeezing, there was room in the fortress for all the Roman troops. No one, the military count ordered, would be left outside the walls and exposed overnight to harassment or attack by the Goths. The fortress provided space for stables, workshops, a Christian church, a hospital, and some barracks. The spaces were designed for a much smaller force. Shelters were set up in the fortress courtyard for those who the rooms could not house. The senior officers took possession of the barracks.

An aide led Bitorix to the space assigned to him and his staff. He kept with him a few of his guards and senior slaves, including Elodia. His area consisted of a small common room, where a slave was already building a fire, and a tiny adjoining bedroom, which was dark and cold. Other slaves were there, busy lighting torches. They set up a desk and a bed and covered the stone floor with rugs. In front of the desk, they unfolded and placed a plain backless wooden stool, which surprised Elodia. *Did Bitorix deem it his curule seat?* Roman consuls and generals—men with real authority—had such seats, but theirs were carved from ivory. *It would be like Bitorix to lug around a pathetic replica.*

Bitorix told Elodia to wait on the bed and then left. Fat Old Woman came in to inspect the arrangements. She saw Elodia sitting quietly and directed a younger slave to bring Elodia a cup of wine. After the day's long ride, its fine flavor lingered on her tongue. Fat Old Woman stood in front of her, hands on hips, and said, "Well, girl?"

Elodia had no idea how to answer. "Well, what?"

"I do so very much hope you're happy with these arrangements."

Elodia was not. It was evident she would be Bitorix's companion again that night. She had hoped he would pick a woman who was not "boring in bed." Albia or some other slave. Any other slave. If Fat Old Woman could be sarcastic, then she could act obtusely. "Well, it *is* nice to be indoors with a fire rather than stuck in a cold tent in the courtyard."

"Nice for *you!*" Fat Old Woman said tartly. "Nice for you, a slut who gets to sleep in this room. Not so for the rest of us. His other servants *are* in tents in the courtyard." She noticed Fat Old Woman referred to herself and the other slaves as "servants." Perhaps using a euphemism to describe their station had less sting. She also saw in the outer room some of the young women slaves drinking wine with the bodyguards. She surmised that *they* would not be sleeping in a tent. Perhaps Fat Old Woman bitterly recalled an earlier time when she was less fat, less old, and was invited to drink wine with strong young men.

Before Fat Old Woman could spout any additional bile, Bitorix entered the room. "Come with me," he ordered, indicating Elodia, and ignoring Fat Old Woman. She followed him around the courtyard perimeter, past sheds, and workshops, until they came to a barracks suite considerably more extensive than his. It, too, had a common room several times the size of Bitorix's, one that was warmed by a fire and occupied by men she did not recognize, but many of whom wore the insignia of senior officers

The one man she *did* recognize was Lupicinus. He was sitting in an ivory curule seat, a symbol of actual authority and much more impressive than Bitorix's wooden one. His fat overflowed the chair. *It must be very uncomfortable.* He faced a semicircle of low stools occupied by senior officers. Everyone else sat on the stone floor, which had been made less cold, if not more comfortable, by thick rugs. Bitorix took a stool that some inferior officer, with a look of irritation, vacated to accommodate him. Without being told, she knelt on the rug at his feet.

When she was settled, she was provided with another cup of wine. She had no sooner sipped it, and begun to appreciate the vintage, which was even finer than Bitorix's wine, than the military count spoke. "Helen," Lupicinus said. "Come and stand by me."

She rose deftly to her feet and, being careful to avoid spilling her wine, stepped over the legs of other rug-sitters to where Lupicinus sat. *This is all very puzzling.*

Lupicinus spoke to the room at large. "Men, if you have not seen Military Tribune Bitorix's most recent trophy, let me introduce Helen. Once you have seen her, you will not soon forget our Helen of Troy, reborn."

She no longer blushed or squirmed at this kind of exaggeration. Instead, she stood erect, chin up, and stared impassively across the room at an arbitrary spot on the far wall. When he added, "Helen, you may kneel," she gracefully knelt at his feet. Sipping her wine again, she looked over the rim at Bitorix. He was perched on the edge of his stool, looking mystified.

As if rehearsed, a slave came to Lupicinus, who handed him some coins. Then the slave approached Bitorix and pressed the coins into his hand. He glanced at them, turned to Lupicinus, and asked, "What is this, sir?"

Lupicinus said, "That is two denarii. I am purchasing our lovely Helen from you. Helen told me you paid one denarius for her just yesterday. So, think of it, you have doubled your investment in just one day!"

He laughed and laughed, which obliged everyone to laugh except Bitorix, who was speechless. He sat for a few moments, mouth agape. He made little gurgling sounds. Then he closed his mouth.

At the same time, the joke caught her off guard with a sizable swig of wine in her mouth, a volume she was forced to quickly and quietly spit back into the cup. Then she clamped her jaw shut, took several deep breaths through her nose, and managed to suppress the laughter that threatened to overwhelm her. She cringed to think what would have happened had she been swallowing.

Could Lupicinus do this? Forcibly "purchase" her from Bitorix without his consent? Of course. Lupicinus, military count of Thracia, Macedonia, and Moesia, could do whatever he wanted.

Lupicinus continued, "I have big plans for Helen." Now she cringed again, realizing this implied something worse than another night with Bitorix. Her new owner—a man-shaped bag of fat—said he had "big plans" for her. She could guess what those plans were. As bad as it sounded, there was always an option. She could stab herself. Or she could stab Lupicinus in his sleep. However, the Romans would locate and kill everyone she knew, basically everyone in her squad, before they crucified her. Stabbing, attractive as it seemed, was out.

While she was mulling her dismal future, Lupicinus was discussing the plans for tonight and tomorrow. He and his bodyguards would attend a banquet hosted by Chieftain Fritigern. Evidently, Fritigern had set up a banquet tent just outside the fortress gate. This was a compromise location. Fritigern had first suggested hosting a dinner in his command tent at the bottom of the hill, an idea that Lupicinus rejected. Lupicinus commented, "As a wise man once said, 'Even a lion does not dine in a wolf's den.'" The aphorism made no sense to Elodia, so she suspected Lupicinus himself was the wise man.

She wondered if her handsome old owner would accompany her fat new owner to the banquet. She glanced at Bitorix. He was staring daggers at Lupicinus. She could imagine those visual daggers becoming real if Lupicinus failed to watch his back.

Lupicinus moved on to review tomorrow's march. "We're only one-third of the way to Marcianople, and there is no fortress between here and there large enough to protect us all. Therefore, we will leave two hours before dawn and not stop until the gates of Marcianople are safely closed behind us." They discussed how to deal with Goths who might impede their progress: those who got in the way versus those who posed a threat.

Lupicinus said his men should avoid provoking armed resistance; killing a few Goths didn't matter, except it would slow their progress.

"Now," Lupicinus stood and said in an overly loud voice, "Helen and I have some *big planning* to do."

This witty announcement was greeted with whoops and cheers, a humorous moment shared by almost everyone. Her face became stony again, and she bit her lip to keep silent. Lupicinus reached down to where she was kneeling and drew her up. He led her by the hand into the adjoining bedroom amidst general applause. They were followed by two women, his body slaves. He also called in several of his officers. She sat stiffly on the end of the bed, watching as his slaves helped him out of his armor and overcoat, leaving him in only his tunic as they washed his hands, face, and feet. There was a stunning green silk dress on the bed beside her. *Why was it there?*

He spoke quietly in Latin to his officers, so quietly she had trouble making out his words. She heard him mention "banquet in Marcianople," "archers ready," and "Fritigern." Were they hatching some treachery? She did not react. After all, she was not meant to know Latin. Their conversation lasted only a few sentences before Lupicinus waved the officers out of the room. Then he turned his awful attention to her.

Resigned to the coming indignity, she stripped off her outer clothes. The room was still cold. She sat shivering, wearing only her tunic, wondering whether she should shed it too just to get it done.

She'd lifted her tunic and was fiddling with her loincloth belt when Lupicinus looked over and, for the first time, noticed what she was about.

"Here, girl, stop that!" he said in Greek. "Put those things back on. And put on that green dress. We're going out in a short time."

She gladly did as he ordered. Confused, she asked, "You don't want to bump me, lord?"

"We don't have time for that. Anyway, I like more flesh on my girls," he chortled. *Small breast jokes. Always funny.*

But a glance at his body slaves confirmed his preference. Either of them would have fifty pounds on her. The green dress did not fit her well, having been made for a girl with more flesh, but she delighted in the fabric. She'd never worn silk before.

Once he was comfortably undressed and holding a large wine cup, he dismissed his slaves and sat in a chair facing her. He waited while she pulled her socks back on. Even with rugs, the stone floor was cold.

Not one for small talk, Lupicinus started right in. "You told me you would kill a man if the emperor ordered it." He paused, waiting for some acknowledgment.

She hadn't said anything of the sort. "Yes, I would, my lord," she lied.

"The emperor has a man who needs killing: this Fritigern, the chief of this mob of barbarians following us. We need these barbarians to settle down, to become good Romans. Like you."

She was not and never would be a good Roman. The man was talking to her like she was a simpleton. He went on, "You've seen what the barbarians are doing; the fires they've lit, the farms they're destroying? Their plundering?" *Yes, because they're starving.* "And raping." Her face grew red with anger. *As if Romans never do that?* She calmed herself before Lupicinus noticed her loss of composure.

"Fritigern has told his people to wreak havoc," he said, "But it must stop. We want the barbarians to join with us, for everyone to become one people, to become Roman citizens. But they will not, not with that man as their leader. Do you understand?"

Yes, you want me to kill Lord Fritigern.

Looking wide-eyed and innocent, she asked, "What can I do to help, my lord?"

"You might not need to do anything. I have heard there is a plot to kill him," which meant *Lupicinus* had a plot to kill him, "but should that fail, we need a backup plan. That would involve you. Could you kill Fritigern?"

"If the emperor desires it, then yes, I could do it. It would be my duty. Even though it might cost me… cost me my life?"

"Yes, there is a slight risk," Lupicinus said in his best soothing and calming voice, "but there is also a great reward." She looked at him questioningly. *Here comes the manumission offer; he will offer me my freedom.*

"If you agree to my plan, I will reward you generously. If Fritigern is dead within a week, I will grant you your freedom and give you a pound of gold. You might not have to do anything. He might be killed in the plot I heard about."

She opened her eyes wide in apparent wonder and disbelief. *He must think me a total idiot.*

"If that plot succeeds, you get the gold. No risk. If that plot fails, and you will certainly know if it fails, then you must kill him in his sleep."

"I could do that…" she said while trying to look thoughtful. "I *will* do that, my lord!" she promised, this time with profound resolution, complete with a tight jaw and clenched fists. She wondered if she was overacting or if he would notice if she did.

"How can I get him in his sleep, my lord?" she asked as innocently as she could.

She knew what Lupicinus was going to say, but she wanted to hear it from his own mouth. "Tonight at the banquet, I will gift you to Fritigern. I will tell him you are my Helen of Troy, the most beautiful woman in the world. I expect he will accept you graciously or as graciously as a barbarian can. But he will not know you are also my Trojan horse. When he takes you to bed, you kill him."

"And if he doesn't want me in his bed?"

"He will, once he sets eyes on you. You must show him your great love-making skills. Which, I regret, I will have no opportunity to sample."

What makes him think I have such skills?

When she betrayed a quizzical look, Lupicinus clarified, "Yes, Bitorix claimed you were a cold fish. Which demonstrates how desperate he was to keep you for himself. I have never met Chieftain Fritigern, but," he rattled on, "no doubt he is a better lover than that oaf, Bitorix. And more attractive than me," he said, looking down at his rolls of fat."

At least that was true.

"Will you do this?"

"Yes, my lord," she lied again.

The plan from her point of view could be summarized like this: she would trade a Roman master for a Gothic master. Who would soon die in some sort of nefarious Roman plot. And should that plot fail, another plot, which would probably cost her her life, could earn her a pound of gold. Which the Romans, being Romans, would never pay.

It was pitch black when they left the fortress by a postern gate. A half-dozen guards lit their way with torches. The guards were understandably nervous. Six guards would be ineffective if the Goths meant to kill them, but, as Lupicinus correctly reasoned, they were in little danger. Fritigern's priority was to get provisions in Marcianople. Slaying the province's military commander would not be helpful.

Fritigern's large tent, twenty by thirty feet, was surrounded by a dozen warriors holding torches. The entrance flaps were up, revealing two men in the opening with several other men clustered behind. A handsome young man stepped forward, holding his hands wide, and, with a big smile, began speaking in atrocious Greek. He pointed at himself and said, "Fritigern, chieftain Balti of Tervingi Goths," then pointing at the stooped gray-haired man beside him, "Him, King Alavivus, Biggest Tervingi."

Fritigern was a man of perhaps thirty years of age, a big man, about six feet tall, with broad shoulders. His muscular arms bulged under golden bangles. His black hair was long in the back, but he was clean-shaven on the sides and front. His beard and mustache were neatly trimmed, odd for a Gothic chieftain. Through the torchlight, he peered at them with penetrating eyes. The light was too dim to make out their color.

He's big. A match for Caius, but Bitorix is much more handsome. He seems warm and sincere. Or acts that way.

By contrast, King Alavivus was old, probably sixty or more. His hair, what was left of it, was a mop of gray. His beard matched his hair both in color and dishevelment. If he'd been tall once, he was no longer. He stooped and walked with a staff. There was nothing warm and sincere about him. King Alavivus did not smile. He scowled and looked ready to spit.

Fritigern said, "Friends. Welcome. Come. Eat. Friends," taking a step back and waving them into the tent. Lupicinus smiled, touched his forefinger to his forehead in salute, and stepped forward. King Alavivus blocked him, putting an arm in front of Fritigern. The king turned to Fritigern and said in Gothic, "Just the fat one, not his guards. And he must give up his weapons."

Fritigern, obviously irritated, replied, "Old Father, we have discussed this before. We will *not* disarm them. We have two guards for each of theirs. We must be gracious hosts."

"We must show these ugly frykers our hatred. They starve us, kill us, steal our children."

"Hush, Old Father. You have already forgotten what we decided earlier." Fritigern reached up and gently pushed the king's arm out of the way. Turning to Lupicinus, he said in his broken Greek, "King Alavivus old. Now stupid like child. Come," and waved them once again into the tent.

The king reluctantly dropped his arm. "Fine," he said, "Let the crap-eating bastards eat real food for once."

Since King Alavivus did not respond to being called old and stupid, Elodia determined he had no Greek. And since none of the Romans responded to being called ugly fryking crap-eating bastards, she determined they had no Gothic. *This should be a memorable meal.*

After they entered the tent, Fritigern indicated the other men standing there. "Tervingi chieftains," he said by way of introduction. Lupicinus pointed at her and said in Greek, "Helen of Troy." She kept silent at this ludicrous name and kept her face expressionless. Lupicinus's single introduction was done; his guards did not warrant an introduction.

Fritigern reached for her hand and, bowing, kissed it. "Beauty," he said in Greek.

While retaining her neutral expression, she replied in Gothic, "A most gracious compliment, but undeserved." Fritigern smiled.

After that, she acted as the translator. Fritigern welcomed it; he said it was a relief to avoid using his poor Greek. He introduced the other Gothic chieftains by name, which she translated into Greek for Lupicinus. He saluted each one in turn, repeated their name, and added in Latin "Goth turd one," "Goth turd two," and so forth. She did not translate Lupicinus's words, which she pretended not to understand because, as far as Lupicinus knew, she did not speak Latin.

Fritigern's introductions complete, Lupicinus introduced a topic that deeply concerned her: her. He said in Greek to Fritigern, "It would be most improper of me to come as your guest without giving my host a present," which she translated. Some chieftains responded by touching their swords, worried that said "present" might be some unpleasant Roman surprise.

Thinking of Lupicinus's plot to assassinate Fritigern, she thought, *No, you'll have to wait for* that *surprise!*

Lupicinus, oblivious, carried on in Greek. "Allow me to gift you my most valued possession, the most beautiful woman in the Roman Empire, my Helen of Troy," an inflated statement that she dutifully translated. She added in Gothic, "Forgive me, Lord Fritigern, but that is what he said."

Fritigern looked at her and said, "Tell him I accept his beautiful gift with pleasure. Tell him when we Goths get an opportunity, we will destroy all things Roman, both ugly and beautiful. By accepting you, there will be one fewer beautiful Roman thing to destroy."

She said, "Excuse me, Lord Fritigern, but I am, in fact, a Goth," to which he smiled and laughed. She added as neutrally as possible, "And you do me a service by accepting me as your humble slave."

"Good," he said and laughed again. "Tell him I accept his gift with thanks. And you may add any other typical meaningless phrases Romans use when accepting a gift."

After translating that diplomatically, Lupicinus instructed her to go and kneel at Fritigern's feet. She was Fritigern's property now.

The ramifications of this change finally came home. She traversed the distance in four steps. With each step, she felt her heart lighten. Oh, to be away from Bitorix and Lupicinus! She felt light, lighter. She glided weightlessly down the length of the tent and mused, as she started to kneel, whether she would descend to the floor or float above it. That silly idea made her smile. She quickly reverted to a grave appearance but not before Fritigern saw her initial reaction.

Goth servants carried in the feast. It was a collection of meats, breads, and root vegetables served with sweet sauces and many bottles of wine. The Gothic chieftains ate little and drank much. Their conversation was subdued, but its tone proved that King Alavivus was not the only Goth seething with rage. But because Elodia could speak Gothic, they had to temper their remarks. Still, she heard them uttering anti-Roman sentiments, remarks she avoided translating.

Lupicinus complimented Fritigern on the excellent quality and quantity of the food. She accurately translated this to Gothic even though it was clear Lupicinus was mocking the starving Goths. To her translation, she appended, "I am sorry the military count feels he can ridicule you."

Fritigern replied in Gothic, "You may tell the military count that an excellent cook, who trained in Rome itself, prepared the meal. We found him today in the nearby estate of a Roman nobleman. All the food you see here came from that estate. Once we plundered it, we burned it to the ground. The henchmen who were charged with guarding the estate have joined my army. As have all the nobleman's slaves. The nobleman, his wife, and his children were all slaughtered. I am pleased you are enjoying the meal. Were it otherwise, I would slay the fine Roman cook."

It took her a minute to formulate an acceptable translation, something that would not result in bloodshed. "My lord, Fritigern says the credit for the meal belongs to his new and excellent cook. The ingredients were all acquired locally from a nearby estate for a very reasonable price. To ensure they were brought here safely, they were carried by servants from the estate who were guarded by the estate's soldiers. Unfortunately, the estate's owner and his family cannot entertain you since they are not in residence."

As the evening wore on, Lupicinus began to set the stage for the upcoming plot. "You have provided me with a most sumptuous feast—actually, it's been quite mediocre but don't translate that—one that I will long remember. You must allow me to reciprocate. Tomorrow, when we have all reached Marcianople, I will hold a banquet to celebrate Roman and Gothic reconciliation. It would give me great pleasure if you all," and here he waved his hand to encompass King Alavivus, Chieftain Fritigern, all the other chieftains, and her, "would do me the great honor of attending," which she translated literally.

Fritigern said they would be most pleased to attend. Farewells were extended. Lupicinus and his guards headed back to the postern gate. She was left in the company of the chieftains with a small bundle of her possessions. The other chieftains left the tent, followed by Fritigern and her. Some warriors started breaking down the banquet tent while the rest accompanied them on the road leading down from the plateau. Once Fritigern was sure the Romans were well out of earshot, he said, "You are an excellent translator." She was about to thank him when she realized he'd spoken in flawless Greek. She began to laugh. She watched him smiling by torchlight.

She replied in Gothic, "And you can speak the most atrocious Greek," making him laugh too.

The night was clear and bitter. Above were myriad stars flickering in the blackness, far more than could be seen from the outpost on the Danube, where the river mist obscured the night sky. Back at the fort, she and Caius would be in bed soon after dark. Pressed against each other on a cold night like this, sharing their warmth. Where was he tonight?

As she gazed up at the sky, her steps took her to the road's edge. Before she could step off into a black void, Fritigern gently took her elbow and guided her to safety.

A few minutes later, they had descended to the plain and into the Gothic camp. His guards led the way to his command tent. "We will sleep here," he said. The tent was divided into two rooms. The front room was a sizable audience space with a wooden seat at the back, for Fritigern's use, she assumed, and rugs on all sides for clients and petitioners.

They walked through the audience room, and Fritigern, pulling aside a canvas partition, waved her into the rear room, his private quarters. She had an idea of what would happen next, but Fritigern surprised her by saying, "You sleep there." He indicated a pile of rugs and furs on one side, opposite his cot. She watched as he stripped down and held the single torch, which provided the light for her to do likewise.

Clad only in her loincloth, she crawled under a pile of furs and watched as he extinguished the flame. Within a minute, she could hear him breathing deeply, fast asleep. *What a day. So much to think about. I will never be able to fall…* were her last waking thoughts.

She was lying awake staring up at the tent roof with a fur blanket pulled up to her chin. Vapor had condensed inside the canvas and formed little streams that ran down the stitched seams. Some streams stalled until joined by other streams. Some streams would hit a wrinkle and split in two. The fortune of any stream was unpredictable, much like her life. It continued to change. Had it changed for good or evil? Being yanked away from her limitanei squad, especially Caius, was definitely evil. Being taken away from Bitorix was fortunate, but it would have been evil if Lupicinus had tried to bump her. Being given to Lord Fritigern? Fortunate so far.

Even if he decided to bump her, that would not be so bad, especially compared to bumping Lupicinus. She shuddered.

Still, what would Lord Fritigern do with her? He probably didn't know. She could tell he was surprised to be given her. She knew nothing about him. Was he married? Did he have children? He was a man of strength, power, and prestige: the kind of man her dear father should have found for her. She needed to know this man.

The room flap was pushed aside, and a short blond man stepped in. He was carrying a large bowl of water, which he set on a washstand. Fritigern climbed off his cot and, apparently half asleep, tottered over to it and splashed cold water on his face and chest. He whooshed from the shock and jerked erect. Now fully awake, he turned, looked around, and focused on her. She sat up, keeping the blanket under her chin. He called out to the servant who was bustling about in the outer room, "Bron, bring hot water for the girl!"

She said, "Not necessary. I can wash with cold."

Fritigern called again, "Bron, never mind the hot water." And then to her, "Just as well. We have no time to waste lighting a fire. It is many miles still to Marcianople. We need to be on the road as soon as possible."

Calling once more to Bron, "Bring me fresh clothes. And clean clothes for the girl." And then to her, "My good clothes from last night show traces of the banquet. I spilled gravy and splashed wine. Perhaps I was a little tipsy."

She scoffed. She had watched the Romans drink to excess, but Lord Fritigern, perhaps on the lookout for treachery, had only sipped. She drank far more wine than him.

His servant, Bron, appeared shortly with fresh clothes over one arm and a towel over the other. In his hand was a block of soap. The

143

odor of roses filled the tent. Where could he get perfumed soap and women's clothes at such short notice?

Fritigern stripped off his loincloth, splashed water over his limbs and privates, and dried himself with the towel. She did not react openly to his nudity, but her heart jumped. His physique was magnificent. Bron handed him each of his garments as he dressed: clean loincloth, gray wool tunic, leather trousers, cotton over-shirt, and cloak.

He left the water for her to use. Unlike him, she did not splash. She dipped a corner of the towel in the water, dabbed it with the soap, thoroughly washed, then, rinsing the cloth, wiped her body clean, leaving it slightly damp.

Fritigern evaluated her body throughout this. She did not react. After finishing her wash, she noticed he was still viewing her. With a wry smile, she asked, "Not exactly the beauty promised by Lupicinus?"

He said, "I'm sure some men would think so, but I do not. You are short, even for a woman, your shoulders are too broad, and your arm and leg muscles are brawny like a man's." He scrutinized her as if he were purchasing a horse. But he was not yet done.

"You might be taken for a young man from the back except for your wide hips. They are too wide for a man but probably not wide enough to bear children. Your breasts are small but taut. Sufficient to nurse a child, but by all appearances, have never done so. You will never be a wet nurse."

She began to turn red at his frank evaluation but then shrugged it off. "I never claimed to be Helen of Troy. If you dislike me, free me."

"No. I like your face. Even if you do not have Helen's body, you have her face."

This time she did turn red, a deep blush.

"But enough talk," he said, "We need to get moving. Bron has brought your clothes for today. Give your green gown to him. He will clean and return it when we reach Marcianople for you to wear again tonight. You will accompany me to the Roman banquet. Is that clear, Helen?"

She frowned. "Do you understand my name is not Helen? I am Elodia, daughter of Gordric, chieftain of the Fontal clan."

Without bothering to look at her, he said, "Girl, understand me, you are my slave, a gift from Lupicinus, and I shall call you whatever I choose."

She bared her teeth at him and gave a low growl. He looked up and returned her frown with a grin. "Oh my, what beautiful teeth you have!" That almost made her laugh. It was true; they were perfect. Somehow, she'd avoided the problems of missing or rotting teeth that afflicted many people.

As she watched Fritigern pull on his riding boots, she thought of Lupicinus, who was probably awake and dressing at the same time. Or being dressed. It was typical of the Romans who, considering themselves too lofty to garb themselves, relegated that task to their slaves.

He saw her staring at his boots. "We have no time to argue. We need to be heading south by dawn. Can you ride, Elodia?"

Hearing him say "Elodia" placated her; it brought back her smile. "Of course. All daughters of Gordric were taught to ride. And shoot. And use a knife."

"But of course," he said sarcastically, "a veritable tribe of Amazons."

Before she could think of a retort, Fritigern called out, "Bron, find the girl a horse."

"She won't be walking with the other slaves?" Bron asked.

"No, this slave will ride," he said, emphasizing she was still a slave.

Better to spend the day riding than walking. Walking would leave her exhausted at tonight's banquet.

An hour later, the sun was up, and Palmatis was miles behind. She rode quietly beside Fritigern, listening as he, a very busy commander, dispatched orders to his lieutenants. When those duties subsided, he pulled a loaf of bread from his saddlebag, tore off a chunk, and handed it to her. She thanked him with a weak smile. He followed the bread with a lump of soft cheese and a flask of watered wine.

The food cheered her. With a heartfelt "Thank you" and a genuine smile, she tried to return the flask.

"Keep it. I have another."

They rode halfway along the column of refugees. As far as she could see, ahead and behind, a line of carts and people on foot stretched out into the distance until they disappeared into the frosty morning haze.

A few inches of ice-encrusted snow covered the ground. The road passed through bleak rolling hills, but there were few shrubs and no trees to block the wind. The trace of snow that had fallen the previous night swirled and blew in their faces. The cold wind whipped around her ears. She tightened her hood's drawstring. The

146

road was frost-covered, but it would melt as soon as the sun rose. It would be a crispy, cold winter day.

They resumed riding in silence. A thought whirled round and round in her mind. Finally, she got up the nerve to say it aloud, "And thank you for not touching me last night."

"It was only because I was exhausted. I look forward to bumping you tonight."

Was he joking? He was not. That was disquieting. But she had a day's journey ahead. Perhaps she could talk him out of it. Or something may intervene.

Fritigern said, "You are quiet this morning. Come, I would like to hear your story. It will help us pass the time."

And perhaps it might move him to treat her as the daughter of a chieftain, not as some village wanton.

"I don't want to bore you."

"I doubt I'll be bored."

"Fine. I shall start at the beginning."

Taking a deep breath, she began. "You might think my childhood was one of privilege, being the daughter of a clan chieftain. And in time, it was. But my earliest memories are of hunger and fear."

She lifted her flask and sipped the wine to wet her tongue.

"My first memory is of traveling up into the mountains, day after day. I was forced to walk. When I complained of being tired and hungry, I was slapped and told to keep walking. There was no food in the mountains, and the food we'd brought ran out, and we were all hungry. Other families suffered more, but we in the chieftain's family always ate. Not a lot, but enough so we didn't starve. Well, some did. When my grandmother saw how hungry I was, and my siblings too, she gave us her food. She was courageous."

Elodia paused to utter a silent prayer for her grandmother's soul. "After she died, my parents renamed me, giving me her name. I am proud to be Elodia. That's why I got angry when the Romans kept calling me 'Helen.'" At least Lord Fritigern now called her Elodia.

"When I grew older," she continued, "I learned we had fled from the Christians."

"My people," Fritigern interjected.

"Yes, you and all the Christians, both Goths and the Romans. But you, the Christian Goths, rebelled against our king, Athanaric. You fought him and all loyal to him, including my father, Gordric. You took our land and pastures in Scythia and drove us up into the barren Carpathian Mountains."

She did not speak with anger or bitterness. She was just reciting a story as it had been passed down to her.

He interrupted her again. "You do know, don't you, we only rebelled after Athanaric began killing us Christians. He killed hundreds before we rose against him."

"I've heard this," she said with a shrug. "It was a long time ago, and I was just a baby."

That seemed to surprise him. Perhaps twenty years did not seem so long for someone as old as him.

"But the days of hunger passed?"

"Yes, my clan found fertile fields in Dacia occupied by a few Iazyges tribesmen. After killing the men and enslaving the others, our days of want were over. We even earned silver by selling the excess slaves. We ended up wealthier than we'd ever been back in Scythia."

"Did you grow up fearing Christians?"

"Oh yes. Athanaric said we could expect attacks at any time, though it never happened. By you Christians or by the Huns. We were trained to defend ourselves. Both boys and girls. Back when we lived in Scythia, we all farmed. We were very poor. My older brothers and sisters worked the fields. I was too young for most jobs except gleaning, looking for the few fallen wheat kernels the others missed. But in Dacia, we had slaves for the fieldwork."

"Then your life grew easier?"

"We were not hungry, but my father worked us hard. The boys trained to be warriors. The girls trained to manage a home, raise a family, and defend ourselves if necessary. We all practiced archery. The boys practiced spear and sword; the girls practiced knife fighting. Father ensured all his children could ride. He insisted we groom, feed, and muck out our own horses. We enjoyed hunting. I shot my first deer from horseback."

"I can see you sit a horse very well."

"Of course." Elodia reached down and caressed her horse's side. "Also, there was bookwork. I learned Christianity and Latin. A wandering missionary from Rome came into my father's village. He was lucky to pick our village. Most followers of Athanaric would have executed him on the spot, but my father found him amusing, so he kept him on. He was of no value at hunting or in the fields, but he was keen to preach. He taught my brother Boltus and me Latin, which I enjoyed but Boltus hated. He tried to teach us the Jesus religion."

"With little success?"

"With no success. He taught me that god is three equally powerful gods, but they came together to form one god, which is just nonsense. He said the first god is a real god, but the second god is a ghost, which is laughable, and the third is Jesus, the son of the first god by a virgin. That last one seemed reasonable to me. Jesus might well be the son of a god, after all, it is well known that Rome's Romulus was the son of Mars. But three gods? It makes no sense, does it?"

Fritigern just shrugged. "I am an Arian Christian, but you may believe whatever you like."

Elodia said, "The missionary said he was a true Christian, a Catholic Christian, and people like you, the ones who follow the preacher named Arian, claim Jesus is a lesser god. He said Arian Christians should be tortured and killed until they believe like him."

"How would he tell what I believe after he's killed me? Never mind. What do you believe?"

"I don't believe any of the Christian gods are real except perhaps the Jesus God. Sometimes, when I need help, I pray to him."

"Did the missionary teach you Greek?"

"He didn't know Greek, so I didn't learn that until I crossed the Danube."

She realized at that point she was telling her story for her own benefit. She cast her mind back to events from years ago and from a hundred miles to the north. Painful events. How much did she really want to tell this man? She stopped talking. They paused at a small river. Several ox carts were queued, waiting for a chance to ford. Elodia and Fritigern moved out of the way until the way was clear. Their horses took advantage of the pause to pull up clumps of brown grass. The sun had melted the night's frost, leaving the landscape wet and glistening. Its thin overnight veneer of ice cracked and broke as horses and carts crossed the river.

"How did you end up south of the great river?" Fritigern asked.

His question startled Elodia back to the present. "That really *is* a long story."

"Go ahead. We have time."

"My father kept in touch with another clan, the Dunlana clan, which was led by a remote cousin. They had fled Scythia at the same time as us, but they settled just north of the river. When I was fourteen and just coming into my womanhood, the cousin came north with a dozen of his men. They came to renew ties with my people, exchange news, and so on. The unmarried men sniffed around our girls, looking for possible brides. If not brides, then at least women they could bump."

Fritigern smiled at her frankness. As a soldier, he did not need a story decorated with polite phrases. She went on, "I was not interested in them. There was a boy I liked who lived nearby. His family was quite common, so I knew my father would never let me marry him, but I still dreamed of it. Father told me his plan was for me to marry his cousin's son, a man who would probably be that clan's next chieftain."

"Were you intimate with this boy you liked?"

"Intimate? You're asking if I bumped him?" He nodded. "Oh no. Not that I didn't want to. But my father made it quite clear he needed me to stay a virgin. Being a silly girl, I didn't care what he wanted. But he said if we bumped, he would kill my boyfriend. I paid attention to that!"

She went on, "This cousin showed up with his son, my prospective husband. I immediately did not like him. He treated me with disdain. Why would I like him when all the other boys buzzed around me like bees near a flower? And they did! Men found me beautiful, and for the first time, I appreciated it. This princeling was so arrogant. He talked down to me and instructed me how things would be once we were married."

Elodia reined in her horse, which was tired of standing still. She let it walk into the creek, upstream from where the carts were crossing. The horse drank noisily while the young woman quietly drained her wine flask.

"One day, we had an archery contest. I bested him. I really was excellent. Still am. He felt humiliated and made nasty remarks about my body, the muscles in my shoulders, back, and arms. He called them 'bulgy.'"

"Which they are," Fritigern said, "but such a very attractive bulgy. The kind of bulgy muscles one needs to draw a Hunnish bow while riding."

She ignored Lord Fritigern's clumsy compliment and continued her story. "If my cousin's son was trying to provoke me, he succeeded. I asked, 'Are you as poor at arm wrestling as you are at archery?' We ended up arm wrestling. I was within a hair of beating him when he reached with his other hand across the table and poked my teat. Of course, I was distracted. He slammed my hand down to the table with a yell. Everyone considered it a great joke.

"I was humiliated and furious. I pulled the knife from my belt, the knife my father gave me on my last birthday, and jabbed it in his arm. Not very deeply, but far enough for blood to ooze out. That

152

certainly silenced the onlookers. My father heard the story. He was furious!"

"For stabbing a guest? I'm not surprised."

"No, not for stabbing him!" Elodia said, "For challenging him, for making him lose face. As punishment, to make me lose face, Father humiliated me. He ordered me to work in the fields beside the slaves. For a week. Everyone else continued to enjoy themselves. They hunted, feasted, drank, and danced while I was confined to the fields and slave quarters."

"Did you learn your lesson?" Fritigern asked.

"I learned several lessons. For example, always keep your knife handy. One of the princeling's bodyguards suggested he would like to arm wrestle me. The first time he said it, it got a laugh. I mean, the man was twice my size. But he kept suggesting it when no one else was around. It stopped being funny, especially when he switched to wrestling. I ignored him. I complained but was told he meant no harm. He was a half-wit and a nobody.

"On the last day of my punishment, I encountered him again. It was dusk. I was late coming in from the fields when he blocked my way. No one else was around. He told his 'wrestling' joke yet again. I ignored him and tried to walk around him, but he kept blocking me and telling his joke and giggling. I grew worried. I reached for my knife and realized I'd left it in my bedroll."

Talking was thirsty work. Fritigern's saddle bag was within reach, so Elodia snatched his wine flask and took a mouthful. If he noticed, he didn't object.

"What happened?"

The last of the carts had cleared the river ford. She rode ahead of Lord Fritigern and crossed. Now clear of ice, the river came up only to her horse's hock. Once she crossed, she pulled off the road again. When he caught up, she looked him square in the face, paused, and said, "He raped me."

The silence hung between them. At last, in a soft voice, he asked, "And…?"

"At first, the princeling claimed it wasn't rape because I was a slave that week. Everyone knows you can't rape a slave.

"My father rebutted that foolish assertion and demanded compensation. After some hesitation, the princeling backed down. They negotiated. They quickly discarded any notion that the princeling would marry me."

"Because you were no longer a virgin?"

"Exactly," she said. "Father vetoed the usual practice, where the rapist would be forced to marry the woman. He wasn't going to force that half-wit on me. After a day of talking and yelling, and with the prospect of a feud hanging over them, my father and the princeling agreed I would marry the half-wit's brother."

Fritigern nodded. "What of the half-wit? Was he punished?"

"Oh yes. Both Father and the princeling agreed he must be executed. But they argued over who would do it. The princeling wanted my father to do it to avoid a division within his own clan. Father just wanted to put the whole affair behind him, but when I urged him, he agreed to take care of the half-wit."

"Was he hung?" For a dishonorable person, that would be typical.

"That was the original plan, but I said he didn't deserve that kindness. At my insistence, he was taken to the hanging tree and tied. Then I killed him with my knife."

"Quick and painless?" Fritigern asked. She glanced at him, confirming he was being flippant. When she didn't reply, he asked, "What did your husband say?"

"We weren't married yet. The princeling and his retinue had gone home. Father promised that I'd follow along shortly, and I did. I don't blame my father for any of this. He did precisely what custom requires. He was a kind father."

"Did the cousin witness the half-wit's execution?"

"No. But of course, he found out about it later. Not long after, we married. It was not a good way to start a marriage."

"Are you still married to the half-wit's brother?"

"No. He abused me even before learning how the half-wit died. After that, he beat me regularly. I think he would have killed me if I hadn't killed him first. So, I did. Then I fled south to the great river, which was nearby, and rafted across. Some Roman frontier guards gave me sanctuary. And they gave me a job as their squad's provisioner. That was a peaceful, happy time. It lasted a couple of years. It ended a week ago."

"When the Roman limitanei abandoned their river forts?"

"Yes. My squad, like the others, was ordered to march to Durostorum. Once we got there, I was seized by a Roman military tribune named Bitorix."

"I've met him. He's on Lupicinus's staff. He seems like a man of honor."

"He's not. He's a snake. If I get a chance, I'll do him with my knife," she said bitterly, "after ensuring it's dull."

"He raped you too?"

Twice. She nodded.

155

Fritigern laughed, "On consideration, I am glad I did not touch you last night." She did not laugh. It was not funny.

"How did Lupicinus get you?"

"He simply seized me from Bitorix. Another treacherous Roman enchanted by my *pretty face*."

"Why do you spit out 'pretty' that way? Most women would kill to be as beautiful as you."

"Kill. Yes, killing is what my beauty has forced on me. It is a curse, not a blessing. I don't doubt if I were less pretty, I might be happily married and living with a husband and children."

"More likely, you'd be walking along this road with the rest of our nation. You would have no food except what your husband received from the Romans. Which he'd have got by selling your children."

Lord Fritigern was probably right, she decided. What was her rape compared to the horrors faced by all the people—her people—tramping along this road?

"Why did Lupicinus seize you from Bitorix? Was it just to have a gift for me?"

"Probably. But also, Lupicinus got great pleasure in it. It's not quite true Lupicinus seized me from Bitorix." She gave a short chuckle. "He bought me for two denarii. And just to further humiliate Bitorix, he announced it in front of all his staff. They laughed. Even I laughed."

"Why does he hate Bitorix?"

"I don't know if it's hate, but it is surely contempt. Lupicinus is from an old family from Italia province. He looks down his nose at non-Italians like Bitorix, whose family comes from Galatia province. Bitorix claims descent from Galatian royalty. I was told when Lupicinus heard that story, he just hooted. Galatian royalty? He was scornful. It means nothing to an Italian. That story made him dislike Bitorix even more."

"All right. Then why did Lupicinus give you to me?"

"This may sound stupid, but here's what I believe: he wants you dead. Something he heard about me made him think I'm an assassin. That I'd be willing to kill you in exchange for my freedom. That's our agreement. I kill you, then I'm free. But I'm not so stupid as to trust him!"

"Aren't you an assassin? You did kill your husband."

"True. And some others since then. But they were bad men."

Fritigern laughed. "Sure, just like all the people I've killed have been bad! When a person needs killing, you kill them. Bad or good has nothing to do with it. But how would killing me gain you your freedom? It would gain you your death."

He rode quietly for a few minutes, thinking that over. "So, you don't plan to assassinate me?" he said with a smile.

She saw his smile and returned it. "My plans are flexible," she said.

There was silence for a while until she asked, "What are your plans for me?"

"I haven't really considered it. Other than bedding you!"

"And then? Sell me to slavers?"

"No. I'm done with the slavers gorging on Gothic flesh. They got their fill and more outside of Durostorum. Anyway, we might all get sold to slavers. Or killed. I don't trust the Romans. I especially don't trust Lupicinus. This banquet, tonight, for example. What might keep him from killing me and all my chieftains?"

The answer seemed obvious to her. "I expect he will."

"Why do you say that?"

"Lupicinus discussed with his officers a plot to kill you. When else would he get such a good opportunity?"

"You heard this? They spoke in front of you?"

"Yes. They were speaking Latin, thinking I didn't understand."

"But you said the plan was for you to assassinate me!"

"That was their backup plan in case the banquet treachery fails."

Fritigern looked at her skeptically, wondering whether she was lying. Or thinking she had some other motive?

"Why are you telling me this? And why now?" he said.

"It has taken me this long to judge you. When I awoke this morning, I didn't care whether the Romans killed you or not. They are pigs, but you're a Christian. I don't like Romans, and I'm suspicious of Christians. I have finally decided you're less bad than the Romans."

They rode along silently for a few minutes. Then Fritigern called to an aide. "Instruct the commanders to meet me here as soon as possible. We need to talk." The aide rode off to convey his order up and down the column.

It took almost a half hour to gather all Fritigern's top lieutenants. They pulled off the road to avoid blocking the column and dismounted. There were some raised eyebrows when he said she would be joining them.

He recounted his conversation with her and explained his dilemma. If the top Gothic leadership attended this banquet, it seemed possible, even likely, they would all be massacred. If they refused to attend, the Romans, including perhaps the emperor himself, could claim themselves gravely insulted.

The emperor had invited the Goths into the empire and said he would provide them with land in Thracia. He must want mutual trust since, without it, war was inevitable. Fritigern certainly did not want war. His people had suffered enough. Also, he did not think his warriors, many disarmed and all hungry, could stand up to the well-trained, well-equipped, and experienced legionaries.

The discussion went round and round. A few men distrusted her and believed that the Romans, while not generally trustworthy, would never dishonor themselves by massacring banquet guests. It would violate the universal law of hospitality.

The idea that Elodia might serve the Romans as a backup assassin was generally dismissed. In fact, it led many to reject all her story, including that a massacre was being planned.

On the other hand, no one could casually dismiss the grave risk to the Tervingi Goths should the Romans decapitate its leadership. The best idea so far—and the idea the leadership was drifting toward—was to attend the banquet but fully armed and hypervigilant for signs of treachery. If it came to a fight, they would fight. And die.

Just as the discussion was ending, Elodia stepped forward with an idea. While not without risks, every idea was risky, her idea was novel. It was quickly adopted.

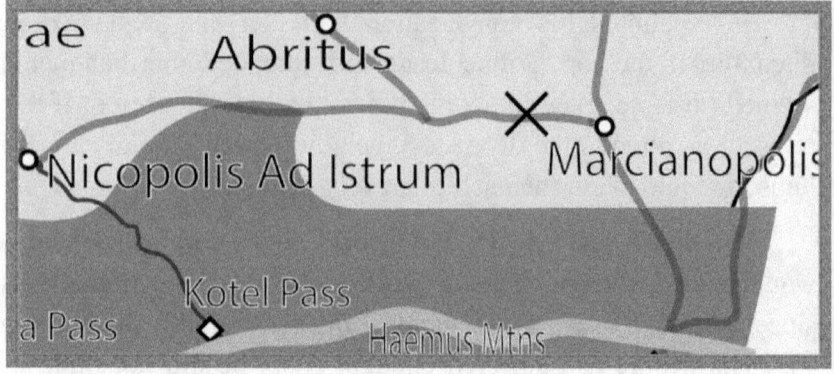

7. Roman Treachery 376 CE

*H*aving invited King Alavivus [Gothic King] and Fritigern [Gothic Chieftain] to a dinner party, Lupicinus posted soldiers against the main body of the barbarians and kept them at a distance from the walls of the town, and when they asked with continual entreaties that they might, as friendly people submissive to our rule, be allowed to enter and obtain what they needed for food, great wrangling arose between the inhabitants and those who were shut out, which finally reached a point where fighting was inevitable.... He [Lupicinus] put to death all the attendants of the two leaders.... [Fritigern was] allowed to go out with his companions to quiet the people, who, believing that their leaders had been slain under pretense of friendly entertainment, had blazed out into turbulence.

From Res Gestae, Volume XXXI 5.5, by Ammianus Marcellinus

The Goths on horseback arrived at Marcianople well ahead of those who came by cart or on foot. As Fritigern moved south, he noticed the barren lands around Palmatis gradually giving way to thick forests near Marcianople. He appreciated the mildness of the winter there compared to what his people faced on the bleak heights near Palmatis. Though the nearby Black Sea helped moderate the climate, the nights would still be frosty and cold. But at least there would be wood for campfires.

Fritigern sent scouts ahead to stake out a hilltop campsite some six miles from the city walls. His scouts chose a place where many natural springs bubbled up from the chalky earth. When the carts arrived, he ordered them placed in a circle, a wagon-fort, to provide some defense should things turn hostile. He hoped relations with the Romans would remain cordial. If so, this was a campsite where his people could remain indefinitely.

At the campsite, the scouts set up tents where Elodia and the Gothic leadership dressed and prepared for the Romans' banquet. Then they waited until a large number, several hundred armed warriors, arrived. The banquet attendees, accompanied by this large entourage, proceeded to the city gates. As the slave Albia had said, Marcianople was much larger than Durostorum. The walls were thirty feet high, with towers every two hundred paces. It was no surprise that the gates were closed. The Romans did not intend to allow Goths to flood the city. Once the Gothic chieftains were recognized, a gate was opened, but the guard commander demanded they leave their arms with him. Fritigern refused. The standoff continued for half an hour until the commander's demand was quashed by someone higher up, perhaps Lupicinus himself. The Romans agreed to let the leadership, plus a token number of armed bodyguards, enter.

Before entering, Fritigern explained this arrangement to the gathered crowd of Goths who waited outside the gate. The large crowd was not having any of it, claiming the banquet might be a trap. As Elodia had planned, Fritigern addressed them, telling them he felt perfectly safe. A lie.

At last, their party of eight leaders, a dozen bodyguards, and she entered through the gate. It was ominous to hear the gate slam closed behind them. *Like a trap snapping shut.* From the other side, she could hear yells and wails of protest. A Roman centurion, trying to ignore the racket, welcomed them and asked them to follow him. As he led them away, the shouts and protests continued and increased.

The gate centurion led them across a courtyard and directed them into a nearby hall where a long table was set for a vast meal. The table was laden with platters of meat, bread, and fruit. None of their Roman hosts were present yet. While they waited, slaves gave them delicate silver goblets filled with first-rate wine.

Military Tribune Bitorix came in and greeted and shook hands with the Gothic delegation. He approached Elodia as if to give her a kiss on the cheek. She was standing beside Fritigern. When Fritigern noticed her back away, he turned to stand between the two and said to her in his poorest Greek, "Slave, wine more me."

She took his wine cup. Before she could move, a Roman slave came forward with a jug and topped it off, frustrating Bitorix's advance. His smile turned sour. From then on, she moved and dodged to keep Fritigern between Bitorix and herself.

Bitorix, using his execrable Gothic, tried to engage the Goths in polite but strained conversation. However, the noise from outside the gate soon grew so loud their words could hardly be heard.

Fritigern, doing his worst to communicate with Bitorix, pointed at the food-laden table and, in a loud voice, said, "Eat now?"

Bitorix responded, almost yelling, "We are waiting for his lordship Military Count Lupicinus to come!"

Fritigern feigned he could not understand. He brought Elodia forward to translate. Before she could start, everyone heard methodical hammering at the gate. A Roman legionary rushed in and spoke with Bitorix. He turned to Fritigern and shouted, "Your countrymen have apparently started battering the gate."

Using Elodia to translate, Fritigern hollered, "Please forgive my followers. They are simple barbarians. They foolishly fear for our safety. Let us go and quiet them. With your permission, we will leave temporarily to settle them and then return."

Elodia continued to translate, trying to be heard above the noise.

Bitorix seemed nonplussed. He said, "Perhaps one of you," here he indicated King Alavivus, "could talk to them?"

Through Elodia, Fritigern replied, "That would not help. The protesters would assume the rest of us are being held hostage. I am afraid we will all have to go, if only for a short while. We will go and calm them, then come back. And then eat!"

That was where Elodia's plan hung by a slender thread. If the Romans were well-intentioned, they would be allowed to go and return. If they planned treachery...

Without waiting for Bitorix's agreement, Fritigern motioned to his party, and they all moved swiftly to the door. They left the hall, hustled across the courtyard, and reached the gate. The gate centurion was still there. Though surprised to see them again so soon, he ordered it open.

At that point, Lupicinus finally appeared, emerging breathless from the dining hall, panicking to see his prey escaping from a trap he believed was already sprung. He was wearing only one greave and sandal, the other foot bare, and his chest plate was only half attached, so it jiggled with his fat as he hurried.

The gate opened a small amount. Fritigern's lead bodyguards were just able to squeeze out. Then, from behind, Elodia heard Lupicinus call out, "Shut the gate! Cut them down! Kill them!"

Two dozen legionaries, who had been standing by, streamed out into the courtyard and charged them. At the same time, a dozen arrows flew toward the Goths, shot by guards standing on the banquet hall balcony. Several of the Goths were hit, including King Alavivus. And Elodia.

She cried out and collapsed to the pavement. She was conscious when Fritigern scooped her up, threw her over his shoulder, and headed for the gap in the gate. An older warrior named Boderus helped up the fallen king, and those two made it out immediately after Fritigern and her. Because Lupicinus had apprised only a select few men of his secret plan, the outbreak of violence took the gate centurion by surprise. Recovering quickly, he drew his sword. Before it cleared his scabbard, a Goth stabbed him through the guts. Fritigern's bodyguards had been ready for anything.

The advancing legionaries reached the gate just as the last of the bodyguards exited. Elodia saw a few soldiers stop to finish off the fallen bodyguards just as the closing gate blocked her view.

Outside, their men had shields ready to protect them from any archers on the walls, but the shields weren't needed. Perhaps there weren't any archers, or maybe the wall guards were as surprised by their sudden exit as the gate centurion had been.

The Goths moved quickly away from the walls and into darkness and safety. Some warriors stayed behind, preparing to ambush any Romans foolish enough to pursue them.

Elodia's world was turning black as Fritigern mounted his horse. Still carrying her, he galloped back to the wagon-fort. Boderus followed right behind, carrying King Alavivus.

Elodia fell in and out of consciousness as she rode, slung over Fritigern's shoulder like a flour sack. The periods of insensibility were bliss compared to the intervals when she felt his horse's every jar and jolt. The ride from the city gate to the medical tent, only a few miles, never seemed to end. By the time they reached the Gothic camp, she was fully awake.

They quickly approached a large tent well-lit by multiple torches. Fritigern called out to a man standing near the tent opening, "Medicus Nedarcus, here is the king. Also, this slave girl. Both hit by arrows. See to King Alavivus first. He is bleeding out. There may be other wounded following." The Gothic chieftain smoothly dismounted and laid her on a mat in the medical tent without causing Elodia much additional suffering.

Boderus laid Alavivus beside her and left. Nedarcus knelt next to the king. "He is already dead." The medicus pointed out the wound to Fritigern. An arrow had struck the king's thigh and pierced an artery. He must have died within minutes. In comparison, her injury, an arrow had struck her left shoulder, was less severe but very painful. She writhed on the mat. Nedarcus turned his attention to her. "A nasty wound. I'm surprised you don't cry out!"

"Here, bite on this," he said as he placed a strip of leather between her teeth.

"She has not screamed, but she has cursed," Fritigern said. "She cursed from the moment she was hit until I got off my horse. She filled my right ear with a non-stop stream of cursing. She demonstrated her linguistic skill by cursing in three languages. I can now recite in Latin, Greek, and Gothic the phrase, 'Crap-eating-mother-bumping-Romans.'"

He paused and said slowly, "Elodia, I need to go and leave you in Nedarcus's hands. He is our finest medicus. I must organize a retreat of our forces from here. By dawn, the Romans will feel safe leaving the city. They will come after us."

Nedarcus said, "Stay a moment, Fritigern. Hold the girl while I dig out the arrow."

Fritigern gripped her tightly while the medicus's knife widened the wound, allowing the arrowhead to be extracted. Then she did scream, though it was mostly muffled as she bit down on the leather strip. She did not struggle against Fritigern's grip.

While Nedarcus stitched the wound, Fritigern said to her, "You suffered bravely, as a Goth should." Perhaps so, but he could see tears blurring her eyes as she looked up at him. "This wound is an unfair reward for your clever plan. Yes, we lost King Alavivus and several other brave warriors, but not the rest of our leadership. Had the Romans been honest, as unlikely as that now seems, no lives would have been lost today and no insult given or taken. Now, the Romans and we are truly at war."

She began to relax, but Fritigern had more to say. "Finally, before I go, I must apologize to you. This morning I promised you a night of pleasure. Obviously, we must postpone that delight until later," he said with a smile.

166

She didn't know whether to laugh or be angry, so she spat the leather strap from her mouth and laughed. Which hurt a lot.

They [the Gothic leadership] were received with applause and rejoicing, and mounting horses hastened away to set in motion the various incitements that lead to wars. When report, that spiteful nurse of rumors, spread abroad what had happened, the whole nation of the Tervingi Goths was fired with ardor for battle, and amid many fearful scenes, portentous of extreme dangers, after the standards had been raised according to their custom and the doleful sound of the trumpets had been heard, predatory bands were already rushing about, pillaging and burning the country-houses and making whatever places they could find a confusion of awful devastation.

From Res Gestae, Volume XXXI 5.7-8, by Ammianus Marcellinus

The news of the Roman treachery spread quickly. By dawn, each clan was planning how it might survive the winter. The Romans had promised food, which the clans desperately needed. Indeed, that was the promise that drew the Goths in their tens of thousands to Marcianople. Now it was clear the promise was a lie. The Roman treachery had gone beyond trying to decapitate the Gothic leadership. Its actual goal was the extermination of the Gothic nation by starvation and enslavement.

It wasn't as if Marcianople had no food. The harvest south of the river had been excellent, but the Romans had gathered it from the area around the city. Now it was locked behind stout stone walls. The city was effectively impregnable. The Goths had no siege engines, minimal expertise in manufacturing them, and, in any case, no resources to sustain a long siege. The clans understood this and realized their only hope for survival was to disperse and live off the land. To pillage.

Fritigern had an even more immediate concern. He understood the Romans would take by main force what they'd failed to achieve by stealth. He expected Lupicinus would gather his troops in Marcianople, burst out from the city, and like a lightning bolt, destroy the Gothic leadership. He would count on the Goths being surprised and disorganized, an expectation Fritigern knew was justified based on how the Goths had behaved at Durostorum.

Some clan leaders stayed near the medicus's tent to learn King Alavivus's condition, while others left to organize their own people. Those who remained were not surprised when the medicus came outside the tent and pronounced, "King Alavivus is dead." They had seen the thick trail of blood leading to the tent.

The old man had been the Gothic leader for years. Even the clans who questioned his decisions and refused his orders paid lip service to his experience and wisdom. Fritigern had no similar following among the clans. He was young, and his concessions to Valens, which he made in exchange for permission to cross the Danube, rankled many clan leaders, notably his agreement that the Goths would convert to Christianity. Some had asked, "Where was your Jesus God in Durostorum when we were forced to sell our children to the Roman slave traders?"

Fritigern worried that this whole debacle would be laid at his feet, starting with the retreat from the Huns to the Danube crossing and now this exhausting and fruitless march to Marcianople. He knew the Romans would soon emerge and sweep through the refugees like scythes through a wheat field, a massive sacrifice to Victoria, the goddess of victory.

The silence that followed the medicus's announcement was finally broken. Fritigern called to the clan leaders, "The Romans are marshaling now. That city gate will open at dawn, and they will march out in their thousands. Do not remain here. You will be slaughtered."

The crowd grew hushed. He continued, "Gather your people and head west to Abritus City." It was a city they all knew, even though most had never been there. It was a city where their forebears had utterly destroyed Roman legions.

"Send your families and carts on ahead but keep your warriors here to guard our rear," he continued. "Hurry. Your clan—all our clans—depend on our haste. And our unity."

The hilltop camp was empty by dawn except for a few scouts who remained behind. A train of carts was visible off to the northwest, with the last cart only a mile away. A cloud of warriors followed along, mostly on foot. The Gothic army spread out on either side of the road and trudged along the land, still frozen from the night's frost.

While most of the tribe headed northwest toward Abritus, not a few sought easy pickings near at hand. They were driven by hunger, the desire for loot, or simply for revenge. Those who lost children or women to starvation or Roman slavers had sworn an oath of hatred for all things Roman. Now they had an opportunity to act. It showed as plumes of smoke rose from burning villas, near the road at first, farther afield as time went by.

The plundering Goths, fearful of being overtaken by Roman cavalry, moved fast. They bypassed estate villas having a wall or stout fence—they could be plundered later—but there were many wealthy estates with no defenses or only a dozen bully boys left behind as guards. Opulent owners possessing any sense had long since taken refuge in the city, but owners who valued their property above their lives risked finishing up with neither.

The Goths were not well-armed. The Romans had forced many of them to surrender their weapons before ferrying them across the Danube. But they made up in numbers and fierceness what they lacked in swords. An estate's guards, confronted by a dozen angry Goths, might find it advisable to surrender their swords and join in the pillaging. If the Goths questioned their loyalty, a simple loyalty test was available: the guards were told to demonstrate their new allegiance by killing their old master and his family.

Some young Goths veered off the road to Abritus for a different reason: to be free from their leaders.

Clan leaders, attempting to make peace with the Romans, trying to obtain their protection from the Huns, and hoping to secure lands they could subsist on, had appeased the Romans. The clan leaders now had to swallow a shameful truth. Any notion that they could live side-by-side with the Romans had proved false. The young men and women had said as much, but the leaders had not listened. Their deafness had resulted in countless deaths. Now the farce was over. Now it was time to seize the freedom they'd been promised.

As they marched along the Abritus road, the young could see wealthy estates in the distance. The lure of food, drink, and gold was strong. The fear of a pursuing Roman force was also strong.

But the need for food dominated. It had been weeks since many had had a decent meal. And a full stomach? That was a distant memory.

Clodia looked at her shoulder. It was tightly bandaged. There was no sign of bleeding. Her arm was confined by a sling to immobilize it. She had fainted after Nedarcus dug out the arrowhead and then fallen into a restless sleep. She could tell by the growing eastern light that there remained a few hours before Sól would ride her brilliant chariot into the sky.

Boderus knelt by her side. He was old and gray and majestic. His face was kind but resolute. *He must be a clan chieftain.*

When she was fully awake, he led her to a filly tied up outside the medical tent. Carefully, he helped her up into its saddle.

"Can you stay on?" he asked. "These pre-dawn hours are calm but frigid."

"Yes," she said. "The cold will keep me awake." *I hope.* She wasn't feeling steady. She just wanted to sleep. "Where are we going?"

Boderus said, "We must leave and be far from this place before dawn. The Romans will be out as soon as it's light enough to march. They will want to kill our leaders, the ones they missed last night."

Her head was groggy. It took her some time to recollect the evening's events. She remembered Lupicinus shouting orders, telling his soldiers to slaughter them. Everything after that was just a fog. "Lord Fritigern?" she asked.

"He's fine. He left me here to escort you and Nedarcus," indicating the medicus with a nod, "to somewhere safe." With that, Boderus mounted, took her horse's reins, and led off.

She slumped forward and rested her head on the horse's mane. She might have fallen asleep, but trotting jogged her wound. She grit her teeth until her jaw hurt. She wished for another strip of leather to bite on.

At dawn, Boderus stopped for a break. Her shoulder pounded dully, but the worst of the pain was gone. He addressed the medic, "Take this girl to Abritus and set up your medicine tent somewhere along the road. Look after her, she belongs to Lord Fritigern, but get ready for new casualties."

Though it angered her when people assumed she belonged to some man, she didn't say anything. She was too tired.

"We expect there will be many wounded today. Most will need your help more than she does."

With that, he handed her horse's reins to Nedarcus, turned his mount around, and started back toward Marcianople, the way they'd come. He looked back over his shoulder. "Take care, girl."

Elodia didn't reply. Perhaps she should have said the same to him. She worried she would see him later in Nedarcus's medicine tent.

She watched as Nedarcus tied the reins to the back of a mule cart. It contained the canvas medical tent, now disassembled, and the grisly tools of his craft. His tunic was stained dark brown, a product of last night's bloody work. His face and hair were clean, recently washed. He was beardless, and his gray hair was trimmed short, factors that made washing easier. Forty years old, she estimated. The creases on his face revealed each of those years.

He worked quickly but hobbled as he moved. Some old wound? He showed surprising agility for an old man. He noticed her studying him and smiled. Ignoring the ache in her shoulder, she returned his smile. He had a kind face that must have been very attractive in his youth. Still attractive in some ways, she decided, though he was no Caius.

Their medical cart joined the long train of carts and folk heading to Abritus. It was almost dusk by the time they reached the city. Many Goths had arrived before them and were camped along the road. The Roman garrison had barred the city gates when the Goths showed up. A smaller city than Marcianople, Abritus was surrounded by a moat and massive walls. Elodia learned that Emperor Constantine built these after her ancestors butchered a Roman army there some generations earlier. That bit of history made her feel good.

Nedarcus helped her, and she helped him. He cleaned the blood off her torso, found her a practical woolen tunic, the arrow and blood having ruined her lovely silk banquet gown, changed her shoulder bandage, and retied her arm sling. She watched as he erected the medicine tent. It was a big tent with room enough for six ground mats for the wounded, a table to hold his bandages, saws and knives, and jars of water and beer. Being one-handed, her help was limited to organizing the tent, not erecting it. He dug a fire pit just outside while she gathered brush and kindling. It took some time, but she discovered a trick to using flint and steel with only one hand and two feet. If many wounded were arriving, they would need warmth. At the fire's edge, she placed a small pot of tar. They would need hot tar to cauterize amputations.

Even this minor effort exhausted her. She lay on one of the ground mats, carefully protecting her aching shoulder. Nedarcus placed a blanket over her. She slept.

The young Goths should have stuck to the road. Among the Goths fleeing toward Abritus City was a tight group of five led by Arbrun. The group's sixth member, its patriarch, had drowned during the Danube crossing. He had been unwell and weak when the Roman shipmen pushed their group and forty other Goths aboard a small ferry. With all the jostling and shoving, Arbrun's father slipped overboard and under the rough water. There had been no opportunity to mourn him. Within a day of landing, a mass of legionaries had appeared and herded the thousands of Goths southward toward Marcianople where, as far as Arbrun had understood, food and shelter awaited. But nothing awaited but enslavement or death. The Romans had lied. As usual.

Arbrun was the first to notice the gate at the end of the driveway. His little group had left the Gothic hilltop camp near Marcianople an hour earlier. At first, they walked alongside the steady stream of their fellow refugees, a noisy mixture of young and old. The crowd moved slowly, and Arbrun's group was impatient, so they avoided the congestion by simply walking a score of feet away from the hedge-lined road. It was a small distance but enough to let Arbrun see what those on the road, whose views were blocked by the hedge, could not. There was a driveway and, at its end, a gate.

Silvan, walking beside Arbrun, sensed him looking at her. She looked up, caught his glance, and gave him a tired smile. He smiled back and took her hand. "We'll find food and a place to rest. Soon," he encouraged.

Silvan nodded silently. They'd eaten the last of their food on the march to Marcianople. There they'd expected to receive more from the Romans. Instead, they received nothing but violence. She did not go on and on like brother-in-law Bort, who ranted endlessly about his hatred for the Romans. But she felt it. If anything, she had as much reason to hate them: a decade earlier, legionaries had killed her parents during their war against the Gothic king Athanaric.

Bort boasted how he would kill every Roman they encountered, stab them in the guts, and leave them lingering in pain and praying for death. But Bort had no sword or knife. The Romans had taken his sword before the ferry trip. Somewhere along the way, he'd picked up a cudgel. He'd wielded it dramatically on the march south, destroying many frozen flower buds beside the road. Now he just carried it. He, too, was tired and hungry.

During the chaos of boarding the ferry, Arbrun had been able to keep his sword and Jellena her bow and quiver. Karl had a hunting knife and a cudgel. Silvan was the only one completely weaponless. She knew it, and it made her feel useless.

When Arbrun noticed the gate, he whistled to catch the others' attention and led them down the driveway. After a few hundred feet, the view opened to reveal a long brick wall on either side of the gate. It was solidly constructed from oak beams.

The driveway descended from a small hill as it approached the gate. The hill's prospect revealed the wall was just a dozen feet high. It enclosed a small compound containing several buildings, including an extensive villa. A man was visible, peering over the wall. As they moved closer, he called out a warning. But whether it was Greek or Latin, they could not tell since none of them spoke either language.

Senator Tosca Volesus had not expected to defend his villa by himself. When he met his friend Licinius Sabinus the previous autumn, he doubted any defense would be necessary. When he saw motion on his driveway, he hoped it would be the twenty legionary veterans he'd hired. Instead, a small ragtag party of Goths came up his driveway. He trusted that he, his two grown sons, and his reliable slaves could keep them at bay until the hired veterans appeared.

One of his slaves, an ex-gladiator named Lomas, had served as his personal bodyguard for more than five years. Lomas had been training the other slaves in spear fighting. *A small group but sufficient to deal with these shabby barbarians.*

Still, when Volesus called over the wall, warning the intruders to stay away, he wondered whether he'd made a mistake. A friend from Marcianople had ridden out a few days early with the news that the Goths were trekking south. They'd discussed whether it was wiser to stay behind his walls or seek shelter in the city. If he left his compound empty, he knew he would return to find it looted and burned. If he stayed to defend it, he risked his and his family's lives.

Before his friend returned to the city, Volesus asked him to send out at least twenty veterans, men familiar with weapons. He provided his friend with a purse of gold aurei for the veterans, promising more to come. Now, as Volesus looked around the horizon, he could see many plumes of smoke rising. Those plumes indicated neighbors who had opted for the safety of Marcianople. Volesus would congratulate himself on choosing wisely if the promised veterans appeared. Thus far, they had not. In their stead, this party of Goths was approaching. They were either unwilling or unable to talk.

Lomas stood beside Volesus on the wall walk. "Shall I fetch the others?" Lomas said. Volesus could picture the other slaves, who had never previously held a weapon, cowering in the villa.

"Indeed," he ordered. Lomas jumped down from the wall walk, it wasn't a long drop, and sprinted to the villa. The minutes passed, and the Goths drew nearer, but Lomas did not return. Instead, Volesus's wife, Prisca, ran out the villa's main door.

"Ran" was inaccurate. "Waddled" might be better. Both Volesus and his wife showed the effect of a lifetime of luxury, each weighing twice as much as either son, who were still lean, tall, and athletic. Prisca waddled as fast as she could, each leg swinging forward in an arc that avoided brushing the other. She was halfway to the gate when she called her husband. "They've gone. They've all gone!"

Volesus said, "Who's gone?"

Prisca, still puffing, explained she'd watched the slaves fleeing up a ladder at the back wall of the compound, some still holding their spears. "What about Lomas?" Volesus asked.

Prisca wailed, "He held the ladder steady. I called him, but he ignored me. He was the last one up the ladder."

Lomas deserting? He'd always been a sketchy bastard. Now everything truly did depend on just his boys and him.

Volesus considered throwing open the gate and welcoming the Goths. Would they take what they needed and leave his family in peace? Or would they massacre everyone? He decided not to take the risk. He'd heard horrific stories. These were barbarians.

So far, he could see only a few Goths approaching. Volesus felt alone even though his two sons—Tosca Major and Tosca Minor— were well-trained fighters. Even his wife Prisca could wield a knife. If it came to a fight, it would be him, his boys, and his wife against the… half-dozen Goths.

He nocked an arrow, and his sons, standing on either side of him farther down the wall, did likewise. He indicated they should hold their fire. Let the Goths start the hostilities.

Volesus looked over the wall again and shouted, "Goths, do not come closer!" They continued to approach but more slowly. Apparently, they could now see his bow. "Tosca Major," he called down the wall, "How many do you count?"

After a short pause, his older son called back, "Five. Just five. And the one with a bow is just a girl."

This should be all right. Just let them come a little closer. Then he heard the twang of a bow. "Damn," he shouted at his sons, "Hold your fire until I signal!" But they had not fired.

Arbrun's party heard the man on the wall shout again. Bort said, "He knows we're Goths. I heard him say 'Goth.'" Then two other heads appeared above the wall, one on either side but at some distance from the first man. They heard shouting. Bort, who knew his Latin numbers, said, "The other one shouted 'Five,' so they've counted us."

Jellena asked, "When we get in, what should we do?"

Her younger brother Bort said, "Kill them."

She looked to her older brother Arbrun for confirmation. "Yes," he said, "if they fight us."

Jellena saw the three men on the wall holding their bows. "They have arrows nocked," she said, "That's close enough to fighting." Without being prompted, she nocked an arrow, drew the string, and released. Her shaft sped toward the man on the left. She heard his cry and saw him reel backward off the wall. A shot to the neck.

A moment later, they heard a woman scream. "Got him!" shouted Silvan. The first man's head disappeared. "And the other guy's gone to check on your victim." The third man also turned his head to look at his fallen comrade. Then he ducked out of sight just in time to avoid Jellena's second shaft.

Seeing no defenders visible, Arbrun ordered, "Rush the wall." Jellena and her husband Karl headed to the spot below where the wounded defender once stood. Arbrun and Bort ran to the far side. Silvan, left alone, had no idea where to go, so she sprinted to the gate and waited. *Should I have gone with Arbrun?*

When Karl reached the wall, he boosted his wife to the top. Jellena was relieved to find no one right there waiting for her. Below, the defender lay in a pool of blood. As she surmised, her arrow had pierced his throat. The tip protruded from his nape. She steadied herself, stepped down to the wall walk, and readied another arrow. The first defender was kneeling beside the body. He had gray hair. The victim's hair was straw-colored. Father and son, she guessed. Their bows were on the ground beside them. He clutched his son's head to his chest and rocked back and forth, oblivious to the ongoing fight.

The third defender, given his hair color, had to be another son, younger. He looked about fourteen years of age. He was on the wall walk coming toward her, hunching to avoid any arrows that might come over the parapet. She drew the string, aimed at the father, but held her fire when the younger son noticed her and cried a warning. The father came out of his daze and launched himself toward the villa. A woman—his wife?—had been running toward the fallen son. Her husband turned her around and pushed her back.

Jellena turned and released her arrow at the younger son. It missed but shaken, he dropped his bow, which fell off the wall walk to the ground. He then unsheathed a short sword.

She had no sword nor even a hunting knife. She should have taken Karl's knife. He was still outside the wall, unable to scale it without a boost. She considered leaping to the ground, about ten feet, when both she and the boy were distracted by Arbrun, who came vaulting over the wall, having been shoved by Bort. The boy turned to face Arbrun and raised his sword. An inexperienced fighter, he stayed hunched, unable to defend himself when Arbrun swung his sword, dealing a heavy blow.

The boy raised his bare left arm above his head as if it might block the blade while ineffectively thrusting his sword at Arbrun. Arbrun's sword cut off the boy's arm before crashing through his unprotected skull. The mother, witnessing her other son's death, screamed again and sank to her knees.

The father ignored her scream and reached for his bow, only to see he had left it by his older son's body. He looked over when Arbrun jumped down from the wall walk.

The Roman drew his own sword and prepared to avenge his sons. But then he fell to his knees with an arrow through his chest. Jellena had sprung down to the courtyard and immediately shot the Roman. She walked over to unbolt the gate, letting Silvan, Karl, and Bort in. They looked around to see two young Romans lying dead, one old one on his knees impaled by an arrow and an old woman near the villa on her knees weeping. Soon it was three lying dead as Arbrun walked over and decapitated the wounded father.

Silvan felt diminished. She had done nothing useful in their assault. Would the others scorn her? She leaned over toward her brother and took his hunting knife. Karl said nothing as his sister quietly walked over to the kneeling mother and prepared to cut her throat. She'd seen it done often enough. With little hesitation but with tears streaming down her face, she leaned in and cut, quickly stepping back after getting hit with a spray of blood.

"Well, that was easy," Jellena said with a nod of satisfaction. "There'd better be some food here. Killing makes me hungry."

The others laughed, though Silvan's laugh was forced. Bort did not laugh. "That's four Romans dead and a million left to kill," he said. Out of spite, he dragged the bodies, one by one, to the pig pen, which occupied one corner of the compound, and manhandled them over the fence.

There was food. Food aplenty. And drink. There were breads, cheeses, and fruits. There were nuts, honey loaves, and cured meats. There were spicy pastries and sauces, which none of the Goths could identify, so all avoided. Best of all, there were casks of beer and wine.

The young people carried armloads of victuals into the villa's dining room and laid them on a large table in the center. Jellena saw the table was surrounded on three sides by wide couches. "Oh!" she said, "We must dine like Romans, lying on couches."

Silvan said, "But first, I must wash." She was splattered with the Roman woman's blood.

The five wandered through the villa until they found the atrium. It was a large room, open to the sky and brightly lit on this cloudless winter day. In the center was a large bath, several feet deep and six feet on a side, large enough to hold them all. Steam rose off the water. Stripping down, with no concern for modesty, they submerged themselves and washed off the stink of the morning's fight and the long march.

Jellena spotted a soap jar on a shelf near the bath. She got out of the bath, fetched the jar, and, holding her knees to her chest, jumped into the center. The resulting wave splashed everyone in the face. Bort, who had been inhaling at the wrong time, coughed and choked. A water fight broke out amidst much laughing and yelling. It only ended when Arbrun and Karl submitted to being dunked by the women.

The play might have lasted longer, but the water was cooling off. Karl suggested with no slaves to stoke the boiler furnace, it had gone cold. They were hungry and the recollection of all the food waiting in the dining room drove them on.

Jellena said, "We must also dress like Romans!" Leaving their soiled clothes behind, they wandered until they found the family's private quarters. The men found togas. The women tried to help them dress, but no one knew how to don a toga. The men wound the garment around and around themselves, like human sausage rolls. In the Roman mother's rooms, the women dressed in gold bracelets, jeweled necklaces, and silk dresses. The dresses did not fit well, having been made for the stout Roman matron, but the women were enchanted by the fine silk, a novel texture for them both.

They made their way back to the dining room. Jellena climbed onto the central couch beside her husband Karl; Arbrun and Silvan reclined on another couch while Bort lay by himself on the third.

With no ceremony, the feasting began. In short order, they were all stuffed and quite drunk. When their hunger pangs had subsided, they could feel their exhaustion. Jellena suggested to her husband that he might enjoy the exotic feel of her silk dress. It soon became clear Karl was more interested in what lay beneath the silk. Arbrun followed Karl's lead and began exploring Silvan's dress, both over and under the silk. Though she was nervous, she did her best to relax. It hurt when he entered her, but the wine helped.

Unwilling to witness any more, Bort announced he would go outside and watch the gate. Everyone else was too busy to notice his departure.

He sat on a step by the villa's main entrance, equipped with a cup and a whole cask of wine. He drank, recalled the image of Silvan frolicking in the bath, and drank some more. In time he lay back and passed out.

*A*gainst them [the Goths], Lupicinus mustered all his soldiers in tumultuous speed and, advancing with more haste than discretion, halted nine miles from the city, ready to join battle. On seeing this, the barbarians rushed recklessly on crowds of our men, dashed their shields upon opponents' bodies, and with lance and sword, ran through those who opposed them.

From Res Gestae, Volume XXXI 5.9,

By Ammianus Marcellinus

By noon the Goths' carts were no longer visible from the walls of Marcianople, and the road was empty. Even their scouts had withdrawn. Shortly after, the city gates were flung open, and the legionaries marched out. First, the comitatenses forces emerged four abreast, forming a column of six hundred ranks. They were followed by the limitanei forces, another two thousand men. The latter were the soldiers from the Danube forts.

They looked like amateurs compared to the comitatenses. Rather than marching with discipline, many walked at a casual pace, their equipment often in poor shape or missing. Some men were partially disabled, missing a hand or an eye, infirmities that would have forced their retirement from the comitatenses legions. In fact, this was the case for more than a few who accepted reassignment to the limitanei. The reduced status and pay were preferable to no pay whatsoever.

Not surprisingly, the morale among the frontier forces was poor. They missed the comfort of their forts and the amenities they'd become accustomed to. They missed their home-cooked meals, now replaced with tasteless army food. They missed their women and children. They hated the humiliation of being inferior to the field army forces.

Few frontier legionaries had lower morale than Grainus, Caius, and the rest of their squad. Caius was exhausted. He'd spent nights looking for Elodia rather than sleeping. People had spotted her during the march to Palmatis, but no one had seen her since. Rumor had it that a woman had been involved in last night's clash at the Marcianople gate, a woman who resembled Elodia. No one knew any details.

Grainus's squad found themselves near the end of the column. Only a single century of comitatenses legionaries followed them, a unit of eighty men who served as the column's rear guard. Military Tribune Bitorix rode up and down along his frontier troops as they marched, barking at them from time to time when their slipshod behavior particularly embarrassed him. Caius overheard the comitatenses centurion of the rear guard speak, "Shittiest officer of the shittiest legion." *Probably true.*

To say he had no love for Bitorix was an understatement. All his inquiries related to Elodia's disappearance started and ended with Bitorix. He would love to interrogate Bitorix if the opportunity arose, removing finger after finger and toe after toe. This fantasy occupied his mind as he marched along.

After being on the road for an hour, Bitorix rode down the column and pulled Grainus's squad aside. He gathered the eight men together and dismounted to speak with them. "Military Count Lupicinus has ordered me to inspect the villa of his friend Senator Tosca Volesus. It is just off the road over there," he said, indicating a narrow driveway that led off through a thick grove of trees. Remounting, he said to Grainus, "You lead the way."

Bitorix was not expecting any trouble, but if they were walking into a Gothic ambush, he'd rather someone else take the first arrow.

Caius led the squad down the driveway. In the distance, they could see a gate. When they were near enough, they saw it was partially open. Suspiciously open. With sword drawn, Caius carefully squeezed through the opening, trying to avoid touching the gate. *It might squeak if pushed.* The other men quietly followed suit except for Glabius, who stayed behind to hold the reins of Bitorix's horse.

Bitorix approached the gate and gave it a tremendous shove. The heavy gate emitted a loud squeal as it budged a few inches, enough so Bitorix could easily pass through.

Caius spotted a man lying motionless on the ground just outside the villa door. He approached him quietly and had closed half the distance when he heard Bitorix blundering into the courtyard. Caius knew it was Bitorix even before looking back. *So much for secrecy.*

He dashed the remaining distance to the man who, by this time, had propped himself up on his elbows. He looked like a Goth by his dress, but it was hard to tell. It was plain he was very drunk. Caius put his blade on the man's throat.

Speaking Gothic, Caius said, "Good morning, brother."

The man replied, "Good morning. May Jesus bless you."

Caius recognized the accent of a Goth raised northeast of the river. He called to Bitorix, "He's a Tervingi Goth," and waited for orders. The man stayed frozen. Caius's sword was razor sharp and left a red streak where it brushed the man's neck.

Grainus was crossing toward the building when he noticed a trail of blood leading toward a far corner. He followed it and saw where it converged with several other bloody tracks. The tracks ended at a pigpen. He looked over the rail and saw the partially consumed remains of the Volesus family. Grainus called to Bitorix, "Four bodies, all Romans. Two men, a boy, and a woman. Pig food."

Bitorix caught up with Grainus and peered down at the dead family. He turned to Caius and said, "Kill him." Which Caius did without hesitation, a slice across the Goth's throat.

Grainus saw a man looking out the villa's main entrance. As the Goth gurgled and died, the main door slammed. They could hear it being barred.

Grainus said to Bitorix, "How many Goths are in the building?"

When Bitorix didn't answer, Caius said, "I don't know. At least one. Someone shut and bolted the door."

In a disbelieving tone, Grainus said to his officer, "You didn't ask before you had him killed?" He rolled his eyes.

Ignoring the question, Bitorix said, "Surround the building. Don't let them escape," which was a good idea and one that Minicius and Evander had already considered. They had positioned themselves around the villa. Marius joined Polybius at the back of the building, where they guarded the slave's door.

For the next few minutes, there was no activity. Bitorix ordered Grainus and his squad to break into the building and kill the occupants.

"This could be a trap. We don't know how many Goths are inside. We might all be killed," Grainus protested.

"You've heard my order. Now obey it."

"Aye, sir. Might I suggest you draw your sword, sir? After we've gone in, if Goths should come out, you will need to defend yourself."

"Perhaps," Bitorix said, "it might be better if…" but by that time Grainus was hammering on the door without noticeable effect.

"You need to smash it down," Bitorix said helpfully.

"And then the Goths will escape out some other way. Perhaps we should just torch the place."

"This villa is owned by Senator Tosca Volesus, a friend of Military Count Lupicinus. Our orders are to secure it, not destroy it."

Pointing to the pigpen, Grainus said, "Tosca Volesus is probably over there, talking to the hogs, and is no longer concerned for his villa."

Evander, standing some distance away, overheard the argument. He decided to settle the dispute himself. He quietly walked around the building and pulled out his flint and steel. Once out of Bitorix's sight, he gathered a small pile of kindling and started a fire.

Marius and Polybius were alert and prepared when a man and a woman charged out the slaves' door. The woman immediately released an arrow, which struck Polybius in the chest. At the same instant, Marius shot an arrow at the man, who collapsed with the shaft penetrating his stomach. Marius dropped his bow, drew his sword, and ran at the woman.

When he descended on her, she had already nocked an arrow and was drawing the bowstring. His blow caught her by the neck and cut a swath all the way through her from shoulder to hip. The man lay beside her, writhing in pain. He reached out for her hand and brought it to his lips. Marius stabbed him up under his rib cage to finish him off.

Marius turned back to Polybius. He was lying on his back, breathing shallowly. The arrow shaft quivered with each breath. As time went by, the quivering grew less and less. Polybius tried to speak, but no words came out. Some blood trickled from his mouth, and his breathing stopped.

Minicius, who had watched this fight from a corner of the villa, ran back to inform Bitorix and Grainus. Those two were still discussing how to proceed. Grainus argued that the death of two Goths did not change anything. They still had no idea how many Goths remained in the villa. As they argued, Bitorix issued a stream of contradictory orders, and Grainus responded respectfully yet patronizingly.

The argument ended when a plume of smoke appeared from the far side of the villa. Within a few minutes, the entire building was engulfed. The roof collapsed. No one tried to escape the inferno. There were no screams of barbarians being incinerated.

The squad gathered to watch the flames die. Bitorix turned to Grainus and sneered, "You were so afraid of nothing. Just one man and his girl. And for them, you destroyed the villa of Senator Tosca Volesus!" Grainus did not bother to reply.

Marius found a shovel in a nearby tool shed. Using it, they dug a grave and, praying to Jesus, rolled Polybius into it. They tossed the bodies of the three dead Goths into the pigpen, where they could keep company with the Volesus family. Then the squad formed and marched back up the driveway to the Abritus road.

The road was empty in both directions. Bitorix looked up at the sun and saw it was only midday. It had been a busy morning. He dismounted, dropped the reins, found a broad rock to sit on, and called on Grainus to bring him food and drink. Grainus suggested there might be marauding Goths in the vicinity and that it would behoove them to catch up with the main Roman column as quickly as possible. Bitorix suggested that Grainus piss off and that it would behoove him to provide food and drink as soon as possible.

Grainus delegated the task to Minicius, who looked in Bitorix's saddlebags. They were empty. Of course. Minicius retrieved food and drink from Polybius's pack, seeing as its owner no longer had any use for them. The other squad members relaxed, opened their packs, and refreshed themselves. Once Bitorix was replete, he leaned back on his sun-warmed rock and dozed off.

While the others also slept, Grainus and Caius sat quietly, eating and talking.

"He was a fine companion," Caius said.

"Polybius?"

"Yes. A bit of a fool, but good for a drink and a song."

"He'll certainly be missed by that young barmaid at the Ruptured Duck," Grainus said.

"Yes, I can believe that. Whenever he got his pay, he would hurry into Transmarisca and tuck most of it into her bodice."

"And his fish! No one could catch fine salmon like Polybius."

"They were delicious. ... Except when Elodia cooked them."

Grainus nodded. It was true.

When that topic was exhausted, Caius turned to discuss Elodia.

"Where do you think she is?" he said.

"Being held in Marcianople by either Lupicinus or *him*," Grainus said, referring to the snoring tribune. "There's nothing we can do about it."

"I'm inclined to get up from here, go back to the city, and knock heads together until I find her," Caius said.

"I would go with you but…"

"But?"

"We'd be arrested for desertion and scourged or even crucified."

"It was just a thought," Caius said.

After an hour, Grainus decided it was time to wake up Bitorix and continue their march to Abritus. Then in the distance, he spotted a small party of horsemen riding swiftly from that direction. He called to Bitorix. Bitorix awoke and jumped to his feet. He ordered the squad to immediately form up and begin marching. "Make it look like we've been marching all along," he ordered.

Within a few minutes, three horsemen drew near. The first one had a bloody bandage wrapped around his chest. He held the reins of the second horse. On its back was a fat man lying face down over the horse's saddle where he'd been secured. He looked dead, as far as Grainus could tell. The third man had a tourniquet around one arm, which ended in a bloody stump rather than a hand. The horsemen carried on toward Marcianople without stopping, without even speaking, except for the one-handed man who croaked out as he passed, "The Goths are coming back."

Had Arbrun any formal military training, he would have taken some simple precautions, like closing the Volesus compound gate and posting a watch. But he did not. Instead, the five young people made up for recent hardships by eating and drinking themselves insensible.

We've slept too long. That's what a feast will do. Silvan awoke with a start, still curled up next to Arbrun, who was asleep. She looked over to the other couch where her brother Karl and Arbrun's sister Jellena were also sleeping, wrapped around each other and breathing heavily. Everyone was here except Arbrun's younger brother Bort. It was his voice that awoke her. He was talking. To whom?

"Wake up!" she shouted.

Karl raised himself on an elbow. "What?"

"There's someone outside talking to Bort." Silvan dashed toward the main door along with Karl and Arbrun, who were forced to lift their togas above their knees as they ran. "How did the Romans conquer the world wearing these silly things?" said Arbrun.

They reached the door and, looking out into the courtyard, saw a legionary, tall with a massive body, bending over Bort. With one hand, he firmly gripped Bort's hair, tilting it back to expose his throat. Against that, he held a sword.

Nearby stood another man wearing the uniform of a military tribune. The young Goths stopped at the villa's open door, wondering what they should do, then realized there wasn't anything they *could* do. One could not fight in a toga. Anyway, they had left their weapons behind in the dining room. Before they could react, the legionary cut Bort's throat.

Arbrun let out a short cry as he watched his brother die. Then, when he'd had time to catch his breath, he filled the air with a great shout. In his fury, he flung himself out the door as if planning to attack the Romans with his bare hands. Two pairs of hands pulled him back. Jellena caught up, bringing with her the men's weapons.

Once they yanked Arbrun back and out of the way, Karl pushed the great oak door closed and barred it. Addressing Silvan, Karl said, "You and Arbrun stay and guard this entrance. Jellena and I will guard the slaves' door."

Karl handed his sister his knife. Silvan took it gingerly, with distaste, as though it were still covered in the Roman matron's blood. She did not want it and did not know how to use it, especially against a legionary armed with a sword. It all seemed hopeless.

When Karl and Jellena were gone, Silvan peered through the two small glass windows flanking the main door. She saw another legionary, from his uniform she could tell he was a decanus, approaching the military tribune and Bort's killer. She watched as he waved his hands, arguing with the military tribune who was pointing to the door she was standing behind. The decanus was flailing his hands in opposition. Several other legionaries moved out of sight along the side of the building.

For several minutes the two Romans argued. Then two things happened. First, she heard a cry and the sound of fighting from the far end of the villa. Then she smelled smoke.

"We need to check on my sister," Arbrun said. He and Silvan left the main door and moved back through the building, passing around the atrium to the utility area. Their view out the slaves' door was obscured by billows of smoke. It cleared momentarily, allowing Arbrun and Silvan to see Karl lying face down just outside the door. The point of an arrow was protruding from his back. Arbrun gasped in horror. Silvan started to cry out but instead began coughing and choking.

When the view cleared again, they caught a glimpse of Jellena. Her torso had been sliced almost in two. Farther from the door were several Romans clustered around the body of one of their own.

The Romans noticed Arbrun, who made no attempt to back into the burning building. When Silvan saw one of them nock an arrow, she pulled Arbrun away from the door. Now they could not see anything, and the heat was intensifying. Arbrun stood stunned by the sight of his little sister's and best friend's bodies.

Silvan looked to him for direction. Seeing his dazed expression, she pulled him firmly back to the atrium. The air was slightly better there as the fire sucked down fresh air through the open roof. She stepped down into the shallow pool, pulling him after. They pulled their garments up into makeshift masks. Submerged and below the smoke, they could watch as the house disintegrated around them. Burning beams, embers, and clay tiles rained down. They tried sinking to the bottom of the pool, hoping the water would provide protection from the falling debris.

In time the embers died down. A few scorched timbers lay across the pool, trapping Arbrun in the water. He pushed them aside and clamber out. He looked around for Silvan, but she was stuck under fallen beams. Fortunately, he spotted her under the water. He jumped back in, pushed the beams out of the way, and dragged her out. She'd been floating face up, so she could breathe, but her forehead was cut, and, as head wounds do, it bled freely. He ripped off a piece of his toga, now dirty and sodden, and pressed it to her wound.

She was too dazed to walk, so Arbrun carried her out to the courtyard and left her while he surveyed their situation. The entire house was a flattened ruin. Only the kitchen chimney jutted up from the ashes. Thankfully, no Romans were in sight.

All the corpses were gone. A quick search found a fresh grave and a shovel. Arbrun dug up the grave. It contained the body of the legionary killed by Jellena's arrow. Silvan sat stunned and silent. She watched, incapable of helping, as Arbrun disposed of the Roman's body, dragging it to the pigpen. She wept openly as he returned carrying the body of Jellena.

"You could help, you know," he barked. "Dig that grave deeper. I'll go back for Karl and Bort."

Arbrun made two more trips to the pigpen, bringing back a body each time. Silvan still felt dizzy and sick. She scratched at the grave. Her whole body was shaking. Arbrun finally said, "Give me that," and seized the shovel from her. When the grave was deep enough, she cried as he tenderly placed the bodies of Bort and the newlyweds in the grave.

She watched as he walked to the slaves' quarters, some distance from the ruined villa. Nobody was there. Based on things left behind, it looked like the owner had moved the slaves, probably into the city. He found clothes, which they needed having lost their own in the fire. They had to discard their "borrowed" Roman garments, his toga and her silk gown, and replace them with practical working clothes. Of course, there were no weapons among the slaves' things, but he did find an axe and knives in a woodworking shop.

When he returned, Silvan had calmed down and was no longer dizzy, but she was suffering a terrible headache. At least her head wound was no longer bleeding. Arbrun said, "It doesn't look bad. It will scar, but your hair will cover it in time."

The two knelt and prayed to Jesus and Odin for the souls of their lost siblings. Now even Arbrun wept.

"This morning, we were five," she said. "Now, just two. It seems unbelievable," she added bitterly, her voice quavering. She was here, alone with Arbrun, the man who said he would lead and protect their little group. Her indifference to him was turning to dislike.

"We need to go," she said. "We need to find our clan. We'll starve out here by ourselves."

Arbrun agreed, adding that with just two of them, they'd likely be killed before they starved. They set off up the driveway, with Arbrun taking her arm to steady her. She shrugged off his assistance. *I need to be strong.*

"You're feeling better?" he asked.

"Shush, listen!" she whispered. They heard men's voices and horses. They moved off the driveway and crept quietly up to the road just in time to see a Roman squad move away from them, marching toward Marcianople. It was the squad that had attacked them in the villa. After the Romans were out of earshot, Arbrun looked over to see tears running down her cheeks.

"Oh gods," she said, "it was all I could do to keep from attacking them. All I have is Karl's knife, but I wanted... I wondered if I could have brought down one before they got me!"

"I felt the same," Arbrun said.

He reached to comfort her, but she pushed him away. "We need to move. Now," she said, "but not on this road. Do you know another way to Abritus?"

He said, "We'll head northwest across the fields."

Titus was a common Roman soldier. Common soldiers trusted their generals to lead them to victory, not to annihilation. Sometimes that trust was misplaced.

He was a highly competent squad member of a relatively competent squad of a less-than-competent limitanei legion. His legion was here, a few miles outside of Marcianople, marching fast, very fast, in pursuit of, rumor had it, the king of the Goths. Rumor also said Military Count Lupicinus had the king in his grasp last night, but the fat bastard allowed him to escape.

As Titus looked around, he could see other legionaries flagging. It was cold but dry. Many of the men had already finished the water they'd carried. The men near him were unaccustomed to long marches wearing full armor and carrying swords and heavy shields. Glancing behind him, he could see the comitatenses soldiers of the rear guard. *They* did not seem to be tiring. It grated on him to admit it, but perhaps, just perhaps, those fryking field army men were generally better soldiers than frontier guards like himself.

Titus noticed when the limitanei squad behind his pulled out of formation. That left his squad as the last in the column except for the rear guard. It was mildly irritating. He knew the members of that squad. He'd shared food with its leader, Grainus, before they left Marcianople. By "share," he meant he provided Grainus with half a chicken; in return, Grainus promised to share his cured pork whenever the column took a break. Now the column moved on, leaving Grainus and his squad behind. Titus looked over his shoulder and saw them standing beside the road talking to Military Tribune Bitorix.

With Bitorix standing beside the road, who would lead them? As far as Titus was concerned, it could be anyone because anyone would be an improvement over Bitorix. The man was a mentula. His absence almost made up for the missing cured pork. Pork, Titus now knew, he would probably never see.

The few times Bitorix had appeared in Titus's life, he fryked things up.

Take, for example, the squad games last year. Titus's squad and the squads from four other Danube outposts, including Grainus's, had gathered for contests of skill. Typically, wreaths of ivy were bestowed on the winners of each athletic contest. But in honor of the tenth anniversary of the emperor's reign, there were additional prizes: purses of gold and first access to whores specially procured for the games. Military Tribune Bitorix was responsible for organizing the games and had secured an allowance to purchase the prizes. Titus's squad won the distance sprints and weightlifting events. They even came in second in archery, which Grainus's man Marius won. A friend of Titus placed second in the knife-throwing event. The best knife thrower (and a very pretty knife thrower she was) was Grainus's provisioner Elodia. However, the judges disqualified her, saying the events were open only to limitanei, not slaves, so Titus's friend won that prize by default.

When the winners of the games claimed their prize purses, they found them light by one coin in ten. Bitorix confessed to taking a "surcharge," as he called it, saying he needed the extra funds to acquire the best class of whores. Given his rank, there was nothing the prize winners could do. Titus's friend grumbled but took his gold and enjoyed his whore anyway. He reported to his squad something his whore had said; that Bitorix had "sampled" each of the whores before selecting them to, in his words, "ensure the finest quality."

Titus was roused from his recollections by a commotion near the start of the Roman column. A cavalry group rode off the road to deal with a dozen Goths who had come too close. The Romans had previously passed small groups of Goths standing well back, groups that did not present an imminent threat. A centurion came by to say the column should march on without pausing; today's mission was to capture or kill the Gothic leaders believed to be near Abritus, not to exterminate every Goth encountered. Titus watched with interest as the horsemen closed on the Gothic warriors. He wondered how the barbarians were armed. He could see spears, cudgels, a sword or two, and at least one bow. It was the latter that had provoked a Roman response.

The Goths began to back away once they saw the cavalry deploy, but it was too late. Within a minute, they were surrounded. The Goths with spears raised them, which would have thwarted a cavalry assault had there been more spears. The Romans charged with heavy lances, evaded the spears, and overran the barbarians. The lone Gothic archer got only one shot away, which skewered a horseman just as his lance impaled the archer.

The action was over quickly. The cavalry returned to the column, leaving behind a small pile of bodies plus, separately, the body of their comrade, which they would collect later.

The Goths did not seem to learn a lesson from this skirmish. More Goths soon appeared on the column's flanks. They kept pace with the column but maintained a respectful distance. The road, which ran roughly northwest, was bracketed with low hills on both sides. Soon the hills rose and began to close in. The column stopped, and from the front, a whistle blew. A rumor came that there was a barricade across the road. Titus heard another whistle from the rear. A large crowd of Goths appeared behind the rear guard, which was redeploying for defense in response to the whistle. The column began to move again. Evidently, the troops had not stopped to clear the barricade. Instead, they were going around it on both sides by trudging up and along the steep hillsides.

A swarm of Goths came over the hillsides above the troops on either side. Titus heard the shriek of their war cry and watched as they approached on the run. Another whistle, an order crying "Testudo," and Titus raised his shield over his head just in time to block a flight of arrows. Screams came from some soldiers who deployed their shields too slowly. The tortoise defense did not work well for troops in line of march when the direction of incoming fire was unclear. On the column's edge, the comrade to Titus's right crouched under his shield, but the man's uphill flank was unprotected. On the second flight of arrows, he took a shot to his chest and toppled over into Titus, knocking him to the ground.

There were no more arrows because the Goths were on them, stabbing with swords and spears, hammering away with cudgels. The men around Titus defended themselves as best they could, but these were frontier troops, not regular army. They had less experience with hand-to-hand combat and had been trained in the traditional style, where men fought in a line, using shields to bash their opponents while reaching around their shields to stab the enemy. Here there was no line and, for many, no shield. While the

Romans wore mail and had swords, most Goths had only leather vests and clubs, having surrendered any better equipment during the river crossing. But the Goths had surprise, numbers, and fury on their side. Each fallen Roman provided his killer with a better weapon, one the Goth had spent hours using in practice and combat back in their homeland, north of the great river.

Titus watched numbly as the men in his squad were struck down one by one. He defended himself against several barbarians. Titus was small and fast. His opponents towered over him. Those with swords used them like clubs, slashing at Titus while leaving themselves open to a stabbing counterattack. A thrust to the gut, a step backward to avoid the wounded opponent's fall, and a glance around to look for imminent danger; it soon became a rhythm.

Yet the Goths kept coming. Titus was forced to retreat down the slope step by step toward the road. He found himself up against the Goths' road barrier, hemmed in by other retreating comrades. The barrier blocked his view to the west, so Titus had no idea what was happening at the head of the column. To the east, back along the road, he could see the rear guard putting up a fierce defense but slowly retreating toward him.

As the Romans retreated, they began to crowd against each other. Only a few rear-guard soldiers separated Titus from the nearest Goth. He had no one to fight and no space to move. Increasingly, Titus found his arms pinned against his sides by the crush of his comrades. He could not fight; he could not move; he could only watch as the wave of advancing Goths drew closer, destroying the buffer of legionaries who surrounded him. He watched as the tall legionary to his left had his head crushed by a club blow. The man did not fall. There was no room. He stood limply, propped up by the Romans around him.

Titus struggled with the effort but was able to turn, which left a gap into which the dead man collapsed. With him down, Titus could finally see his killer. He saw the Goth looking at him and raising his bloody club. Titus glimpsed the club descending toward him. It was his last vision.

... And in the press of mad and bloody strife, the tribunes and the greater part of the army perished, with the loss of their standards, except for their ill-omened leader [Lupicinus], who, intent only upon saving himself by flight while the others were fighting, made for the town in hot haste. After this, the enemy put on the Romans' arms and ranged about, devastating sundry places without opposition.

From Res Gestae, Volume XXXI 5.9, by Ammianus Marcellinus

Caius was stunned by the sight. The three horsemen had galloped past them without any news except the cryptic warning, "The Goths are coming back." *Really? And who was the dead man?*

Bitorix watched as the horsemen vanished toward Marcianople, leaving behind a screen of dust.

He turned to Caius. "Now what?"

Caius said, "'Now what' what?"

"What do you mean, 'Now what what'?"

"Why, Military Tribune Bitorix, are you asking me what we should do?"

"I mean," Bitorix said, "should we continue to march toward Abritus to help our comrades? Who, seemingly, have all been killed by the Goths? Or should we march back to Marcianople to warn everyone of this apparent defeat?"

Caius said, "Well, those horsemen who just passed us will convey any warning to the city long before we can."

"True, but if all the city's garrison now lie dead up the road, who will defend the city walls?"

"Your decision, Military Tribune."

"Of course," he said. "Obviously." Bitorix stopped and looked up the road, then down toward Marcianople. He stared in that direction.

After a while, Marius sat down. Then Grainus. Soon the squad was all sitting or squatting. Bitorix turned and stared up the road again. "I don't see any Goths."

Marius leaned back against his pack and began to doze. Bitorix looked back toward the city again. "No sign of those horsemen," he informed the squad, referring to the horsemen who had passed at a gallop ten minutes earlier and were long gone.

He finally proclaimed, "Never let it be said I could not arrive at a difficult decision. Up, men, we march back to the city. If the Goths have destroyed our army, well… there's no point in throwing away more valuable lives. Form up!

"And where's my damn horse?"

The squad spent a quarter hour trying to catch Bitorix's horse, which had wandered off in search of good pasturage. It let Glabius approach, but when Bitorix came near, the horse would shy and bolt. Finally, with the horse caught, Bitorix mounted, and the squad formed up two abreast in three ranks, and they began marching back to the city.

They'd no sooner started when Arruntius shouted, "I see eyes peering out from the bushes! Over there, beside the driveway!"

The rest of them looked in that direction but couldn't see anything. Nevertheless, Bitorix was spooked. "It is nothing! And did I order you to stop? Keep marching! Double time!"

When they reached the city, other retreating Roman troops were catching up with them. Unlike those troops, their uniforms were clean, their weapons unblooded, and none of them were injured. Bitorix ordered them to break formation and mix in to avoid drawing attention to their pristine selves.

By dusk, it was apparent the losses had been catastrophic. A roll call revealed well over half the force that left Marcianople in the morning had not returned. Almost all the frontier troops were missing. Some of the regular forces had fought their way back. Caius was shocked. He blamed the difference on the limitanei's inferior training and equipment.

Among the missing and presumed dead on the road to Abritus was a majority of the city's garrison. To bring the garrison back up to strength, the city's legate picked through the returning troops, selecting men who seemed least affected by the fighting. Of course, he chose Grainus's squad. They remained garrison troops until reinforcing legions arrived from abroad, and the infamous Traianus, *Magister Peditum* (Master of Infantry), began his terror offensive to drive back the Goths.

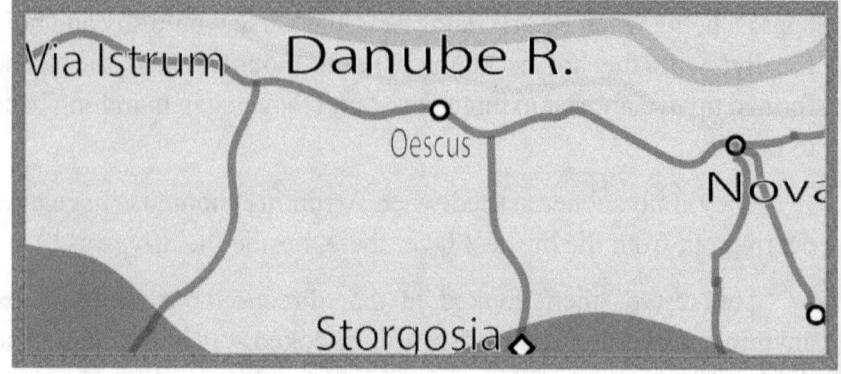

8. Elodia Survives
376 CE

When Elodia awoke, she understood, after a moment of disorientation, that she was in Nedarcus's medical tent outside of Abritus City. It was not the rising sun that woke her but the noise. She was still exhausted, but further sleep was impossible given the cacophony of horses, carts, men cheering, and men crying out in pain. As the old warrior who had helped her predicted—*What was his name? ... Boderus. Yes, that's what he was called*—as Boderus had expected, there would indeed be more wounded warriors. A trickle of men arrived, a trickle that quickly became a flood. Growing up in her father's camp, she had seen the aftermath of a raid but never anything on this scale. The preparations Nedarcus and she had made were laughably inadequate. Six floor mats? They could have used sixty or six hundred.

The wounded mostly suffered stab wounds. Legionaries were trained to use their swords for stabbing, not slicing. The Goths she saw had punctures in their heads and legs, those portions of a foe that a Roman could reach from around the edge of their large shields. Not much could be done for warriors with head wounds other than stitch, re-bandage, and pray. Such wounds were already bandaged on the battlefield. The warrior would have died before reaching them if more than a bandage were required. She and Nedarcus quickly ran through their supply of bandages. Then they cut strips off from the wounded man's own clothes.

She'd learned to stitch wounds when still a girl. Boys would invariably do some fryking stupid thing requiring stitches. And men would often return from raids with open wounds. She was good at stitching. Too good for some men who would prefer having a boast-worthy scar.

Her wounded shoulder ached. That arm was held tight in a sling, but she could stitch using the other hand. She needed someone to pull the wound's severed edges together, but she did what she could. A Roman would yelp and jerk when stitched, but Gothic men quietly endured the pain, especially when a young woman was wielding the needle. She stitched using their supply of cotton string until it ran out. Then she put her silk banquet gown to good use, tearing off thin ribbons. When Nedarcus worried their supply of silk ribbons would be consumed, he told her to bandage, but not stitch, gut wounds. Such victims usually die. "If they're still alive tomorrow, we'll stitch them," he said. A few were lucky. A very few. The gut contained a person's spirit, she knew. If the spirit was pierced by a sword, the person died.

One of the first gut-wounded was a young man, really a boy, a couple of years younger than her. He reminded her of her brother Boltus in so many ways. They both had piercing blue eyes. They had the same laugh. The young man had a sister her age. As she tied the young man's belly closed, she noticed the new wound crossed an old white scar. "Yes," he said, "Belly wounds seem to be my favorite injury, though I got that one when I was drunk and stumbled onto my father's spear. But there's another scar just around on my back. My best friend stuck me there when he caught me bumping his sister!" he said with a laugh.

"If that were the punishment in my village," she replied with a grin, "most of the boys would have back scars!" He laughed and moaned. Laughing hurt. "Lie still while I get you some water." She found a cup near the water jug and returned a few minutes later. The young man was dead.

She cried out and dropped the cup. Kneeling by him, she took his hand. "Oh, Boltus!" She wept. She never learned his real name.

Nedarcus came over and stood behind her. Gently gripping her good shoulder, he said, "Come along, girl. Others need your attention. You will see many more die today." She prayed for the boy's spirit and returned to work. Though she saw dozens more men under her care die, young and old but mostly young, it was the boy she called Boltus she remembered best.

Many men required a leg or arm amputation. Nedarcus postponed those for a day or two. When a blow just left a limb immobile, it might recover if properly anointed and massaged and if the gods could be convinced to intervene. But when it came to restraining a man, while Nedarcus sawed off a dead limb, Elodia, having only one good hand, was not useful. Nedarcus could always find men more able for the task, though she did become skillful at brushing hot tar on open wounds. She found the trick was to persevere in applying liberal amounts of tar even when the patient jerked and screamed. They seldom struck her.

When they finished tending to the seriously wounded, they had time to address those with lesser injuries. By the time they saw them, the wounded were drunk. They were *very* drunk, raucous, and happy to boast of the dozens or hundreds of Romans they had personally killed. By their accounts, not a single Roman had been left alive.

She wanted this to be untrue. She hoped and prayed that the gods would have told her if Caius had been killed or wounded. They had not sent her a message, nothing to indicate that Caius was in trouble. She even prayed to the Jesus God to keep Caius safe.

Elodia also hoped the rest of his squad was unharmed. Perhaps they had been left behind in Marcianople. With some luck, the rest of the Romans had been killed, especially Bitorix and Lupicinus, leaving only her boys to garrison the city. She prayed that Bitorix had suffered a slow and painful death. That prayer was directed at Odin, not the Jesus God who dealt in love. Praying to the right god was essential.

She mulled over these thoughts, fantasizing about the possible terrible fates that might have befallen Bitorix while she stitched up the last of the wounded. It was dusk. She'd been tending the hurt and dying for a dozen hours without a break. She and Nedarcus finished together. They took clean garments, food, and blankets from his supply cart, washed thoroughly in cold water, dressed, ate by the fire, and fell asleep under the cart. They snuggled for warmth. *So tired.* Her shoulder still ached. All of her ached.

Very early the following day, Elodia awoke to find Boderus lying in the tent with his belly bandaged. His face was pale and sweaty, and his eyes were closed. She sensed his spirit was preparing to depart. She squatted by him and took his hand. He started at her touch and looked up at her. "Ah, Lord Fritigern's girl," he said. "I see you survived the fighting."

"I was here at Abritus, where you sent me. There was no fighting here."

"Oh, in Abritus? Did someone carry me here? Who brought me here?"

"I don't know. I just awoke, and you were already here. But I'm glad you survived and that you're here. Now I can look after you as you looked after me."

"Yes, but only for a little while. I'm dying, aren't I?"

His bandages oozed and smelled like shit. A bad wound. As a veteran of earlier fights, he would recognize his wound as fatal. He would not want to hear a lie, and she did not want to tell one.

"Yes, you are," she said. It was remarkable that he was even here. Most warriors with such a wound would be left to die on the battlefield unless their kin were on hand to bring them away. She was surprised someone had made the effort to bandage Boderus rather than mercifully speeding his journey to the other side. They must have recognized him as a leader of note, someone worth rescuing, notwithstanding his wound.

"Do you have kin?" she asked.

"Yes, my son Rodericus should be nearby with our clan, clan Dondori. If he survived yesterday's fight."

"I will find him and bring him," she said with more confidence than she felt. The Gothic camp around the walls of Abritus had grown to thousands over the last two days, and she had no idea where the Dondori clan might have erected its tents. While she searched, Boderus could die at any moment.

Elodia wrapped herself in a thick sagum, pulled a wool cap down over her ears, and walked through the forest of tents. Every dozen paces, she called out, "Dondori! Clan Dondori! Where is clan Dondori?"

She received many responses, mostly like "Shut the *hell up*! It's fryking early!" But after walking less than a mile, she received an answer from a man of clan Dondori. He escorted her to the chieftain's tent and announced her. As she suspected, Boderus was the clan's chieftain. Entering, she met Rodericus and Boderus's wife. Both looked haggard. It was clear neither had slept.

She tried to introduce herself. "I am Elodia of…," and there she was stumped. Elodia of what? She had no clan name, at least none that she wanted to use. She refused to be associated with her dead husband's clan. Caius, being Roman, had no clan. If she mentioned Fritigern, they would assume she was his concubine. Which, shortly, she probably would be. But mentioning him would provide her with some authority.

"I am Elodia, slave of Lord Fritigern. And," she paused, unsure how to proceed, "I am currently working with Nedarcus in his medicine tent. We are caring for Boderus. He is badly wounded," which brought a small cry from his wife. "Please come."

When they returned to the medicine tent, Rodericus and his mother knelt on either side of her husband. He was obviously in great pain, yet his face showed relief at seeing his wife and son, a look apparent even as he grimaced. He took his wife's hand in one of his and extended his other hand to Elodia, which she grasped. "Thank you, Fritigern's girl." He never did learn her name. "I can journey on now." He kissed her hand and released it.

With tears in her eyes, Elodia said goodbye and left them to their private farewells.

She returned to Nedarcus's campsite. The smell of roasting lamb drew her to his cart. He'd built a fire and was cooking meat and turnips, which he shared with her. She must have looked downcast. He said, "Yesterday was a hard, hard day. Are you all right, girl?"

Elodia shrugged without answering. She was not all right. She had seen death before. Goths grew up with death all around them but not in these numbers. It was especially distressing to see the young men and even boys die. She wondered where her own people were. Perhaps, off in the mountains north of the Danube, where she imagined they were safe. Except for the Huns. And the Sarmatians, Gepids, and Vandals. She sighed. No one was safe anywhere.

"I'm sorry we haven't had a chance to talk before," Nedarcus said. "You were hurt, and then we were so busy, there was never a good time. At least I should have thanked you for your help."

"I did what I could, what my mother trained me to do. What any Gothic woman would do," she said.

"Perhaps. But you did it without complaining or stopping, even when I could see you were in pain yourself. You were brave."

Elodia shrugged and stabbed a big chunk of turnip.

"And I don't know anything about you, except they call you Elodia," he said. "Who are your people? Where is your husband?"

His questions were difficult. To ask them of an unaccompanied young woman was reasonable, but she had no ready answers. She deflected. "Do you not have a wife and family to help with your surgery?"

She studied Nedarcus, seeing details she had missed before. His left profile was handsome, but on his right, the tip of his ear was missing, and beneath it, where his skull had stopped a blade, a long white scar stretched from ear to chin. He walked with a limp due, she later learned, to having half his foot cut off.

She wasn't surprised that they hadn't talked before. Nedarcus had issued orders, so many orders. He oversaw the wounded, those who carried them in, and those who removed the bandaged or dead bodies. To her, other than his orders, he'd said little. He seemed enveloped in a cloud of sadness, even misery.

"No," he finally answered, "No family here. I have two grown sons, but they are off with Fritigern's bodyguard. And a daughter. She's away with her husband somewhere. I haven't seen her in more than a year."

"And your wife?" she asked tentatively. If all were well, he would have named her first.

"She died a month ago on the far bank of the Danube. There was a fever."

Before she could say anything, he repeated. "And your husband? Where is he?"

Time to come clean. Partially.

"My husband, a Goth, is dead. As to my clan, as far as I know, they are with Athanaric somewhere up in the Carpathian Mountains. I haven't seen them since my husband died." No point in elaborating any more. "As of yesterday, I am now owned by Lord Fritigern, but previously I was owned by a limitanei squad. I am… the woman of a Roman frontier soldier. Or was until yesterday. His body might lie on the Marcianople road."

She watched as he considered that.

Finally, he said, "I'm sorry to say that is more than likely. I have heard from several people, including Fritigern himself, almost every legionary who left the city yesterday is now dead. Our warriors caught them in a trap. Few escaped. A count of the bodies suggests the entire garrison was deployed and killed. Some of

211

Fritigern's lieutenants say the Romans do not even have sufficient soldiers to man Marcianople's walls. They say there will be no better opportunity to take the city than now."

Her breath caught. What did she care about taking the city? Where was Caius? Where? He must be alive because she'd had no message from the gods, nothing telling her he was dead. Perhaps...

"What of prisoners? Or men left wounded on the field?" she asked.

"We did not take prisoners. The Roman wounded were put down."

She covered her face with her hands. Maybe Nedarcus was right. Maybe Caius was dead. There were so many dead, both Roman and Goth. Perhaps the gods were too busy to send her a message. Or they don't care about Roman deaths.

She sat downcast, considering these possibilities. There was no way to know.

She began to cry. For the first time, what she wanted—really, *really* wanted—she could hardly say it; she wanted Caius returned to her. When that longing filled her mind, she wanted to howl at the sky, the unseen unfeeling stars, *bring my Caius back*. Instead, she just cried softly.

Nedarcus sought to distract her. "Do you have any children?"

"No." She took several deep breaths and calmed herself.

Whether because his curiosity was satisfied or because he saw the pain on her face, Nedarcus asked no more questions. They sat together, eating, not talking. When the meal was finished, he said he would begin to break down the medicine tent. She offered to clean up the cook site. She washed the big black pot in a nearby stream, packed the cooking gear into the medicus's cart, and sat by the fire. She was still exhausted from yesterday. But now warm. Replete. She tucked her chin down and slept. She awoke mid-morning with a neck crick.

Somewhere Elodia had developed a nose for detecting deceivers and a talent for evading them.

She heard men talking, men working. She looked over and saw Nedarcus and another man taking down the tent. It was Rodericus. They pulled down and rolled each panel of hemp cloth, folded the support poles, and put the lot in the medicus's cart. One man tethered her horse to the cart while another harnessed the mule.

Rodericus saw her stirring and came closer. "The camp here is breaking up, scattering. My father, at the end... he talked about you. He was worried about you."

"How did he go?" she asked.

"He died an hour ago. We talked until we had nothing left to say. Then, after he sent my mother away, he asked me to start him on his next journey. He was in great pain. I sent him off."

She nodded. "What did Boderus say about me?"

"He said Fritigern recently bought you because you have no family and no husband. He charged me with protecting you."

She was immediately suspicious. It was true she told Rodericus she was owned by Fritigern, but she never mentioned any payment or anything about her family or husband. In fact, she and his father never had a personal conversation. Boderus died without even knowing her name. He just called her "girl." *Why would his son offer her his protection?* It wasn't an offer. He phrased it as a filial obligation. *Why?* She'd often received spontaneous offers of help or friendship from men. These became more frequent once she developed breasts and hips. Yet what he said was true. She had no family and no friends other than the casual acquaintance of Fritigern and Nedarcus.

Rodericus was about twenty-five years old, some years older than her. He was short for a man, about her height, but with broad shoulders and thick muscles everywhere. The build of a fighter. He was clean, a wonder in this environment, with his long black hair knotted behind his head and his beard trimmed short. Not a handsome man like Bitorix, nor a plain man like Nedarcus.

"What are your plans?" Elodia asked.

"My clan will move west toward Nicopolis Ad Istrum. Like everyone else, we are heading for any town where we might get food and shelter. I went to Nicopolis some years ago. They have large warehouses and granaries, which should be full this year. The harvest was good. If the Romans won't trade with us… well… the city's walls are old. We will take what we need."

"You say you would protect me. In what role? Servant? Concubine?… Wife? Or would you give me to someone in your clan?"

"We will discuss that when we have more time. But for now, let me say I would not give you to someone else. I would ask Fritigern to gift you to me and keep you in my household, perhaps as a servant and companion for my wife," Rodericus said.

He waited, looking at Elodia, expecting some response. He stared into her eyes. She kept her face impassive, hoping he would look away. He studied her, his gaze moving from her mouth to her ears and then her neck. His glance dropped down to the rest of her body, which was modestly covered by her cloak.

214

"How long have you been married?" she asked.

"Not yet ten years."

"Would she want me to look after your children?"

"We have no children." She continued to silently stare until he felt obliged to talk. "She is in good health, but Jesus God and Freya have not blessed us with babies."

Elodia could not imagine that his sterile wife would react well to another young woman in his tent. She remained quiet, hoping Rodericus would still be inclined to talk. Which he did. "Perhaps you could provide me with a son. If so, I would marry you." She raised a quizzical eyebrow. "The leaders of my clan often have several wives?" He turned a statement of fact into a question as if asking her whether being a second wife would be acceptable.

"And if she doesn't want another woman in your tent? A second wife?" she asked.

Now it was his turn for silence and staring. Elodia watched as a wave of scarlet moved up from his neck to his brow. "She does as I say!" he declared. He was irritated. Was he annoyed at her for her question? Or at his wife, imagining her disobedience?

Elodia looked down as if she were considering his offer. When he calmed down, she went back to staring into his eyes and remaining silent. In a pleading tone, he finally said, "I would put her aside if you insist. I could send her back to her parents."

He looked nothing like her late husband, but they were ever so similar. Passionate. Quick to anger. There was no way she would subject herself to such a man, given a choice. She was cautious. She'd been there before. He might get violent if abruptly denied.

Elodia glanced toward the medicus's cart. It was now loaded. Nedarcus climbed up onto the driver's bench. He picked up the reins, then paused and looked over at her. Had he overheard her conversation with Rodericus? Possibly. She stood up and walked over to the cart. As Nedarcus reached down to help her up, she looked over her shoulder at Rodericus. "I thank you for your kind offer," she said. "I need time to consider it."

She squeezed onto the bench beside Nedarcus. He flicked the mule's reins, and they were off.

"Where are we going?" she asked.

"Northwest, toward Sexaginta Prista," Nedarcus said.

"Is that anywhere near Nicopolis Ad Istrum?"

"Not really," he said.

"Good."

The mule trotted off, leaving Rodericus behind, mouth gaping like a fish.

"Glad to be away from him?" Nedarcus asked.

"Oh yes."

"Actually, we go wherever Fritigern and his staff go. Fritigern says any place he goes, the Romans will follow, and any place the Romans go, there will be fighting. I go where the fighting is," Nedarcus said with grim determination. His face and neck were rigid. He did not complain, but Elodia could see he was in pain. A medicus for whom the work never got easier.

Silvan finally ignored Arbrun when he continued to rant about killing Romans. She was more worried about her own survival.

The two traveled northwest from the burned Volesus estate, where they'd buried their siblings.

Buried? Dead and buried? How is that possible? Jellena and Karl just got married. And they were so happy. Oh, how she would miss Jellena. Karl too, of course, but Jellena? She was the older sister she never had. Sister, companion, and friend. And her defense against Karl.

Karl changed once their father died, taking over his role in managing her life. She resented it. He pushed her toward Arbrun as if cementing their friendship was more important than her happiness. It wasn't even a friendship between equals. Arbrun always dominated her brother. And he accepted being subordinate. Yes, Arbrun was stronger and smarter, but Karl was not weak or stupid. He need not be the minion. Arbrun would have respected him more if he'd stood up for himself.

But Karl was gone, and Jellena too. And so was the future that she had expected for herself. Now she could find herself a man, one who could guide and protect her. A man she could endure. Not Arbrun.

It took them two days to reach Abritus. On the first day, they walked only a few miles. Silvan was still reeling from her head wound. They found shelter in an unoccupied villa that had been recently looted but not burned. Arbrun started a blaze in a fireplace using the broken furniture that littered the floor. They found torn rugs, which they used as blankets.

The next day they walked parallel to the road to avoid all traffic until they came to a vast battle site. The ground in all directions was littered with unburied corpses, all Roman. It was clear the Goths had won a great victory—there were smoking pyres where the Gothic fatalities had been cremated—while wild dogs were eating the Roman dead. Dozens of Goths were scavenging through the chaos, looking for anything of value. Arbrun and Silvan joined in, hoping to find better clothes, weapons, and above all, food. They'd had nothing to eat since their ill-fated banquet at the villa.

When the Goths crossed the Danube, the Romans confiscated most people's weapons. Now, this vast field of victory provided an opportunity to re-arm a thousand warriors. Arbrun wanted a sword. He had been able to keep his sword during the chaos of the river crossing, but now it was lost under the charred wreckage of the Roman villa.

The scavengers had already picked over the best things, especially the weapons. Still, Arbrun secured a good Roman sword from under the body of a legionary. He first had to chase off the carrion birds feeding on the dead man's eyes.

As the sun set, they joined other scavengers near one of many campfires by the battle site. It was good to have warmth and the security of numbers. People shared the food they'd been able to scrounge. The next day they moved on to Abritus. A Gothic tent camp surrounded most of the city, but it was starting to break up. Everyone was short of food, so the people dispersed in whatever direction they hoped would prove promising. The only way for the Gothic nation to survive was to spread out and live off the land.

Silvan and Arbrun walked through the remaining tents looking for their clan. They learned their people were already gone, heading northwest to Sexaginta Prista, an important fortress along the

Danube River. It would surely be well stocked with food and other supplies. Their ancestors had conquered it, or so the stories said. Perhaps they could do it again.

Silvan wondered if the Romans had abandoned the fortress at the same time they withdrew the frontier guards from all along the Danube. "I hope not. Where is the satisfaction in that?" Arbrun said. "My new sword must taste Roman blood. When I look at it, I ask it, 'How many of my people did you kill?' To cleanse it, I must use it to slay *that* many Romans. I have asked Odin to preserve me until then. And then I must kill a dozen more in memory of Karl, Jellena, and Bort."

She had no reply. Any pleasure she felt watching Romans die ended when she slit that woman's throat. She felt no more shame or satisfaction than she felt when slaughtering a calf. She understood killing was necessary to survive in this hostile land. She had known that as a member of their little team, she had to do her share of unpleasant tasks. But it wasn't something she wanted to ever do again.

What Silvan did want was a normal life. A strong husband who would treat her kindly and only punish her for good reasons. One who would let her manage home and hearth. One who excelled at both plow and sword, providing food and safety for her and their children. She wanted children desperately. Many boys who would grow up strong and become good men like their father. A few girls to keep her company, to learn her skills, girls who, in time, would become good wives and mothers. Girls to care for her in her old age. This was the life she wished for, that she had anticipated, until the Huns came.

Arbrun and Silvan spent the night in a tent outside of Abritus. They huddled for warmth, but when he began to touch her, she pushed him away. She did not want to marry him, or anyone so filled with hate. Now she regretted bumping him back in the Roman villa. As much as she wanted children, she did not want one until life returned to normal.

It was a long cold walk the next day to Sexaginta Prista. For protection, they attached themselves to a group from a different clan heading that way. When they arrived, they found another tent city outside the walls. The city gates were closed and guarded. That dashed their hope of spending a warm night indoors by a fire. But they did find the rest of their clan living in the tent camp, kin who welcomed and fed them and made room for them by their campfires and who mourned with them the death of their siblings.

Their clan had done better scavenging than they had. It had acquired two carts and livestock to pull them. Both carts were loaded with food, clothing, and other valuables recently appropriated from Roman estates. Silvan talked with their clan chieftain; a tall, heavily built man named Bandar. He wore a blood-stained bandage around his neck. "You did not take any Romans as slaves?" she asked.

"No, we do not need extra mouths to feed," he said, his voice low and raspy. She could not keep from glancing at his throat bandage. His voice had once been deep and rich, a gift from the god Bragi.

She turned her attention to his face. "I suppose we can go back and capture them later when the slave market opens in the spring?" she said.

"They would have starved before then. That would be cruel. So, we killed them. Fast and painless. We are not barbarians!"

Silvan did not think he was joking.

They discussed how the Romans would treat them should the tables be turned. Bandar said, "With luck, they will kill us rather than enslave us."

Silvan disagreed. He was old, and she was young. She had a lot of life ahead of her. She was sure she'd rather live as a slave than die free. She did not share this sentiment with him.

A few nights later, Bandar came to her. "I understand you are not bumping Arbrun. Before we crossed the river, Karl told me that you and Arbrun would marry."

Silvan explained she did not want to have a baby until life became normal again. Also, when that happened, she wanted a different kind of man than Arbrun. This angered Bandar, who was a great admirer of Arbrun. "You seem to think you have some choice in this matter. You do not. Your father or a brother should choose your husband, but Karl is dead, and your father is dead. As the clan leader, the responsibility now falls on me. I will abide by your late brother's choice."

He went on, "It is not good that you deny Arbrun your body. Abstinence is not good for a young man. Men have needs, especially young men. You will talk to him. Tell him you will accommodate him. That is my decision. Whether you are blessed with a child, that is Freya's decision."

That night, as she lay close to Arbrun's warm body, his hands began to caress her breasts and thighs. She took his hands in hers, brought them to her lips, and kissed them. "No, Arbrun," she said, "Not yet."

He said, "Bandar spoke with you? Spoke to you about me? And us?"

"Yes. But still," she said, fumbling for an excuse, "it's too soon after my brother's death. Give me time."

He seemed to accept her reason. He said he would not force her, that he would wait. If Bandar told him that she did not want him for a husband, he did not let on.

Thousands of Goths moved south from Abritus, across Moesia, and over the mountain passes into Thracia, searching for food, clothing, and loot. But mostly food. The winter was growing harsh. The Goths were hungry, cold, and angry. It was an unfortunate Roman who opposed them. As the Gothic horde swept across the land, its numbers grew. Every Roman estate yielded enslaved people, frequently ethnic Goths. These people often exercised their new freedom by slaying their former masters, overseers, and the despised house slaves.

As brutal as estate slaves might be, it was nothing compared to how mine slaves, once freed, treated their overseers. As the mining districts were overrun, a battalion of harsh, solid, and angry ex-miners joined the tribe.

Fritigern and a thousand Goths, including Nedarcus and Elodia, made the trek from Abritus to Sexaginta Prista. Arbrun and Silvan followed only a few days later.

Since Elodia had become, in practice, Nedarcus's assistant medicus and he her protector, she stayed with him as they moved north. They followed Fritigern to provide him with any medical care needed.

The road from Abritus to Sexaginta Prista followed a small river that meandered this way and that. The hills on either side were bare of trees but thick with shrubs, and the valley floor was heavily forested. The road was well maintained where it cut through the woods. It crossed the river many times, mostly by fords, not bridges. Nedarcus was grateful for this because fords would impede any pursuing Roman cavalry. Though Elodia didn't argue, she imagined cavalry horses could gallop across the shallows without pausing. In any case, they reached their destination with no sign of pursuers.

Sexaginta Prista was a massive Roman fortress on the Danube River. It was the home for the river's guard ships, which controlled the Danube River from the Black Sea up to Oescus City.

Fritigern decided that conquering the fortress was necessary. While it remained in Roman hands, the guard ships could block Goths trying to move across the Danube between Dacia and Moesia. He spoke to the leaders of the Greutungi, their eastern Gothic cousins, who were only starting to cross the river. He viewed their support as essential. It would be a disaster if the Romans blocked their passage.

There was another prospect that worried Fritigern. Although the Goths beat the Romans in the recent battle outside Marcianople, he knew his warriors could not stand against the Romans in open battle. His men had inferior weapons, some were still unarmed, and had no armor to speak of. More importantly, the Romans were trained to fight in formation. He'd seen a Roman legion slice through a horde of his tribe like a sharp knife through a trout's belly. His recent victory at Marcianople was due to the rough terrain, surprise, and numbers. The Romans had been vastly outnumbered. Fritigern also credited the blessing of Odin. Without the god's aid, the other factors would have made no difference.

223

Fritigern could picture an army of his warriors retreating north across Moesia to the Danube. If his men were pinned with their backs to the river, they would be slaughtered if Roman ships landed soldiers behind them. Alternatively, if he could capture all the Roman ships, the Goths could be evacuated across the river if necessary.

He soon realized it would be almost impossible to take Sexaginta Prista by storm. The walls were too thick and high, and the garrison too numerous. As a young man, Fritigern had seen Roman siege engines, the fearsome ballistae and onagers, which could hurl great rocks against walls. The Goths had no such weapons and no tools or expertise to make them. Nor was there any hope of besieging and starving the Romans. They had more food than the Goths and could bring in more by boat.

Yet Fritigern was surrounded by energetic young men eager to prove their worth. One of his lieutenants, who had served in a Roman legion, knew how to construct a battering ram. The idea of smashing the fortress's main gate generated immense excitement. A dozen men were dispatched with carts to fetch a great log. Others constructed a frame on wheels from which the ram would be suspended and swung. Iron chains, plundered from some estate, were readied and attached. A rough peaked roof was built over the frame, turning it into a small shed to protect the warriors working the ram from archers above. Fritigern's lieutenant cautioned the crew to wait until the roof could be covered with wetted hides to protect against fire. He said when he was in the legion, he had watched flames quickly engulf a ram shed, trapping the men beneath.

But he was overruled by his crew. It had taken more than a week to gather the necessary materials and to construct the battering ram. The impatient young men were eager to put it to use. Not even Fritigern could stop them.

Bending to their will, Fritigern organized a force of archers to provide cover fire while an enthusiastic group of forty men pushed the ram up to the fortress gate. It took a full minute for the crew, straining at the chains, to retract the great log back but only one second to release it. It smashed against the gate timbers. One timber split but did not break. Again, the log was cocked and unleashed, hitting the same timber. Its split grew wider, but the timber stubbornly remained. Seeing signs of progress, the crew pulled back a third time, pulling even harder to raise the log still higher.

But before they could release it, the defenders hefted a boulder over the wall directly above the ram shed. It fell thirty feet, smashed through the shed's roof, landed on the log knocking it from its frame, spinning it about, and releasing the strain on the chains. As the great log spun, its chains whirled and scythed through the men standing on either side. Splinters from the roof hailed down on the crew. They skewered many of the men who had been spared by the spinning chains. The boulder was followed by a shower of arrows from on high, impaling most of the crew who had somehow survived the ram shed's destruction.

Of all the men who'd manned the battering ram, only five made it back to safety. Even they sustained wounds, mostly minor, but one man's arm was ruined. A whipping chain had struck him above his right elbow, leaving an open wound and exposing the broken ends of his bones.

Members of his clan carried him on a stretcher to the medicine tent. Elodia helped Nedarcus staunch the bleeding and then press on the dressings until the dripping stopped altogether. Nedarcus noted the injury had not severed the arm's blood vessels. "If those blood tubes are cut, the patient always bleeds out before I can help him."

The man was alive but groggy when Nedarcus started to set the bones. As he instructed, Elodia placed an oak stick between his teeth and held his jaw closed to stifle any screaming. It was hardly necessary. The man only screamed a few times before passing out while Nedarcus forced his bones into proper alignment. Then she used cotton thread to sew up the wound. Finally, she held his arm steady while Nedarcus attached several splints to keep it immobile. When he was done, the man began to come around.

As they were finishing up, a young woman came into the tent and squatted by his head.

"Who are you? Do you know him?" Elodia asked.

"I am Silvan." She spoke in a hushed voice, little more than a whisper. "He is Arbrun, a man of my clan and the father of the child I am carrying. Will he live?"

Elodia studied her waist. There was no bulge, no sign she was pregnant.

"I will ask Nedarcus, the medicus. I am only his assistant. My name is Elodia," she said. Nedarcus had moved to the far end of the tent to wash his hands. "Will he live?" she called, echoing Silvan's question.

Nedarcus said, "He might live unless that wound festers. Normally I would amputate a limb where the bones have pierced the skin. But not in this case. The break was too close to the shoulder. He would bleed out before I could seal the blood tubes."

Silvan said, "I will pray it heals cleanly. He would probably rather die than lose his arm. He is a warrior."

Nedarcus had returned to where Arbrun was lying. "With that break? Not anymore," he said. "I doubt if he will ever lift a sword again. He'll be lucky if he can feed himself."

Silvan said nothing. She just looked at the groaning man, showing no emotion, not even a wet eye. "Is he your husband?" Elodia asked.

"Not yet," she said. "And, given a choice, not ever."

"You're pregnant? You don't look very far along."

"We bumped. One time. Maybe ten days ago. And now my bleeding is late."

"Well, you might be pregnant. Or not. With such wide hips, it's too early to tell."

Silvan looked at Elodia's slim figure and bristled. She was sensitive when others commented on her body, a legacy of her brother's mean remarks. "Are you a midwife that you know such things? How many children have *you* had?"

"Two, but I lost them before birth."

Silvan saw a brief look of sorrow pass over Elodia's face. "Oh, I'm so very sorry," she said.

Elodia looked surprised when Silvan began to weep softly. She recovered enough to say, "After what we endured, I'd supposed things could not get worse."

Elodia knelt beside her and put an arm around the young woman. "Come," she said, "Let's go outside and sit by the fire. It's not too cold today."

When Silvan was comfortably seated, Elodia brought some bread and cheese, which they shared. They talked quietly for an hour. Silvan asked Elodia about her life, starting with her pregnancies and branching out to cover much of her life story. Elodia talked about her friend Salonia, the baker's wife, and her baby. "It's been only a few days since we said goodbye, but so much has happened. As if that life happened years ago."

Silvan watched as Elodia relaxed, lying back on the grass, her hands clasped behind her head. "You must miss them."

"I do, but good things have happened too. Though I am sick with worry for Caius."

For her part, Silvan talked to Elodia about her ordeal, starting with her clan fleeing their land north of the river when the Huns attacked. At first, her voice quavered with emotion, but as the thread of her tale began to unspool, she spoke more confidently, sharing her ordeal with her new friend. When she recounted the death of her brother and friends, she wept. The mention, even the thought, of Jellena made Silvan shake with grief. They had been friends and confidantes since childhood. Her death in a matter of seconds still seemed unreal. "I wake every morning expecting to see her nearby. 'Where is she?' I wonder. Until I remember."

Finally, Nedarcus came and reported that Arbrun had awoken. Silvan and another man from their clan walked him back to her tent.

Over the next several days, there were no more foolish attempts to storm the fortress. With so little fighting, their medicine tent emptied of patients, and Elodia looked for ways to keep busy. She started to visit the tent Silvan shared with Arbrun, as much to keep her company as to check his wound.

Silvan was always relieved to see Elodia. Arbrun was not an easy patient, she said. He found his new status as an invalid unbearable. Somehow in his mind, he decided he could blame her for his condition. His demands on her were endless. She told Elodia their clan chieftain was no longer pressing her to satisfy Arbrun's "manly needs." Perhaps no one expected a severely wounded man to have such needs, or maybe the clan chieftain was less concerned for a man who was now an invalid, not a useful warrior.

Within a few days, Arbrun was out of danger, health-wise, but still demanded care from Silvan. When he began to demand bumping, she'd had enough. She tried unsuccessfully to get a tent of her own, a small tent like Elodia's. Nedarcus had requested a tent for Elodia when they first arrived in Sexaginta Prista. Fritigern's regard for the medicus was such that he was granted any reasonable request.

Silvan was less fortunate. Pointing to Elodia's tent, she'd asked Bandar for one just like it. The clan chieftain just sneered, saying she'd done nothing to deserve it.

Early one morning, while Elodia was asleep in her own tent, Silvan came and begged to be allowed to stay. While they'd only known each other for less than a week, Elodia felt they had created a strong bond. Silvan was her friend. She had no others. Although it was a small tent, Elodia agreed.

Silvan came with nothing but her clothes and a knife. Such bedding as she'd shared with Arbrun, she left with him. Elodia acquired blankets for her from the medical cart, explaining to Nedarcus that Silvan would pay for them by caring for their patients. Elodia also got her a change of smallclothes, which Silvan would need during her monthly bleeding.

As it turned out, Silvan never needed them. Indeed, she was pregnant.

Fritigern frequently visited the medicine tent to check on the
wounded and to "ask after my newest slave, Elodia." His visits
started after the abortive assault on Sexaginta Prista. Though he
claimed to be visiting the wounded, Nedarcus said this was never
his practice before she joined his team. Even when the medicine tent
became empty, Fritigern continued visiting, especially around
dinner. They knew he planned to come because he'd first send over
one of his men in the early afternoon with enough meat, flour, and
beer to feed them, him, and his bodyguards.

It was fortunate that Silvan was an accomplished cook because
if it were left to Elodia, they'd be eating burned meat chunks on a
stick. The additional victuals were welcome. Although people were
no longer starving, no one was getting fat except perhaps the leaders
and their favorites. Fritigern's people always had plenty to eat.

After eating, they entertained themselves by singing, dancing,
and drinking. When Fritigern sang, everyone else was obliged to
sing. Or try to. He had a pleasant voice, unlike many of his men. He
claimed Elodia had a fine voice, so he insisted they sing many songs
together, just the two. During these duets, the others were told to
keep quiet.

Elodia enjoyed singing the songs of her people again. She had
not heard them for years, not since leaving her father's village.
There were war songs praising the heroes of old, love songs, both
tragic and cheery, and songs of foolish people making trouble for
themselves. When they ran out of Gothic songs, the warriors would
ask her to sing a Roman song, one of the many songs she learned
while living on the river with Caius and the other frontier guards.
Those songs were generally bawdy, which delighted Fritigern's
men.

Elodia sang an old song, a tale of Beauty, Fire, and War, in which the passionate and erotic Goddess of Beauty was unhappily married to the God of Fire, an ugly cripple. He suspected, correctly, that his wife was having an affair with the strong and handsome God of War. The song told how Fire fashioned an unbreakable net of the finest gold. With this, he trapped Beauty and War in the act of love. Still naked and entwined, he summoned all the other gods to watch their humiliation. The gods' laughter could be heard throughout the world.

Fritigern enjoyed the song so much he requested that Elodia sing it again.

Besides being an excellent cook, Silvan was an accomplished musician. She could play the flute, and when a warrior provided a lute and an aulos, looted from some estate, Silvan mastered them quickly. Perhaps she didn't play well enough for the emperor's court in Constantinople, but she was good enough for a party of Goths sitting around a campfire. Once a dance got going with Silvan on the flute, all the warriors kept time, banging on war drums or clapping their hands. All the children in the camp would join in, dancing around the fire while hooting and hollering. Their fathers, uncles, and other warriors would come, forming chains with everyone holding hands and all singing or chanting the words to each song while stamping their feet. Some songs had well-known steps, with the participants kicking, squatting, and twirling in unison. The children seemed to have bottomless energy, but the adults would grow tired and need to sit and drink. And drink! Silvan and Elodia would often hold hands and join in the dances. They got drunk more than a few times.

One evening Fritigern and Nedarcus sat talking with Silvan and Elodia. Fritigern said the camp would be breaking up soon. "There's nothing to be done here. We cannot take the fortress, and we cannot all stay together here. We have foraged this area to exhaustion. We need to spread out toward less ravaged pastures." Turning to Elodia, he asked, "What will you do, Elodia?"

The question astonished her. He was asking her as if she had ownership and control of her own person. *I am your property, yours to command.* But, in response to his question, she had no ready answer. She had no family and no clan to support her. Unlike Silvan, she had few practical skills other than those she learned from Nedarcus, such as attempting to keep wounded warriors alive. She was a skilled archer, which, for a woman, was not considered a practical skill.

"I will stay with Nedarcus if he will have me."

Nedarcus answered immediately, saying he would. She exhaled and relaxed. She had been holding her breath. "What about Silvan?" she asked.

"She, too, will be staying with me," Nedarcus said. "With the medical cart," he quickly amended. "She and I have already spoken."

Elodia understood. Nedarcus, the medicus, needed Silvan's hands and expertise. Nedarcus, the man, needed Silvan's company.

Elodia and Silvan smiled at each other. As a new dance started, she held her hand out to Silvan, and they joined the dance line. The two men joined them in a minute, with Fritigern taking Elodia's other hand and Nedarcus holding Silvan's. Nedarcus was partially crippled, so he did not dance well and quickly grew tired. When he left the line, Silvan left too. "After Nedarcus has rested, we will rejoin the dance," she said.

Or not. Elodia felt cheerful, watching them go off, just beyond the firelight, sharing a bottle.

232

Usually, when someone left the line, it would reform with the empty hands relinking. But that night, Fritigern turned and took her other hand in his. They formed a chain of two as they danced facing each other. As the evening progressed, they continued to dance but drew closer.

They were almost touching when she looked up and saw him peering steadily into her eyes. She would have dropped her gaze if she was a proper young virgin, but she was not and did not. She returned his steady look with her own.

By and by, the fire died down. People retired to their tents. Elodia looked around for Silvan and Nedarcus. Who had left. So, they did too.

In the morning, she pulled on her clothes and left Fritigern's tent. He'd already gone without waking her.

Caius. Her eyes turned red and hot. She wiped away a tear. *Dismiss him. He's gone forever.*

Fritigern. He was a good and powerful lord. He treated her well. She should pray and thank the gods for bringing them together. He was the gods' gift to her, recompense for Caius's death. Weeping over Caius would show ingratitude to the gods. It would only tempt them into ruining her life again.

She made her way back to her tent. Silvan was not there, nor was there any sign that she'd slept there. Elodia lay kindling for a fire and visited a neighbor's cookfire to borrow an ember. The neighbors bid her good morning but provided little other conversation. They were busy taking their tent down and packing. They said the order had come. The camp would break up that day.

Starting her own fire, Elodia had just finished cooking porridge for breakfast when Silvan showed up. She seemed radiant but said nothing about her night's activities, and Elodia didn't ask. Silvan had also heard the orders and said they should start packing after breakfast.

Elodia dished Silvan a good portion of porridge. Silvan took one bite, turned green, stood, and lurched away from the campfire. A nearby bush was the beneficiary of her vomit. Elodia brought her a cup of beer. She took a large swig, rinsed her mouth, and spat. After returning to the campfire, she squatted and went back to work on her porridge. A few mouthfuls later, Elodia caught her eye. Silvan shrugged and smiled. "I'd hoped Arbrun was out of my life. But it looks like he's left me with a keepsake." Then she returned to her porridge.

They packed their tent and other possessions and added them to the medical cart. Elodia harnessed the mule and, when Silvan and Nedarcus were ready, led the way to where the command tent had stood. Soon Fritigern's group headed west along the river to Nicopolis Ad Istrum.

Traianus [Roman comes rei militaris] invited [Papas, king of Armenia] with great respect to a luncheon. The king came, fearing no hostility, and took his place in the seat of honor granted him.

And when choice dainties were set before him, and the great building rang with the music of strings, songs, and wind instruments, the host himself, already heated with wine, went out, under pretense of a call of nature. Then a rude barbarian, fiercely glaring with savage eyes and brandishing a drawn sword, one of the class called scurrae [scimitar], was sent in to kill the young man, who had already been cut off from any possibility of escape.

At this sight the young king, who, as it happened, was leaning forward beyond his couch, drew his dagger and was rising to defend his life by every possible means, but fell disfigured, pierced through the breast like some victim at the altar, foully slain by repeated strokes.

By such treachery was credulity basely deceived, and at a banquet, which ought to be respected even on the Euxine [Black] Sea.

From Res Gestae, Volume XXX 1.19-22, by Ammianus Marcellinus

A ny sliver of hope Fritigern had of restoring peace with the Romans vanished when the emperor appointed the perfidious Magister Peditum Traianus to crush him and his Goths.

Messengers brought the news of the disaster outside Marcianople to Constantinople within a day and to the emperor in Antioch within a month. Upon his orders, reinforcing legions began to move west from Asia Minor toward Europe. The first to arrive, legions and cavalry from Armenia, came by ship across the Black Sea and disembarked at Constantinople and Dibaltum. Leading them was Traianus, who was subordinate only to the emperor. This general was infamous for having invited the king of Armenia to dinner and then, treacherously, having him killed.

Traianus took control of the local troops, including the scraps that remained of Bitorix's legion, including Grainus's squad. Bitorix was demoted from military tribune to centurion. He claimed this was due to politics in Galatia province, saying, "Traianus mocks all members of the Galatian royalty, like me." Caius doubted whether the emperor's court in Constantinople was even aware of the long-defunct Galatian royal line. He suspected the demotion was due to Bitorix emerging unscathed from the battle of Marcianople, the only tribune to do so.

By early March, the Romans were ready to push the Goths back. They were still vastly outnumbered by the Goths, who were now scattered across Moesia and Thracia. To avoid a repeat of the earlier disaster, Traianus adopted a new strategy: terror. He would deploy his cavalry widely across the land, slaughtering any Goths encountered. Any but not all. The horsemen always ensured enough Goths survived to spread terror back to their tribesmen. If the cavalry encountered a knot of Goths who resisted strongly, they would pass the word to the legions who would march to the site and massacre everyone, absolutely everyone. Rumor had it that

Traianus would reward the soldiers with a gold coin for each Gothic skull produced, just as the master of infantry did a decade earlier during another war with the Goths. In the end, many skulls were produced, but no gold coins were forthcoming.

Soon Roman scouts reported seeing long trains of Gothic carts, loaded with loot, retreating north and east along all possible roads. The Roman generals speculated: would the Goths move back across the river at its delta, or would they stand and fight?

Sueridus and Colias, Gothic chieftains, who had long since been received [by the Romans as auxiliary troops] with their peoples and assigned to keep winter quarters at Adrianople, considering their own welfare the most important thing of all, looked with indifference on all that took place. But when on a sudden a letter came from the emperor, in which they were ordered to cross to Hellespontus [into Asia Minor], without any arrogance they asked for money for the journey, food, and a postponement of two days.

From Res Gestae, Volume XXXI 6.1-2

by Ammianus Marcellinus

The distance from Sexaginta Prista to Nicopolis Ad Istrum was just a long day's walk. Elodia led the mule pulling the medical cart, while Silvan and Nedarcus walked ahead, chatting quietly.

Elodia couldn't hear what the new lovers said, which was fine. Her mind was busy, filled with thoughts of Fritigern.

Life was so hard now. The nights were cold, and it was miserable being separated from the one you love. People should be forgiven for seeking comfort. *Would Caius forgive her?* That night with Fritigern meant nothing special. But she did find warmth and comfort. And pleasure. Surely, were Caius alive, he would not deny her that. Jesus God, please make him welcome in your Christian heaven.

Fritigern had not suggested there was anything special about taking her to his tent. They both found a balm that could only be met by deep sleep, wrapped in another's warm limbs. And a long bump. Probably in the other order. Better still, in both orders. Would this happen again? Possibly. Probably. Hopefully. But perhaps not.

Silvan stopped several times when her baby made her vomit. When that happened, Nedarcus was very attentive, more lover than medicus. Clearly, he knew she was carrying another man's child but did not seem to care. He was much older than her. Elodia knew he had three grown children. She'd met his two sons, members of Fritigern's bodyguard. What would they think of their father taking a young—younger than her—pregnant woman as a lover? Elodia hoped they would be generous.

Fritigern told her he had a woman. He never said who she was or where, but Elodia doubted the other would want to share him. Until that happened, she could fill her time thinking about, perhaps anticipating, what another night with Fritigern might be like. She wished it would be a long time before she encountered his woman. Such were her thoughts as she walked and led the mule cart.

It was late when they arrived in Nicopolis Ad Istrum. For a change, they did not find the city's gates locked against them. A company of young Goths had rushed the city just before word arrived of the Roman defeat at Marcianople. Since the locals did not know war had erupted, the gates were open. The company slew the garrison and secured the city to prevent a counter-coup.

This success turned out to be enormously important. The city contained several large storehouses, which the Romans kept stocked with all the supplies needed by their Danube forts and guard ships. Just as important, the Romans had gathered all the crops after the last harvest from this region of Moesia. Fritigern claimed the ever-looming threat of starvation had been pushed back for months, at least until the current year's crops were ripe. He did not realize there would be no crops this year. With war raging, no crops would be planted.

The Goths threw the rich out of their elegant villas to make room for themselves. Fritigern took the home of the duumvir, the city mayor. It was spacious and beautiful. The walls were covered in frescoes depicting scenes from Greek mythology. The central atrium had a deep pool. Its bottom was covered by a brilliant mosaic featuring Apollo bringing dawn to the world. The ceiling, supported by aisles of Corinthian columns, was painted cerulean blue and featured nymphs and satyrs at play in a stream. Fritigern provided a large room that, he told Elodia, was for the two of them. *That answers* that *question.*

Another large room was set aside for the leadership cadre. Fritigern had a large table installed with a map of the Balkans carved into it, a map showing the cities, rivers, mountains, and roads.

After a night's rest, the cadre, now led by Fritigern, met to discuss strategy. Many clan leaders were present, but many more were out foraging with their people. Elodia watched from a distance, sitting on a marble bench beneath the colonnade. She had no expertise in strategy, nor would the gathered clan leaders tolerate advice from a woman, especially one who shared Fritigern's bed. Her role in preventing a massacre of the Gothic chieftains was forgotten.

Fritigern began. "The Romans have suffered a setback. For them, it is a minor setback. While we can now range freely over Moesia and Thracia, it won't last. We have a limited period to prepare for the Romans' return. Which they will do. They will come in great force."

He continued, "We know Emperor Valens plans to wage war on the Sassanids in Syria. We can hope it has already started. The longer he is embroiled in the east, the longer our breathing space. Otherwise, I imagine the emperor is already ordering troops here from Asia Minor. I would not be surprised to hear he himself is on his way to Constantinople from Antioch.

"And we must deal with his nephew, Emperor Gratian, in the west. He will work with Valens. Legions from both east and west will attack us. How soon? We don't know. But being nearer to us, the western legions will arrive sooner. The question for this group is how best to use the breathing space we have. Our future, our survival, and the survival of the Tervingi Goths as a nation depends on it.

"Knowing all that, I am eager to hear your ideas. What advice can you give me?"

Elodia smiled. *That's the right question! Seize the leadership!*

King Alavivus had been acknowledged as the Tervingi Goths' king, but he was dead. As she'd suggested, Fritigern was moving to become the new king. If he was accepted, then he could demand that all clans follow him.

240

Several voices spoke up immediately, but Rodericus, now clan chieftain of the Dondori and one of Fritigern's advisors, spoke loudest. Since he and she met outside Abritus, she had not encountered him until today. On entering the room, he'd passed without speaking, but he acknowledged her with a smug smile. Hearing Rodericus's loud voice, Fritigern called out, indicating he should be allowed to speak.

"I know the Romans," Rodericus said. "Their soldiers are well armed, well trained, and well led."

He added, "Well led but not perfectly led. Every army has a Lupicinus or two!" That raised a cheer.

Someone toasted, "May they have three or four more!"

Rodericus went on. "We fought the Romans in open combat ten years ago. We lost. Our warriors were bigger, stronger, and braver, but they died just as easily. I cannot suggest what we should do, but I know what we should not do. If we go head-to-head with the legions, we will lose unless we can overwhelm them with our numbers as we did outside of Marcianople."

When Rodericus stopped, others called to be heard. The next leader acknowledged by Fritigern was one named Pondorian. He said, "If we cannot defend ourselves in the open, then we must do it from behind walls. Our folk here in Nicopolis are safe, those lucky enough to be here. We need to move across the two provinces and take all the cities we can. We need to conquer until we have shelter for every Goth. Remember that every city taken is a treasure. Each comes with food, weapons, and gold."

Elodia did not know Pondorian or anything about him. Now she knew him to be a fool. Nicopolis was not an example of what they should do. It was an exception. Taking it had been a bold move aided by luck. Taking a city required a siege. Sieges took time, equipment, and experience. The Goths had none of these, especially time. Any city that might fall quickly to them would fall even faster to the Romans when they returned in force. The Romans had advanced siege engines. The Goths' most advanced tool was the ladder.

Yet heads around the table were nodding to Pondorian's words. Even Fritigern seemed to agree. She realized then that none of these men really understood the scope of the Roman Empire, its physical size, or the resources at its disposal. Caius had talked about the empire during those long nights when they sat by the campfire and watched the river. He described an empire with a half million men under arms, a number she had trouble visualizing. She knew Fritigern could only create a Gothic army one-tenth that size, even if he could unite all the clans. As she listened to the clan leaders shout and argue, an all-clan army seemed unlikely.

Fritigern lost control of the meeting when Pondorian regained the floor and demanded they support the regiment led by Sueridus and Colias who were busy besieging Adrianople City.

This Gotho-Roman regiment had faithfully served the empire for generations. Now Valens doubted its loyalty, without any evidence linking it to the Gothic invasion. It was serving as the garrison troop of Adrianople when he precipitously ordered it to move to Asia Minor.

The city's residents, echoing their emperor's suspicions, had rioted, forcing the regiment out of the city. Some soldiers, who'd been caught when the gates closed, were killed, and their heads flung down among their comrades, who were milling about outside. And so, the siege began.

For the sake of justice and Gothic pride, Pondorian said the clans were honor-bound to support their ethnic brothers' siege. And

242

Adrianople, he pointed out, would provide a safe shelter for thousands of Goths. "To Adrianople. To Adrianople," he chanted.

Soon the chant was taken up by a few more clan leaders. It spread until the entire cadre was chanting and shouting. Finally, Fritigern waved and called for quiet. He asked the gathering if anyone opposed besieging Adrianople. Only one person present considered the idea foolish, and that person, a slave girl sitting on a marble bench beneath the colonnade, was not permitted to speak.

That night, in bed with Fritigern, Elodia risked telling him her misgivings. She said Pondorian was a fool. She repeated her earlier opinion that sieges take experience, equipment, and time, of which the Goths have none, especially... She was about to say "time" when Fritigern told her to hush.

"Do not talk, girl. You know nothing about warfare," he said. She felt humiliated and angry. They bumped without pleasure. For the first time, she wondered whether he was truly a gift from the gods to her.

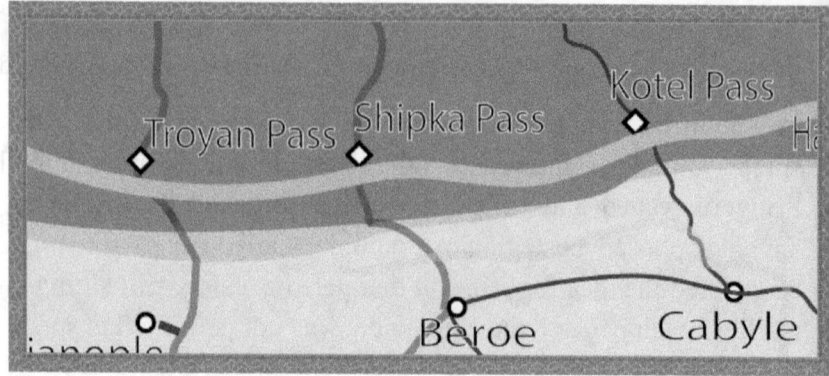

9. Elodia's Arrows
377 CE

*F**ritigern beleaguered the city [Adrianople], visiting it with all the horrors of a siege. Remaining in this difficult situation for some time, they made scattered and promiscuous attacks; the conspicuous audacity of some perished unavenged, and many lost their lives from arrows or from stones whirled from slings. Then Fritigern, seeing that his men, being inexperienced in conducting a siege, were carrying on the struggle with such loss of life, left a sufficient force there and persuaded the rest to go away without finishing the task...*

From Res Gestae, Volume XXXI 6.3-4, by Ammianus Marcellinus

It took almost a week to take the medical cart south to Adrianople. The challenging part of the trip was crossing over the Haemus mountains on Shipka Pass. The track was frozen, and many warriors were willing to push the mule cart over steep stretches. Elodia could only imagine how difficult it would be in a few weeks when the track turned to slush. After traversing the pass, their journey took them south to the Via Militaris, which they followed to Adrianople.

At Adrianople, the road continued southeast to the capital city. The land was flat and forested along the road, broken only by the occasional village and farm. Many had been ravaged and burned earlier by passing Goths. The untouched villages looked impoverished, too poor to pillage.

As usual, Elodia led the mule while Nedarcus and Silvan walked. On the rare occasions when she was sick, she rode. They were accompanied by a group of seven warriors tasked with guarding them, men who resented that assignment while all their comrades had rushed ahead to the siege. Nedarcus said drily there was no point in arriving at Adrianople before some young fools got themselves damaged.

During that week, Elodia did not see Fritigern. He had ridden ahead. Even when they arrived, Fritigern did not acknowledge her. Some evenings she would see Bron, Fritigern's body servant, come by her tent. She hoped he would stop and deliver a summons from Fritigern that he wanted her company. But Bron would walk by, offering her only a nod. *The man can certainly hold a grudge.*

When they arrived, the Gothic legionaries had already attempted two ladder assaults.

It broke Elodia's heart to see all the losses from arrows, falls from scaling ladders, and crushed skulls. The walls were high. Those who fell invariably died or broke bones. Nedarcus taught

Elodia to set bones. The handicapped were loaded into carts, carts purloined from nearby estates, and sent back north. Those with compound fractures usually died on the way.

Most of the other injured had suffered arrows or crossbow wounds. Quickly learning the medicus art, Silvan became adept at patching them up. They, too, were sent back north.

After the third assault failed, Fritigern gave up. Without siege engines and expecting an imminent Roman counterattack by Traianus, the attempt to capture Adrianople was costly, dangerous, and pointless. Fritigern did receive some benefits; there were arms factories outside the city waiting to be plundered. Finally, after so many months, all his warriors were equipped with swords and spears.

Fritigern announced he and his warriors were heading northwest, back up the Via Militaris, to support the Goths who were besieging Philippopolis City. He had received a message saying its defenses were in disrepair, and if only the current besiegers had Fritigern's support, the city must soon fall.

Silvan was grieving. Arbrun's arm had re-broken a week earlier, and the wound reopened. It became infected, and he had just died. While Silvan wept, Nedarcus sat beside her, trying to comfort her. She said she had not wanted to marry Arbrun, but she still harbored feelings toward him, that he was the father of her unborn child and was her last link to their peaceful life in Scythia before the Huns arrived.

Her sorrow made Elodia angry. Like all the new casualties from the pointless siege of Adrianople, his death had been a waste. *That fool Pondorian was wrong.*

Before Fritigern left, he came by the medicine tent where Nedarcus, Silvan, and Elodia were talking.

Despite it not being her place to vent, Elodia did.

"Arbrun has died," she said to Fritigern.

"Arbrun?" said Fritigern, looking puzzled.

"Silvan's brother-in-law!"

"Oh, right," he said dismissively.

His tone angered Elodia even more. "He died in a stupid venture for which your men had neither the equipment nor the training. They had no plan except to mindlessly attack."

Fritigern threw up his hands as if to disavow the failed assaults. "These ladder attacks began before I got here."

"You could have stopped them. You could have devised a real plan, one that would have succeeded with fewer deaths," Elodia retorted angrily. Tears began to stream down her face.

Fritigern tensed. "These warriors are Goths, not Romans. They will not sit still for training. They want to attack. If I am not aggressive, they will find a leader who is!"

His anger erupted. He raised a fist to her face. She knew better than to respond. She cowered and cast her eyes down, hoping it would placate him. "You will not criticize me, especially in public! I told you before; you know nothing about warfare. You know nothing about anything!"

Silence filled the tent for several minutes. When Fritigern had controlled his breathing, he said, "I came here to give you orders.

"I will lead my men to Philippopolis. Nedarcus, you take the medical cart back the way you came, north to Nicopolis Ad Istrum, and wait for me there. You will have the same guards. Silvan will go with you." Then he turned and looked at Elodia.

"And you too," he said. "I do not need you dogging my heels. You will stay with Nedarcus if he will have you. Just do not forget who owns you."

His words stung. Was she just an ordinary slave? She decided her criticism galled him: he could not listen to a girl. A slave.

Nedarcus instructed Silvan and Elodia to reload the medical cart with their tent, cots, and remaining bandages and splints. She harnessed the mule, and they began the long trip back northwest to Nicopolis Ad Istrum. The same small group of guards accompanied them, but its count was now reduced to four. One of the seven original guards had fallen with a crossbow bolt through his brain. The other two guards had suffered broken legs when their scaling ladder fell. Rather than guarding the medical cart, they were riding in it. Silvan had stopped vomiting. She and the mule had become friends, so she took her turn leading it. Elodia walked along in the rear. Despondent.

As Nedarcus, the medical cart, and its entourage made their way north, no one suspected the Romans were close on their heels.

The trail back over Shipka Pass to Nicopolis Ad Istrum was a sea of mud, just as Elodia had foreseen. Spring was mud season. The melted snow collected on the road, waiting to be churned into mud by each passing horse, cart, or warrior. The resulting muck did not seem to drain. It stood stubbornly, slowing the medical cart and making life miserable.

Fritigern's warriors had long since marched past them, leaving them alone in the rear, unguarded except for their little, and now dedicated, guard detail. There was no sign of the long-expected Roman counterattack. Not until they reached Shipka Pass.

The muddy road was relatively flat from Adrianople to Beroe City. After Beroe, it started climbing the hills. In the hills, they went from trudging through stagnant water to slogging through a torrent of cold muck. As the road grew steeper, they climbed a series of switchbacks. Nedarcus and Elodia stood behind the cart, pushing. Silvan was ahead, leading the mule. The guards had gone on to check the road condition.

They reached a point on the hillside where they could see down the way they'd come. A wounded warrior lying in the back of the wagon suddenly called out, "Romans!" Elodia peered over the edge, down past several switchback bends. Far below was a squad of seven legionaries making double time, hot on their trail. Though it was her first glimpse of them, they had obviously seen Nedarcus's little party. Elodia watched as the distance quickly closed, made easier for the Romans because they were not encumbered by a heavily laden cart pulled by a tired mule.

Where are our guards? "Andagis!" Elodia shouted, looking up the hill for the guards' leader.

"Coming!" he answered just before she saw his feet, sliding on the dirty muck, go out from under him. He fell flat on his back, taking down a second guard as he tumbled. The other two guards stopped to help their comrades, which initiated another round of all four warriors going down in the mud.

"Hurry!" she urged. In these conditions to go fast, it was best to go slow. Would the guards reach them before the Romans? Yes, but it was close. Since the wounded could not be moved, they would have to make a stand by the cart.

"Silvan!" called Elodia. Her friend was standing beside the mule, frozen in terror. "Quickly! Unharness the mule and take it up the hill! Hitch it to a tree or something!" Elodia was less concerned with the mule than with her pregnant friend. When the fight came, Silvan was useless except as a target.

With Silvan's shaking hands and frozen fingers, it took her endless time to unhook the mule. Then, with soft coaxing words, she led the animal up the road, past where the mud-covered guards were on their feet again and lashed the reins to a shrub. Silvan turned to look down as a skirmish was unfolding.

Elodia chocked the cart's wheels so it couldn't roll back down the hill. The two wounded warriors each grabbed a spear and staggered out of the cart. For them, the spears served more as crutches than weapons. The Romans came around the last bend and headed toward them with swords drawn. They, too, struggled through the mud. One short legionary stopped to pull his shield off his back. Lifting it, his feet slipped sideways. He landed on his back, sending up a great splash of dirty water.

The Romans could see the Goths were disorganized. Their guards were still rushing downhill. The two men with leg wounds were leaning on their spears and propped up against the cart. To the Romans, the two women and the unarmed gray-haired man must have appeared harmless. With so little opposition, the legionaries did not bother getting into formation. They simply charged.

The four Gothic guards drew their swords. Inching their way through the mud, they moved around the cart, using it to steady themselves. Without further mishap, two guards stood on either side of the cart next to the wounded men. Elodia moved gingerly, her feet slipping to the front of the cart. She grabbed a side rail and hefted herself into its bed. There, under the driver's bench, was her bow, wrapped in a tarred cloth to keep it dry.

She risked a glance down the road. The first of the legionaries were almost upon them. Not panicking, she carefully unwrapped the bow. Mercifully, the string was dry. She strung the bow and pulled off a small tarpaulin that covered her quiver. A surge of excitement passed through her. Moving quickly, she selected an arrow and nocked it. She turned to face the enemy. The odds were unfavorable, with seven legionaries against her four able-bodied warriors, but there were two things in their favor. First, the Romans were fighting uphill, and second, they were standing in a shallow river of mud while weighed down with shields and armor.

Taking her time to aim, she shot an arrow through the chest of the leading legionary. He fell in a cartwheel, knocking down another legionary. *That improves the odds.* She bent to fetch another arrow from her quiver. Stand. Nock. Pull. Pause. Aim. She watched as the next legionary struggled back to his feet. *Good. Lying down, he'd be tough to hit.* Once erect, he turned to face her and began approaching. *A perfect target.* Her arrow penetrated his armor and came to rest deep inside his chest. It was still quivering when he toppled over.

Things moved quickly now. She made her third arrow ready and released it. Its victim was a legionary who had finally reached the cart. The legionary died quickly, with a shaft through his eye, but not quickly enough to stop his blade thrust. He toppled backward as his sword punctured the belly of a wounded guard. The guard released his useless spear and sank to the ground.

Now the odds were even. Elodia's fourth shot was off, striking a giant legionary in the shoulder. She'd been aiming for his neck. He fell to his knees in the mud. He pulled off his helmet and pulled the arrow out of his shoulder. It must have barely penetrated. Perhaps it had deflected off his chest plate? When the arrow came free, his shoulder spouted blood. The legionary collapsed face-first in the mud.

His companion, the one who had initially slipped in the mud, caught up, rolled his companion onto his back, and, in a herculean effort, lifted the wounded man, threw him over his shoulder, and staggered back down the road. If the wounded man cried out, she didn't hear it. Her ears were full of the screams of their crippled guard, who was busy pulling the dead legionary's sword out of his stomach.

This left just two legionaries facing the four able-bodied guards. When they realized they were now outnumbered, they turned and ran. All four legionaries would have been easy targets until they were out of range. But Elodia was too stunned to nock another arrow.

She recognized the soldier she had wounded and the soldier who carried him off. They were Caius and Grainus. Through the intervention of some benevolent god, she had failed to kill her own lover.

Pandemonium erupted. Later, Elodia would confess to yelling hysterically. She was joined by a screaming warrior. He lay on the ground with the legionary's sword beside him. The sword lay in a growing pool of blood and was wreathed in a thick blue rope, his guts. His leg splint, intended to protect his earlier injury, broke when he fell, allowing his lower leg to project from his knee at a horribly wrong angle.

Nedarcus came from behind. As he passed her, he stopped, gripped her shoulders, and shook her until she shut up. She did her best to regain her composure and explain that she'd just shot and maybe killed her lover. The medicus shook his head and silently moved on toward the dying warrior.

Had he not heard what she was saying? Or perhaps he thought she was going crazy? He didn't seem to care so long as she stopped yelling. She stopped.

Kneeling by the dying warrior, Nedarcus held his hand. The warrior stopped screaming. In a raspy whisper, he spoke to Nedarcus, who spoke quietly in return. She couldn't hear what they were saying, but she'd witnessed this conversation in the past. After several exchanges, the warrior finally nodded and looked up at the sky. Nedarcus drew a knife from his belt. He opened the man's throat in one fast, firm motion. She saluted and said a silent prayer to Odin, asking that the young man be guided directly to the warriors' feasting hall.

When his comrade's suffering was ended, Andagis worked quickly to get their little party moving again. Silvan retrieved the mule and harnessed it. Two other guards helped the surviving lame warrior back into the cart. The fourth guard approached her and earnestly congratulated her on her kills.

As the other guards finished their jobs, everyone gathered around, offering praise and thanks for her fine shooting. She tried explaining about Caius and Grainus, but no one seemed to hear or believe her claims. Her voice rose. She felt herself getting hysterical. In as calm a voice as she could muster, she insisted she must go back and find Caius.

Andagis refused. He told Silvan to start leading the mule up the road. Nedarcus took Elodia's hands in his. He explained she was in shock from having killed so quickly and effortlessly. That he'd seen that reaction previously when warriors killed for the first time. Neither her avowal that she'd killed men before nor any other argument swayed him. The cart was moving uphill, and she was not permitted to go down.

One of the guards pointed out that if she could overtake the legionaries, they would surely kill her. "They would recognize you as the archer who slaughtered their companions." Even if the Romans believed she was Caius's lover, they would kill her anyway. She realized that was true, stopped arguing, and followed along numbly.

They continued their struggle up the pass, always looking downhill, fearing a return of the Romans. After a half hour, they heard men and horses coming down from above. A few minutes of worry were followed by great relief. It was a patrol of Goths sent to help them. They said Fritigern had noticed their absence and sent them an escort.

It was well after midnight before they emerged from the north end of the pass. Fritigern had organized a campsite along the Etar River for the several thousand Goths lately arrived from the Adrianople siege. One of their new escorts guided them to a spot not far from the river, where they unloaded the medical cart and erected the tent.

Nedarcus suggested they bathe before sleeping. It was a good idea in principle, they were covered in mud, but the river was freezing cold. He persuaded Silvan, so the two headed off by torchlight, but Elodia was spent.

She laid out her sleeping blankets in her tent when Bron came and informed her Fritigern wanted to see her. Though weary, she had no choice but to follow.

Bron pulled aside the outer tent flap, allowing her to enter the tent's council room. As she stood there, he left, and Fritigern opened the inner flap.

"I heard what happened on the pass today," he said. "The whole camp has heard. You must be exhausted."

His demeanor was kindly, as though their past arguments were now forgotten. It was the end of a very long day. The time was not right for apologies. They both seemed ready to ignore their fight and move on.

She was too tired to say anything, so she just nodded.

"And, as I expected," Fritigern said, looking her up and down, "you are extremely dirty. I've had my slaves prepare this for you."

He stood aside to reveal a large bronze tub. Steam rose from it. Nearby stood several waist-high jugs, all steaming. If there was anything she wanted more but expected less, other than a reconciliation with Fritigern, it was a hot bath. She still couldn't speak but stumbled into the tent's private room, moving toward the tub. Fritigern grasped her arm to steady her. She reached up and put her arms around his neck. He pulled her to him. After a short embrace, she kissed his mouth and gasped, "You're standing between me and my tub!"

She kicked off her sandals and, leaning on Fritigern, stepped into the bath. Within seconds she had stripped and was squatting in hot water. "I'm sorry it's not hotter," he said, "but I wasn't sure when you'd arrive."

She gasped as the sizzling water soaked her frozen limbs. "It is glorious." A slave came in to carry away her soiled clothes. When she left, another came in to scrub her. The slave poured hot water over her head, vigorously rubbed all her exposed skin with a rough cloth, and then poured on more water to rinse her off. The slave wrapped a clean towel around her when she stood and helped her out of the tub.

Though it was not luxurious, complete with lotions and unguents like her Roman bath, it was the perfect bath to end a horrific day. While she was bathing, Fritigern lay on his cot, head propped up on one elbow, watching.

The slave rubbed her dry and then swapped the towel for one of Fritigern's clean tunics. It came down to her ankles. She sat beside him on the cot. The first slave returned with her newly washed clothes and hung them from a line to dry in the outer tent. When they were alone, he said, "Will you sleep with me?" He indicated his pile of rugs and blankets in the tent's corner.

The second slave returned with a tray of bread, cheese, sweets, and beer. She helped herself to a small bowl of honeyed apple cake drowning in thick cream and a mug of warm beer. She ate quietly but greedily while she tried to consider his question. But her thoughts kept returning to the day's events. She kept picturing a man with an arrow through his neck, unable to cry out, blood gushing from his mouth.

"I shot my Roman lover today. Maybe killed him," she answered. A non-sequitur, but it did not seem to puzzle him.

"I heard you killed a half-dozen Romans today."

"Only three. Plus, perhaps, my lover."

"So you say. But I doubt it."

"You think I don't know what my lover looks like?" She couldn't help being miffed.

"I think from the moment you strung your bow, you worried one of those soldiers might be him. When you saw three men die by your hand, you convinced yourself the fourth was your Caius. You are an excellent archer, so your fear caused you to pull your shot."

She sat quietly beside him. Surprisingly, Fritigern remembered Caius's name. Was he right? She'd seen men lose it after killing someone. Vomit. Nightmares. The trauma of fighting affected people in different ways. Killing had never bothered her before. Maybe this was different. Maybe after killing three, she *was* shaken? How could she tell? "Perhaps you're right. I don't know. I *believe* he was Caius. He was gigantic, like Caius. And his comrade, the short, stocky one who carried him off, looked like Grainus."

"How likely is it that of the thousands of Romans in Thracia, the ones who came after you included those two men?"

She shrugged. "Not likely," she agreed. She leaned into him. They kissed. She put her arms around him, and they kissed again.

"What happened at Philippopolis?" she asked.

"Impregnable walls and too few of us to mount an assault. We didn't even try. That's why I'm here before you."

Perhaps her opinion about ladder attacks had sunk in. Fritigern seemed to have forgotten that he had raised his fist in anger when they parted in Adrianople. She would forget it too.

"You don't have to sleep with me," he allowed. "You can sleep here on this cot if you'd rather."

But cots were cold and uncomfortable. Elodia walked over to his bed, lay down, and pulled up a bearskin rug. He joined her, and they huddled together against the cold. She pressed her back into his chest while he wrapped an arm around her. He caressed her, and she began to respond. But the long day's events intervened, and she fell into a troubled sleep. So much killing…

She was awoken by the sounds of the camp being broken down. They were on the move again. Fritigern was already up and gone. There was a tray left with her breakfast. She ate, then entered the tent's outer room, looking for her clothes. They were still on a line, slightly damp.

As she felt them, Fritigern entered from outside. He smiled. "You're up, I see." She nodded. He came to her, and they quietly embraced.

Seeing her touch her garments, he said, "And your clothes?" He felt them and summoned a slave. "Dry them over a fire. Don't scorch them, and keep them out of the smoke," he ordered.

"You cried out in the night," he said.

She shrugged. "I have no memory of it. I remember nothing from when my head hit the pillow until now. I slept the sleep of the dead."

"That's what you think. You talked, you wept, you kissed me, and then you punched me. And you stole all the blankets."

"And what did you do to defend yourself? Besides sneaking out of bed this morning. Leaving me with nothing, not even a kiss?"

"I think if you check, you will find I may have left you with a baby."

She checked. He was right. "You bumped me in my sleep?" she asked incredulously.

"Believe me, Elodia, you started it, and I didn't think you were asleep. You rolled onto me, and you wouldn't get off."

"I suppose you tried hard to push me off?" she said with a smile.

"I tried some. A little bit."

"And this happened when I was sound asleep?"

"It happened after you kissed me and before you punched me."

She laughed. "That is so typical of my men. They get pleasure, and I get nothing. Almost nothing," she said with a grin.

Raising a skeptical eyebrow, he asked, "Your *men*? How many men have you had?"

Turning back to the tent's private room, she said primly, "I keep a list, which we can discuss later. With your many responsibilities, you don't have enough time to hear it all now."

He came close and rubbed her shoulders. "All true. I must go, but it will be an hour before they break down my tent. You can sleep until then."

No, I can't. But she did; she was so very weary. Fritigern was right; her sleep had been unquiet. *Are the gods trying to tell me something?*

She woke up fully when his slave came in with a jug of hot water. She washed in a basin and put her clothes back on. Now they were warm and dry. And smoky. *Oh, well.*

She found her way back to the medical tent. Silvan and Nedarcus were taking it down and reloading the cart. Elodia harnessed their mule, and they were on their way. They joined a long line of carts heading northeast to the Via Istrum. The sky was blue; the wind was fresh. It was good to be alive.

———◆———

The Greutungi took advantage of this favorable opportunity, and when they saw that our [Roman] soldiers were busy elsewhere and that the boats that usually went up and down the river and prevented them from crossing were inactive, they passed over the stream in badly made craft and pitched their camp at a long distance from Fritigern.

From Res Gestae, Volume XXXI 6.3-4, by Ammianus Marcellinus

———◆———

The problem with showing great ability, as Elodia did on Shipka Pass, is it attracts additional burdens.

When they reached the Via Istrum, they found springtime along the Danube was well-advanced and particularly lovely. Marshes lined the quieter portions of the river. The carts moved slowly, continuously squealing, disturbing all the wildlife, and driving flocks of herons, pelicans, and ducks into the air. A boar came out of the underbrush, snorted, and crossed the road in front of their mule. Elodia jumped, but not too high, as though confronting boars was an everyday event. One day, a man in the cart ahead of theirs stopped his mule and jumped down to piss. As he stepped off the road, a swan charged out of the reeds and attacked him. They all laughed as he hid behind his mule until he could make a running leap for his cart's bench.

As they moved east along the road, the column of carts and wagons grew longer. The word had gone out that Roman legions were flooding Thracia and killing every Goth they encountered, not only Goths but also the many slaves who had fled their absent owners. When a master left their estate seeking safety in a fortified town, a slave might see this as the chance of a lifetime to gain their freedom. Slaves the Romans found on the roads were assumed to be runaways and routinely slaughtered.

Thracia was a wealthy province, a rich source of plunder. A single rural villa might provide silver and gold worth more than two hundred slaves. Rural estates were also well supplied with farm carts, good for hauling plunder. The Goths, who managed to retreat north across the Haemus mountains ahead of the advancing Romans, joined a river of riches that flowed beside the Danube. The fleeing carts provided the Romans with a reason to advance quickly. The Goths heard stories of legionaries overtaking heavily loaded carts, cutting down their occupants, and seizing the cargo. The troops kept any goods they recovered, distributing them among themselves.

After that first night below Shipka Pass, Elodia saw little of Fritigern for a few days. He was busy organizing the nation's defense. He had formed a flying squad of cavalry to push back any threatening Roman force. He was arranging a stronghold for the tribe's defense, a location in the highlands of Dobrudja called Ad Salices. This stronghold was protected on two sides by the Danube delta and on a third side by the Black Sea. Fritigern explained all this one evening when his squad was heading east, having just destroyed a Roman force coming through the Iskar Gorge. That was the day she first met Gosvintha and Artos.

Fritigern's squad arrived late in the day at the river site where the medical cart had stopped for the night. As folks were preparing their evening meals, several hundred Goths rode in from the east. The group was led by Lord Farnobius, a leader of the Greutungi. That eastern tribe of Goths had crossed the Danube in large numbers and was now moving west up the Danube. For Fritigern, meeting Farnobius and reaffirming the alliance between the two great Gothic tribes was vitally important.

Elodia was excited to see the Greutungi because they brought horses. If Fritigern could purchase one for her, she imagined herself riding with him on patrols.

The Greutungi were much more of a horse people than the Tervingi. Maybe it was because they'd come from the broad plains north of the Black Sea, good horse country. Or perhaps, to survive the onslaught of the Huns, they'd adopted Hunnish tactics. Whichever, the Tervingi found themselves with an ally who fought from horseback and who could provide their leaders with horses. To her excitement, Fritigern bought Elodia a horse, which she named Bridie in honor of her favorite mule, now long gone.

Farnobius and his staff gathered around a large bonfire with Fritigern and his officers. It was a chilly, dreary afternoon, hinting of rain. Fritigern talked the Greutungi into camping near them. He promised a great feast indoors if it rained. The people, mostly men but a few women, stood with their hands outstretched, warming themselves by the fire. Everyone, Tervingi and Greutungi, talked and watched as slaves erected Fritigern's large tent. Its public room was large enough for everyone to sit and eat.

Elodia noticed a boy pushing through the adults to a place by the fire. He was about seven years of age, short and skinny, all head, hands, and feet as if readying himself to sprout to manhood. A woman came behind him and rested her hands on his shoulders. Clearly his mother by their common features.

She looked ten years older than Elodia. She was compact with broad shoulders. Her short black hair framed a handsome face which was marred by a scar that ran from cheek to ear. Her hair covered any scar above that. She wore black leather riding gear. Around her waist hung a sword belt. Its scabbard held a gladius, a shorter sword than the spatha, which most cavalrymen preferred. The gladius's lighter weight was more manageable for most women to wield. Her outfit and demeanor suggested she was a warrior. A warrior and a mother, it wasn't common.

She stared into the flames without glancing around, but her son scanned the leaders until he spotted Fritigern. Then he moved from under his mother's grip and rounded the fireside until he stood before Fritigern. "Artos!" said Fritigern, finally noticing the boy. He gave him a manly handshake, which Artos returned awkwardly. As Elodia stood aside, Fritigern introduced them. "Artos, this is my warrior mistress, Elodia. Elodia, Artos is my son."

Elodia, who had been looking down at Artos, jerked and looked at Fritigern. "Warrior mistress? What do you mean? What happened to 'slave'?"

He answered in a voice that rose so everyone nearby could hear. "Your deeds, Elodia, on the Shipka Pass were not those of a slave but of a warrior. You have earned your freedom and the name 'warrior.'"

From the gathered Tervingi came clapping and cheers of acclamation. The Greutungi, though they had no idea what Fritigern was talking about, joined in.

Elodia hid her surprise and tried to carry on as if nothing had changed. She offered the boy her hand and said, "Greetings, Artos."

He took hers, gave it a single solemn shake, and said, "Greetings, Elodia, Father's warrior mistress." It left her speechless.

"Artos, where is your mother?" Fritigern asked, just as he saw a woman moving around the fire toward them. When she came close, he said, "Elodia, this is Artos's mother, Gosvintha. Gosvintha, Elodia is my warrior mistress."

Gosvintha and Elodia greeted each other. There was an awkward pause as they looked each other up and down. It was broken by Fritigern saying, "Oh, Artos! You have doubled in size! It's been, what, two years since I last saw you?"

"Three," Gosvintha said.

"I have my own pony now, Father," Artos said. "Her name is Liuva. Would you like to see her?"

"Of course."

"Can we go now?"

"Later, Artos. I have important matters to discuss with Lord Farnobius."

"Liuva *is* important!" Artos's voice became shrill, almost whiny.

"I said *later*. Elodia, control the boy!" *Isn't that a job for his mother*? She might be his warrior mistress, no longer a slave, but it seemed he had no difficulty in giving her orders.

Elodia took Artos by the arm and pulled him away. Although that ended the argument, it left Artos on the verge of tears.

It was starting to rain. Fortunately, the tent was now erect. All the leaders of both tribes were making their way inside. Elodia indicated the tent to Gosvintha and Artos. They followed the leaders. Nodding toward Fritigern, Gosvintha said to Elodia, "He had no such fine shelter when I last saw him. He has grown important indeed."

The tent, as big as it was, had little free room remaining when Gosvintha, Artos, and Elodia entered. Men were sitting on rugs, knee to knee, facing a central cook fire. A slave poured warm ale into cups, which the sitting men passed around.

Elodia moved to the rear room's door. When Artos started to follow, his mother pointed to an empty corner of the main tent. "Sit there. Stay here with the other men. But don't speak."

Artos looked pleased. Elodia guessed he'd rather be there with the council than with two women. She closed the room's door flap behind them. This room was chilly, but there were plenty of rugs and blankets. As they wrapped themselves comfortably, two slaves entered. One brought them tankards of hot ale, and the other carried embers for the brazier.

Elodia felt, as the hostess, she should initiate the conversation, but she wasn't sure how to start.

"You are Greutungi?" she asked. "Oh, that's a stupid question. Of course, you are. Excuse me."

"No, not stupid. I am Greutungi, and most of us are, but some Alans ride with us. Even a few Huns."

"Huns? Didn't you come to Moesia to escape the Huns?"

"Mostly true. But there are Huns, and then there are Huns. They have clans, just like we Goths, clans that sometimes disagree, feud, or even war with each other. Rather like Fritigern and Athanaric."

"And these Huns hate the Romans as we do?"

"Yes," Gosvintha said with a laugh, "but they fear the other Huns more than the Romans. The Huns here were fast losing a blood feud with another clan and hoped to save themselves by allying with Lord Farnobius."

"And the Alans? Are they fleeing a rival clan?"

"That's not what Batraz says. As much as I can understand him. I'm just learning Alanic, and his Gothic is poor. But he says he is here for silver. The Romans are rich, and he wants riches. Also, the Huns have conquered his homeland, and he will not bend a knee to them."

"Batraz?"

"He is my current lover," Gosvintha said. "You probably saw him outside by the bonfire. He was the gorgeous tall blond warrior wearing a black and silver mink cape."

Elodia nodded as though she'd noticed him, but she hadn't. There were many tall blond warriors of varying degrees of gorgeousness by the bonfire.

"We met while our people were crossing the Danube," Gosvintha continued. "He and I helped each other get our horses across. He poled the raft while I kept the animals calm. We couldn't speak each other's tongues, but the crossing was something we could do without speaking. Later, we found other things we could do without speaking."

"But which used your tongues?" Elodia suggested. Gosvintha laughed in agreement.

"Where did you cross? And when?" Elodia asked.

"We crossed many miles downstream from Durostorum. Perhaps two weeks after your tribe crossed."

"People said the Romans were only allowing Tervingi Goths to cross."

Gosvintha laughed again. "We did not seek their permission. Once they had their hands full dealing with you, we just went. The few Romans we saw avoided us. But after you killed them all at Marcianople, we only saw them peeking out from town walls. Which was fine with Batraz. He has been able to scoop up more silver these last several months than he could ever have taken back home."

Their conversation lapsed. Elodia stared at the brazier's glowing embers. Finally, she said, "Fritigern told me when we first met, he had a woman. Are you that woman?"

"That's a blunt question," Gosvintha replied with another laugh, which made Elodia smile. *She laughs a lot. I like her.*

The Greutungi woman resumed, "I cannot tell if he was referring to me. I have not seen him for years. That was when he last saw our son. Perhaps, since then, he has taken other women before you. That would be like him. He is a man who loves women. Do not despair when he sets you aside and takes up with another. He might come back to you. He always came back to me. And then we parted as we always do."

"May I ask what came between you?"

She waved her hands, indicating it was no great matter. "I am a warrior. He wants a wife."

"You are not married?"

"Only in the warrior's way. We take what we need, what we must have. By violence if necessary."

"And Artos?"

"I am a warrior, but I am still a woman. Women who bump get babies."

"Did you love each other?"

"Love? We were excellent together. We enjoyed each other. Whether for fighting or bumping. Or just riding and drinking."

"And yet?"

"He went crazy when he imagined me being hurt again, or killed." Gosvintha briefly touched the scar on her cheek. "He wanted me to stop fighting. I told him I am a warrior. A warrior fights until they can't. A broken leg or a scar on the cheek didn't stop me from fighting. He wouldn't see that. He returned to his people here in the west. And I kept our son and remained east with the Greutungi."

"What are your plans for Artos now that you've come west?"

"He's not a baby anymore. And I am not made to be a mother. I have brought him here to live with his father. It is time for Fritigern to do his duty by Artos, to train him in the ways of men, and to leave me free to serve my Lord Farnobius as a warrior."

"Does Fritigern know this? He has no time to be a father. You must understand, he now commands all the Tervingi. He is trying to save our tribe from annihilation."

"I understand all this," Gosvintha said dismissively.

"He will not have time to train Artos," Elodia warned her. "He is always on the move, riding here, fighting there, or organizing a camp or a fort. Even I rarely see him. A boy needs that much time and more."

"Now hundreds of warriors answer to him. Training a boy? That is something Fritigern can assign to one of them."

Gosvintha's decision to walk away from her son exasperated Elodia. "He has seen only seven winters. Surely, he still needs a mother," she said.

"I'm sure there is someone here who can care for Artos while his father is busy." Gosvintha looked Elodia straight in the eye. She stared back and wondered, *How has this boy become my problem?*

Gosvintha took her silence as acceptance. "I shall inform Fritigern of this when he is less busy. Before we leave tomorrow."

The warrior woman drank the rest of her ale. "Now I have told you my story. You must tell me how you came to be with Fritigern and sleep in his bed."

Elodia told her a brief version of her history. She did not mention the men she'd killed or her recent fight on the pass. Despite Fritigern calling her a warrior, she was not one. Killing did not define her. She was sure if they compared numbers killed, Gosvintha would come out ahead.

"You have not mentioned Shipka Pass. What happened there?" Gosvintha asked.

Reluctantly, Elodia told the story as briefly as she could. When she finished, Gosvintha just nodded as if her story was acceptable, as if Elodia had somehow passed muster. They could hear the conference in the outer room breaking up by then. The room flap was lifted. They stood as Artos and Fritigern entered. Gosvintha stepped forward and, with two hands, pulled Fritigern's face down to hers and kissed him fully on the lips. "Fritigern," she said fondly.

"Gosvintha?" he asked suspiciously, unsure what her kiss meant.

"We must talk later before I go. I will leave Artos here with you and... Elodia?" she said with an inflection, as though she wasn't sure of Elodia's name.

Elodia said, "Yes," confirming her name. Fritigern looked at her quizzically. She realized he thought she had just agreed to take care of Artos.

Gosvintha said, "You will take care of my boy? Protect him?"

Elodia said she would. It was a simple statement, but it took on the weight of an oath and would change the rest of her life.

Without further explanation, Gosvintha slipped past him out of the tent, where Elodia could see her tall, blond, gorgeous warrior waiting. The encounter left Elodia puzzled. She had been denied a child, but as if in compensation, Ithunn had provided her with a boy. Perhaps a stepson?—and made her the mistress of her tribe's leader. *Was this her fate?*

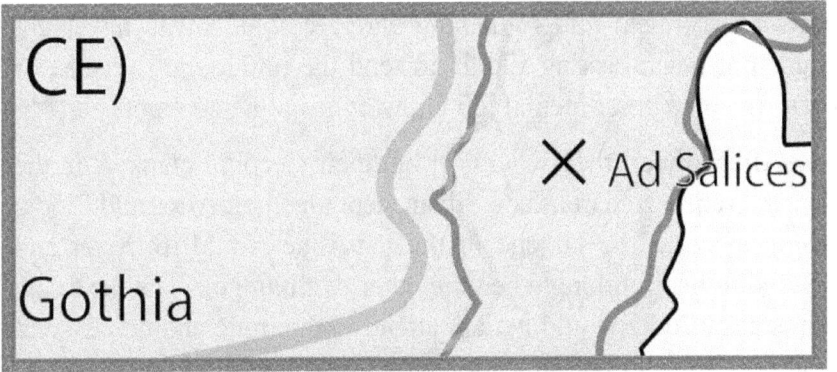

CE)

X Ad Salices

Gothia

10. Ad Salices
377 CE

The Greutungi left them, heading west up the river. Fritigern and his cavalry squad sped east toward Dobrudja to block any Roman advance north from Marcianople. He said it was a race to gather the tribe in the stronghold at Ad Salices. "If we are together, we will survive the Roman onslaught, but divided as we are now, they will defeat us in detail."

Their column, now numbering hundreds of carts and wagons, including Nedarcus's medical cart, was heading east at the pace of a mule, trailing far behind Fritigern's galloping warhorse.

Every evening when they made camp, Nedarcus, Silvan, and Elodia would set up the medical tent. Artos soon learned to help. He replaced Silvan in the heavy lifting. There were always injured people needing Nedarcus's care. The medicus attended them, and Elodia assisted as needed. Silvan would cook dinner for the four of them. It mystified Elodia how Silvan transformed a few ingredients into a delicious repast. Elodia tried to help her when Nedarcus didn't need her. Sometimes her assistance would turn what would have been a tasty meal into something barely edible. Silvan never got angry but began asking Elodia to tend the mule, chop greens, or perform some other menial job far away from the cookpots.

After dinner, they would set out their sleeping blankets in the tent and retire. Nedarcus and Silvan slept together. Artos and Elodia would sleep at the far end of the tent. She would roll over and pretend to hear nothing when the other two bumped. The next day, Artos and Elodia would get up, attend to the mule and horses, and help pack the cart before resuming their journey.

Artos slept with them and came by for meals, but the rest of the time, he attached himself to a group of older boys. They would run along the road, playing, hunting, getting into mischief, trying not to get caught. When hurt, he would turn to Elodia for the mothering he'd never had. Elodia provided it gladly. It didn't take long for her to love the youth and for him to call her "Mother."

*C*ount Richomeres, by common consent, took command of the whole [Roman] force and was joined by [General] Profuturus and [Magister Peditum] Traianus, who were encamped near the town of Salices. Not far from there, a countless mass of the barbarians had arranged their numerous wagons in the form of a circle and, as if enclosed in a space between city walls, were enjoying their rich booty at their ease.

From Res Gestae, Volume XXXI 7.5, by Ammianus Marcellinus

*E*lodia's journey from their camp on the Etar River to the stronghold took three weeks. Fritigern and his flying squad passed by them several times but did not stop except to drop off wounded men. There had been clashes to the west between the flying squad and Roman scouts.

Nedarcus's two sons accompanied Fritigern: Gotheric and Gavar. Gotheric moved on when Fritigern left, but the younger son, Gavar, stayed behind one night. He was short, well-muscled, and more handsome than his father, with a strong chin and broad forehead. He had a ready laugh, unlike his father, who tended to be grim. The two brothers could pass for twins, but Gotheric claimed to be one year older. He had flaming long red hair, hastily tied in a ponytail, and an unkempt red beard. By contrast, Gavar was shaved clean, head and face, because he said it avoided people confusing him with "my older, uglier brother." Gotheric's retort was Gavar kept close shaved in a hopeless attempt to keep his lice at bay.

Elodia was interested to see how Gavar would react to Silvan. She was heavy with child, and apparently, Gavar knew his father was not the father. And yet Silvan made no secret that she and Nedarcus were lovers.

Silvan, Elodia decided, was staking a claim to Nedarcus, irrespective of what Gavar or anyone else might think. Silvan had told Elodia of her desperate need for security for herself and her unborn child. Nedarcus filled that need. Elodia wondered if her friend's choice was wise. He was old. What if he died or was killed? Would a younger man of greater rank be better?

On the other hand, a younger man would fight in the warriors' shield wall, where it was more likely he'd be killed. It did not occur to Elodia until much later that her friend and the old medicus might genuinely have feelings for each other. In addition, Elodia assumed men would always be available for the picking, like apples on a tree. This idea might be accurate for Elodia, who came to men's attention with no effort on her part, whether she wanted it or not. Not so for plain Silvan.

The following day, Gavar rode west to catch up with Fritigern while Elodia and the long train of carts and wagons marched east to the stronghold. Just before Gavar left, he warned Nedarcus, "You must move with all possible haste."

Nedarcus said, "Because of the Romans? Are they that close?"

"Yes, their cavalry is only a few days to the west."

Elodia said, "I understood the enemy would come north from Constantinople along the Black Sea coastal road."

"Indeed, they will, but those are not the ones who will catch you. The ones you need to fear today are Western Emperor Gratian's bodyguards. And right behind them, Count Richomeres is leading legions from Gaul."

"They would be foolish to attack us," Elodia said. "We have hundreds of wagons, and each wagon has one or more warriors."

"And all those warriors are spread out along the length of your column. Against a body of professional legionaries, it would be a bloodbath. The Romans would work up the length of your column and slice it to ribbons."

"What should we do?" asked Nedarcus.

"As I said, you need to move with all possible speed. Get to the stronghold. If any place can provide a haven, that is it."

The stronghold was in the highlands of Dobrudja, a hilly region that blocked the Danube's eastward flow, forcing that great river into a sweeping path to the north and east, where its delta drained into the Black Sea. The wagon-train continued east into the highlands when the river curved north.

Along the river, they'd become accustomed to thickets of willows, marshy areas of rushes, and small ponds covered with lily pads. In the evening, when the din of wagons and people ceased, the air was full of bird song, the endless whirring and buzzing of insects, and the squeaks of small animals. The area flooded often. Any farms were set on higher land, well back from the river. In many places, the Romans had built the road up on a thick bed of stone and gravel to keep it usable in all seasons. Bridges, which had been well-maintained in the past by the limitanei, crossed the river's tributaries where fording was impracticable.

But as they moved up and away from the river, the land grew quieter and less lush, and the road quickly degraded to a wide dirt track. The willows gave way to ash and elm. These grew denser until they covered the land in a thick tall forest, which squeezed the road into a narrow passage through cliffs of dark wood. The many streams cut deep gullies across their path which became masses of rutted mud, made ever wider by the many wagons looking for an easier route to cross.

Elodia and Nedarcus pushed their cart through the mud when necessary while Silvan coaxed the obstinate mule to pull. It was reminiscent of their Shipka Pass experience, but the hills were less steep, and there was plenty of help from other travelers to bull through the challenging spots. Still, Elodia kept looking to the rear, fearful of seeing Roman cavalry charging from behind, swinging their deadly swords, slaughtering everyone within reach.

After weeks of travel, they finally reached the stronghold. They were all stunned by its size. It was an enormous ring of wagons, thousands of them.

Crews were busy digging a deep ditch around the outside. Children were packing the area beneath the wagons with brambles. Carts and smaller wagons were turned on their sides to form a six- or eight-foot-high barrier. It was a formidable defense. Any legionary who survived the ditch without being shot was likely to be clubbed trying to climb over the wagon-fort.

The wagon-fort enclosed a quarter-square mile. Nedarcus's wagon was one of the last to arrive, and notwithstanding the fort's enormous size, Elodia worried if there was room for their wagon, tent, and provisions. Fortunately, expecting them, Fritigern and his staff had set aside an area near the main entrance. Tents and people, tens of thousands of them, and pastures for the innumerable animals occupied the rest of the space.

Over the next week, the Goths made final preparations for a siege. The last of the foraging parties returned. They had gathered vast amounts of food, yet people were still worried. There were so many people, and no one knew how long a siege might last.

Crews were cutting logs for palisade sections to defend weak spots in the perimeter. Other teams worked on the ditch. Initially, slaves did the digging, but as time grew short, Fritigern's lieutenants requested assistance from the clans. Their leaders did not respond favorably to direct orders. Most clan leaders obliged, but one leader deemed digging beneath the dignity of his warriors. However, his clan's women shamed their men when the women showed up with shovels saying, "If it is beneath you to defend your women and children, then we will defend ourselves."

Finally, the flying squad, led by Fritigern, passed through the main entrance. The gate guards promptly sealed it with wagons and a palisade section. Hot on their heels was a Roman cavalry squad. It stopped out of bowshot. The riders stared. They, too, were as stunned by the size of the stronghold as Elodia had been.

Time weighed heavily on everyone. The Romans waited, hoping to provoke the Goths into fighting in the open beyond the protection of their wagons.

The Goths waited impatiently for the Roman attack. Fritigern resisted the temptation of an open battle. They had the advantage in numbers, but that was their only advantage. Notwithstanding the quantity of combat kit they'd salvaged after the battle outside Marcianople and from the Adrianople arms factories, they were still deficient in swords, spears, shields, and armor. Clans that had missed those engagements had only the weapons they'd successfully smuggled across the Danube. They fashioned cudgels and spears using the timber they feverishly cut from around the wagon-fort. That stopped when the Romans surrounded the stronghold.

The Goths knew Romans were lurking in the woods when they attacked a party of woodcutters. They had felled a tree but were set upon when trying to retrieve it. The Romans crucified them outside the main entrance just beyond bowshot and taunted the Goths to come out and save their brothers or at least retrieve their bodies. Fritigern would not permit it, standing fast against the fury of their kin.

The one problem they did not face, not immediately, was a lack of food. The foraging teams had gathered provisions for several weeks. They later learned that the Romans, seeing the countryside barren, assumed the Goths had minimal provisions. It turned out the Romans were the ones going hungry. The Gothic foraging teams, after gathering anything that might prove useful, torched or spoiled everything else. They lit fields of wild grain, leaving the Roman cavalry without fodder, and they polluted streams with rotting carcasses, forcing their besiegers to travel several hours for water.

Initially, Elodia was surprised and not a little disappointed when Bron never appeared to summon her to Fritigern's bed. At first, she would delay laying out her sleep blankets, hoping for a message. With camp gossip as effective as it was, she soon learned the truth. Fritigern was sharing his tent with another, a woman named Athena.

Athena was young and beautiful. Younger and more beautiful than Elodia, she had to admit. That was reason enough to dislike her. In addition, she was Rodericus's sister. Elodia seethed with resentment.

Her rival was tall, slender, and curvaceous, with a long gold braid of hair that fell to her waist. Whether she spoke or sang, her voice was melodious. Elodia heard her singing one evening when she just happened to go by Fritigern's tent. No, it wasn't happenstance. She was spying, trying to learn more about this young woman who had replaced her in Fritigern's affection. And in his arms, for she saw the two of them sitting near his bodyguards around his campfire, Fritigern seated on a rug, Athena sitting on his lap, his arms wrapped around her.

As Elodia watched, Athena started a well-known tragic song. It told the story of a dame goose who lost the love of her mate to another. In the first verse, Athena sang how the gods have ordained that geese mate for life, and yet her gander had left her for another with whiter plumage. Fritigern joined in on the second verse and sang the part of the hunter, who noticed the dame goose, in her sadness, was refusing to flee as he approached. Fritigern and Athena sang the third verse together, where the hunter simply walked up and wrung its neck. They'd performed it well, and the audience clapped and cheered.

It was a beautiful, sad song. Elodia had sung it with Fritigern. Not as well as Athena. Now she was the dame goose. Gosvintha had warned her this would happen, but, oh, the pain. How could she have imagined Fritigern was a substitute for Caius? She returned to her tent in tears but determined not to sit quietly while her neck got wrung.

Artos showed up one evening, looking for a place to sleep. "That new woman," as Artos called Athena, "told my father she could not sleep in the same tent as 'that bastard.'" Fritigern hadn't argued. He told Artos to stay somewhere else. Angry and sad, Artos returned to Elodia.

He began sleeping again in the medical tent with Nedarcus, Silvan, and her. They gave him affection, of which he got none from his father.

Artos began to make a nuisance of himself. Nedarcus asked his older son, Gotheric, for help. Gotheric was a member of Fritigern's bodyguard but had few chores within their camp. He had developed an affection for Artos when the boy and his father were on better terms, so he was happy to include him in his daily combat training.

At first, the boy was resistant to the discipline, but after a few thrashings, he came around. As he felt his strength and skill improve, he became enthusiastic. He was younger than the other boys in the class but was big for his age and demonstrated a natural speed and agility. Gotheric would devise team skirmishes pitting half the boys against the other half. Initially, Artos was the last to be picked by the team leads. Soon he became a team leader himself.

In the end, neither side could consider the battle of Ad Salices a victory.

It took a week for the Romans to torment the Goths into attacking. A dozen children had ventured into the woods to gather firewood. They were captured. Their heads were catapulted into the stronghold the following day.

The pressure on Fritigern to attack was enormous. He resisted the young warriors who were swearing revenge and hatred of all things Roman. They called him a coward. For all their passion, they were also the least trained. Few had any combat experience. Fritigern knew if they faced veteran legionaries, they would slaughter them like the children they'd only recently been. But his ability to check them, already strained, finally snapped.

Ignoring Fritigern's orders, the young warriors unblocked the main entrance. All the warriors, young and old, streamed out and formed a shield wall to face the Romans. They had taken the bait. The Romans were waiting.

Fritigern held his bodyguards in reserve and used them to ensure women and boys did not follow the men out the entrance. He and his lieutenants organized the women into perimeter guards. There was little to stop the Romans from attacking over the wagons far from the fort's main entrance. The ditch was just an impediment. It was neither wide nor deep enough to block an attack.

The women in each clan had a pool of weapons. They had virtually no swords, the men had taken them all, but there were clubs and spears aplenty, many having steel points, and everyone had knives. The children piled pyramids of stones around the perimeter. Each group of women stood on guard near their own clan's wagons. Artos and Elodia joined the group farthest from the main gate, where Elodia guessed an attack would occur. Nedarcus argued with her, saying he and Silvan would soon be knee-deep in blood; they needed her near the gate at the medical tent. But Elodia knew Artos would not stay there with her. He would seek out the fight. Preserving the life of Fritigern's bastard became her top priority.

As she predicted, the Roman attack hit her station. The women detected the danger even as the legionaries were vaulting the ditch. The tops of ladders appeared over the wagons, and Roman helmets appeared above the top rungs. Each helmet would provoke a hail of stones. Often these had no effect unless some stone struck with sufficient force to knock a man off. The ladders were short, no higher than the wagons they were meant to scale, ten feet at most. Often a soldier, knocked down by a stone, would soon reappear, not seriously hurt but angrier and with blood running down his face. If the blood streamed over his eyes, he might not see the spear that killed him or the woman who thrust it into his eye.

Many legionaries succeeded in scaling the wall of wagons, but they were overwhelmed by mothers and teens before they could arrive in numbers sufficient to form a shield wall. A Roman soldier might slaughter several before a swarm of screaming Goths buried him. It reminded Elodia of a carpet of ants streaming over the struggling body of a wounded rat.

When a cluster of legionaries succeeded in crossing the wagon barrier, they would stand back-to-back. The Goths would back away, using their spears to keep the soldiers at bay. Then the reserve force, Fritigern's bodyguard, would intervene and kill the legionaries. Goths with bows would help take them down. Elodia had downed seven, by her count. The women would snatch up swords and shields from the dead Romans. Elodia was one of the few with the strength to wield a sword and shield, though it was a struggle for her.

She tried to keep a protective eye on Artos, but in the thick of battle, defending herself against a legionary's sword required all her concentration.

Eight soldiers scrambled over a wagon at one point and stood with their backs to it. They were armed with swords and shields, adequate for protecting themselves but not ideal for penetrating a forest of spears. Fritigern's bodyguard was busy fighting an encroachment elsewhere. It was up to the women and teens.

They closed in on the soldiers. The Romans looked scared, and rightly so. A young Roman standing before Elodia was struck by an arrow, penetrating his chain mail. He toppled forward face down on the ground. Artos, standing slightly behind her, stepped forward, knife in hand, and plunged it into the prone body. The victim's two mates standing on either side of him advanced, swords ready, and began to thrust at Artos.

Moving to protect him, Elodia hit one legionary with her shield, forcing him to fall back onto the wagon, and thrust her sword through the other. That shattered the Romans' little shield wall, allowing the other women to charge in.

The resulting melee was over in moments. All the Romans lay dead. Artos had no idea how close he'd come to joining them.

Finally, some of the [Roman] dead, who were men of distinction, were buried in such manner as the present circumstances allowed; the bodies of the rest of the slain were devoured by the foul birds that are wont at such a time to feed upon corpses, as is shown by the plains even now white with bones. However, while it is a fact that the Romans, who, far fewer in number, struggled with that vast multitude, suffered great losses, yet lamentable was the distress with which they afflicted the barbarian horde.

From Res Gestae, Volume XXXI 7.16, by Ammianus Marcellinus

After the great battle, the Goths were all stunned. More than a thousand were dead and many times that wounded. Though there were healers besides Nedarcus, each with many assistants like Silvan and Elodia, the casualties overwhelmed them. The carnage visible on the battlefield was soon replicated within the wagon-fort as the healers cauterized wounds and lopped off smashed limbs. The survivors walked through rivers of blood. The screams of the wounded and cries of new widows and their children filled their ears. The smell of funeral pyres, metallic blood, and the sweet odor of gangrene filled their noses.

The Roman losses were a fraction of theirs. Fritigern had been right: his undertrained, undisciplined, and poorly equipped men were no match for the legionaries. And yet, the great action must have stunned the Romans too. Their losses weighed more on them because they were so outnumbered.

The Goths did not see the Romans again after the battle. For a period, they lurked nearby expecting the wagon-fort to break up and move on, leaving them vulnerable to attack. But the Goths were patient, waiting and waiting, always expecting another assault, which never came.

After waiting a week, the Romans ran out of food and fodder. Soon, the Gothic scouts reported they were gone.

The Goths had captured a few Romans. They expected them to bargain for their release. They did not. Fritigern ordered Gotheric to oversee them. He put the prisoners to work digging a mass grave for their own dead, which took a week. When they buried the last of them, Gotheric killed the gravediggers and topped off the graves with their bodies. That satisfied Fritigern.

Fritigern visited the medical tent most days, checking on the wounded and saying a comforting word to each. On one visit, Athena accompanied him. He introduced Elodia to her as his "woman warrior" without ever mentioning their history. Elodia offered her hand, but Athena ignored it, leaving her rival standing, angry, and looking foolish. Athena had nothing to say to Elodia or, for that matter, to the wounded warriors. Privately, Silvan asked Elodia, "Does their suffering mean nothing to her?" Elodia had no answer.

When Fritigern spoke to Elodia, he was cool, verging on indifferent. She replied similarly, but she was not indifferent. She'd offered him love, which he'd discarded as a thing of no value. His own son worshipped him, but that did not touch him. Instead of accepting these gifts given freely, he'd attached himself to a beautiful, talented woman with no heart. Though he might be a great leader of men, she could not understand his soul. It saddened and angered her. For Athena, she felt nothing but contempt and would relish the day when Fritigern found yet another woman.

By the end of a week, the healers had done what they could. The injured had been treated. The dying had died. Food was running low again. People wanted to move on.

Fritigern moved west along the river, harassing the retreating legions until he reached the outskirts of Durostorum. Elodia and the medical cart trailed the squad by some days.

The people who lived near that city said it was strongly held by its Roman garrison. The retreating legions had stayed for only a few days before withdrawing south to Marcianople. The locals said the retreating troops were sullen and discouraged, and there had been desertions. The deserters had plundered and killed civilians living near the city. The civilians kept watch and killed any they found.

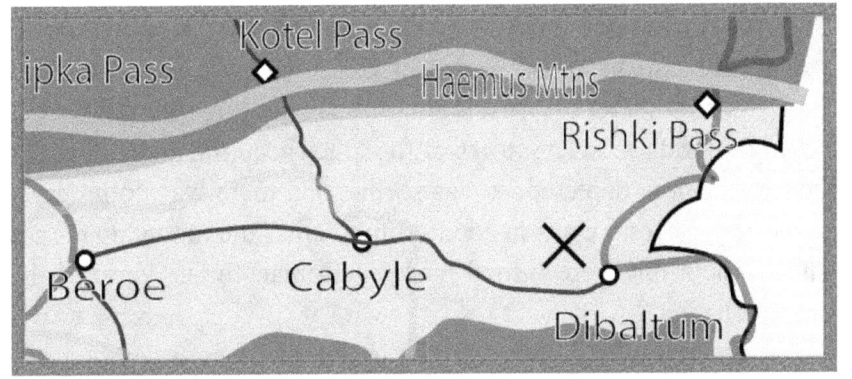

11. Elodia & Gosvintha
377 CE

... Our soldiers, having thus found an opportunity, shut in the other huge hordes of barbarians within the narrow passes of the Haemus range by building high barriers. They doubtless hoped that the dangerous mass of enemies, crowded together between the Hister [Danube] and the waste places, and finding no way out, would perish from lack of food; for all the necessities of life had been taken to the strong cities, none of which the enemy even then attempted to besiege because of their complete ignorance of these and other operations of the kind.

From Res Gestae, Volume XXXI 8.1, by Ammianus Marcellinus

Fritigern realized any attempt to besiege Durostorum would be futile. Instead, he set up a defensive wagon-fort a few miles from it. From there, the Tervingi Goths spread throughout Moesia, hoping to find food. The stores of food they accumulated before the siege were now depleted. It was spring, and there was nothing yet to harvest. Several clans headed south to cross the mountain passes into Thracia but were turned back by Roman forts. Were all the passes blocked?

Fritigern sent scouts to all five passes to find out. He took the flying squad south from Marcianople, where the road into Thracia crossed through the coastal hill country. He ordered Nedarcus to wait at the Durostorum camp until he returned with more information, so Artos and Elodia waited too.

Time weighed heavily on the medicus team, who had nothing to keep them busy except treating accidental injuries. Inactivity pressed harder on Elodia, who was still trying to deal with Fritigern's disregard. Only Artos kept busy, playing rough games with other small boys. But he continued to press Elodia. "When can we go riding?"

When they'd been trekking toward the stronghold, he and Elodia had enjoyed riding together every day. But that wasn't possible when cooped up in the wagon-fort. The danger of brigands or deserters was too great.

The tedium was alleviated by the reappearance of Gosvintha. She and a party of fifty Greutungi led by Farnobius were heading west but stopped at the wagon-fort to enjoy the hospitality of their Tervingi cousins.

When the hugging and joyful weeping of reunion were done, Gosvintha sat talking to Elodia by the campfire outside her tent. She'd had Artos bouncing on her knee, but he was too big for that, so he escaped her kissing and grabbing in favor of a game of kickball with his friends. An old cow's skull served as the ball.

"So, Fritigern has moved on. I warned you this would happen," Gosvintha said to Elodia.

"True, but that didn't reduce the sting."

"At least you have other skills to fall back on," her friend said. "You can stitch a wounded man back together, and you can hunt any creature, animal or human."

"And I can cook!"

Gosvintha laughed. "From what I hear, this Athena girl has only her beauty, and beauty fades in time."

"Did my beauty fade?"

"Of course not. But Fritigern is fickle.

"Forget him," Gosvintha said, "and think of our next great adventure."

"*Our* adventure?"

"Yes. Artos complains he wants to ride his pony. Then he shall. You and my son will join our little party of horsemen when we leave your depressing ring of wagons. We are heading up the great river and will join Lord Alatheus, who is crossing the river at Oescus. From there, we plan to ride up the Iskar Gorge, past Philippopolis, through the Succi pass, and into the endless grasslands of Pannonia. I have been there before, Elodia. There is no finer horse country in the world."

It only took one minute's consideration for Elodia to agree. Would Fritigern be angry if she left without his permission? Did she care? She did not. He had publicly freed her, with great praise, and then humiliated her by taking up with another woman. He felt nothing for her, and she felt contempt for him. As for Artos, a boy he hardly acknowledged, she would not be stealing his child but returning him to his mother. There was no reason to stay and every reason to go.

The only person who objected was Artos. "I cannot go *now*," he complained. "I have just made a new friend. I like her, her name is Heva, even though she is a girl and very old." It was true Heva was a girl, but she was only fourteen. His objections crumbled when he learned she was Greutungi and would be coming along. Her father, a man named Avagis, was Gosvintha's current lover.

And so, after a tearful farewell to Silvan, Nedarcus, and their other Tervingi friends, they mounted their horses and rode west.

The Goths living in the wagon-fort outside Durostorum were beginning to panic. Food was running short. They had exhausted the nearby area. The Roman blockade of the Haemus mountain passes had its intended effect of preventing the Goths from moving south.

Fritigern was surprised at how quickly the Romans recovered from Ad Salices. Though they had far fewer losses than the Goths, their losses had cost them dearly. Their quick retreat after the battle showed they no longer had enough strength to go head-to-head with the Goths. The Roman strategy became clear when Fritigern found the Romans had fortified all five Haemus mountain passes. They meant to starve the Goths in Moesia until reinforcing legions could arrive. The longer the Romans could hold the passes, the stronger their blockade became, and the weaker the Goths would grow.

The Goths had defended themselves adequately at Ad Salices. Despite heavy losses, they had averted the worst possible outcome:

annihilation. Now they faced their constant enemy: hunger. The fertile fields of Moesia would offer no harvest this year. The Moesian farmers had taken refuge in the fortified towns, fled from the Goths, or died. Fritigern needed to lead his people south into the broad expanse of Thracia. From there, they could spread out to Macedonia, Greece, and the other Balkan provinces to find food, plunder, and, more importantly, pressure the Romans to bargain for peace. All this depended on breaking out of Moesia soon.

Fritigern would have to attack one of the five passes in force, but which one? Several of his cavalry squads had not yet reported. When he could determine the weakest, he would make a lightning thrust there with all available force. Until then, the Durostorum wagon-fort remained in place.

Silvan sorely missed Elodia. Silvan's time was drawing near. She hoped the baby would come soon and not when they were busy trying to push the medical cart over some treacherous pass, especially since Nedarcus did not seem well.

The situation changed abruptly when a messenger arrived on a lathered horse. "We've taken Shipka Pass!" The scouting party assigned to reconnoiter that pass found it indifferently guarded. For some reason the goddess Eir found fault with the Roman garrison there and scattered the seeds of a curse on them. When the seeds sprouted, the victims began to puke, shit, and die, leaving so few of the garrison on their feet that the Gothic scouts could simply walk in and take over the fort.

Some Roman slaves appeared untouched by the curse seeds. The scouts put these to work, digging a great hole into which all the Romans—dead, dying, or living—were thrown. There was some question of whether slaves were also cursed, but, finding some of the slaves among the dying, it was clear Eir had scattered her seeds widely. The scouts decided to play it safe by also throwing all the slaves into the hole. The Goths backfilled the hole and, sacrificing a horse on the burial mound, prayed to Eir that the goddess would spare them her wrath.

Fritigern, upon hearing the news, gathered his forces to surge across Shipka Pass, a nine-day journey back along the Via Istrum, a route they had traveled in reverse just a few months earlier. With Silvan riding on the driver's board and Nedarcus leading the mule, they were just joining the line of carts and wagons when the whole column stopped. Orders came back that instead of heading to Shipka Pass, they would go south to Rishki Pass, a substantially shorter trip. After the column got moving again, a rumor passed from wagon to wagon, often accompanied by a cheer. Apparently, the Romans had withdrawn from their fortifications at Rishki Pass. The road to Thracia lay open.

The end of the first day's travel found the Goths making camp twenty miles south of Durostorum, back in the hill country near the Roman Palmatis fortress, which they'd passed less than a year ago. Silvan could hardly recognize the countryside; it had changed so much. So had she. Evidence of spring was everywhere. Small founts flowed from the rocky outcrops that had been bone-dry in winter. The shrubs and trampled grasses, which she'd assumed were dead, proved her wrong with their abundance of new verdant growth. She saw fresh stalks everywhere from the road, topped by a carpet of forsythias. It was the season of rebirth, a fitting season for her baby to arrive.

This year she rode in a cart led by an old man she loved. She wasn't starving. She wasn't stumbling along with her brother and their three friends, struggling to put one foot ahead of the other, desperate to reach Marcianople, where they'd been promised food. A lie. Five close friends quickly cut down to just herself. New friends were added and lost, and, finally, a new, very little friend was due any day. Silvan didn't know whether to smile or cry, so she did both.

Silvan helped Nedarcus set up the medical tent. It was difficult. He wasn't feeling well, and she was very pregnant.

Fritigern was making his rounds from tent to tent, chatting with as many of his people as he could. He found Nedarcus and Silvan just starting their dinner. He squatted by their campfire with his bodyguards standing behind him. Nedarcus made a show of offering him some of their fare. Fritigern accepted a mouthful or two. He had always enjoyed Silvan's cooking, but he could see their pot did not have enough food for three, let alone for two and a half.

After exchanging pleasantries, Nedarcus said, "That is a bit of good fortune, finding the Rishki fortifications abandoned, isn't it?"

Fritigern answered, "Good in one sense, bad in another. Good that now we can look to all Thracia for food and supplies. Bad that it dashes my hopes of crushing the garrisons that were guarding the other passes. We could have hit them from both north and south. We could have slaughtered them and finished what we started at Ad Salices. It's also bad because it shows I am facing a Roman general who saw that danger and has withdrawn those garrisons. This man is no Lupicinus. We must move carefully."

He continued, "I see you've retained your cooking skills, Silvan. That was delicious. Good for you and good for your baby too. When is it due?"

"Any time, really, my lord."

"How are you feeling, Nedarcus?" The medicus was frequently short of breath and often felt faint.

"Couldn't be better, my lord," he lied.

"Of course. Well, I'm assigning your son Gotheric to stay with you until we're through Rishki Pass. I want my two best medici healthy and available should we see action."

His comment made Silvan blush. *There* was an acknowledgment that her medical skills might be compared with her master's.

"And I'll also send over some extra victuals. Gotheric has quite an appetite."

Gotheric stepped forward from among the bodyguards and squatted on the ground beside his father, putting an arm around the old man. Silvan looked at the pair with affection. She'd come to love the old medicus. He hadn't seemed so old when they first met, but the last year had been hard on him.

Fritigern got up to go. "Any word from Elodia?" he asked.

"None since she and Artos rode off with Gosvintha, my lord," Nedarcus replied.

"Very well. I trust she's looking after my boy." With that, he walked off to the next campfire, trailed by his bodyguards.

The plan was for Gosvintha's party to rendezvous with the Greutungi Goths led by Alatheus at the Ford of Constantine. There, Alatheus would cross the great river in one of the few places where it was wide and slow enough for the Greutungi horses to swim across.

Elodia expressed concern that the Roman garrison in the nearby fortress of Oescus might interfere, but Gosvintha said that garrison, along with all the other Danube limitanei, had been withdrawn the previous year.

Nevertheless, out of caution, Gosvintha avoided approaching Oescus along the Via Istrum. Though it was the shortest and best road, running beside the Danube River, it went right through Oescus City. Instead, they planned to travel a minor inland road, one that intersected the Via Istrum just upstream from the fortress.

A week after leaving Durostorum, Gosvintha's party arrived on the hills above Oescus. From their vantage point, they could see the great width of the river.

Elodia informed Avagis that the Roman Emperor Constantine had once built a bridge across the river linking Oescus with Dacia. Avagis asked her to repeat her story about the bridge in front of everyone. "Tell your tale aloud so all can hear," he said. With that wide river in plain sight, she could hardly repeat her story, at least not without laughing. Perhaps a god could build a bridge that long, but no human, not even a Roman, could span that distance. The others all hooted at her foolish story.

The Chi Rho banners of Emperor Valens flew above the city walls, indicating it was once again in Roman hands.

They could see horses and the occasional rafts crossing the river. Heva, Avagis's teenage daughter, said, "Look, there is fighting!" She must have had good eyesight because, from this distance, Elodia could hardly see what she meant. Indeed, as the rafts and animals came ashore, they were assailed by men on the bank.

"The men on this shore are Romans. I can just make out their aquila," Heva said. Elodia could see the sunlight reflecting off that brass standard, but unlike Heva, she could not identify it as an eagle. "And the people coming ashore are wearing barbarian dress."

Far below was the Via Istrum, the imperial river road, which closely followed the river upstream and down. And they could see their road going downhill to the west of the fortress, where it joined the Via Istrum. They quietly walked their horses downhill on a stretch of road flanked by trees, blocking the view of the fortress and the riverside fight. As they neared the shore, Avagis, Heva, and Elodia left their horses behind and crept ahead to reconnoiter. They confirmed the barbarians were Alatheus's people, and their foes were Roman legionaries, doubtless part of the garrison from Oescus.

The Romans were having the best of it. The Danube's rushing current pushed the rafts and horses into a muddy stretch of beach, where Roman swords greeted them. The rafts ran aground a dozen feet from the shore, leaving the Goths to trudge through ankle-deep mud. The mud sucked at their sandals, making every step a trial. Every time a raft landed or a horse struggled ashore, the warriors would struggle out of the mud and try to establish a beachhead. But the Romans would redeploy and wipe them out.

There seemed to be no end of horses and rafts on the river. The river was so broad that those crossing had no idea what was happening to those who'd crossed before, nor could they know their landing site was terribly dangerous.

The three scouts risked moving close to the junction of their road and the Via Istrum. To Elodia's surprise, their road continued beyond the crossroads and up a wide concrete ramp, which rose high above the river. They crawled through the crossroads and up the ramp, where it ended in an abrupt drop, falling thirty feet to the river below. They peered over the east edge. The Romans were directly below, quietly waiting for the next group of Goths to land and be slaughtered. They backed away from the edge far enough to where they could stand without being seen.

The scouts quickly returned up the road to where everyone else stood waiting. "What can we do?" Avagis asked. "We should help, but what can our few warriors do against a cohort of legionaries?"

Elodia answered, "I have a plan."

It only took a few minutes to trot down the hill and across the crossroads, and up the ramp. There they quickly established a defensive line across the bottom of the ramp using logs, brambles, and loose bricks from the ramp itself. The ramp provided protection for their flanks and rear. When their defenses were as secure as possible, their archers leaned over the ramp's edge and opened fire on the Romans below.

A large group of Goths struggled to come ashore. None got more than two steps out of the water before being cut down by the waiting legionaries. One warrior, who had fallen to his knees in the mud, looked up to see a Roman raise his sword, readying a killing blow. He watched, frozen, expecting to see the blade arc forward. Instead, the Roman collapsed, an arrow protruding from his chest. Elodia smiled a grim smile, her first kill of the day.

The Romans did not notice Elodia's archers until a dozen of their comrades had already fallen in their midst. At that point, their vaunted discipline fell apart. A few left their shield wall and retreated away from the shore to attack up the ramp. When others saw their comrades retreating, they assumed the attack was coming from the rear. Perhaps their imaginations magnified a few warriors into a thousand. In any case, the retreat became a rout. This allowed the Goths to establish a secure beachhead, which they reinforced minute-by-minute as additional men came ashore. Elodia dropped ropes, allowing warriors to climb to their position atop the ramp and strengthen her defensive line.

The Romans retreated in poor order to the fortress. Elodia had won not by killing but by making them panic. There was an interval where they might have counterattacked, but they did not, letting the advantage shift in her favor. The garrison's primary mission was to defend the fortress. They only ventured outside its gates when the risk was minimal. They would not come out again.

The losses to Elodia's people were light. None of their warriors were killed, but Heva was wounded, and Artos had a narrow brush with death.

Elodia had just finished treating a warrior's wound when Heva and Artos approached her. She was hobbling with a crude bandage around her thigh. At first glance, it looked like she was leaning on Artos for support, but then Elodia could see Heva directing Artos's movements, steering him by pulling hard on his ponytail, this way and that. She looked angry. He looked downcast.

Elodia could see blood through Heva's bandage. "Sit down. Let me look at that." Heva did so, while retaining her hold on Artos's hair. Elodia cut off the bandage. "You're lucky. It's just a shallow slash. How did it happen?"

Heva, looking sourly down at Artos, said, "You tell her, you idiot."

Artos looked up at Elodia. "Me and Heva was guarding a log when a Roman jumps up on it. I sees him and am just about to cut his balls right off when Heva pushes into my way. So, I pokes her by an accident with my knife." Then he turned to the young woman. "I'm sorry, Heva. Sorry you wasn't watching what you was doing," he said defiantly.

Heva reached down and smacked him. She looked at Elodia. "A legionary was just about to split this little shit's skull. I lunged and put my spear through the soldier's face. And what thanks did I get for saving his useless life? He stabbed me! I came within a hair of killing him!"

Nearby warriors, hearing this exchange, burst into laughter. Seeing how high the wound was on her thigh, one exclaimed, "The boy came close to cutting *her* balls off!" The crowd found that hilarious, but Artos looked around and felt confused and embarrassed. He turned bright red. He looked at Elodia. "Is Heva going to be all right?"

Elodia assured him, "She will be just fine." She saw a tear in his eyes.

He moved close to Heva and, putting his arm around her, said, "I am sorry, Heva. I would never try to cut your balls off." He realized how stupid that sounded the moment the words were out. So did the gathered crowd, who roared with laughter.

Elodia pulled both young people into a hug. "That was very brave of both of you."

Heva relaxed her grip on Artos's hair, replacing it with a kiss. "Especially brave of you, Artos," she said, "attacking a swordsman with a knife. Such an idiotic thing to do."

Now reconciled, the two were the subject of many toasts once the ale barrels were opened. One warrior even composed a song about the incident. By the next day, no one could remember the lyrics. *Probably just as well.*

———✦———

The plan described by Gosvintha faltered when the Greutungi Goths were turned back at the Succi Pass. The Romans had fortified it heavily. It lay on the Via Militaris and was the most significant choke point for travelers moving in and out of the Balkans.

Alatheus was carefully studying the Roman defenses, planning with his lieutenants a strategy to overcome them, when Farnobius, ever impatient, led a frontal assault against the Roman palisade. That thoughtless attack killed a dozen fine warriors and led to an argument between the two lords. The argument did not result in physical violence, but it fueled the long-time rivalry between them.

Farnobius announced that his clan would head east and sack Beroe City, which his spies said was ripe for the plucking. Alatheus countered, saying his forces would move to the sweet grasslands just west of Dibaltum, a Black Sea port.

Gosvintha, maintaining her long allegiance to Farnobius, said she would follow him, whereas Avagis sided with Alatheus.

Elodia asked Avagis, "Why do you side with Lord Alatheus when your woman sides with Lord Farnobius?"

"Precisely because Gosvintha sides with him."

"Things are not good between you two?"

"No. She has taken up with another, that big Hun, the one they call Octar."

Elodia was not surprised. One night while she and Gosvintha were well into their drink, she'd asked how many lovers Gosvintha had enjoyed. The woman warrior tried to count them but ran out of fingers.

"Will you fight him for her?"

"Fight for Gosvintha?" Avagis laughed. "No, she does her own fighting. I would be fighting both Octar and her. Even if I won, I would lose. No, I have graciously surrendered her. It is time for Heva and I to find another woman."

Elodia saw him looking pointedly at her. She had longed for a warm companion on cold nights, but her fantasies never included Avagis. Yet he was as tall and broad as Caius, with a short black beard and a single eyebrow that framed his face. He stayed bald by scraping his scalp clean. He was not unattractive.

She ignored his stare, but she weighed his decision as she considered her own, Lord Alatheus or Lord Farnobius?

Artos lobbied to go with Alatheus because of his friendship with Heva. For Elodia, a more important consideration was the two men's characters. Alatheus came to decisions with cool deliberation. Farnobius was a hothead, someone who had shown he would throw away young lives. For Artos's sake, she picked Alatheus.

Elodia made a point of telling Gosvintha when the two women were working side-by-side grooming their horses.

"Gosvintha, my friend, you intend to accompany Lord Farnobius when he rides east to Beroe?"

"Of course. I am pledged to his service. Oh, he would release me if I asked, but Octar admires him, and I," she licked her lips, "greatly admire Octar."

"This makes me sad," said Elodia, "I will miss you. I intend to follow Alatheus. And plan to keep Artos with me, unless as his mother, you object."

"I can understand your choice. Alatheus is a good man, but a timid man. Farnobius is bold, a man of action, as the late skirmish at Succi Pass showed. That appeals to Octar and me."

More foolish than bold.

Gosvintha continued, "But I am not one to mother a small boy. It is proper for you to first consider Artos's safety. I trust you to keep him safe.

"I will also miss you. We women warriors are few. It has been a joy to ride by your side."

"We will meet and ride together again," said Elodia. "I am sure." But she was wrong. Once they parted ways, Elodia would never see her friend or Artos his mother again.

The large party of Greutungi split into smaller groups, each looking for good pasturage and for settlements they could profitably plundered.

Within a week, Elodia evicted Artos from her tent in favor of Avagis. The boy joined Heva as her new tentmate. Elodia enjoyed cuddling with Avagis and rubbing his bald pate in the tent they shared.

The barbarians, however, like savage beasts that had broken their cages, poured raging over the wide extent of Thracia and made for a town called Dibaltum, where they found Barzimeres, tribune of the targeteers, a leader experienced in the dust of warfare, with his own men, the Cornuti, and other companies of infantry, and fell upon him just as he was pitching his camp. He at once, as the exigency of imminent destruction compelled him, ordered the trumpet to sound the attack and, having protected his flanks, charged out at the head of his brave soldiers, who were ready and armed for battle...

From Res Gestae, Volume XXXI 8.9-10, by Ammianus Marcellinus

Women reasoned that Loki, the prankster god, considered it a great joke to start a woman's labor at the worst possible time.

Silvan had prayed to Jesus that the baby would not come while they struggled over Rishki Pass. The pass was difficult and certainly harder than Nedarcus and she could have managed without Gotheric's help.

Late on a warm spring day, they were two days south of the pass in the hill country overlooking the Black Sea city of Dibaltum. *The sun sinks so slowly into the western hills. It's as if evening might last forever.* Not true, Silvan knew, but there would be time enough before nightfall to descend from the hills and camp in the plains below.

Her reflection was interrupted when a messenger charged past, shouting, "Form wagon-fort! Warriors to the front!"

"Why?" yelled Nedarcus. The messenger didn't stop to reply but continued galloping down the column shouting the same order. It did not take long for the answer to arrive by rumor, passed from wagon to wagon. The scouts had spotted Romans. How many? The number grew as the rumor progressed. What started as a single cohort was, by the time the talk reached the last wagon, four legions.

Before the circle was complete, all the warriors had disappeared to the south, prepared for battle. An hour later, a messenger came back carrying a wounded warrior. On his sword arm, he wore a makeshift bandage and tourniquet. Nedarcus looked him over and decided that the crude dressing was adequate for now. He said they needed to move the medical cart closer to the battle so they could quickly treat the wounded before they bled out. The messenger guided them—with Silvan riding in the wagon, Nedarcus leading the mule, and Gotheric walking alongside, sword drawn— three miles south to where a scene from Hades was unfolding.

They stopped on a hilltop well short of the action. Nedarcus said, "Never mind the tent. Just make my battle instruments ready." By that, he meant a table where he could strap a warrior down while amputating a limb, a second table where Silvan could stitch up and bandage wounds, and the saws, clamps, and dressings they would need.

Silvan could see the Goths outnumbered the Romans, who were in complete disarray. There was a log palisade, typical of a Roman camp that they would erect nightly, but some sections were not yet up. A ditch in front of the barrier also had gaps. Around the ditch were dead Roman soldiers, caught off guard by the Goths' surprise attack. The dead soldiers had been armed only with shovels. The Goths had rushed through the gaps in the ditch, past the partial palisade, and laid waste to the Romans inside the camp. Had the Romans another half hour available, they would have finished their night camp and been safe from such a devastating attack.

As Elodia watched, a line of Romans inside the camp moved toward the gaps in the palisade, advancing in proper formation, pushing back the Goths. The Goths retreated through the gaps out of the camp. When the Roman line reached the gaps, a whistle blew, and the line paused. Even from her distance, she could hear men shouting and screaming. Some of the Goths had been caught with their backs to the palisade. Unable to retreat through a gap, the Romans were killing them.

After a short period, she heard the whistle blow again, and the line advanced beyond the palisade and then beyond the ditch. The Goths' efforts to stop the Roman advance failed. They could not form a shield wall of their own, having neither the shields nor the training. Some tried to flank the Roman line, but that proved difficult in the failing light. The Romans numbered more than the Goths, and as their line advanced, they had no trouble extending it at either end. Indeed, it was the Goths who were in danger of being enveloped.

Gotheric said, "We need to move. The Romans will be on us in no time."

Nedarcus didn't argue. He took the mule's reins, but the animal locked its legs and wouldn't budge. Gotheric and Silvan had loaded one table and were loading the second when she cried out, "Oh Jesus, not now!" Her water had broken. She dropped her end of the table and moaned under the blow of the first contraction.

Gotheric said, "Fryke the fryking table." He carefully lifted Silvan and put her into the cart. Then he went to help Nedarcus with the obstinate mule. Try as they might, it would not move. Gotheric looked back and saw the Roman line only a few hundred yards away. The Goths holding them back were quickly dissolving. He returned to the cart, gathered up Silvan, and began trotting toward the wagon-fort, with Nedarcus following right behind.

"My tools!" moaned the medicus. It had taken him years to find just the perfect saw for amputations, and now it would fall into Roman hands.

The three had not gone more than a hundred paces when a horde of Gothic cavalry streamed past into the fray. Now it was the Romans' turn to shout and scream. The horsemen kept coming, squad after squad. Silvan could hear the battle until she was lost in her own world of pain. Nedarcus had hoped to reach the wagon-fort, where midwives would be available, but the three of them were still well short of it, and the baby wasn't waiting. He had Gotheric put her down and asked her to squat. Nedarcus stood behind her to keep her upright and put his arms under her armpits to take her weight. After a minute, he gasped to Gotheric, "I can't do this. She's too heavy for me."

Gotheric, who had been standing around feeling useless, was happy to take over from his father. Nedarcus moved around in front, ready to catch the baby.

In all the commotion, no one could hear Silvan's screams. But her cries ended far sooner than Nedarcus would have expected. Soon he was holding a baby girl. Later Silvan swore, despite all the racket, she could hear the baby's first cry.

It was dusk, and the Greutungi were approaching their own camp when by chance, they encountered Fritigern's wagon-fort outside of Dibaltum and heard, just beyond it, the sounds of battle. They leaped to their cousins' aid.

Avagis and Elodia found themselves well back in the galloping body of horsemen, which passed by their ally's wagons and charged toward the Goths' common enemy. The cavalry rode past the Tervingi forces and smashed into the Roman line. The lead riders trampled through the legionaries and wheeled to assail them from behind. By the time Elodia entered the fight, the Romans were scattered and running toward the doubtful safety of their incomplete palisade.

She noticed, a few yards on, a small cluster of men standing on a hillock, not retreating. With a shout to Avagis and his cousins, she charged them. Each warrior picked their own opponent. Elodia chose the tall man whose armor glittered in the failing light. Though his fellows closed to protect him, her lance caught him in the chest. Avagis and the other warriors quickly killed the others with sword and lance. She'd slain the Roman commander, Tribune Barzimeres.

In Silvan's opinion, the Goths suffered a despairingly large number of casualties. The first day after the battle, Gotheric had to substitute for her as a helper while Nedarcus performed amputations and stitched wounds. By the second day, she could advise Gotheric though she was too busy caring for her baby to do much more. By the third day, she could leave baby Jellena—for she had named the baby in honor of her late sister-in-law—with Nedarcus while she and Gotheric worked as a team. Nedarcus was always exhausted and complained of ongoing chest pains. Silvan became the lead medicus, and Nedarcus an adviser. The trip over the pass and the battle had taken so much out of him. No amount of sleep seemed to help.

As horrific as the Gothic casualties were, the Roman deaths were much worse. Of the three cohorts engaged, the Goths had killed almost all of them. Some survivors escaped fleeing south into the forests. Others fled east into Dibaltum, only a few miles from the battle site. That was an unlucky choice, for, in the dark, some Goths mixed among the fleeing Romans.

Once inside the city, they blocked all efforts to close the city gates, allowing a large force of barbarians to enter. The Goths sacked the city, killing all the soldiers they could find and any civilians who stood in their way.

Among the Romans captured was a Marshal of the Court named Aequitius, a top-ranking figure in Valens's imperial court. He was able to identify the body of the Commander of the Guards. "It was Barzimeres," he said to Fritigern, "who rallied the troops and pushed you out of our camp. We would have beaten you if those Huns hadn't shown up at the last moment." Later he was paraded before the Gothic troops, publicly humiliated and tortured.

Fritigern didn't argue with Aequitius's opinion. He might have taken exception with the marshal's description of the cavalry as Huns. They were his Greutungi allies, but if the Romans wanted to believe the terrifying Hun cavalry destroyed Barzimeres, so much the better.

... And by his [Barzimeres] valiant resistance, he would have withdrawn on equal terms had not the charge of a large force of cavalry surrounded him when he was breathless from fatigue. And so he fell after having slain not a few of the barbarians, whose losses were concealed by their great numbers.

From Res Gestae, Volume XXXI 8.9-10, by Ammianus Marcellinus

Several days after the battle, Elodia and Avagis rode to the Tervingi wagon-fort. They left their mounts hitched to a friend's cart and walked through the warren of tents, looking for the medical tent. It was simple to find: they followed the moans of the many wounded. Avagis pointed to it as Elodia watched Fritigern and Athena go in. Just the sight of her made Elodia bristle. But she quieted when she heard a baby crying.

"Silvan had her baby!"

When they reached the tent, Elodia could hear Fritigern talking to Nedarcus, his voice marked with genuine concern for the old man.

"You look tired, my friend."

Nedarcus said, "Isn't everyone? It's been a busy week. I'll be better after a night or two of rest."

Elodia chose that moment to poke her head into the tent. "Resting is for the dead!" she proclaimed.

Silvan shrieked in joy and threw herself at her friend. A brief melee followed, with Elodia being passed for kisses and embraces from Gotheric to Nedarcus and back to Silvan, as Elodia struggled to hold the new baby. Avagis stood off to the side, looking self-conscious, until Silvan noticed and pulled him into the scrum of hugging limbs.

Fritigern stood well clear of the throng and wore an uncomfortable smile. Athena stood behind him, hands on hips, with a sneer on her lips.

When a semblance of calm was restored, Fritigern asked Elodia, "Were you with the cavalry?"

"With them? I led them!" she said, exaggerating slightly, "and it was my lance that destroyed the Roman general!" With that, she seized a spear, brandished, and shook it.

Gotheric had never met the great strapping barbarian who seemed glued to Elodia's side. "It's Avagis, isn't it?" he said. The two men exchanged handshakes.

Elodia turned her attention to her former lover and the woman he now seemed to favor. She handed Avagis the spear, strode across the tent, threw her arms around Fritigern's neck, and gave him a prolonged and probing kiss. Silvan glanced at Athena, who turned red and furious as she watched a rival feverishly embrace her man.

Silvan whispered to Gotheric, "It's good *she's* not holding the spear."

Finally, Fritigern pulled his tongue from between Elodia's teeth and pushed her back. "Phew! That was more exciting than seeing your warriors arrive!" he said with a grin.

"And this man is Avagis?"

"Indeed! This is my new lover. Avagis, meet my old lover Fritigern." Avagis grunted a greeting and punched Fritigern's shoulder in a manly way, a gesture that Fritigern returned.

Fritigern said, "Avagis, this is my wife, Athena."

Avagis did not offer her his hand—he'd been warned—but gave her a slight bow. "Elodia explained *all about* you. When did Fritigern start marrying his women?"

Elodia smiled at Avagis's comment. She said to Fritigern, "So, this is the breeder you married. She has a pretty face. And those hips should be good for a dozen boys. It's hard to believe you traded me for this one!"

Athena looked ready to spit. She turned to Fritigern, a look demanding that he do something to protect her honor. He did nothing but show an embarrassed grin.

For the first time, Elodia felt a tinge of shame. *Perhaps I said what he can't. Theirs is not a happy marriage.*

There may have been more to say, but Nedarcus butted in, "I have work to do, and these wounded warriors need rest and quiet. Please take your talk outside." Which they did, leaving him, Gotheric, and Silvan alone with the wounded.

After the Roman defeat, the wagon-fort remained near Dibaltum for the rest of the summer. Within its great circle, the Goths erected a forest of tents; campfires abounded, and the smell of cooked pig and sheep wafted throughout. The celebrations continued night and day with singing, dancing, and wrestling contests. The quantities of beer and wine looted from the city fueled the festivities. Only when the casks and jugs were empty did life return to normal. There were serious matters to address, such as the division of the arms and armor taken from the Roman dead and the plunder procured from the city. As a Black Sea port, Dibaltum had many warehouses. These contained enough grain and other foodstuffs to allow Fritigern to proclaim the Goths would not go hungry for the rest of the year. There was no need to torment Thracia further.

Of course, parties of young men, bored with camp life, would set out for an adventure. These excursions began as simple banditry, robbing any travelers or traders foolish enough to move without adequate guards. Later, as the year wore on, they started to harass the long columns of reinforcements, who had come from afar to relieve the garrisons of Roman-held towns.

One such town was Beroe, which Farnobius conquered and sacked. His marauding did not go unchallenged. Roman general Frigiderus attacked Farnobius and then retreated across the width of Thracia to the Succi Pass with Farnobius in hot pursuit. It was a trick. Once at the pass, the Roman general turned around and destroyed Lord Farnobius.

Silvan learned of subsequent events when a half-starved boy, one of Farnobius's followers, appeared at Fritigern's wagon-fort.

"My Lord Farnobius thought we'd chased away General Frigeridus. But a day came when the Romans appeared without warning. It was as if they'd sprung from the ground and silently surrounded our camp in the night.

"I fought by my lord's side until a Roman horseman broke through our line and impaled him on his lance. Then the fight went out of us, and we threw down our weapons and begged for mercy."

Silvan was aghast at hearing this news. "Did you see what became of the lady Gosvintha?"

"Yes, she was at her lord's side, along with her Hun lover, a giant of a man. He died first when a Roman spear caught him in the side. Then I saw her fall when a legionary rang her steel helmet with his hammer as if it were a gong."

"Did she die?"

"I don't know. I was struck down moments later. The Romans left me for dead, or perhaps they thought me too insignificant to be worth capturing."

Silvan doubted that. The Romans captured and enslaved children much smaller than the boy. She imagined the boy took advantage of the battlefield confusion and ran away.

He had no more information, but Silvan later learned that many of Farnobius's people survived. They were sold as farmworkers to the great landed estates in Italy. No one knew if Gosvintha was among them, and no one ever saw her again.

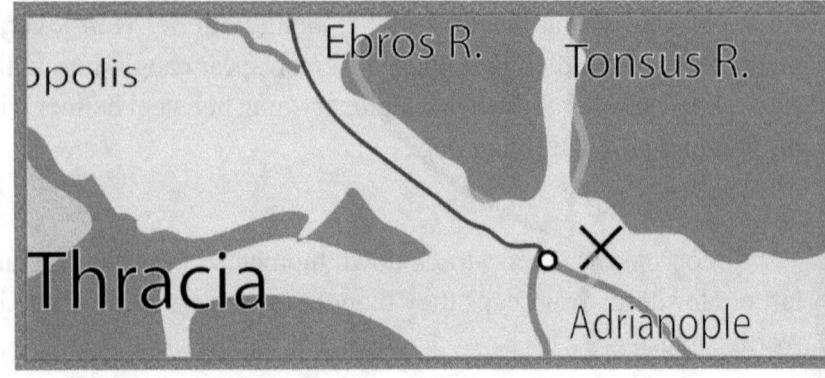

12. Battle of Adrianople 378 CE

Clodia and Artos walked slowly toward the gatehouse of Licinius Sabinus's estate. In one hand, she held a heavy canvas bag; in the other, Artos's hand. Two hundred yards behind her, ranged along a ridge overlooking the gatehouse, were hundreds of mounted warriors, Alatheus's Goths.

Alatheus's forces, after their victory at Dibaltum, turned south. His forces divided, with small groups living off the land by marauding all over the Balkans, from Greece to Lake Lychnidus. In the autumn, they returned north, hoping to pass along the Via Militaris into Pannonia, where they could spend the winter. But again, the Roman forces turned them back at the Succi Pass. They retreated southeast to Philippopolis and, finding that city's gates barred against them and its walls crowded with men-at-arms, turned to the green fields north of the Maritsa River. They met only minor opposition before arriving at the vast estate of Licinius Sabinus. Within its thousands of acres, only a few acres were surrounded by a wall, a wall that protected the patrician's opulent villa.

Elodia, by bringing the boy along, indicated to the gatehouse guards that she was no immediate threat, unlike the force that backed her. As she approached the guards, several leveled their spears at her. She addressed the one without a spear and who wore a gold medallion, the guard captain. "I require speech with Lord Sabinus."

She was expensively dressed, walked with the poise of a queen, and her beauty surprised him as much as her crisp Greek diction. He answered in a respectful tone. "I can convey any message you might wish." He spoke confidently, but she noticed him glancing nervously over her shoulder at the mass of barbarians on the hill.

"I wish to give him this." She opened the heavy bag, showing him the contents.

He jumped back, composed himself, and said, "I shall take it to his lordship."

"No," said Elodia, "He must come for it himself."

Within a few minutes, Licinius Sabinus stood before her and, hands shaking, accepted the bag. "How?... Why?..." His voice cracked as he spoke.

"This was your son Julius?" she asked, referring to the bloody, severed head in the bag. He nodded.

"He and a small band of men, I would not even call them fighters, tried to block our road. He had courage; I'll give him that. He had launched into a speech about Roman citizenship and the rule of law when one of my impulsive friends silenced him with a spear. Perhaps if he'd spoken Gothic, my friend would have been more patient."

She continued, "One of his comrades, who wisely dropped his weapon, explained who he was. I thought it would be a kindness to deliver his head to you."

Licinius Sabinus, still clutching the bag, sank to his knees. "What do you want?"

"We would like to purchase your estate. To avoid further bloodshed, we can offer you a fair price."

The aristocrat stifled his sobbing. "And what is that?"

"Safe passage for you and any who wish to accompany you to Philippopolis."

"And…?"

"That is it. We will move in and try to avoid burning the place down, as happened with the Volesus villa."

Licinius Sabinus had not heard the fate of his friend Senator Tosca Volesus. Elodia swiftly recounted the story as told to her by Silvan. Perhaps it was the picture of ending up as pig fodder that convinced Licinius Sabinus to accept Elodia's offer.

The Goths moved into the villa. With its many rooms, each family needed to share with only a few other families and their horses. The high ceilings meant the small cookfires they lit in each room were not too smokey, although they ruined the ceiling murals. The villa provided Alatheus's Greutungi with a good shelter for the coming winter.

As the summer of 377 CE came to a long and turbulent end, as all the lakes and rivers began to freeze, Fritigern led his Tervingi into winter quarters in the city of Cabyle, which the Goths had seized earlier in the year. After the total destruction of nearby Dibaltum, the fearful duumviri of Cabyle threw open its gates, hoping to escape a similar fate, a largely successful tactic. Fritigern decided the city would make an ideal headquarters. Its defenses were intact, the local harvest was bountiful, and the nearby Black Sea promised to take the edge off the worst of the winter storms that blew south from the Haemus mountains, only twenty miles to the north.

Cabyle served as a center of operations for the Goths. Spies and traveling merchants provided intelligence of Roman strength and disposition. Legions continued to pour in from Asia Minor, making the Gothic hold on the roads to Constantinople tenuous. Yet the Goths continued to poke at the Romans, hoping to draw them out of the capital city in strength. At least one such raiding party got caught in the open and crushed. This was the first time Silvan heard of the victorious general, Magister Peditum Sebastianus, the master of infantry.

With the medical cart parked in the city, Nedarcus and Silvan had few patients. Gotheric returned to serve in Fritigern's bodyguard, but he frequently came to enjoy an evening meal lovingly prepared by Silvan and to bounce little Jellena on his knee. He would sing her songs and keep the two medici up to date on events.

"He knew their target and was lying in wait," Gotheric said, referring to the destroyed raiding party.

"Who is 'he'?" asked Silvan. Gotheric and Nedarcus were talking. Silvan had come late to the conversation.

"Sebastianus is his name. One of Valens's most seasoned generals and now his master of infantry. We wouldn't know it was him, but the man is a great boaster. He loudly brags of his victories in Egypt, Persia, and the north; and that he has never been defeated. His troops are said to love him and almost raised him to be the Western emperor after the death of Valentinian."

"I'm sorry, Gotheric, but who was Valentinian?"

"He was Valens's brother, and the father of Gratian. So, Western Emperor Gratian is the nephew of Eastern Emperor Valens."

She shook her head. "It's all so confusing. Why don't they have real names like 'Gotheric'?"

Gotheric laughed. "An excellent question. I don't know. Perhaps their names mean something in Latin."

Silvan continued to sleep with Nedarcus, but that was all the two did. The medicus was old now and tired and needed her warmth under their shared blankets. Even if he had the will to do more, he no longer had the means and hadn't since the battle near Dibaltum. She loved the old man—he had not seemed old when she first met him—and she had counted on him for status and protection for herself and now, for her daughter. *But he is dying. When he's gone, what shall I do?* Then, with guilt tempered by necessity, her eyes turned to Gotheric.

Looking at Gotheric reminded her of the lusty nights she and Nedarcus had once shared. Being a dutiful son, Gotheric had never, as far as she'd noticed, looked at her in that way, but now if he did, her willpower would melt.

Winter passed and turned into the spring of 378 CE. The Gothic raiders returned to Cabyle from all over the Balkans, from wherever they had ventured. Some had gone as far as Macedonia and Greece. Master of Infantry Sebastianus used guerrilla tactics to assault the Goths on the move.

The pressure grew on Fritigern to take decisive action. Reports from his spies within Constantinople said the emperor was also under tremendous pressure from its citizens to act against the Goths. The people blamed him, justifiably, for the devastation of the Balkans since it was Valens who granted the Goths permission to cross the Danube. By May, Valens imagined he had sufficient forces to crush them, but a few of his generals disagreed. Even his nephew, Emperor Gratian, leading armies from the west, cautioned him to wait until their forces could unite. However, Magister Peditum Sebastianus, confident after a series of small victories, said the time to act had come. He asked why Emperor Valens should share the brilliance of the inevitable triumph with his nephew.

As a final provocation, Fritigern led his Tervingi out of Cabyle and headed down the Via Militaris toward Constantinople. Nedarcus and Silvan went along, with Gotheric leading the medical cart.

Nedarcus was worried. "Where are the Greutungi?" he asked, a rhetorical question. Those horsemen from the east had not wintered with the Tervingi, which was fortunate. Having the Tervingi cooped up in the city was bad enough. Much of Silvan's bone-setting resulted from fights among bored young men unused to city living. Mixing with clans from another tribe, one used to living on the open Scythian plains, would have stirred more fights, possibly feuds, and even inter-tribal warfare. But Silvan worried about Elodia. *Where is she?*

"Lord Alatheus promised their support when the time is right. They will come," Gotheric declared.

"Well, they haven't, have they! Despite Fritigern dispatching messengers to Alatheus!"

"I wouldn't worry. Alatheus knows we must stand united if we don't want the Romans to destroy us, tribe by tribe."

Silvan said, "Yes, that is what the Romans do. Remember the Roman king, Yulius Kaiser, and how he conquered the Gauls?" The story of Kaiser versus the Gauls was the stuff of legend passed down from generation to generation. Even campfire songs recalled how, a hundred hundred years before, Kaiser had defeated each Gaulish tribe one by one. Soon he had defeated all the Gauls except the one led by their great hero Vercingetorix.

The songs said that after a long siege of Alesia, the Gaul's capital city, and with the help of the Roman gods, Kaiser took the city and captured its leader. They told how the Roman king tied each of Vercingetorix's limbs to a horse and laughed as the four horses tore him apart. During the whole execution, the hero never uttered a cry. But when his limbless body fell to the ground, Vercingetorix jumped up onto his legless hips and cursed Yulius Kaiser before falling over dead. Within a year, Odin struck down Kaiser with a lightning bolt, fulfilling Vercingetorix's curse.

Silvan knew the song and, with encouragement from Gotheric, sang it that evening when the column of wagons had circled for the night. The adults clapped their appreciation. The children enjoyed reenacting his grisly death and trying to outdo each other in ever more hideous versions of Vercingetorix's final fate.

... But on the dawn of that day, which is numbered in the calendar as the fifth before the Ides of August, the army began its march with extreme haste, leaving all its baggage and packs near the walls of Adrianople with a suitable guard of legions; for the treasury, and the insignia of imperial dignity besides, with the prefect and the emperor's council, were kept within the circuit of the walls. So after hastening a long distance over rough ground, while the hot day was advancing toward noon, finally at the eighth hour [after sunrise], they saw the wagons of the enemy, which, as the report of the scouts had declared, were arranged in the form of a perfect circle. And while the barbarian soldiers, according to their custom, uttered savage and dismal howls, the Roman leader so drew up their line of battle...

From Res Gestae, Volume XXXI 12.10-11, by Ammianus Marcellinus

Nedarcus sniffed the air. "A battle is coming. A big one. Soon, very soon."

After three days, the Gothic column reached the vicinity of Adrianople. Fritigern's scouts reported a mass of Roman troops to the south. One scout even reported seeing the imperial standard of Emperor Valens himself. Other scouts disputed that, but Fritigern believed it, saying, "The man thinks himself invincible. He has surrounded himself with flatterers who constantly remind him of his greatness. Of course, he wants to be present at the glorious battle. He sees no possible outcome but triumph."

Nedarcus, feeling glum, decided Valens might very well be correct.

Fritigern formed the wagon-fort on a hilltop northeast of Adrianople near the banks of the Tonsus River, a hard day's march over rough terrain from the city. "Let the legions come to us," he said. "A long brisk walk under the hot summer sun will do them good." He knew the Romans would be thirsty and exhausted when they finally faced his Tervingi warriors.

Nedarcus and Silvan dealt with the stress by setting up the tools of their morbid trade. They had strapped little Jellena into a corner of the wagon. She howled. Silvan took a moment to look down the hill and across the waving red plain. *An odd color.* She rubbed her eyes and looked again. The plain was covered in legionaries in their red cloaks. The view rippled and wavered in the heat as the legions, a dozen or more, marched ever closer.

Gotheric returned from Fritigern's side to update Silvan and Nedarcus on the situation. He was feeling pessimistic for a change. There was a rumor that the Greutungi had arrived during the night after riding hard down the Tonsus valley, but come the light of day, there was no sign of the Gothic cavalry. Gotheric did not stay long but returned to Fritigern. Nedarcus and Silvan watched their warriors deploy in a well-formed shield-wall downslope from the wagon-fort.

Silvan remembered Gotheric's words. These were not the undisciplined warriors, he had said, who had thrown themselves at the Romans during Ad Salices. These men (and a few women) were now well-equipped with weapons and armor. They had had a year to train, working together in teams. They performed proper maneuvers as signaled by whistles and war drums. Silvan wasn't so foolish to say the Goths were a match for the legionaries, but she hoped and prayed they would not slaughter her people again.

The hardest part was the waiting. Rumors abounded. It was said that Fritigern and Valens were negotiating for peace. Some said Master of Infantry Sebastianus had ambushed and butchered all the Gothic cavalry. Others said Fritigern, faced with that disaster and suing for peace, was picking hostages to exchange with the Romans. The only thing Silvan knew for sure was the hillside between the foes was now on fire, obscuring her view of the enemy. The long brown winter grass, burning hot, generated mountains of smoke, which, thankfully, the north wind blew from the wagon-fort onto the Romans below.

It all changed in a moment with shouts and screams. The Romans started the battle by launching an archery assault. Warriors dragged back wounded comrades up the hill to the medical tent. Silvan and Nedarcus set to work digging out arrowheads and bandaging gaping holes. Soon the wounds became ghastly as the two forces came to grips and fought with sword and spear. The wounded lay on the ground near the tent, waiting their turn to be treated. Children distributed leather thongs for the badly injured to bite on. Other children carried flasks of water to the wounded. Older youths performed a much more perilous version of the same job, taking water to the warriors on the front line.

Then, in the early afternoon, as suddenly as it started, it stopped. Not the battle, to be sure. Silvan could hear the clash of arms, the shouts, and the screams, but all the clamor was more distant. Newly wounded warriors stopped arriving, giving Nedarcus and her a chance to help the wounded who had been waiting, some for hours. For many, their turn would never come, having bled out on the ground.

It was after nightfall when the noise of battle finally ceased. Silvan saw Gotheric returning, carrying a man over his shoulder. He gently laid him down on a mat in the tent. Silvan looked at the wounded man and shook her head. "It's a nasty gut wound. There's nothing we can do for him."

Gotheric said, "I know, but he wants to see Nedarcus."

Silvan was puzzled. She looked at Gotheric and then at the dying man. Suddenly she recognized him. It was Gavar, Gotheric's younger brother. Nedarcus, hearing the commotion, came over and kneeled by his younger son and took his hand. Gavar was in great pain but did not cry out. He mouthed a few words. Nedarcus leaned in, putting his ear next to his son's mouth.

Silvan went to fetch him water. The old man still gripped the young man's hand when she returned. Silvan could not hear what Gavar might have said. "Leave them," Gotheric said to Silvan. They moved out into the dark, found shelter under a wagon, and pulled a blanket over themselves. Despite the day's traumas, sleep took them instantly.

The messages from Fritigern to Alatheus had been explicit. The Goths, both tribes, Tervingi and Greutungi, would meet at Adrianople and crush Valens's vast army.

Elodia saw two faults with the plan. First, Alatheus's force had arrived at the city at dawn and were milling about beneath its walls. but where was Lord Fritigern's army? And where were the Romans?

Second, Elodia had watched her people go up against the superbly-trained and well-equipped Roman legions and win. But she would never use the word 'crush.' Every victory had been hard-fought and bloody.

After wasting an hour in confusion, Alatheus realized he'd led his cavalry to the wrong place. The battle would take place twenty miles to the northeast. He led his forces in that direction at a good trot, one that would eat up the distance by early afternoon without exhausting their mounts.

To learn the disposition of the Romans, he sent out a dozen boys on swift ponies to scout ahead. Artos was among them.

Elodia was sick with worry, but she had her own safety to consider. She rode beside Avagis and just ahead of Heva and her new beloved, a short compact warrior named Tolton. Heva was now seventeen, five years younger than her lover.

All were equipped with spears and swords. Shortly after noon, a pair of scouts returned to report that the rear of the Roman forces was only a mile ahead.

The scouts were shaken. Several of their number had been chased down by the Roman cavalry, caught, and killed. In her heart, Elodia knew Artos was among the dead.

Alatheus deployed his force in two lines, one to charge each Roman flank from the rear. Smoke from grass fires kept the Romans from noticing their approach. Elodia's horse shied when choking smoke blew in its face, but she had trained it well. Nothing slowed her attack.

The Roman line slowly dissolved under its impact. The Gothic cavalry shredded a path through a group of red-cloaked soldiers, then turned about and tore another route back the way they'd come.

Roman foot soldiers dashed toward the horsemen, swinging their swords, hoping to bring down both beast and rider. Occasionally they succeeded, but more often, the horsemen, working side-by-side, would slash and kill their foe and emerge unharmed.

Elodia spotted a group of boys making a stand inside a circle of slain ponies, expertly wielding their spears as they'd been trained, trying to keep their attackers at bay. The legionaries seemed to hold back and taunt the scouts. Did they think this was a game of cat and mouse, that they could toy with the youths before killing them?

One of the boys—Oh, Odin, it was Artos!—darted out, gutted a legionary, and retreated back into the relative safety of his comrades. For the legionaries, the death of a fellow brought the game to an end. They charged. But now she was there along with Avagis, Heva, and Tolton. This was a melee fought on foot, with swords and no quarter. It did not last long.

None of the boys' assailants survived. In the end, Artos survived, though two of his fellow scouts did not, and Avagis suffered a terrible slash to his chest.

Elodia knelt on the ground beside him, pressing her bare hands to his wound, trying to stop the bleeding. She looked up and around for help. She found herself surrounded by Gothic soldiers, looking down helplessly as she struggled. Where were her bandages? And her needle and stitching thread? The battle was over. But if the battle was over, why was Avagis still bleeding? It made no sense. She pressed down on his chest with both hands, her fingers spread, but blood flooded out between them. Where is Nedarcus? She needed her friend, the medicus. Her tunic was soaking up his life, turning red.

Heva knelt beside her father and pulled Elodia's hands away. "He's gone," she said. Which was impossible. But then Artos came over and held her. "Avagis is gone," he said, so she knew it was true.

*A*t the first coming of darkness, the emperor [Valens], amid the common soldiers as was supposed (for no one asserted that he had seen him or been with him), fell mortally wounded by an arrow and presently breathed his last breath; and he was never afterward found anywhere....

Amid this manifold loss of distinguished men, the deaths of Traianus and [Magister Peditum] Sebastianus stood out. With them fell thirty-five tribunes, without special assignments, and leaders of bodies of troops, as well as Valerianic and Aequitius, the one having charge of the stables, the other of the Palace. Among these, also Potentius lost his life in the first flower of his youth; he was tribune of the promoti respected by all good men and honored both for his own services...

Certain it is that barely a third part of our army escaped. The annals record no such massacre of a battle...

From Res Gestae, Volume XXXI 12.12,18-19, by Ammianus Marcellinus

---

*W*hen Silvan and Gotheric awoke the following day, they walked to the brink of the hill and looked over the battlefield below. He knew what he would see, but she did not. Silvan was shocked into silence. The plain was covered with bodies, broken spears, shattered armor, and more bodies. The devastation went out in all directions for at least a mile. Gothic women and children were working among the fallen, knifing any Roman wounded, respectfully dispatching any fatally wounded Gothic warriors, and searching the bodies and debris for objects of value.

Silvan's stomach turned at the gruesome sight. She said, "I knew we were victorious. Otherwise, the Romans would have overrun our camp last night, but such a victory? I could never have imagined!"

Gotheric said, "It was a near-run thing. We almost lost. The Romans would have beaten us, but the Greutungi finally showed up. They surrounded the rear of the Roman army. Once the Romans knew they were being attacked from the rear, they fell apart."

"How many died?" she asked.

"A thousand? Many thousand? Much higher than I can count," he said. "And we have found the body of Magister Peditum Sebastianus. Emperor Valens will have to find another master of infantry." Only some weeks later did they learn from sources in Constantinople that among the fifteen thousand dead was Emperor Valens himself.

The next few days were hectic. Gavar had died in the night. Silvan hardly knew him, but Gotheric was severely shaken. The prevailing story was that Fritigern, Gavar, and the other bodyguards were making their way back up the hill in the dusk when a Roman suddenly arose from a heap of bodies and ran Gavar through. Perhaps he had mistaken Gavar for Fritigern since they had a similar height and build. The other bodyguards ensured it was the Roman's ultimate blow. Gavar's body was consigned to a large burial pyre along with the hundreds of other Gothic dead.

"Are you saying that wasn't how Gavar was killed?" Silvan asked Gotheric after the funeral rites were complete.

"Not according to Father. He heard Gavar's last words. Gavar said Rodericus was standing beside Fritigern, that he saw the Roman coming and, rather than engage him, he nimbly stepped out of the way. That left only Gavar shielding Fritigern, Gavar who couldn't even see the Roman before he was wounded."

"Did Gavar think Rodericus deliberately moved aside?"

"Yes. Well, Gavar didn't say so, but why else would he mention it? Gavar and I had talked in the past. He, too, questioned Rodericus's loyalty to Fritigern. Gavar said Rodericus might be scheming to have himself declared king of the Goths."

"Do you think you should warn Fritigern?"

"He would talk to his wife, Athena, and she to her brother, Rodericus, and I would wake up with a slit throat."

Silvan smiled, saying, "I shouldn't like that," and patted his hand.

"I hope Elodia can keep Artos alive. As king, that boy, having noble parents, a Tervingi father, and a Greutungi mother, could bring all the Goths together," he said.

"I still have nightmares," she said. "In my dreams, I see the mutilated bodies of Elodia and Artos floating down the great river. Since they left with Gosvintha, we have heard nothing from them. Do you think they're alive?"

He smiled. "Of course they're alive. Elodia is a survivor. Artos could not have a better guardian."

Silvan and Nedarcus continued to tend the wounded, but after two days, Silvan found him kneeling immobile beside a young warrior who died even as Nedarcus was bandaging him. She tried to stir the old man, but he was incoherent. She would have called for Gotheric, but he had left with Fritigern and the rest of the fighting force to assail the city of Adrianople. *A stupid waste. Besieging the city will succeed no better now than last time.*

With help from friends, they moved the old man to a mat farther down the tent, away from the wounded. He responded enough to take a sip of water, then turned to lie down on his side. Silvan covered him with a blanket and kissed his face. She continued her duties but checked on Nedarcus from time to time.

In mid-afternoon, she found him dead. She cried silently, pulled the blanket over his head, and waited for Gotheric's return, hoping it would be soon.

After only two days, Fritigern and his bodyguards returned. Their siege of Adrianople had proved as useless as Silvan expected. Gotheric, hearing of his father's demise, wept silent tears. He recited the burial prayers, which he addressed to both the old gods and Jesus. Fritigern attended. He reminded his followers that praying to Jesus was appropriate since they were all Christians now. Then Gotheric lit his father's funeral pyre.

Silvan organized a funeral feast in honor of the dead medicus. As they had done in the past, Fritigern ensured there was sufficient meat, spices, fruit, and vegetables to properly dignify his old friend and to feed all the people who came.

Gotheric sat quietly beside the campfire when Silvan, duties complete, came over and sat with him.

"You seem to be taking his death in stride," she said.

"As do you. I was just his son, but you were his beloved."

"I may seem serene, but in truth, I ache. I ache until my whole body shakes, and I cannot breathe. We had a wonderful thing, but he and I knew he was nearing his time. I have been waiting for this for a while. Ever since Ad Salices. He could no longer shrug off all the pain and death."

"Yes," was Gotheric's only spoken answer, but he took her hands in his.

That night they eased each other's pain and became lovers.

The vast assemblage of Goths soon broke up, having thoroughly exploited the area around Adrianople for food. Each clan went its own way. The Greutungi went north toward Pannonia, where Alatheus had long coveted the vast grain fields.

With Avagis dead, Elodia did not seem to care where she went. Artos led her as they followed their lord, but he only took her as far as the Sabinus estate, where she and Avagis had been happy together. Artos said it was a place where they could live among friends and Avagis's family. A place to settle for good, or so he believed.

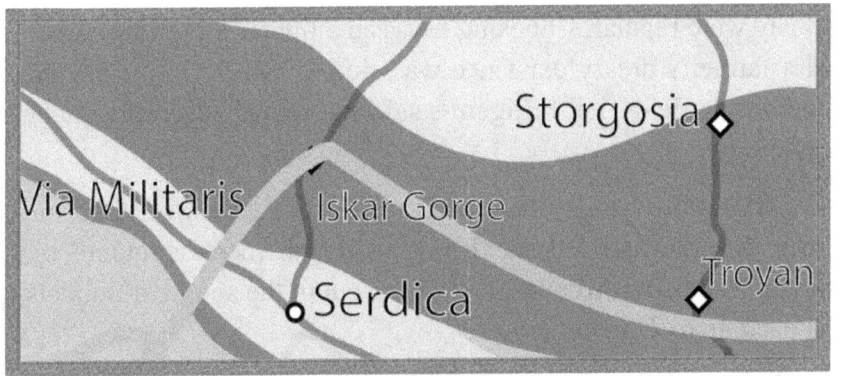

13. Hot Pursuit of Fritigern 382 CE

Several years passed, during which the Tervingi Goths were able to control the southern countryside. Fritigern's wagon-train meandered around Macedonia and Greece, living off the tribute coerced from frightened towns.

Gratian, emperor of the west, appointed a general named Theodosius to rule the eastern empire. He began the slow process of rebuilding his army by summoning legions from afar and constituting new legions, a mixture of useless raw recruits stiffened by veterans and barbarian mercenaries.

Emperor Theodosius promoted two competent generals named Bauto and Arbogast. These men were not proud Italians but pragmatic Franks, another Germanic race. They began, paradoxically, to recruit Goths into their ranks. After several years of plundering and chaos, the Balkans were destitute. For a young Goth, there were no more easy pickings. He was left with only two prospects: take up farming or join a Roman legion. He had no qualms about switching to the Roman side, especially since the food and pay were regular. Choosing between a fighter's exciting career and a farmer's dreary existence was simple. Other Goths, having found fertile fields, left Fritigern's side and settled peaceably under Roman rule.

Lord—now King, since Adrianople—Fritigern witnessed his forces dwindle and felt the Roman strength increase month by month. Bauto and Arbogast drove him out of the southern Balkans and back up to Thracia.

He knew he'd lost control of the countryside when he learned that Emperor Theodosius, accompanied by new veteran legions, had freely traveled from the western empire, down the length of the Via Militaris, and entered Constantinople without meeting any armed resistance. This dashed his dream of extending Gothia to include Moesia and Thracia.

It was inevitable that if his Goths stayed within the empire, they would live under the thumb of the Romans. While that might be an option for his people, it was not available to him. The Romans, bitter and vengeful after his victory at Adrianople, would not rest until they saw him crucified.

King Fritigern led his remaining supporters, including Silvan, Gotheric, Rodericus, and several hundred warriors with their families, back north up the Via Militaris toward Philippopolis. They planned to traverse Troyan Pass to the Danube River and ferry across to safety beyond Rome's reach.

When Fritigern's wagon-train passed by the Sabinus estate, it stopped for a week. Silvan was surprised and delighted to find Elodia and Artos living there. It was a joyous reunion. They each had a lot of news. Silvan mourned the death of Avagis while

Elodia was saddened by the death of Nedarcus. But she cheered the union of Silvan and Gotheric. She immediately fell in love with three-year-old Jellena and, as she played with the toddler, secretly envied her friend. She wanted a baby.

Gotheric resumed training Artos as they'd done before the Battle of Ad Salices. But now Artos was almost twelve and a veteran of Adrianople, where he had killed his first man. Based on that encounter, Artos assumed the air of an experienced warrior. It took some serious sprains and bruises before Gotheric convinced Artos that he still had a lot to learn.

Gotheric took on the duty of teaching Artos the arts of sword and spear. He left the arts of archery and knife fighting to Elodia, whose knowledge of those weapons was unsurpassed.

When it came time for the wagon-train to move on from the Sabinus estate, Elodia and Artos joined it.

Military Tribune Caius Coelianus arose stiffly from his cot while it was still dark. He stretched, left his tent, and walked over to warm his hands at the campfire. He knew there was no hope for more sleep that night. His shoulder ached. It had been five years since he caught an arrow in his shoulder during a skirmish on Shipka Pass. His squad had attacked a party of Goths. What should have been a simple operation turned into a fiasco when a Gothic archer, with what he had to admit was great skill, took out three of his comrades and came within an inch of killing him too. Only fast action by his decanus had saved his life. After a painful year in Constantinople, waiting for the wound to heal, he returned to duty. His shoulder, perhaps a little less solid or flexible, only bothered him on damp winter mornings like this.

His plan for the day would have the whole camp up, saddled, and in pursuit of the Goth wagon-train before dawn. They were not far ahead. Perhaps his corps could harass them again today.

He had chased Fritigern's wagons across the barren and snow-covered Thracian plain, past the city of Philippopolis, north over the frozen Maritsa River, and into the forested hill country just south of the Haemus Range. The fugitives appeared to be heading straight north toward Troyan Pass. It was clear that they intended to find safety by crossing over the Danube and out of Roman territory.

Caius needed a win. He needed to be the man who brought Fritigern, the Gothic king, bound in shackles, to Constantinople. There would be a triumph, where he would occupy a place of honor, standing in a flower-covered chariot pulled by two snow-white horses, riding through the capital's streets to the emperor's palace. He would escort Fritigern, now totally humiliated, to the executioners who would garrot or crucify him or whatever punishment pleased the new emperor Theodosius.

A log burning in the fire cracked, starting Caius. Yes, he needed this win. The empire needed this win. It needed some good news to counter the lingering shame of Adrianople.

Caius fought in that disaster and saw hot action. By then, he'd been promoted to centurion. Through good fortune, his century was one of the very few to extricate itself from the deadly Gothic pincer. The generals called it skill, but Caius knew he'd been lucky.

He was now a tribune leading a corps of two hundred horsemen, charged with capturing Fritigern, preferably alive. He had confidence he could do it. The days were gone when Fritigern could lead a thousand wagons to wherever in the Balkans he might choose. He and all the Goths knew Theodosius's ire was focused on him personally. Clan leaders still honored Fritigern for his leadership and pledged their allegiance to him, but they found it expedient, safer, to put distance between their own people and the king of the Goths.

A soldier of the watch, walking by on patrol, silently saluted him and moved on. Caius knew his men needed their sleep. Yesterday's attack had been successful. They'd caught Fritigern's wagon-train on the march, slain several oxen, torched two wagons, and killed a warrior and his woman before retreating unscathed. This was not Caius's preferred method, but it worked better than the more conventional means he'd tried the previous week. Then his force attacked the Goths in their camp, with their wagons in a circle. He'd lost a half-dozen men. The battle-hardened Gothic warriors had easily destroyed their Roman opponents. His men were raw recruits, inexperienced. Pitting them against Fritigern's men had been reckless. So now Caius used hit-and-run tactics.

Today would be another such mission. Burn some wagons, kill as many draft animals as possible, the mules and oxen were essential for the wagon-train to move, and retreat before the enemy could fight back. With luck, they might find some Goths outside their protective circle and kill them too.

The tactics had proved fruitful. Fritigern's northward retreat slowed because the Goths feared an attack every time they maneuvered their wagons from a protective circle to a vulnerable train. Caius wondered if they would buckle under his pressure and simply abandon their wagons and flee to the Danube. That seemed unlikely. The wagons held years of loot, which no Goth would leave behind. They had few horses, so they would have to flee on foot. On foot, men, women, and children would be easy targets for Caius's cavalry. He could only imagine the despair the Goths must be feeling.

He did not relish his mission. This was not personal. He was a soldier obeying orders.

He walked to the camp's kitchen fire and spoke to the cook. Soon he was squatting near the fire, enjoying its warmth while spooning up a large bowl of porridge and gnawing on a pork leg.

His mealtime reverie was interrupted when he heard a commotion. An aide appeared. "Sir, a messenger has come."

The imperial messenger arrived at the head of a squad of horsemen. The orders he carried turned Caius's mission on its head. They came directly from Magister Militum Arbogast, the empire's Master of Soldiers. Without explaining why, Caius was now ordered to negotiate a ceasefire with Fritigern, offer him safe conduct, and return with him to Constantinople. He read and re-read the parchment. The orders were written in the classical style, the document was signed, and the wax seal clearly showed the imprint of Arbogast's signet ring.

Caius stayed informed on the interminable Gothic war, its skirmishes, and massacres. He knew how the imperial court operated. The court had finally decided to stop this costly and endless fight and to make peace. It was a singular offer. Never before had an emperor negotiated with invaders while they remained within the empire. It would be too shameful. And yet that seemed to be the proposal.

In mid-morning, as the rising sun was melting the night's frost, Military Tribune Caius approached the Gothic wagon-fort holding a white flag. He was there to talk, not fight. He stood outside the ring of wagons just beyond bowshot, a single bodyguard at his back, and patiently waited until a Gothic warrior came out to parley. Caius spoke Gothic with his harsh Italian accent, but the warrior seemed to understand.

"I come offering terms to Fritigern. I am unarmed," Caius said.

Saying only, "Wait," the warrior turned on his heel and returned to the wagon-fort. Fifteen minutes later, a pair of Goths emerged, King Fritigern and his brother-in-law, Rodericus.

"I understand you are offering terms," Fritigern said.

"Do you promise to stop killing our people," Rodericus interjected, his voice dripping with sarcasm, "if we promise to stop killing those little boys you throw at us?"

Fritigern waved, silencing Rodericus.

Caius was a patient man. He and these warriors knew Caius's war of attrition was taking a daily toll on the Goths. Fritigern's wagon-train was unlikely to reach Oescus and the Danube crossing without being sliced to ribbons somewhere on that long distance. If this warrior wanted to make a joke, Caius didn't mind. Anyway, his comment was correct about the "little boys." The legionaries Caius had lost had never seen combat before.

"I have ordered my forces to stand down until dawn tomorrow, a truce while we talk. I am Military Tribune Caius Coelianus. What are your names?"

"I am Fritigern, King of the Goths."

Since Fritigern did not introduce the other man, Caius assumed he was a bodyguard. But he wondered when he watched the other man bristle at being ignored.

Fritigern looked Caius up and down. The man was a giant. "You speak good Gothic."

"I learned it as a young man from a Gothic girl in Aquileia. She taught it to me as we lay together in bed. Her language was only one of many things she taught me."

Fritigern grunted a laugh. "What are these terms you offer?"

"First, we need wine. And chairs so we can sit and talk."

When Fritigern nodded, Caius signaled. A young legionary ran into the clearing carrying two stools, and a second man brought out a flagon and two cups. Caius and Fritigern sat. Rodericus was left to stand behind his king. Caius filled the cups and sipped from each to show the wine was safe. They began to talk and drink.

After their second cup of wine, Caius and Fritigern were ready to discuss terms.

Caius said, "The emperor wants peace with the Goths. He is willing to reaffirm the promises made by his predecessor."

"Which Emperor Valens broke."

"Which Military Count Lupicinus and his greedy confederates broke. The empire has always welcomed immigrants. They are our strength and future."

"Can we cut the rubbish? What are you offering?"

"You, all the Goths, may settle in Moesia or Thracia, wherever unoccupied land is available. There will be no more harassment, no more fighting. I have the emperor's offer right here. I shall read it to you." He pulled out and unrolled the parchment orders. "It starts with the agreement's purpose, 'So that Goth and Roman may forever live side-by-side in true Christian fellowship.' Then it…"

Fritigern interrupted. "Where does it mention safe conducts and bodyguards?"

Caius looked down through the document. "Here. 'So the man known to the Goths as their king may travel to my city accompanied by a reasonable number of bodyguards, sufficient to secure their safe passage, there to learn from Theodosius,' and what follows is his many titles which I'll omit, 'there to learn from *Theodosius* such property, largesse, and gifts his lordship is willing to bestow upon said King of the Goths and his people after receiving from said King vows and pledges of his eternal loyalty to me…'"

Fritigern waved impatiently. "Enough. Does it say we can settle by clan, each with its own chieftain and priests?"

"Yes."

"And what does the emperor want in exchange?"

"That you agree to a typical *foederatus* agreement, a covenant. You will become Roman allies. You will be permitted to settle in the empire. In return, you will provide military assistance when asked. You can negotiate the details later when you meet the emperor's officials in Constantinople."

"That's it? I just surrender to you, disappear into the capital, perhaps never to be seen again, and the war is finished?"

"As I said, the emperor is providing you with a safe conduct, and you may have an honor guard." Here Caius nodded at Rodericus, assuming he was just one of the king's bodyguards.

"Roman safe conducts are not known for being safe. I was there in Marcianople when Lupicinus used a welcome banquet as bait to lure me into an ambush."

"Times have changed. Lupicinus is dead. Emperor Valens is dead. His successor, Emperor Theodosius, is a man of honor who sincerely wants to end these years of fighting. He understands the value the Goths would bring as friends of the empire."

"He only wants us to provide him with men who know how to fight."

Caius shrugged, but this was true. He downed the last of his wine and rose to leave. "You will consider our offer? Please send me word by dusk. We will maintain a truce until dawn tomorrow."

The rumor quickly spread that Fritigern and Rodericus had left the wagon-fort to meet with the Roman general and negotiate peace terms. Immediately a large group, including Elodia and Artos, gathered at the far end of the ring of wagons and waited for them to return.

The wait for Fritigern and Rodericus seemed far longer than a single hour. When the two men returned, the crowd drew close.

Fritigern announced in a clear voice that could be heard by the entire throng. "I have met with the Roman leader, a man named Military Tribune Coelianus, who offers what, on the surface, appear to be fair terms. Which, having experienced Roman treachery as I have, is a snare. A trap. He offers exceptional terms designed to persuade us to disarm.

"The Romans have suffered many casualties in this long chase across Macedonia and Thracia. Once we appear weaponless before them, they will slay us all. That is my belief."

Elodia heard little beyond "Military Tribune Coelianus." She shouted at Fritigern over the buzz of the crowd, "Did you say Caius Coelianus?"

"Yes. What of it?"

She did not answer. Instead, she pushed her way through the crowd and hurried over to the ring of wagons. She pulled off her

342

white apron, fastened it to a long stick, and made her way through the woods toward the Roman line, leaving behind sounds of arguing and shouting.

W hen Fritigern finished describing the Roman terms, the crowd erupted in questions and shouting. It took a few minutes before Rodericus, who could shout louder than anyone, calmed them down.

"And what did you say? Did you agree?" Gotheric asked.

"I gave no answer but said I would consider their offer. The Romans expect an answer before dawn tomorrow."

"And what will you answer?"

"I will answer 'no.' This is obviously a Roman trap. They see the Goths as a snake and, as one does when killing a snake, you start by cutting off its head."

The crowd erupted again and again it took several minutes before order was restored.

Athena, Rodericus's sister, asked to speak. "My Lord, as your beloved wife, may I ask a question that no one else dares ask?" This generated a snicker from the crowd. Everyone knew that Fritigern was no longer a slave to her beauty and that the two had not slept together in months.

"Of course, *my beloved wife*."

"It is possible, as you say, that this is a trap. It is also possible that the Romans want peace. Which is it? I suggest they want peace because they have no need for a trap. If they mean to exterminate us, they can simply carry on as they have. Every day they weaken us. In a few weeks, and long before we reach the Danube and safety, we shall all be dead. This must be a real peace offer."

"Or perhaps they tire of this long chase. Are they chasing other groups of Goths? Or just the Goths led by me, your king?" Fritigern said.

"No," he continued, "They hate me, Fritigern. They will never forgive the king who killed their emperor, destroyed their vast army, and humiliated them."

Athena said, "Then, *King* Fritigern, if we were to have a different king, perhaps they would let us go in peace. If your kingship poses a threat to every man, woman, and child here, would it not be better if you left the kingship to someone else? I, for one, think my brother Rodericus would make a fine king."

Everyone knew the king and his wife were alienated, but publicly supporting her brother over her husband drew cries of surprise. And for those like Gotheric, who believed Rodericus had long conspired to overthrow Fritigern, it confirmed that suspicion.

The uproar that followed went on and on. The crowd broke into factions, arguing back and forth, with one faction insisting Fritigern's stubbornness endangered everyone and that this was an opportunity, perhaps the last, for the Goths to avoid being massacred. The other faction claimed loyalty to Fritigern. However, even they could see the approaching threat of annihilation.

Fritigern was too angry to notice how few people were shouting in support of him. "Enough!" he shouted as if declaring the debate ended made it so. He headed back toward his wagon, elbowing his way through the crowd. Rodericus followed him and the crowd watched.

At the edge of the crowd, Theobald, one of Rodericus's brothers, blocked Fritigern's path.

344

"What do you want, Theobald?" Those were the last words of Fritigern, King of the Goths and hero of the Battle of Adrianople.

With no conversation, no drama, and without issuing a challenge, Rodericus struck Fritigern from behind with a war axe, a blow that took his leader squarely in the back. Fritigern collapsed where he stood. With a second blow, Rodericus decapitated him.

Artos watched, stunned, as Rodericus murdered his father. He screamed and called for his stepmother, but Elodia was nowhere in sight.

When Elodia crossed the Roman picket, she was immediately captured by a sentry, who roughly hustled her into Caius's presence. He looked up from his portable desk to see a young woman, a familiar young woman, staring at him.

His eyes deceived him. She was dead, a death confirmed by countless dreams. She had been dead for years, killed by a Roman arrow while trying to flee from Marcianople. But, no, here she was. His hands shook. He dropped his pen. He stood suddenly, knocking aside his desk and spilling his cup of ink. He saw her eyes grow wide and glow. Her arms stretched towards him, and his to her.

Elodia and Caius wordlessly threw themselves into each other's arms. She wept openly. He bent over, burying his head between her head and shoulder where no one could see his tears. They clung to each other for a minute and another, separating only when Caius's senior aide cleared his throat. Repeatedly.

"Our picket reports violence within the Gothic wagon-fort, sir."

As if he'd said nothing, the two resumed kissing, embracing, and babbling insignificant questions and answers, much to the embarrassment of the crowd of legionaries standing nearby.

Finally, the senior aide's words replayed themselves in Elodia's mind. It took great willpower for her to push Caius to arm's length. He could see her face growing serious. "You have offered Fritigern peace terms?"

Caius said he had and recounted his discussion with Fritigern.

"This is not a trick? Not a ruse to disarm us?" He confirmed the offer was bona fide.

"You swear?"

Caius dropped to his knees, took her hands, and said, "By all the gods and by the love I have for you, this is not a deception. The offer comes straight from the emperor! Please, oh please, convince your people to accept it."

She raised him up and kissed his lips again. "I need to go back," she said.

"Must you return right now?"

"Yes. Fritigern is telling the people this is a trap. I must convince them otherwise. I fear there may be violence, and I have left my child, Artos, alone."

She did not even take the time to explain who Artos was. He assumed the boy was hers by another man. He escorted her back to the wagon-fort, which she reentered without anyone taking notice.

Elodia returned to find chaos. She gasped in horror at the sight of a headless body. It took a moment to recognize it as Fritigern's.

Rodericus sat a few yards away, nursing a wound to his left arm. By his side lay Fritigern's bloody head. Its eyes were open, and he looked surprised. At Rodericus's feet lay a knife. She recognized the knife, one of a matching pair she'd given Artos the previous year, and she looked around for its owner. The boy was fifty feet away, struggling. Gotheric was restraining him by sitting on him.

Silvan quickly explained the situation. "He," pointing to Rodericus, "killed Fritigern and chopped off his head. He was walking away with the head when Artos charged after and stabbed his arm. Gotheric dragged Artos away before Rodericus could kill him."

Artos calmed down when Elodia approached. Speaking calmly, he said, "He killed my father. Like a common thief. Without warning and from the back, he killed him. He must die."

Elodia wracked her brain, trying to find a way to restore calm and peace. She knew Artos. He had resolved to avenge his father. There would be no way to change his mind. She would have to take him into exile, away from everyone else. But she knew he would not go.

She was still seeking a solution when Rodericus approached. "The boy has wounded me and must die," he said. "Prepare him." Gotheric released Artos, who stood and drew his own sword. It was a short-bladed gladius. Though a smaller sword than a long-bladed spatha, it was still very heavy for a twelve-year-old to wield, even one who Gotheric had been training daily.

Elodia could see Athena bandaging her brother's arm. Then Rodericus stood and tried to lift a small shield, but his wounded arm couldn't support it. His sister put his arm in a sling and bound it to his chest. Rodericus drew his sword, a spatha, with his good right arm and walked toward Elodia and Artos.

Elodia drew her own sword, another gladius, and stood between Artos and Rodericus. From behind her, Artos said, "Mother, stand aside. I must fight him myself."

"You are still just a boy, and I promised your mother to protect you," she said, over her shoulder.

Rodericus overheard this. "Then, Elodia, you will die. As well as the boy."

Elodia's mind raced. Rodericus was a big man. His reach was longer than hers, and his sword blade added another six inches. When it came to wielding a heavy blade, she did not have the big man's endurance. She could not imagine how she could win.

Then she fell. She was still tumbling when she realized Artos had kicked her feet out from under her. "I must fight him myself," he repeated. He stepped around her prone form and assumed a defensive stance, feet spread, knees bent, and sword pointing at the approaching Rodericus.

Who laughed. "You're a fool, boy," he said. He swept his sword down, a slash that knocked Artos's sword out of his hand and to the ground. But then Rodericus dropped his own sword. His arm flopped down, useless.

Artos, using his own sword as bait, had anticipated Rodericus's slash. When the boy felt the clash of weapons, he jumped to the right, stepped in, and planted his second knife in his opponent's bicep. It was a deep thrust, which rendered his sword arm useless. Rodericus could not pull the knife free because his left arm was bound in a sling.

For a moment, the boy and the man stood facing each other, both disarmed. Elodia lay at their feet, wondering if she should come to her boy's aid. He had been insistent that the kill must be his. Would he hate her if she interfered? Would he survive to hate her if she didn't? The solution came quickly.

Elodia pulled her own knife from its sheath and, taking it by its razor-sharp blade, handed it hilt first to Artos. Her hand bled as she released it. Rodericus was distracted, trying to disentangle his left arm from its sling, when Artos calmly stepped forward and plunged Elodia's knife into his heart.

His father was avenged.

Elodia lay her head on Caius's chest. She had never been happier. A morning filled with killing and death was blotted out by an afternoon of love. At noon, she had returned to his camp, splattered with Rodericus's blood, which he sluiced off in a nearby ice-cold stream. When they were clean, dried, and dressed, he led her back to his tent. Caius ordered that they not be disturbed. They were both still shivering, but under his blankets, found ways to warm each other.

And there they remained, alternating between talking and making love. She asked after Grainus and the rest of his squad.

"Evander died of a fever a few months ago, and Polybius was killed when we tried to stop some Goths who were ransacking a senator's villa." Their deaths distressed Elodia. The three had sung beautifully together. "As for Grainus and Marius, they are with some legion in Ephesus.

"And Minicius and Arruntius are dead. They died several years ago. We got into a skirmish in the Shipka Pass. Those two and another man you never met were taken out by one Goth, a master archer, in a matter of seconds. He could nock, draw, and loose faster than any Roman I've ever seen. He must have tired after killing three, luckily for me. His aim was a little off, so I was hit in the shoulder."

Elodia wondered if she should confess. Yes, but not today. "I'm happy she missed."

"The master archer, you mean?"

"Yes, yes, I mean *him*."

"I spent a year recovering in Constantinople. My shoulder still aches on damp mornings like today."

Elodia kissed his wound. When he claimed he also ached elsewhere, she kissed there too.

The Romans and the Goths soon parted ways.
Caius's orders, in support of the peace mission, required that he return to Constantinople with the king of the Goths. With Fritigern dead, he insisted that his son Artos must be the new king and must go instead.

Elodia insisted her pledge to keep him safe required her to accompany him.

Artos sputtered with exasperation. "Mother, I am twelve years of age. I do not need you hovering over me like a mother hen."

"It would diminish Artos's standing at the court if he arrives with his mother in tow," Caius said.

It took time for Elodia to accept this. Was it already time to let him go? So soon? Where was the little boy Gosvintha put into her arms? At least he would be safe with Caius. And Caius, dear Caius. How could they part again so soon? Because he was a good man, an honest man, he would not promise to come back. He said his twenty-year term as a legionary had another eight years to run. She would have preferred to hear a lie. Find another man, he said. She had had other men. She did not want another man. She wanted Caius. But there was no help for it.

Heva's husband, Tolton, agreed to accompany Artos and lead the Gothic party to the capital city. Heva did not voice her dismay, but now she and Elodia had a common bond, a bond of missing the one they loved.

"When you return, how will you find us?" Heva asked.

"Caius suggests you camp near the abandoned Roman fortress at Storgosia and wait for our return. It is not far beyond the Troyan Pass. He says it is good farm country, green with fine pasturage for the animals. And the fortress is there if you need protection," Tolton said.

And so, with hearts breaking on both sides, the Romans and Goths went their separate ways.

With Fritigern dead, Elodia took over as the party's leader. The mountain pass challenged the Goths and damaged several wagons. Despite her folks' exhaustion, Elodia sensed an upbeat mood. They were no longer being pursued. The never-ending concern that any step beyond the wagon's protection might lead to capture or death, that every day might be their last, all these fears had taken an emotional toll. Her people could begin to relax.

Not that she let down her guard. She issued orders. The wagons were to be circled nightly. Watches posted. Scouts to patrol nearby, looking for signs of trouble.

When the wagon-train reached the Roman fortress of Storgosia, twenty miles south of the Danube, they found it abandoned, just as Caius had said. A passing trader said that years earlier the Roman garrison was transported downstream by boats when Emperor Valens gathered his forces to crush the Goths. It did not surprise Elodia that news of the great battle at Adrianople hadn't reached this remote area. News now traveled so slowly. She could imagine the bones of the fortress's garrison lying, bleached white, on that vast battlefield. Would this fort ever be manned again?

The wagon-train stopped outside the fort for the night. After dinner, Elodia prepared her bedroll. She would sleep alone. She missed Artos, his hugs, and kisses. Even more, she desperately longed for Caius.

To the east and west of the fort were large tracts of fertile and unoccupied land, more than enough for their party. The previous farmers had fled or been killed, and their homes burned and leveled. Forest had encroached on what had been productive farmland.

The fort was theirs for the taking. If the Romans, Huns, or anyone else threatened, everyone could take refuge within. The Goths had originally planned to continue north and cross the river, but this location had one important advantage: it was in Moesia. When peace finally came, they would be within the empire in a land already designated for the Goths.

Elodia suggested that folks claim quarters in the fort, but no one was interested. We are not city dwellers, they said. The various family groups started laying claim to the good farmlands.

Elodia knew little about farming, but Gotheric helped her mark out a large plot for herself and another for Artos, for whenever he might return. Gotheric said she, as the settlement's leader, should

352

have a double-size plot, one worthy of a leader. He marked a regular-size plot next to Elodia's for Silvan and himself.

Elodia's little farm was not the one she'd dreamed of. But she started getting crops in the ground and building a small house. She had no slaves, so she did all the labor herself, aided by the community as needed.

Though last winter had been surprisingly mild, each Gothic family, recalling how harsh winters could be, worked hard to prepare for the next, a half-year hence. Wheat was sprouting, huts too, rising like large molehills across the rolling hills.

Eventually, the brilliant, variegated greens of spring turned into the muted colors of summer. Summer turned to autumn. The harvest was good. The crops were in; the excess livestock had been butchered, their carcasses salted or smoked for the winter. Elodia and Silvan helped the neighborhood men split and stack firewood, sufficient for Moesia's cold winter. Elodia's neighbors planned for a traditional autumn celebration. Even the little gangs of teenage boys were excited and could be bribed into helping.

Silvan and Elodia set up a large trestle table on the festival day, which quickly filled with all good things to eat, as provided by the neighborhood's women. The menfolk did their part by bringing drink and, to Elodia's surprise, tools and timbers of various sizes.

"Are we building something?" she asked Gotheric.

"We are, indeed," he answered. "Two things. With your permission. The neighborhood needs a barn that everyone can use to store crops and secure animals. I considered this when I marked out an oversize plot for you. And, as the settlement's leader, you need a hall, not just a hut."

She knew what he was talking about. He meant a hall like the one her father had. It should have a great room with double doors at one end and a large common area on beaten soil covered with straw. There should be room enough for six or eight trestle tables where all the neighbors could sit and feast. She pictured a raised platform opposite the double doors where she and her family could sleep and eat at the high table. Gotheric said, "It will have a high ceiling and a loft around the common area where guests and your slaves can sleep, whenever you get some. And a central fire pit with a ceiling hole so it doesn't get too smoky."

Elodia demurred, "It is too much. I cannot expect…"

Gotheric interrupted, "It is our gift to you from the whole neighborhood. We have all agreed. Mind you, it won't be finished today. Most of the wattle will get done today, but it will take weeks to apply all the layers of daub. But when we're done, it will be as snug as any lodging…anywhere. And much more comfortable than dwelling in that drafty Roman fortress."

Gotheric made sure the construction work was done before the drinking began. After the drinking started, the local man who considered himself a Christian priest had each of the three couples with newborns come before the company, where he introduced each baby by name to the gathering. He sprinkled water on their heads while the folks tossed back a great quaff of ale in support. That done, he called the two couples who wanted to get married according to what they said was "the Christian rite." They made pledges, sang songs, had their crossed hands bound by a bright red strip of cloth, and then unbound. After that, the priest pronounced them married, and they kissed. And kissed. Again, the pronouncement served to initiate another round of serious drinking.

Elodia was puzzled. This rite bore no resemblance to the one she'd witnessed years before. She decided Christian priests would just invent a ceremony on the spot.

When winter came, it was hard, but no one starved. There was food aplenty at Yuletide. For the Christians, it was a time to celebrate the birth of their Jesus God. For everyone, it was a time to gather in the new hall and share food and stories.

Gotheric began his story, which he made up as he went along, by warning everyone, especially young children, to stay indoors during the bitter winter nights because he said, "These are the nights when Odin leads his Wild Hunt across the land and through the sky."

Once he had their attention, he said, "Growing up in Gothia, I knew a young woman of my village whom the gods had blessed. She was the daughter of the clan chieftain. Her beauty surpassed all the other girls in the village; indeed, she was more attractive than any woman for miles around." He looked at Elodia, while she, blushing, looked at the ground. "Her father captured a Christian priest just to educate her. And she quickly absorbed everything he taught, the way a fine cloth absorbs dye. Soon she could speak almost any language: Gothic, Greek, Latin, even the language of far-off Egypt."

He spoke on. "When she turned fifteen, her father paid the bride price to a man in the next village. He, in return, gave her silver bangles, which made her arms look very fine."

A drunk called out, "Did she have fine teats?"

Gotheric ignored him and continued. "But soon she detested him because he could not speak Egyptian, and he, fine man though he was, came to detest her too. One Yuletide night in the dark of winter, she killed him with a knife and tried to flee in his golden boat across the great river."

Elodia had thought she understood where the story was going, but then it took a turn.

"But Odin and the souls of his dead warriors were hunting that night. The god's frost bridge of lights, pulsing and glowing blue and green, carried the eerie hunters directly from Odin's heavenly palace down to where she struggled, trying to push the heavy boat into the river.

"The young woman knew the hunters had come when she heard Odin's dogs barking and his ghostly warriors' screams. She tried to take shelter with a poor fisherman whose house was nearby, but he barred her entry. With horror, he watched as the lord of the gods himself came to Earth and called to her. She sank to her knees before him and begged forgiveness for being out of doors on Yuletide night. She promised to give him her silver bangles if he would spare her. But Odin spoke a word of power, and his dogs tore her to shreds."

The hall, hearing her dreadful fate, was stunned to silence.

"In the morning, when the fisherman grew brave enough to venture out, he saw nothing was left of the girl, not even a scrap of bone or skin, nothing except her two silver bangles. The fisherman knew they were both cursed, having been rejected by Odin himself, so he took them with a gloved hand, to avoid touching them, and hurled them as far as he could into the river. So, children, on the darkest nights of winter, stay safe in your house. Do not venture out!"

The gathered people clapped at his story of the Wild Hunt. Elodia laughed. She was amused by the story's moral: being out on a winter's night was a terrible crime; killing your husband was not.

Winter was over, and every day, Heva looked up the road hoping to see the men return. While she would be happy to see all the men, it was Tolton she longed for. Their little boy was now four years old and could only remember his father because Heva kept talking about him. Tolton had promised her that he would be back within a year. Now a whole year had come and gone. He was long overdue. Every additional week brought her closer to despair. Gotheric tried to reassure her that a year was only a guess, that many things could prolong Artos's mission. His words did not help.

Then, on an overcast day that promised rain or even a late-season snowstorm, the wait was over. A small party of horsemen emerged from the forest and rode into the center of the village. The watchman's warning was immediately followed by shouts and calls. Tolton did not reach his hut before Heva pulled him off his horse, pinned his shoulders to the ground, and smothered him with kisses. The bodyguards dispersed to their own huts, where their arrival was greeted with shrieks and cries of joy. Artos rode straight into Elodia's farmyard.

At first, Elodia did not hear the horses. She was dealing with a little shrieking and crying toddler of her own. Five months earlier, her little girl had been born. She named her Matilde after Caius's Italian mother. While lifting her, Elodia looked and saw Artos framed in the door. Elodia shouted first in surprise, then in joy. Her arms were already full of baby, but she stretched to embrace him too. She gave and received one kiss before he tried to push away, saying in his best grownup tone, "Hello, Mother. It is good to be home."

She looked him up and down as if expecting to find pieces missing. "Oh," he said, "a baby! Your baby?!" He gently took Matilde from her, lifted her, and kissed her. "A sister for me, like I always wanted." The baby looked up at Artos and smiled. "We have peace, mother. I signed the document right in front of the emperor! They all expected me to simply draw an *X*, but I know how to write. I was going to write *Artos,* but Caius was there, and he said I was signing as All King of the Goths, so I wrote that in our tongue, *ALA RIC.*

"We have peace! The emperor has given us permission to live in Moesia and Thracia. All we must do is pay some taxes and provide troops... Oh Jesus, my sister has barfed all over my tunic!"

If he meant to say more, he was interrupted by someone else coming in the door, a person who blocked most of the sunlight. Elodia turned. Even with the person's face in the shadows, she knew who it was. She leaped up and threw her arms around Caius's neck. The two exchanged hugs, kisses, and happy tears for a full minute.

When Caius finally stepped into the hall, he looked past Elodia and saw Artos holding little Matilde. "You've had a baby?" Through all her tears, she could only nod. "And Artos is the father?" She started laughing and tried unsuccessfully to punch him in the chest. She laughed until she was bent double. Artos didn't see the humor and blushed a bright red.

Caius stepped forward and gingerly took the child from the young man. She grabbed his little finger with a stubby hand, held on tightly, and looked at him dubiously. "Does she smile?" he asked.

"Not at big ugly men who question her paternity!" said Elodia.

"What is her name?" Caius asked.

"Matilde."

358

"A strange name for a Goth." This time her blow did connect with his chest, but lightly. "My mother would be so pleased," he said. "She talked about the day when she would have grandchildren. She hoped one would be named after her. Preferably a girl." Elodia and Artos laughed. Another round of kisses, hugs, and happy weeping followed.

It was getting on to dinner time. Elodia had only prepared a meal for one and a child. She and Caius talked as she prepared dinner for two more mouths. "Why are you here?" she asked. "Can you stay? What about your eight more years of service?"

"Odd thing about that," Caius said. "After the treaty was signed, Artos spoke with Magister Militum Arbogast about the security detail he was providing to see us safely home. Artos complained that I was not fit for service, having been badly wounded. He *ordered* me to strip before the general and show him my shoulder scar." Caius noticed Elodia was not looking at him.

"I mean the wound where I took an arrow in my shoulder." Caius saw Elodia blanch. "The arrow fired by an excellent Gothic archer." She turned bright red and turned her back to him. "You know the wound I mean?"

"Yes," she said, "I know the wound. I know your body very well, including all your wounds."

"And you know the archer I mean?"

She turned again to face him and saw he was smiling at her. "You bastard, you knew!" she cried, closing the distance to wrap her arms around him.

"A good thing she wasn't *more* excellent, or you wouldn't be hugging me."

"Enough, you villain! Who told you it was me?"

"That's a secret. And I promised Tolton I'd keep it a secret."

"What did Arbogast do?"

"He agreed I was unfit for service. I have a parchment showing my release. I am now an ex-legionary."

Then the door was flung open, and a happy Silvan came with her little girl. Gotheric followed carrying a mountain of food. Elodia told Artos to run around to the homesteads of all the newly returned men asking them to come too. Once *their* neighbors heard the commotion, they invited themselves, and arrived just after dark, bringing even more food and drink. It was unplanned, but now there was no doubt this was a bona fide feast.

Several hours later, when everyone was sated, and most were drunk, people sat around the central fire singing softly, rocking back and forth to the rhythm, holding each other, and generally enjoying the snug, convivial ambiance. Despite the hall's sturdy walls of wattle and daub, the cold was seeping in, although the central fire did its best to push it back. Sleet fell through the roof hole and hissed on the fire below.

A knock came on the hall door.

The person nearest the door opened it, allowing a gust of frosty air and a poorly clothed man to enter. "May I beg hospitality for the night?" Over his tunic, he wore a thin cloak. It was damp and flecked by snow. He did not wear boots but rather sandals wrapped in strips of cloth.

Elodia rushed to the door to welcome him, as the law and custom of hospitality required. She took the stranger by the hand and assisted him as he limped to a seat near the fire. She helped him out of his cloak and spread it out to dry, replacing it with a blanket and another blanket over his knees. Someone brought a cup of mulled ale; another provided a trencher layered deeply with meat and carrots. The stranger could not hold both trencher and cup; his right arm ended in a stump. He pulled long from the cup, set it aside, and put the trencher on his lap. He lifted a well-cooked pork leg and gnawed on it with his few remaining teeth. His mouth ejected spittle out a split in his lip where a sword-blow once cut him, leaving a scar from temple to chin.

The code of hospitality prevented Elodia from asking his name or home or how he'd come to their door. Those matters had to wait until he had drunk and eaten his fill. But she had her answers when he pulled a little knife from his belt and set to work cutting a chunk off a succulent bit of pork. The knife was old and inadequate for the task. Its blade had been sharpened so many times that only an inch remained.

Elodia, who was kneeling in front of him, was startled. She stared at the knife and then at the stranger's face. He was gazing back at her. "I found you," Bitorix said. "I finally found you." His voice was deep and gravelly, almost broken, not how she remembered it. "I always loved you."

"You had an odd way of showing it," spat Elodia.

"I wanted you, but you would have nothing to do with me. No matter what I said or did, you just scorned me. I could not break you. I hated you and loved you. And yet, after Lupicinus stole you, I realized your strength drew me to you. I was so stupid. I hated him so much. I still weep to think of it," Bitorix said, his wet eyes matching his words. "After the great battle"—presumably he meant Adrianople—"which left me as you see me, the legion had no use for me. I had only one desire, to find you and beg forgiveness. I hoped if I could find and plead with you, you might find it in your heart…" His voice trailed off.

Elodia looked up into his face. Hers was still filled with hatred. Her heart was racing, and she could hardly breathe. When she calmed down, she said, "You are the one person in this whole wide world I truly despise." It took her another minute to regain her calm. The room was quiet except for the crackling of the fire. Everyone was silent, listening for what would come next.

She had to stop talking to keep control. "However, when you raped me, when you had me lashed and…" here she had to pause again, "when you took my knife! The knife my father gave me. Then I swore, I swore I would get it back someday. I never dreamed you would walk into my hall and slice my food with it."

He said, "I have kept your knife all these years to remind me of you."

Ignoring that, she said, "I also swore you would receive *this knife*," here she drew her knife, "the knife Grainus gifted me back then, so long ago, to replace the one you stole." She held the point an inch from his throat. Her hand began to shake. She and Bitorix locked eyes. His eyes had the silver cloudiness that afflicts the old. He must be effectively blind, she decided.

"This is a day of celebration, so I will not kill you. Or have you killed. The law of hospitality forbids it. But I will take my knife, and as promised, you will *receive* this one, though not in the way I intended." With that, she jerked from his hands the old, tired knife, her father's gift, and replaced it with the fine knife provided by Grainus. "You may stay the night and, on the morrow, go in peace."

That seemed a fitting conclusion to the celebration, though many had hoped for a bit of bloodletting. Most families gathered their children close, donned their outerwear, and returned to their homes. Others, who were too drunk to move, slept on the straw-covered floor as near to the fire as they could manage or up in the loft where it was warmer, albeit somewhat smoky.

Elodia laid out a pile of rugs and blankets on the raised platform, placing baby Matilde next to where she and Caius would sleep. Artos looked at the arrangement and asked where he should lie for the night.

"You take some blankets up the ladder to the loft and sleep there. And guide that old... guide Bitorix up to the loft and make sure he's comfortable."

Artos did as he was told. Snoring could already be heard from the guests sleeping below in the common area. Caius and Elodia quickly stripped and climbed under the blankets she'd laid out. They kissed, relaxed, and held each other close. She pulled in tight to his side and began to caress him. "Let us be together always," he said.

"And no one come between us," she said.

Just as ardor was seizing them both, they heard the creak of someone descending the ladder. A moment later, Artos burrowed under the blankets and came between them.

"I couldn't sleep up there with that smelly old man," he said. Though he was a king, he was a boy still.

Elodia sighed as she sandwiched him against Caius. There would be other nights.

The End

14. Epilogue

It took several violent years before the treaty of 382 CE took hold. But within a decade, both sides were dissatisfied with it. The treaty allowed the Goths to settle in their own communities and to be governed by their own laws and leaders, an unprecedented concession by the Romans, who had previously insisted that tribes admitted to the empire be geographically dispersed and assimilated into Roman society. Theodosius only agreed to these terms because he assumed the time would soon come when his forces would recover their strength and dominate the Goths once and for all.

The Goths disliked the treaty because it obliged them to supply the emperor with warriors upon demand, which Theodosius demanded once too often. In 395 CE, he used them as fodder, not in defending the empire against its foreign enemies, but in a battle against a Roman usurper. When the Goths suffered devastating losses, King Alaric and his men deserted en mass.

The consequences of Alaric's leadership are described in the next book of this series.

The surviving books of the ancient historian Ammianus Marcellinus provide the backbone of *Elodia's Knife* and are quoted in the text.

Sadly Elodia, Caius, and most of the characters are fictitious, as is Artos, the youthful portrayal of the very real Alaric. However, King Fritigern, King Alavivus, and many Roman leaders, including that inhuman fiend Lupicinus, are historical.

Cast of Characters

Gods

Gothic Gods

Eir .... Goddess of Healing

Freya .... Goddess of Love & Fertility

Odin .... God of War & Death

Ithunn .... Goddess of Spring

Skadi .... Goddess of Winter & Hunting

Christian God (Arian Heresy)

Jesus .... Son of God(created, not co-eternal)

Emperors

Eastern Emperor

Gratian .... reign 367 to 383, Nephew of Valens

Western Emperor

Theodosius .... reign 379 to 395, Successor of Valens

Valens .... reign 364 to 378

Goths

Chieftains

Alatheus .... Greutungi Leader

Alavivus .... Old King of the Goths

Bandar .... Chief of Silvan's Clan

Boderus .... Chief of Dondori Clan

Farnobius .... Greutungi Leader

Fritigern .... Tervingi Leader, Chief of Balti Clan

Rodericus .... Son of Boderus

The Young Goths

Arbrun .... Leader of the Young Goths
Bort .... Arbrun's Younger Brother
Jellena .... Arbrun's Younger Sister
Karl .... Friend of Arbrun, Jellena's Husband
Silvan .... Karl's Younger Sister

Other Goths

Artos/Alaric .... Son of Fritigern and Gosvintha
Athena .... Sister of Rodericus
Avagis .... Warrior
Elodia .... Gothic Woman
Gavar .... Son of Nedarcus, Bodyguard of Fritigern
Gotheric .... Son of Nedarcus, Bodyguard of Fritigern
Gosvintha .... Woman Warrior
Heva .... Avagis's Daughter
Nedarcus .... Medicus (Doctor)
Salonia .... Gothic Wife of Roman Baker

Romans

Officers

Aequitius .... Marshal of the Court
Arbogast .... General
Barzimeres .... Commander of the Guards
Bauto .... Magister Militum (Master of Army)
Bitorix .... Military Tribune, later Centurion

Frigiderus .... General
Lupicinus .... Military Count of Thracia
Profuturus .... Military Commander
Sebastianus .... Magister Peditum (Master of Infantry)
Traianus .... Magister Peditum (Master of Infantry)

Limitanei (Border Legionaries)

Arruntius.............. Pedes
Caius .... Pedes
Evander .... Pedes
Glabius .... Pedes
Grainus .... Decanus
Marius .... Pedes
Minicius .... Pedes
Polybius .... Pedes
Titus .... Pedes

Roman Civilians

Licinius Sabinus .. Wealthy Aristocrat
Julius Sabinus ...... Son of Licinius Sabinus
Tosca Volesus ..... Wealthy Senator

Acknowledgments

I am grateful to the many people who helped me finish this who-knew-it-would-take-so-long project: my editors Elizabeth Flynn and Joseph Donley; my cheerleaders at Chanticleer Review (Kiffer Brown and David Beaumier); the Village Books Fiction Writers group, who gently crushed my prose as necessary; and my beta readers (Sonya Fitak, Cheryl Perry, Kristina Smith, Rob Campbell, Ian Phillips, Graham Phillips, James Conroyd Martin, and Strider Klusman).

Also my daughter Martha, who had to endure the recitation of so much half-baked prose and feed me banana bread.

A book would not be complete without a cover. For that, I thank Bob Paltrow for the cover design and Audra Mercille for the author photo.

Author Biography

Robert S. Phillips is an avid reader and history buff. Born in Vancouver, BC, Robert has lived in many places in Canada and the U.S., only returning to the Pacific Northwest in the last decade. Home is Bellingham, WA. His three grown children all live in Washington; two in the State and one in D.C.

"Elodia's Knife" is his first novel, with a sequel in the works.